Sea
of
Broken
Glass

Sea
of
Broken
Glass

JENNA
PINE

SEA OF BROKEN GLASS
Copyright © 2024 by Jenna Pine
www.jennapine.com

This is a work of fiction. Names, characters, places, and incidents either are the product of the author's imagination or are used fictitiously. Any resemblance to actual persons, living or dead, events, or locales is entirely coincidental.

e-book ISBN: 978-1-954466-34-0
Paperback ISBN: 978-1-954466-35-7
Hardcover ISBN: 978-1-954466-42-5

First e-book edition June 2024
First paperback edition June 2024

Book design by dragonpenpress.com
Cover Images: Deposit Photos
Editing: Arielle Bailey

For everyone who's ever questioned

what they were taught as children,

who learned to take care of themselves

when the people they trusted failed them.

For my sister, who is one of my best friends:

We'll always have the Sister Thing.

And my sister-in-law: one of my favorite people ever.

Nasmarya

OSHYA

Flatlands

• Salitas

Ryth
• Hollow

Montalo

• Cliffreach

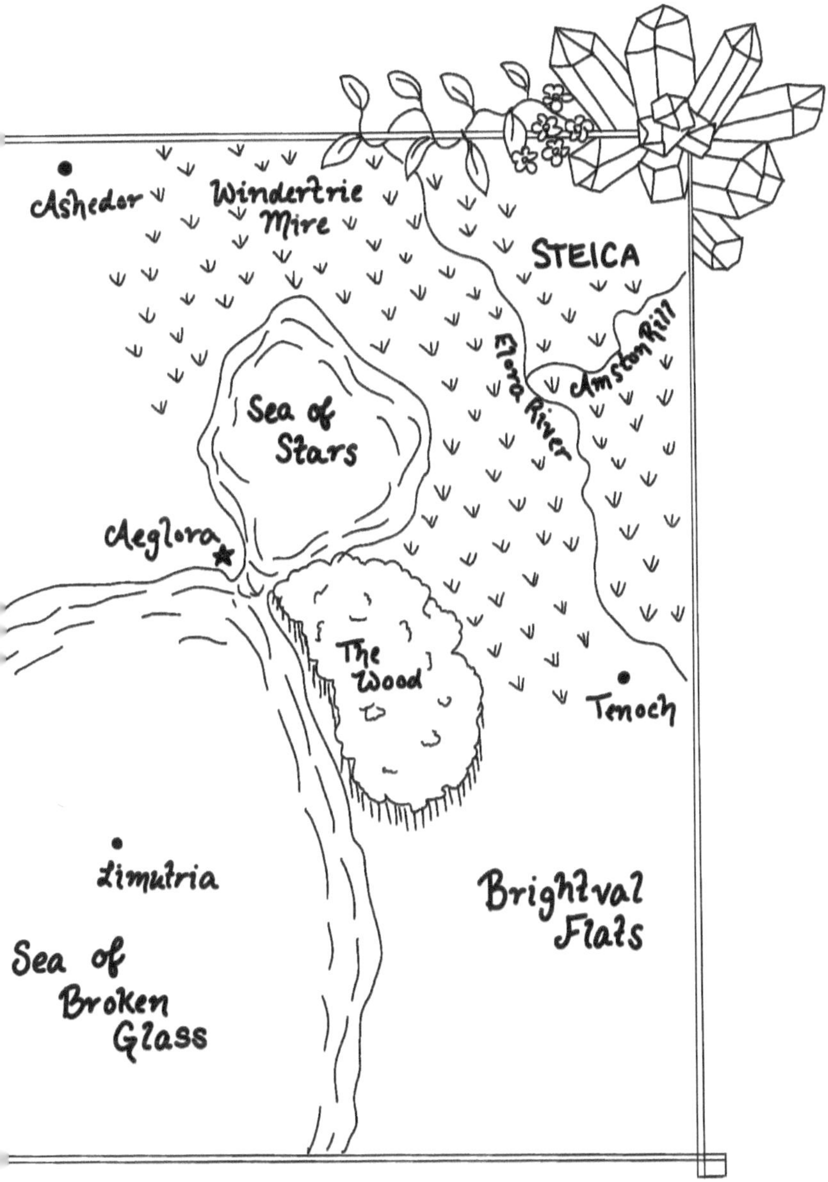

Ashedor

Windertrie Mire

STEICA

Sea of Stars

Elora River

Amston Rill

Aeglora

The Wood

Tenoch

Limutria

Brightval Flats

Sea of Broken Glass

Part One

BURNED

One

ELODIE

The world was born in fire, but forged of crystal. Sefella could not prevail over the power of Ivlene.

Excerpt from *The Records of Bright*

The sky is on fire.

I catch my breath and rub the sleep out of my eyes, jolting up and pressing myself so close to the window that my breath fogs the glass. The sky is burnt orange and soot black, the clouds burning away as streaks of fire rain down at regular intervals. The night had been dimly lit by the storm clouds, but now, well after midnight, it glows with the fire of Sefella herself. From this side of the house, I can see people running along the plank walks, the pounding of their steps sending ripples across the surface of the sea and rocking the entire village where it floats.

The screams turn my blood to ice, my pulse pounding in my ears.

I throw a shawl across my shoulders and rush to the living room. Dad is on his feet, a look of shock painting his face. He sets the mine ledger in his chair as he bolts for the door.

My heart lurches. Where is Loxy?

I follow on Dad's heels, wringing my hands, and burst out into the unnaturally dry air. He takes off toward the mine offices, but I stop, frozen at the door.

Outside is chaos. Small children scream, pointing to the sky as their mothers and fathers tuck them into their arms and try to turn them away, back to their homes, to protect them from the wrath of the Bright One falling on our heads. Each rock that falls shakes the seabed, sending waves toward our little village.

What did we do to deserve this? Again? My heart races, and I push away the foggy memories I have of the last time this happened.

Of Mom…

I have my suspicions about why this is happening again, but I can't think about them now, can't worry about the possibility. I have to find Loxy. Make sure she's okay.

Another boom thunders, followed by a deep splash. Stones hit the sea all around, but this one…this is much closer. A shockwave of salty water surges over the walks closest to the impact, and I yelp as the water rushes over my feet, its temperature several degrees higher than it should be this time of year. The heat prickles my skin, penetrating my numb feet, and I catch my breath, on the edge of hysteria.

I blink back tears. Unbidden, images of the last time this happened flood my vision. Mom, on fire with power no one should have.

Loxy, following her into the danger.

I shake my head, trying to clear the images. The last time Sefella visited was exactly twenty years ago, yesterday. The anniversary of Mother's exile. And now, it's happening all over again.

It's our fault. It has to be.

Especially after what happened before…

I could have done better. I could have found help for Loxy, before it was too late.

Is it too late now?

What will the village think this time?

Maybe I should have *forced* Loxy to seek help. Maybe if I had done that, none of this would be happening.

I shake my head and turn back to the sky, fixing my eyes on the horror before us. The village rocks again where it floats. Since it's been raining for a few weeks already, the entire village bobs and sways with each wave, each impact, at least half a foot above the sea bed. Then it yanks to a stop again, throwing me off balance, as it reaches the end of the ropes that anchor it to the ground or connect this path to the paths and houses around it.

It is almost never this rough, even during the rainy season.

Something tingles across my body, raising the tiny hairs on my arms, and tiny lights drift down from the sky, like the sparks popping off a fire. They buzz as they touch my skin, and I jump back under the awning of the door.

I've seen this before.

The lights follow, drawn to me like feathers on a stormy, static-filled day. I gasp, trying to escape, but it's no use.

Elodieee…

A voice on the still air, floating like the sparks buzzing against my skin, a whisper full of honey. I look around, but the only people I see are villagers, all people I know and none of whom sound so soft, so comforting, especially not now, threatened by the burning skies.

Loxy bolts down the walkway behind me, almost slipping into the sea. I'm so relieved to see her, I can't even think about where she might have gone so late. "El!" she yells, voice shrill and hoarse.

I look over, my eyes still wide as the sparks land on my exposed skin. "Lox!" I reach my hands toward her, and she runs into my arms.

Loxy shakes in my embrace, and I look around for Dad, but he's long gone by now. Would he have stayed if I asked? It is selfish of me to even think it when the mines need him more than we do.

The buzzing sparks are starting to hurt, and I grit my teeth against the pain. I look at the bare skin of my arms—they are covered in tiny round burns, the same kind I get when I stand too close to the fire in the hearth or the cookstove.

Elodie…

The voice tries to numb my thoughts like a sedative, but I shake it away, focusing on the pain of the burns.

"Loxy, do you feel that?" I ask, pushing her back from me.

I see the pain in her eyes before she nods, and I grab her and drag us both through the door into our house. But even here, behind closed doors, the sparks still burn my skin and the red specks still appear on Loxy's arms. We sink down to the ceramic tiles inside the door. The chill of the tiles calms me, but only enough that I am no longer in a blind panic.

I clutch Loxy close to me, and we wait for the fire to cease raining from the sky. For the screaming to stop. For the day to end.

We wait.

The rain pattering against the windowpane pulls me from my exhausted sleep. I blink my eyes open and try to focus on the room, but it is too dark. Not even the coals in the hearth cast light into the room, their dull red glow nearly extinguished. It has to be close to dawn by now, though I don't know how we fell asleep in such fear. And now the screams are silent, and Loxy snores softly in my arms where we lay tangled together on the floor.

The tiles beneath us—a feature of all Limutrian homes to keep salt, water, and sediment from building up throughout the seasonal changes—are too warm beneath us. That must mean the Sea is also too warm.

I rub my eyes again, reorienting myself. It's so quiet.

Then I remember the Burning Rain, Sefella, my fear of what the village will do now.

Ivlene, preserve us.

Heavy footsteps tread down the planks of the walk outside, and the vibrations shake into the house under the entryway's tiles. The steps rattle the wall behind my back, and I watch the crack under the door as the barely visible shadows of feet stop outside. The knob turns, and I shake Loxy awake, not daring to remove my eyes from the knob.

This is it. They are coming for us, just like Mom. They are going to cast us out of the village or, if we are very lucky, kill us.

My chest constricts, and I stumble to my feet, pulling a bleary-eyed Loxy up with me. We step back, away from the door, away from whoever is trying to enter, just as the door swings open and narrowly misses our toes. A large, dark form fills the doorway. He shakes out his oilskin and reaches up toward the lamp by the door, turning the key to illuminate the room.

"Thank the Bright One you're safe," Dad breathes as he hangs his oilskin over the peg on the wall. It's the most I've heard him say in weeks. He turns and looks at us. Though, as has become his habit, his gaze rests more on me than Loxy.

I sigh in relief. It's just Dad. Not a mob, not the wrath of Ivlene. My heart begins to slow again. "Yes, we're fine. Where have you been?"

"Doing what I could to protect the mine office."

I nod and release Loxy, watching my fingerprints appear on her arm in stark red.

"Everything fine here?" His eyes scan the dark room, trying to find anything out of place.

I look around, too. A few pots are on the ground, thrown there by the waves that rocked the house, and many of the crystals fell from the shelves, but overall, nothing of value seems to be destroyed, no food lost.

I make my way to the kitchen and dig around in one of the island's drawers until I find a match. I strike it on the book and hold it to the wick in the kitchen's kerosene lantern. The room is immediately twice as bright, filled with a soft orange glow.

It still isn't enough to reach all the dark corners, but for now, it will do.

"What a mess," Loxy says, her eyes on the shelves of Dad's treasures from the mines. This shelf seems to be the most damaged, with almost every crystal overturned or on the floor. She kicks casually at a broken spire of white with her slippered foot.

"It could have been worse," I say, striding toward the lantern by the hearth. "At least the house wasn't hit."

"A few on the other side of the village were," Dad says. "The brigade is still busy with the fires."

"Where will the families go?" I ask. I hold another match to the next wick, and the room brightens more.

"Their neighbors have offered to take them in. One or two will stay at the guest house. Only one of the houses had been completely destroyed when I left the office."

I shudder at the thought. It could have been our house smoldering on the Sea, but for some reason Ivlene spared us. I lift my eyes skyward and mumble a small prayer of thanks on our behalf.

Maybe our family isn't cursed after all.

Loxy kicks at another broken bit of rock on the floor, then reaches toward the crystal. Her fingers wrap around a bright white tower of selenite, and then it explodes into a million fragments.

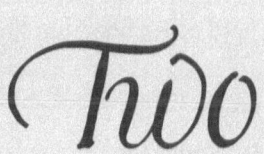

Two

LOXY

The Bright Ones were born sisters, twins of the same celestial blood, two faces of the sky. Ivlene was born to rule the day, the very face of the sun, while Sefella was the moon. And like these two faces, the sisters were to share in the power of the world.

Excerpt from *The Records of Bright*

I jump back as the shards of selenite strike my bare flesh. It stings, but nothing manages to pierce my skin, at least not as far as I can tell. I blink, my heart pounding, and back away from the crystals, stunned.

What was that?

My ears ring, a sound like chimes I hadn't noticed before touching the crystal. The room distorts and dances before my eyes. The ringing grows louder and louder, and I clap my hands over my ears in an effort to subdue it, gasping as it digs into me and forces the air from my lungs.

But it does nothing to quiet the ringing.

The ringing vibrates my skull, shaking my thoughts until they are mush. I squeeze my eyes closed tightly and clench my teeth as the ringing turns painful. I sink to the ground, slamming my knees against the hard plank floor, but I barely feel it over the pain in my head.

Loxy…a voice whispers.

Hands grab my arms, and the ringing begins to fade.

"Loxy! Lox!" I begin to hear again. "Are you okay?"

I open my eyes to the concerned face of El. Dad stands several paces away, and the expression on his face can only be described as horror.

My stomach sinks.

I blink away the last of the pain and rise to my feet. My arms sting, but I'm not sure if it's from the shattered crystal or the sparks from the Burning Rain. I glance down at my arms where the sparks fell. Tiny red dots pepper my skin like spices on a roast.

Where did they come from? The sparks? They weren't red, like the embers of a fire would glow. The sparks were all the colors of the rainbow shining against white light, like tiny bubbles.

Bubbles that burn?

El steps back next to Dad, her eyes almost as wide as his. "What was that?" she says softly.

"Loxy?" Dad says, his voice trembling. I look up into his watery eyes, his image blurring as my own fill with tears.

I study my hands. Nothing seems different. "I don't know."

Dad raises a hand toward me, his eyes wide, and opens his mouth to speak. But no sound comes out.

He looks so broken.

Slowly, he sinks to his knees, his face blank.

I turn to El. "What's going on? What's wrong?"

El glances outside, turning the ring on her finger around and around. Mom's ring. The silver one with the aquamarine stone. Her face is pale, and she doesn't speak, her large seafoam eyes full of pity.

And fear.

"El? Dad? Please! Say something," I plead.

Dad stares at the floor, still in shock, and El forces a wan smile, still twisting the ring. "It's just that…for a moment, you looked exactly like Mom."

My heart flips. Like Mom? Why would Dad…

Then it dawns on me, like the sun when it breaks over the distant horizon and reflects across the water outside the window.

Not just Mom. *Mom.* The mom they drove out twenty years ago.

Mom with her magic out of control.

The Burning Rain brings change. I don't know where the words come from, but the truth burns as much as the fire that fell from the sky.

Tears fill my eyes again, fear squeezing around me like a vise. I look back at my hands, still no different save for the few burns from the sparks. But now they shake, trembling uncontrollably. Panic grips me in earnest.

They are going to kill me, just like they tried to kill Mom.

I turn on my heel and run from the house, ignoring El's cries for me to wait. I sprint down the walk, toward my safe space, toward the apiary's bushes and office and Audrey, *my* Audrey, tears streaming down my face, heart flying like a bird across the surface of the sea. El doesn't follow, or, if she does, she doesn't try very hard to catch me.

The night is close around me, the darkness stretching out in every direction, all the way from the mountains to the faint glow of Aeglora in the distance. The water is inky black, so dark that I fear slipping off the walkway, even though the water would only come to my knee. But even my fear of falling isn't greater than my fear of whatever is happening to me.

And so I keep running, tears blurring my eyes, heart pounding until my chest aches.

I slide around the turn toward the apiary, barely registering the shouts of villagers as I shove past people, hardly smelling the smoke that drifts across the waves. Clouds have moved back in, lightening the predawn sky, and rain begins to fall, first speckling and then drenching my dress.

I stumble to a stop on the walk outside the apiary square and bend over, taking a moment to catch my breath before slipping into the office. I push the door closed behind me, softly, and lean back against it, heart still pounding and breath shallow.

"Loxy?" Audrey says, causing my heart to flop again in my chest. She stands by the desk, sweeping up bits of broken glass. Her dark hair glows in the lamplight.

I raise a shaking hand. "N-no. Stay there. Please."

"Loxy, what are you doing here?" She brushes off her hands over the pile of glass shards and steps toward me.

My heart stutters forward in a panic. What if the crystals come again? What if I hurt her?

What is happening?

"Please, Audrey, something's wrong. Stay there!"

She isn't listening.

"Calm down, Bumble. Deep breath. What's going on?"

The nickname is a bit of familiarity, of comfort in a world that is careening out of control. It is a tonic, and I find my breath burns less in my lungs and my heart slams into my sternum with less force.

I take a breath. "There's something wrong with me."

An unbidden memory of salt crystals sprouting from a door frame springs to mind, and I wince, recalling the way they had sliced Dad's arm. The look of fear on his face. I was so young at the time, barely a toddler. How did I even remember that?

Audrey takes another step toward me, and the panic is back. I gasp and sidestep away from her.

"Then let me help," she says, her voice calm, a balm on my torn soul.

I think of crystals, of the explosion at the house, the cut on Dad's arm years ago. Magic I've always had, though I've kept it hidden, but this is so much worse. This is dangerous.

My magic could really hurt her. For the first time in my life, it is the magic, and not the villagers—not the priestesses—that scares me.

"Please, Audrey. Stay there. I don't want to hurt you!"

But Audrey is already in front of me, taking me by the shoulders. She strokes my shoulder with her thumb. "You won't hurt me. See? I'm fine. Now, what's going on?"

I let out a strangled cry as I push her hands away, then hear a grind of earth as crystals sprout from the door where I had been standing. She pulls one hand to her chest, her face pale, but she is not injured, at least not that I can see.

My gaze moves to her eyes, expecting fear, hurt…but I see neither. Not even surprise. Her eyes are as kind and calm as ever. Did she know? What other explanation is there for her serenity?

"How long?" I say. "How long have you known?"

She takes a step toward me, running her finger gently along my jaw. My skin tingles where she touches it, leaving a warmth that spreads through my body. My heart begins to slow, and I look to her with desperate eyes, seeking the comfort she always brings me.

No one else has this effect on me. No one ever has. Even *she* didn't have that effect on me until I got to know her. Until we were so close I couldn't imagine life without her. That's what it's like to need feelings, to need emotional attachment and bonding and trust before finding out I'm attracted to someone.

Audrey gestures toward the chair at the desk. "Please, Loxy. Will you sit down now?"

I do as she asks but keep my eyes fixed on a jar of honey next to the apiary ledger. Drops of water and more glass litter the book and the desktop. I interrupted her from cleaning up the mess left by the Burning Rain only to bring her a different kind of mess.

Audrey slides another chair across the floor with a scrape and settles in next to me. "Now. Start from the beginning. Tell me everything."

So I do. I tell her about the salt. About how it Sings to me, how it always has. How Elodie has been afraid, how *I* have been afraid. How we've hidden it.

I pull a small pouch of salt from my pocket. I dump cubes of pink halite into my palm and feel the buzz of salt magic at the contact. It's familiar and safe, at least here. As long as no one knows.

I let the Song of the crystals soothe me as I play with the structures, collapsing the crystals and reforming them, pulling the salt out of the impurities, then mixing them back together. Demonstrating for Audrey.

But she already knows.

And then I tell her. I tell her how the magic has grown. What happened during the Rainfall.

Am I a monster?

Eventually, Audrey places her hand over the salt, lowering it and looking at me with such warmth that I have to turn away, hide my tears.

"Everything is going to be okay, Bumble," she says again. She hesitates, and I look back in time to see her brow furrow. "But maybe we should think about backup plans."

"Backup plans?" I say numbly.

"Do you think Elodie will keep this silent?"

I open my mouth, but nothing comes out. I don't know the answer. El is always too concerned with the temple, with the will of the priestesses. She's been trying to have me "cleansed" for years, though I've refused.

I'm not like her. The temple has never accepted me, and honestly...I'm not sure I really accept them, either.

And now? What will Elodie do?

What if she's at the temple even now?

Audrey rises to her feet, pulling books down from the shelf over the desk. "We could leave. We've talked about it before. Just you and me." She tosses a smile over her shoulder, and I can't help returning it. "A fresh start, where no one knows you. Where there's no black cloud over your family and no Elodie to tell you how to live your life."

I lean forward. "There's the capital, Aeglora, where we would merely be faces in a crowd. Or Salitas, by the coast. We could live on the beach and just enjoy the sunsets every day. Or even Ryth Hollows, where I might have a chance at actually becoming a healer."

Audrey smiles again. "That's the spirit! So, a backup plan. If something happens, we leave. You and me."

Me and Audrey. It sounds almost too good to be true. Could Mom be out there somewhere, too? I may never know.

At least, not if I stay here.

Three

ELODIE

In the beginning days, the balance was true. Ivlene ruled the happy occasions of life, the births and marriages, and Sefella held the brokenhearted and carried the dead to the Underworld.

Excerpt from *The Records of Bright*

I run my fingers through my tangled hair as Loxy disappears around a corner. I had tried to follow her, but she's so fast. My eyes are wide, heart pounding as I let her go. What if she betrays our secrets? Is this what will finally bring the eyes of the priestesses back to our family, deciding we are dangerous, kicking me out of the temple?

What if she hurts someone?

I squeeze my eyes closed. I don't know if I'm more worried about her or our family...or my place at the temple. We could lose everything.

She couldn't control just any crystal before now; she had no link to a crystal that wasn't salt. And I know for a fact that the crystals Dad had lined up on that shelf were very much Not Salt. In truth, she's always had a bit too much interest in those crystals, as if she secretly wanted this all along.

My stomach aches. Halosinging, while still a horrible blight, was at least benign. But Crystallosinging? I'm not so sure. Especially since that's how everything had started with Mom. If anyone finds out...

Should we leave and start over elsewhere? Would she even be safe somewhere else?

I know where she's going now, though. She's made no secret of her love of the apiary. And she talks about Audrey nonstop, the only person she's ever seemed to really care about here. Her only friend. More than a friend. I've never had a bond like that. I've never really wanted one: no husband or wife, no life partners. All I've wanted is the temple and maybe a few friends.

Will I lose even that now?

Before, when it was only salt Loxy could control, there was hope the priestesses could help. But I have a horrible feeling in the pit of my stomach. I've heard how they speak of Crystallosinging and other advanced forms of Singing, like the Atmosinging Mom bore. If they find out... And if they learn we've been hiding it all these years...

It will all be over.

I wait a moment for my breathing to slow as tears prick my eyes. I am no warrior. I haven't been in condition for a while, and my lungs burn just from sprinting one block.

As I wait for the pressure in my lungs to ease, I watch the rain fall on the sea, creating infinite ripples on the waves. It's normal rain, just water. I push myself up straight and take my first step toward the apiary as footsteps leap onto the walkway where I stand. The walk lurches under my feet, and I stumble.

I turn to yell at whoever carelessly jumped onto the walk when the runner's voice cuts through the rain.

"Elodie!"

Maisy—Priestess Maisy, just newly initiated from my own class—is running toward me from the direction of the temple. My heart lurches forward, stomach sick, even as I raise a hand in greeting. Surely they can't have found out so quickly!

She slides to a stop next to me, un-winded. Maybe it's just me who's out of shape. Maybe I should be running the walkways so I don't come so close to death every time I have to move faster than a walk.

"Elodie, you're wanted at the temple," she says. "All priestesses and apprentices are required at this time of crisis."

I throw a glance over my shoulder toward the apiary, still yearning to follow Loxy, to protect her. But instead I turn to follow Maisy. The priestesses will not wait long for me, and there will be punishment if I'm too slow. Audrey will have to be enough for my sister. For now.

The rain increases as we walk, and by the time we make it to the steps into the sea, my dress is drenched. I know the delicate fabric is filled with wrinkles and smells from yesterday. I will surely be reprimanded. Priestesses are not to look rumpled, not to look as if they'd slept on the floor. Which I had.

I touch the dry turquoise paint across my nose and feel the cracks, feel the soft edges where it's smudged. It should be a line across my face, just below my eyes, exactly one finger's width. It should be clean and fresh, like me. I should have fixed the markings, added the dark eye paint of mourning, but there wasn't time.

Bright One help me.

I want to be away from the temple like I never have before. Somewhere deep in my bones, I can feel Loxy's need for comfort, for help. As her sister—and a priestess—that's supposed to be my role.

Instead, I am stuck here, placating the priestesses with my obedience. And getting nothing but an anxiety so strong that I feel as if it is crushing me under its weight.

But aren't I here to make a difference? I know I can. I can feel the presence of the Bright One every time I set foot through that glowing pink arch.

Elodie…

The rain increases in intensity, and thunder rumbles. I jump, my heart beating out a hasty staccato.

I have to get to the temple. Now.

Four

LOXY

Magic grew in this world, magic with elements from both sisters, magic of light and power and darkness, magic to control the wilds that existed at the beginning.

Excerpt from *The Records of Bright*

I spend all day with Audrey, and her affection and calm attitude, her unconditional acceptance of me—all of me—soothe me back to serenity. But finally, the afternoon is waning, and she practically pushes me to the door.

"You have to face them sometime," she says gently, brushing my cheek with a kiss.

I give her a shaky smile, panic already building in my chest, and step outside. I drag my feet all the way home, stretching the walk out as long as I can.

How are they going to react to this morning? And what did El do? I don't think she would have given me away to the priestesses, not really, but the flutter in my heart betrays a sliver of doubt.

The house is silent as I approach. Maybe no one is here. Taking a deep breath, hand on the door's handle, I finally push into the living room and strip out of my wet outer garments. I find a place to hang them around Elodie's oilskins, then turn to face the room.

"Lox!" El cries, her cheeks rosy pink and a drunken grin splitting her face. Her turquoise stripe is smudged so that the edges blur onto her golden skin. In some places, it's completely wiped away, even worse than it had been this morning.

I wave, my eyes roving the open hearth. No Dad. That explains the bottle of honey wine on the bricks, cork popped and bottle nearly empty. Did she drink all that herself?

"Are you okay?" I ask, eyeing the bottle again.

El waves her hand absently, wine nearly sloshing out of her glass.

I nod slowly. She is shrugging off her bad day in a bottle of wine, but the bottle—and the broken look in her eye—tell me all I need to know. Maybe she told them, maybe she didn't, but either way, we are still the black sheep of Limutria. Maybe even more so now.

I settle into a chair by the hearth and pull out my sketchbook and pencil box. I ink part of a copy I had been working on of the anatomy of a heart. Duplicating the diagrams from my textbook helps me remember them. For a few blessed moments, the room is quiet save for the ticking of the clock on the wall.

But my heart is pounding. I am trying to keep myself calm with these normal things, my little drawings and studies, even though I can't focus on them. I don't want to ask. I don't want to know.

I *need* to know.

And yet, I'm too afraid. My entire future is in Elodie's hands, as it has been all day. Ignoring the facts don't make them any less true.

I hunch down, closer to the drawing, keeping my eye on my sister. Is she drinking because she feels guilty? Could she possibly have kept quiet?

Those priestesses mean everything to her. She craves their acceptance more than anything else. And I'm the one thing that could stand in her way. She never really understood what it was like for me, how I've never been accepted by them, by Ivlene.

How it feels to be a true outcast.

"Our future is ruined, you know," El suddenly says, breaking the silence and jolting me out of my spiraling thoughts. "There's nothing left for us after this. They are *priestesses*. They say we're cursed. And their words are truth straight from Ivlene herself."

My pen pauses, hovering over the page, afraid to hear more, but also desperate to know the truth. To know what she said. I've never seen her like this, so distraught and *drunk*. El has always been the stable one. The dependable one. I've never seen this side of her, and my heart thrums in apprehension, as if my body knows what she's about to say.

"Or maybe the curse is already at hand," she says, oblivious to my racing heart, my mounting anxiety. She turns her glazed eyes on me. "Maybe it has something to do with *you* after all."

There it is. My heart sinks, and I break out in a cold sweat. "You should sober up before Dad gets home!"

She waves me away and takes a long drink from her glass. "Just go to your room, Lox. You don't know anything. It would be better if you weren't here, anyway."

The comment is like a cold knife into my heart, but I shove the tears down. She acts like I haven't carried guilt and anxiety over being discovered for my whole life. As if I didn't wish I were anywhere but here. As if I didn't have enough to worry about right now without her drunken, loose lips.

She only has to worry about her reputation. But my very survival is at stake. Witches don't last long in Nasmarya, and they haven't for over a millennium. I've done my part to protect us. I've kept quiet. I've allowed her to dictate my future for me. I'm giving up my dreams, all to make sure no one finds out.

Because of her.

Don't I deserve better from her?

I storm into our room, wishing I could slam a door behind me, but the curtain only swings down to cover the opening, its gentle motion too soft for the storm raging within my heart.

A storm that matches the one growing outside.

Five

ELODIE

The balance remained for a time, but Ivlene grew hungry for the power her sister had.

Excerpt from *The Records of Bright*

I finish off the wine as Dad walks through the door. He passes me without a word, without a glance. He just dumps his oilskin at the door for me to clean up later, waves a hand at me, and disappears into his room.

Then it's just me and the priestesses' words and the suspicions of the villagers. Already, they give me a wide berth at the temple and on the village's walks. No one wants to be near the family associated with the last known Singer, especially after a Burning Rain, the very judgement of the Bright One, Ivlene. It's like they're just waiting for evidence that proves them right, that our family is a blemish, is dangerous.

I've given everything to this place. I know what will happen, how they'll treat us all once they know. I see the shattering selenite again in my memory and shudder.

They always leave everything to me. Ever since Mom...

I glance at our room where Loxy is probably moping. Where Mom's portrait hangs to mock us. Anger bubbles up in my gut, and I suddenly can't stand to be in this house anymore.

I drape an oilskin over my shoulders and step out the kitchen door onto the narrow porch. It's separated from the walkways, making it mostly private to anyone outside the household. On a clear night, I can just barely make out Aeglora's lights far in the distance, or at least the skyglow from them, but tonight rain falls too steadily to see beyond the next house.

One day I will see the capital, study with the priestesses there. If we have to relocate, maybe that day will come earlier than I'd thought.

I walk to the railing and rest my arms across the top, letting the rain running off the roof fall on my head. It cools my flushed face, probably smearing my paint even more, but I'm beyond caring. No one but Dad and Loxy will see me tonight, and the cool air and water on my face clear my head. The smell of smoke still hangs in the air, though the fires are all out.

I haven't felt this heavy since Mom left. I close my eyes, seeing again that fateful day.

Strong arms pulling me back, holding me away from Mom.

Mom like a torch, flames of purple and pink and white licking at the air from her body. Crystals sprouting from her open palm like seedlings. Whirling tornadoes spinning around her, rushing past us on either side. Her eyes bright orbs of silver.

There was nothing of Mom in that stare.

My heart pounds. The glow in Mom's eyes was so much like Loxy's. I had no idea what was coming then. What if it happens again, with my sister?

What if the village finds out?

I desperately wish not to remember what happened next, but my mind plays the memory anyway.

Loxy reached out toward the crystal I had broken, touching one stubby finger to the jagged edge of salt. It regrew, reformed, repaired itself back into the shape it used to be.

I looked up at her with wide eyes. I glanced at Dad, but his gaze was fixed outside, at the battle that raged as the temple tried to force Mom out of the village.

Three priestesses with elegant robes and intricate makeup stood between us and Mom. They held their moon-shaped blades in front of them, like they always did when they were protecting Limutria, while Mom hurled fire and wind and crystal in their direction. They knocked away every attack, and Mom backed toward the edge of the village, toward the edge of the plank walks and floating buildings.

Mom let out another roar, and the High Priestess stepped forward. When she spoke, her voice was clear, ringing with power beyond her own. The first time I'd ever heard the Bright One speak through a priestess. "Volta, we will not allow you to live here as you are. But if you let us help you, cleanse you of the magic that infests your spirit—"

Mom let out another great roar, and the sea began to build behind her, like during the worst storms of the rainy season. She hurled another fireball at the High Priestess, and the sky crackled with lightning.

The Priestess deflected the fire with one flick of her weapon as a lock of her hair fell in front of her eyes. "Volta Shayde, you are hereby banished from Limutria."

Mom tried to run at the priestesses, but suddenly it was as if a wall surrounded the village. Mom threw herself against it for what seemed like ages, trying to force her way back into the village. Every time she hit the wall, I flinched. After a few minutes, I buried my face in Dad's shoulder.

The noise eventually died down, and I turned just in time to see Mom running out into the sea, the storm chasing her into the distance. Then she was gone, and all was quiet.

And we were left to clean up the mess, pick up the pieces of what she had destroyed.

I feel the familiar flutter of my heart when I think about Mom's magic, that twinge of anger mixed with fear. If it happened to her, who's to say it won't happen to Loxy, too? We still don't know what changed Mom. Only Ivlene knows if Loxy is also in danger.

Maybe if she hadn't abandoned us, hadn't stayed away all these years, she'd be able to help. We would know.

The cool air and the rain dripping down my face do more to drive the alcohol out of my blood than a tall glass of tonic water would. I knew that remedy already; Illume had taught it to me last year during my first lessons. It tends to be in high demand in Limutria, especially during the rainy season.

The door opens behind me with a creak, then closes with a soft click. Small footsteps pad up next to me, but I do not turn. Loxy appears at my elbow and mirrors my stance at the rail, and I glance at her before turning my eyes back to the rain. I can't help but see Mom in every line of her face, the same proud contours, the same bright, sparkling eyes.

And now the magic, stronger than ever.

For several long moments, neither of us speaks. We simply watch the rain fall.

"Eventually Dad's going to notice you drank a bottle of his wine," she starts.

I roll my eyes. "Please. He doesn't notice anything these days."

She sighs, but doesn't answer. She knows I'm right. I can feel something in her posture that tells me she has more to say, but we don't speak another word for several long moments.

"Do you think Mom's out there somewhere?" she finally says, as if reading my earlier thoughts.

I want to say no. I want to pretend she's dead so we can all move on. Death would be easier than not knowing, than the guilt of having let the priestesses send her out into the wilderness.

The bitterness of knowing she never came back.

"Somewhere," I finally say instead. It's almost the truth. She falls silent again, and I look sideways at her, moving my head only marginally so that my chin still rests on my crossed arms. "Do you remember her?"

Loxy's face falls, and her gaze drops to the rippling surface of the sea. "A little. Every day I forget more and more. You and Dad never talk about her anymore. And I only remember bits and pieces. Truthfully…" She hesitates. "Truthfully, I'm so jealous of you sometimes." She straightens and begins toying with the alexandrite around her neck.

I blink in surprise, then take a step back from the rail and turn to face her. "Why is that?"

"You actually knew her."

"So did you."

"Yes, when I was a kid. But in a year? Five years? I'll barely even remember her face. I'll only know that portrait."

I turn back to the rain rippling the sea to hide my wince. I hate that portrait as much as Loxy clings to it. For her, it is a thread to the mother she misses. To me? Just a constant reminder that my mother is gone, she didn't come back, and all her responsibilities for the family fell on me. "I doubt that."

"Why?"

I sigh. Much as I hate that portrait...Loxy needs her yet. "I won't let you forget."

We fall into silence again. Loxy drops herself down on one of the padded lounge chairs under the roof, and I return my arms to the railing. My thoughts drift, like the ripples on the sea below. They spiral from Mom back to Loxy, back to all my worries.

"Are we in trouble?" Loxy suddenly says a few minutes later, breaking the white noise of the storm. When I glance at her, her face is expressionless, but I can hear the tension in her voice.

She's scared.

Her question ricochets in my aching skull. *Are we in trouble? Probably.* "Of course not."

"Then why were you drinking?"

"It was a stressful day." And a terrifying one. Even thinking of what the priestesses would do if they knew about Loxy makes me sick to my stomach.

"That's no reason to drink. Do you want to know what I think?"

Not really. "What's that?"

"You're too worried what your friends think of you. And the priestesses." She swings her legs over the side of the chair, leaning toward me with her elbows on her knees. "Actually, the entire village."

And she's not worried enough.

"*You* can say that," I snap. What does she really know of what I've done for us all these years? How I've protected us?

"Why?"

"You don't care what anyone thinks." The words are out before I realize how they sound. Maybe the alcohol hasn't evaporated like I'd thought. I hadn't meant to say it, but it's the truth. She gallivants around the village like she hasn't a care in the world, like nothing can touch her.

And leaves me to pick up after her.

She looks hurt, and my stomach drops.

"Of course I care," she says softly. "I care what you think. I care what Dad thinks."

I glance at her, guilt settling in my stomach, even though what I said was true. "But you don't care what the village thinks."

"I do. But you care too much."

"Maybe I care too much so I can protect you." I turn away from the rain again, to face her. The rain increases behind me, like water pouring from a bucket, the cold water splashing at my ankles from the sea over the edge of the porch.

"Why do I need protecting?" Her voice is rising like the sea around us.

The words are out before I can stop them. "Because if they ever think you're anything not…normal…they'll run you out just like they did to Mom."

"Not normal?"

"They already think you're odd. They don't need to find out you're corrupted, too. They might have forgiven the salt, but this?" I spin from my place at the railing, heart pounding. My fear for her is too close, too real, now that she's given voice to it. "Why can't you let me talk to Priestess Cydia? We could help you, I know we could! And if you were cleansed, healed, then maybe…maybe I could get you that apprenticeship with the healers."

"And what, exactly, would this *help* entail?" She drops the loose thread on her skirt that she'd been twisting between her fingers. "You just said it yourself. They won't be so forgiving of me anymore. And if you let them know their suspicions are right? There's no hope of an apprenticeship here. You know that."

"I…I don't know. But there are so many stories, Lox, stories of people cleansed of their Singing. I'm sure we could find you the help you need."

"I don't need help! I haven't needed your help in years; why can't you see that?" She jumps to her feet and plants her hands on her hips. "Why can't you just admit that I have a gift? That if people would see Singing for what it really is, beyond the danger, that we could all be so much better off? If they weren't afraid of me? Maybe then Dad wouldn't be afraid of me, either."

My anger is building like a storm cloud. Is she really that naïve? "Because it's *not* a gift, Loxy. You're deluded if you think so! Singing is nothing but a curse, and Singers are nothing but a danger to everyone around them!"

"Have you ever seen me hurt anyone?"

I hesitate. "Well, no. But you had weak Singing. Practically useless."

"Like me?"

"I never said that."

"You think it."

"Don't you tell me what I think!" I am facing her fully now, my hands on my hips, mirroring her stance.

"Why? Because you don't like that I can read you so easily? You're so selfish, El. You never think of anyone but yourself."

"You know that's not true!" I can feel my face flushing with anger now far more than alcohol. The rain continues its tumultuous downpour behind me. "Everything I do is for you. And you would have everyone know you're a…" I almost say *freak* but bite my tongue at the last minute. The anger in her eye, the salt in the air around her…I can't say it. "Not normal, just so you can feel special!"

She blinks in the roaring rain, silent. The rain is suddenly deafening, and my pulse is far too fast. I bite my tongue, wishing I could take back that last comment. Slowly, she approaches me.

"Do you remember that time in the dry season? When you explained away my magic slip to your friends? Do you remember what you called me later, when no one else could hear?"

I don't answer. In truth, I don't remember whatever event she's talking about. But it must have made an impression on her.

"Do you think I'm a freak?"

For a moment I can't answer. Do I? Did I really say that to her? It had been on the tip of my tongue only a moment ago. I can't argue the truth.

A toddler who can create and destroy towers of salt? A child who can purify and supersaturate drinking water? A young adult who can whip mounds of salt into a frenzied storm when she's angry?

It's far from normal.

"I wouldn't put it that way," I finally say.

"But you do." The air around her sparks with those white crystals again, the ones that appear whenever we fight. Proving my feelings. Proving that whatever control she thinks she has is a delusion.

She could never fit in as a healer's apprentice. Not here. Maybe not anywhere. It's not safe.

I know she would be great at it, if it *was* safe. If she didn't have the Singing. Maybe even with the Singing. She could probably help people.

But I can't say that to her, or she will just want to start an apprenticeship more. And I can't bear to break her heart every day. I won't always be able to protect her if she starts working at the temple.

I give her a broken smile, try to make the truth sound like a joke, try to hide my fear for her. *Of* her. "You're my little sister; of course you're a freak."

It was the wrong answer. I knew that, knew it before I said it, but I couldn't seem to stop the words from tumbling out anyway.

The salt spins around her, and I glance toward the small bit of walkway we can see from the porch. Blessedly, it's empty.

"One of these days," Loxy says, her eyes narrowed to slits, "I'm going to leave, and we will prove you wrong. All of you." She turns and stalks back into the house.

I stand alone, facing Aeglora, for a while longer as the rain falls harder around me. My anger is dissipating as I realize the rift I've once again opened between us. All that's left now is guilt. How do I always say the exact wrong thing to her?

The room is oddly quiet the next morning when I wake. A watery light filters through the window, not quite sunny but not a rainstorm either. I can just barely see the sky from my bed, partially cut off by the drenched brown of the roof. The clouds are a bruised gray-green color, promising more rain, but for now, the storms are still.

I don't move from the bed. I can feel the words of the villagers burning in my ears already, and I can't face the priestesses with their gossiping. The older ones, the full priestesses, aren't so bad, but the younger ones, my peers, the apprentices…their tongues wag at even the suggestion of a good story, anything to jar them out of their boring lives.

I can't go. Not today. Not until this prophecy business all blows over. Not until I know Loxy will be safe, in control of her new self.

My stomach twists into knots, and I roll over to face the wall. Not even a dry day in the middle of the rainy season will make me move now.

"El?" comes a voice over my shoulder. A shadow falls across the dim daylight.

A dry day won't move me, but that voice might.

I roll back over to see Loxy standing over me. "Yeah?"

"I know you didn't mean it. What you said yesterday."

Butterflies flit in my stomach, and I swallow back my relief. I sit up and pull her down onto the bed with me, wrapping her close to me in an embrace. I tuck her head under my chin, hiding my tears threatening to spill over. Her words are a balm to my heart. But she doesn't need to see that weakness in my eyes.

"I *didn't* mean it," I say. "You are wonderful and special. And so like Mom."

She pulls back, and I have to fight myself not to shrink away and hide my face. "You really think so?"

I swipe at my eyes. "Yes. You look like her. You have her magic touch." I smile. "She was a Halosinger at the start, you know."

She smiles back at me, and the tension in my chest loosens just a mite. "Yes. I know." Her smile fades. "If she had been here, she could have taught me so much. What happened to her?"

"I have no idea. There was a Burning Rain." The room fades from around me, the scene replaying itself in my mind.

Mommy! I see my arms reaching for Mom. I see Dad pulling me away.

"Then people started getting sick. And her magic...it grew and grew, and then it exploded."

Swirling wind. Flashing light. Shattering crystals.

Elodie...

I shake my head quickly, ignoring my name. It was only memory. "They thought she brought it down on us. That the Bright One was punishing her. They made her leave."

Her back, disappearing across the sea in the cloud of a storm, was the last I saw of her.

We fall into silence. My mind is on that last day, the last time I saw Mom, but there's no way Loxy will remember that, so I don't know where her mind goes.

"I meant what I said, you know. I can't stay here forever. Maybe I will even find Mom." Loxy's voice rings in the silence.

Six

LOXY

Ivlene fought to take control of all the world, the light and the dark, and cast Sefella out of the sky. Sefella fell to the world in a fiery rain, a Burning Rain, and this Rain returns to remind us of Sefella's fall from greatness.

Excerpt from *The Records of Bright*

I want to find her."

The words are out of my mouth before I can stop them. I've been thinking about this as long as I can remember, feeling the hollow left by the loss of Mom.

Wondering why she never came home.

El turns a pitying gaze at me. It burns through my skin, ignites my bones. I can feel the static tingle of magic buzzing through my body, awakened by my heightened emotion. White fuzzes the edges of my vision.

I shove it down. "I mean it. I want to find Mom. I want…I need to know if she's okay. If she's even still alive. And if not…El, I can't stay here. There's no future for me here." My voice drops to almost a whisper. "You should know that by now."

"Lox, we can't just leave. *I* can't leave." A muscle twitches in her jaw.

Of course. The temple. Even with all the sand-filled things they've said about us, enough to make her hide and cower in our room, even with the new danger my new power brings, she still doesn't see how horrible they are, how much better she can do. We could do so much, *be* so much, somewhere else. The capital. The cities by the coast.

Anywhere but here. This place is a poison.

Loxy…

A voice fills my ears, one I thought I'd heard before. I shake my head, trying to dislodge it, to focus on El's response.

She is still talking. "Maybe we can go look for her when we're older. Take Dad. Have a great adventure together." She laughs, that same high, nervous laugh as her public one. "But I need to finish my training. I'm only a few lessons away from taking my exams and making herbalist and priestess."

Wait. She wants me to keep waiting. As if I haven't been waiting for her since I finished my formal schooling.

My heart pounds, but there's no stopping now. I already laid it all out, bared my soul to her. "You could finish your training somewhere else. You could teach me what I need. We could find Mom, settle somewhere new. Someplace the world will accept us. Accept…me."

"We'll talk about it in a few years, I promise." El squeezes my shoulders, her words closing the conversation.

Anger flashes through my body, momentarily blinding me. "Why? Why not now? This place is killing us. It already broke our family once, and if we stay, who's to say it won't happen again? We could take Dad and Audrey. You could resume your apprenticeship in Aeglora. You've always wanted to see the temple there, anyway. We could start over."

"This is our home, Lox. The people need us."

"Need *you*, you mean. They've never needed me. I don't even think they really *want* me here."

"End of discussion, Loxy. Give it a few more years."

I bite my tongue, knowing she'll never bring it back up unless I do. My chest is tight, my words stoppered until I feel a bursting pressure. I want to fight, to argue, to cry.

But it won't mean a thing.

I stand, part of me longing to curl back into bed with my sister for comfort but another part of me wishing to be so far away from her that her words stop buzzing in my head.

I should have known better.

I stride to the wardrobe while El collapses back into the mattress. She may be content to laze around, to hide, but I don't want to stay here. I quickly exchange my nightgown for a simple pale-violet dress and drape the alexandrite necklace—*Mom's* necklace—over my head. Then I escape the room full of weighted expectations.

Dad sits at the hearth. He glances up as I enter, then quickly looks away.

My heart lurches. El must have been telling the truth, that I am like Mom. Why else can't Dad even stand to look at me anymore?

I can't be in this house right now.

I shove my feet in my boots and flee into the muted daylight.

Most of the village seems to be taking full advantage of the break in the rain, milling about along the walkways. The sea ripples beneath the planks as the people walk, and I think I pass one of the priestesses heading back the way I came, though I duck my head, hoping to avoid her attention. Instead, I focus on the beauty in this small respite in the weather. If the sun had been peeking through the clouds, it would be reflecting rainbows on the walls of the houses.

But there is no sun, and even though the rain isn't falling, the air is chilled.

I pass by the fishing pier where several fishers stand with their lines in the water. I pass by the turn to the temple. I pass the grocer and the mine office and the tailor.

I head straight for the apiary. I need Audrey.

Halfway there, the rain returns, along with a biting wind. The walkway bucks with the waves, and I slip a few times, hunching against the constant gale. Somehow, I manage to keep my footing. I duck my head against the driving rain, but it still finds its way past the oilskin and drips down my neck, freezing me. I can barely even hear the engines of the water purifiers down the block, something we wouldn't need if they'd just accept my Singing.

Finally, the edge of the apiary comes into sight. Much like the garden squares where soil covers the stones and creates the growing fields, the apiary is covered in grass and, in the dry season, flowers. The hives stand staggered in the middle of the square, tightly wrapped in oilskin, but not so tight that the honey bees are trapped without airflow. The pastel paint of the hives almost glows in the dim light of morning, hues of pink, yellow, lavender, and blue replacing the color of flowers.

Audrey is already in the square, checking the hive farthest from the small apiary office. I direct my steps toward her, squaring my shoulders against the wind. My stomach is warm and happy at the mere sight of her, a harsh contrast to how cold the rest of me has become in the rain.

As I approach, I wave. "Good morning!" I call over the storm.

She smiles and lifts her hand in return. A smile just for me. She holds a jar of sugar water in her other hand, and the hand she waves with holds the dropper. The honey stores must be low if she feels the need to feed the bees. And the rainy season has barely begun.

"Help me with the checks!" she yells over the gale.

I nod and approach, peeling back the protective covering to peer into the hive. The honey stores look full, at least ninety of the one hundred pounds we started with still present. Maybe the sugar water is just a precaution. We check the hives for the health of the queens, for any sign of damage or disease, and that they are staying as dry as possible. Once we finish the checks, we hurry into the office.

Audrey places the jar of water and dropper on the shelf above the desk and begins to peel off her oilskin. A puddle forms under her feet. "I think most of the hives will make it, but I'm worried about the queen in number three." She hangs her oilskin on the rack by the door, and her dress beneath it is spotted with dampness where the rain dripped through. My heart stutters at the sight of the few places her dress has grown so damp it clings to her form, and I flush, turning away quickly.

The window has already been replaced, fresh and clean, letting the light into the small office. The rain is diminishing again, unstable as it often is during the rainy season.

I remove my own oilskin and bag and hang them next to hers. She pulls her ledger down from the shelf and sits at the desk, still dripping water onto the floor. Then we begin the tedious task of notes, leaving comments on the condition of each hive and writing care notes for the next week. We will check on the ill queen more often to make sure she survives, but if she doesn't, the hive may fail. It's only one out of twenty, but it will mean beginning a new hive when the rains end.

When we finish the ledgers, Audrey snaps the book closed and spins in her chair to face me, playing with the charcoal pencil in front of her. She pecks me on the cheek, and a warm glow spreads across my face again, but this time from pleasure rather than embarrassment. I duck my head and fiddle with a loose thread on my skirt. I want to kiss her back, to tell her how much she means to me, but my teeth are clamped together so tightly I can't utter a word.

How can I? Haven't I said enough today already? What about last night? Words feel like too much now. I stand and grab the broom out of the corner, and Audrey laughs, taking the hint and fetching a wash bucket from the warehouse connected to the office.

Bright One bless Audrey for not forcing me to talk anymore. I just want to exist for a while.

And Audrey lets me.

By the time I leave the apiary, the world is alive and fresh again. My Singing is amplified, empowered, stronger, and I'm not afraid of the changes the Burning Rain brought anymore. I no longer only Sing to salt; I Sing to all crystal.

It's almost overwhelming. I pull the cool, salty air into my lungs, closing my eyes. It's a familiar breath, laced with Singing as always, but it's also more now. *I* am more. It fills every bit of me. I feel new. Powerful. Like I can do anything. Be anyone.

Isn't this what I wished for all these years? Something more powerful to make all the pain worthwhile? Something I could use to convince the world how valuable Singers could be, beyond purifying the salt from the water of the sea?

And now I have it, and the world feels huge.

I open my eyes and look out toward the mountains in the distance. Yes, the world is huge, but the village is still small.

If only Dad would accept this part of me, if only the world could see us for who we really are. If only they didn't fear us.

But even my brief melancholic thoughts aren't enough to hold my attention for long. For once. I feel reborn, and I look back to the sea with new eyes.

The crystals in the sea, in the air, all seem to glow like they never did before, alive with my new magic. Each one Sings a note that sounds like its name, mostly new and one old. Halite still Sings the strong Song of the Sea. But beneath the halite, I can hear those other Songs. Blödite. Mirabilite. Quartz.

The skies open in a spectacular downpour, soaking me through in seconds. I hurry down the last block, practically dancing. Even the rain can't dampen my spirits.

Yet as I step through the door to the house, Elodie and Dad nowhere to be seen, my spirits come crashing back to the Sea. I would have thought either they'd stay home or they would be home by now. It's almost time for dinner.

Elodie must finally have gone to the temple. My stomach drops to my toes.

What if El isn't here because she's changed her mind? What if she's telling them all about…me? Is that why she was so slow to move this morning? She was preparing herself to do the unthinkable?

My skin goes cold and clammy as I hurry back to my room. Would she go that far? Was I in danger? I didn't think she'd ever betray me, but that was before I had so much power. And in her eyes? I don't think she'd see it as a betrayal.

I curse under my breath. I can't stop her from telling the priestesses. It's far too late for that. I've been gone too long; she's had too much time. All I can do now is wait to know the truth.

How could I have forgotten the danger here so easily?

I change out of my sopping dress and exchange it for a dry one, then busy myself with cleaning up the house and stoking the fire in the hearth. Busy hands calm the mind. El always says that, but I suspect it really came from Mom. But even if it didn't, I don't want to break the illusion.

I feel closer to Mom now than I ever have before. Mom was a Crystallosinger. And more. An Atmosinger, if the stories are to be believed.

The main door hits the wall, and El steps through, her gown completely soaked. She pushes her dripping hair back away from her face and hangs her oilskin, nothing in her movements indicating any betrayal. I turn back to the hearth, letting her collect herself, and hear the door click closed and her steps retreat to the bedroom. Heart pounding, I force myself not to follow.

My stomach is sick, but I move to the kitchen anyway. I fill a kettle and a pot from the sink, placing the pot on the stove and the kettle over the hearth. No matter what she did, or didn't do, we could all stand to have a hot meal and some tea.

I am shredding some dried fish jerky into the stewpot when El appears at my shoulder, now in dry clothes, her wet hair plaited neatly.

"Here, let me help," she says.

She takes vegetables out of the cooler and begins slicing, each stroke of the knife neat and precise. After she accumulates a pile, she dumps them all in the fish broth, adding a few sprinkles of seasoning. We work this way for several minutes in silence, her slicing vegetables and me preparing fish.

She dumps more seasoning in the soup, and I lean over, reaching for the spoon. I don't know what to say, but I do know how bad El is at seasoning soups. Sure enough, I wince as I taste the broth.

El sees, her eyes flicking up to me from the cutting board where she has started slicing carrots. "What, no good?"

"Bland," I say, my voice as bland as the soup. "How can you be daughter to a salt miner and sister to a Halosinger and not know how to use salt?"

"Shh!" she says.

My heart lurches. Right.

I keep talking, hoping to distract from the mention of my magic. "You need how to learn how to cook with salt. It's called flavor."

I run my finger along an assortment of jars, all holding salts of different colors and flavors from green to pink to violet, earthy to fruity to herby, all native to Limutria. All as precious as gold. They are Nasmarya's only bargaining chip with our neighboring countries, the one commodity we can trade for things we don't have here.

"I'd use the pink," I say.

"I was thinking black," she says, reaching for the jar with the large, purplish crystals. It has an eggy flavor, usually nice.

But not in El's hands.

I shake my head vehemently. "No. You're so heavy-handed, El. Do you *want* it to taste like rotten eggs?"

She sighs. "Fine. Pink it is."

She pulls the pink jar from the shelf, the bright purple berries popping out from the salt, and twists off the lid. She adds several pinches of the pink halite and blackberry mix to the bubbling copper pot, and the sweet scent wafts around us.

We fall back into a heavy silence, chopping vegetables again. I want to say more, but the words stick in my throat.

Finally, El breaks the quiet, her eyes fixed on the carrots under her knife. "Are you okay?"

"Yes," I lie.

She doesn't pry any more than that. But the fear won't be silent, growing until it is all-consuming. What did she do? Am I safe?

We cook quietly until I can no longer stand the gnawing fear. I drop the package of fish jerky to the counter with a slap, and she jumps, nearly dropping the knife.

"Where did you go?" I demand. "You seemed pretty content to skip duties this morning."

"I was summoned to the temple again. Just like yesterday. We're still doing damage control from the Burning Rains. A lot of people are scared. And when I was dismissed, I stopped by the apiary. You'd already left."

Summoned. She didn't choose to go.

But she had tried to come check on me. I feel a small bloom of warmth, hope, spreading through my body.

"Would you have gone if you hadn't been summoned?"

Her hands are shaking, and for a moment I think I see a spark beneath the blade as it slices through the carrot. "No. I would have stayed with you."

I turn to face her. "So you didn't tell them? About me?"

She shakes her head, long, stringy bits of wet lavender hair hiding her face where it has already escaped the plait hanging down her back. "No. But they're watching us. Maybe closer than before."

I suck in a sharp breath and turn back to the pot. I hear El's knife thudding against the cutting board again, but neither of us says another word.

El kept my secret. And it terrifies her.

The wind suddenly rattles the panes of glass in front of us, sending a flurry of rain slamming into it. In fact, the rain all around the house is suddenly falling with such intensity that, even inside, it is a roar so loud I wouldn't be able to hear her talking right next to me.

I see a flash of light from the corner of my eye, then the knife clatters to the floor. I jump as El backs away from the counter, staring at her hands as if they are covered in blood.

"What is it?" I yell over the roar of the storm. "What's wrong?"

"You didn't see that?" she cries.

I start to shake my head when an arc of jagged lightning cuts the space between us, jumping between her fingers. We lock eyes.

Elodie is a Singer.

Seven

ELODIE

Ivlene rules the sky above and the world below. She rules the weather and the crystals, the fire and the seas. She is pure and perfect, untouched by the magic that once plagued the world.

Excerpt from *The Records of Bright*

N̊o.

No, no, no. This cannot be happening.

I break into a cold sweat, and my fingers tingle with the effects of the lightning. My entire body is alive, humming with a resonance I've never felt before. Is this what it's like? To be a Singer? To be infected with magic?

Elodie!

My hands spark again, and I cry out in alarm. It doesn't hurt, but it does scare me. The rain is pounding furiously against the glass, and thunder shakes the windows in their panes. Wind howls around the corners of the building. Every bit of the storm outside mirrors my inner turmoil.

It can't be.

"Loxy, what's happened to me?" I cry, backed against the center island counter like a cornered animal.

Loxy raises a hand toward me, her eyes full of sadness and compassion. And something else.

Awe.

Was I ever this compassionate toward her?

My memories swirl. Mom, summoning a storm. Mom's hands engulfed in crystals, in wind, in fire.

Fire sparks in my hand as another arc of electricity strikes my fingers. Something wet falls on my cheek, and I look up. A mass of white vapor has formed above my head. Another drop falls from the cloud, and I touch it where it lands on my face. My fingers come back wet, only water, and lightning buzzes between them like the webbed feet of a water fowl.

I look back to Loxy, but she is backing away from me now, her eyes on the cloud overhead, fear replacing her compassion. Her awe.

Perhaps the priestesses weren't worried about Loxy at all. The problem might not be my sister.

It might be me.

But that doesn't make any sense. Haven't I always been the faithful servant? I've always stayed on the path of Ivlene, done my work as a priestess apprentice, done everything expected of me and more!

Why would Ivlene allow Sefella to curse me this way?

Lightning strikes from the cloud over my head and shatters a vase on the island next to me. Shards of clay scatter, one striking my cheek. It stings and grows warm, then I feel the blood trickle down my face.

I look toward Loxy in horror. "*Help me*," I mouth, but the words don't come.

It's enough.

Loxy leaps into action. She bypasses the lightning, somehow, though every step she takes closer to me, my fear grows. The storm grows in intensity right along with it. She springs toward me, and I close my eyes, expecting pain, blackness, something to stop the destruction I am creating.

I will be the end of the village. I am death. I am doom.

I brace myself for the inevitable, sending a prayer to Ivlene for Loxy to slay me where I stand and free my family from what is coming.

Instead, warm arms wrap around my frame, and Loxy pulls me close. I raise my arms to return the embrace, sobbing into her dark curls. Her hair clings to the water on my face, the tears, the blood. But she doesn't seem to care. She simply holds me in her arms.

And I feel my heart calming. My breathing growing steady. The storm beginning to subside.

And then the cloud, the tingling, the lightning, they're all gone as if they had never been. Even the storm outside has settled into light rain.

The house is another story.

I open my eyes, still clinging to my sister. It looks like a whirlwind swept through the room. Which, I suppose, it did.

Dad will be back soon. And the reality of the entire situation hits me in full force: I have magic. The most dangerous, most cursed kind.

My heart slams into my chest, and I gasp, hurrying around the side of the island to grab the broom, clean up the puddles and the shards of broken porcelain from a vase that my...my *magic*...had knocked over.

Now I am just like Loxy. Only worse.

No one can ever know.

Loxy appears at my side, wordlessly helping me clean up. Like I've done for her all these years. Like I've tried to, at least. We lock eyes for a moment, but neither of us says a word.

What can we say? What do I do? Go to the temple and be cleansed? Hide it, like Mom and Loxy? Try to control it?

None of those sound like good options, and my eyes burn as I fight back tears. I don't want Loxy to see me cry. I have to be the strong one. Like I always am. I have to keep us as normal as possible.

My mind cycles through my options as we clean, as we finish dinner, as Dad finally comes home and doesn't even notice the pile of shards from a broken plate we'd missed. My heart pounds the entire time, my breath shallow. Loxy doesn't mention my magic, and neither do I. It's not long after Dad arrives that I settle on an option. My only one, really.

I know what I have to do. My magic—I struggle to even think the word, disgusted at what I am becoming—must never see the light of day.

I will not be like Mom. I will not be like Loxy. I will keep my magic to myself, hide it, suppress it until it yields to my will.

No one has to find out about either of us. I just have to figure out how to stuff it down.

When morning comes, I make my way to the temple, trembling. I can't bear Loxy's stare on me, the awe, the fear, the astonishment. I can't bear the secrets I'm hiding from Dad. Even though I know I'll have to hide them from the priestesses as well, the temple is the last place anyone would expect to find a Singer.

Right?

I shudder, chewing my lip. Why would Ivlene allow this? What did I do to deserve this curse?

A pang of hurt lances through my heart. If my friends at the temple find out about me, I could lose everything.

How could Ivlene's people act like this? I know what they would do, but I also know that I am a wonderful apprentice. A good person.

The air is humid and heavy and cold. I hunch over under my oilskin, even though no rain is falling, hoping that it will somehow hide my face from the nosy gazes of the villagers. But faces follow my every movement, eyes curious and confused. Everyone can see something is different, like they always did with Loxy.

They just don't understand what. Such is the nature of Singers.

I slip into the apprentices' washroom at temple, using the towels and pots of paint to make myself as presentable as possible without completely losing my calm, only feeling a small tingle of magic in my hand as I touch up my paint.

The magic buzzes louder under my skin as I recall the looks from the villagers, and I almost cry out in pain. Instead, I bite my lip and push against it, forcing it back and away. I smooth the wrinkles out of my dress as much as possible, then hurry to my station in the herbalism room. I take my usual place at one of the benches and begin to prepare a poultice for one of the older priestesses, an easy one that doesn't take long to mix.

This is usually my favorite part of the day, the time I get to be with myself. The time I get to do everything I've always wanted: serve the village, serve Ivlene, help people.

I sigh, almost feeling safe here at my bench, pulling out the first ingredients for the poultice. For so long, this place has felt more like home than home has. I found my first real friends here, and the priestesses allowed me to follow them after Mom was banished, even though…well, despite Mom.

And over the years, they've seemed to accept me. I served out a penance for our whole family and found a place to belong. A reason for being.

I flinch as I start to grind a bundle of herbs. Loxy wanted the same. But it was too dangerous for her here. She was so young, and even with such small magic, how could I trust her to keep it hidden? I hated even bringing her for services, but everyone deserves the love of Ivlene.

But today is different. I feel distant and disconnected from everything around me. And now that I am no different from Loxy, guilt nags at me, guilt that I get to learn what she's always wanted.

And she's lasted twenty years without betraying her secret. Maybe I underestimated her. Maybe she could have found a place here like she wanted, a place where she could help the villagers and learn healing. A place to belong.

Priestess Maisy, the other woman in the room today, says something to me, and I flinch, unable to comprehend her words.

"What?" I say numbly, automatically.

"I asked if you can help me," she repeats. Her voice is calm and patient, but I see the irritation in her eyes. The priestesses aren't used to repeating themselves.

"Yes, of course," I say absently.

I leave the poultice and join Maisy at her bench. She immediately begins pointing out the herbs that need to be crushed and heated. It's a complicated tincture, one that needs precise timing and cooking. A tincture like this requires two herbalists or one very skilled master such as Priestess Illume.

I remove the striker from the drawer and hold it to the gas burner, squeezing the handle to drag a flint and create the spark. Only nothing happens. I try it a few more times with no success, then examine the flint. It's worn down, ready to be replaced.

"Do we have another striker?" I say.

Maisy looks up from sorting. "Not in my bench."

I look at the striker again, and she wanders to the supply closet. I hold the striker to the burner one more time, but, again, no luck. My own striker has been missing for weeks, and none of the other benches seem to have one. Each attempt to make the striker work, or find a replacement, only serves to increase my frustration.

And as the frustration builds, I can feel the magic also building under my skin.

"Not now," I whisper, picking at the worn edge of the flint.

My heart stutters, and I drop the striker to the bench, my hands trembling.

Maisy pokes her head out of the closet, a brown jar in one hand. "Everything okay?"

I nod and force a smile, then after she disappears again, I study my hands. The buzzing is strongest at my fingertips, and the air around me feels electric, charged and full of energy. I turn over one hand, forcing my breathing to slow.

In. Out.

I rub my fingers together as a greasy sensation coats them.

A spark flies from my finger, and a flame no larger than that of a candle springs to life on my index finger.

I jump back, and my heart flutters. I glance over at the closet, and when Maisy doesn't appear, I hold my finger to the burner. It ignites with a whoosh. I close my opposite hand over the flame on my finger to snuff it out, then push the buzzing away.

It's working. The burner is ignited, and nothing has gone wrong. No one knows.

Then thunder claps outside. So much for the clear day.

But the thunder feels different than usual. It pulses with my heartbeat, in time with my breath. As my pulse increases, the rain and the wind begin.

The storm is mine.

Elodie…

My heart races now, the buzzing loud and painful under my skin. I rub at my arms, willing the buzzing to subside.

Priestess Maisy reappears at my elbow. "We're almost out of lavender. We should cultivate more in the garden next season."

I jump, one hand flying to my heart.

"Are you sure you're okay?" she says, her eyes traveling over my face. "You seem pale. Are you ill?"

I shake my head. "Of course not. I'm fine. You just startled me."

She casts me one more concerned look, then turns to the mortar and pestle and begins crushing the first herbs. I place a pot over the flame and add a few drops of rose oil, waiting for it to sizzle. I follow Maisy's movements and recipe automatically, responding without actually hearing a word I say. All the while, my mind spins as I listen to the rain pound on the ceiling overhead.

The storm taps at the windows faster and faster, mimicking the beat of my heart.

"Did you hear Her Eminence's most recent announcement?" Maisy says, breaking a woody stem in half with deft fingers.

The mention of High Priestess Cydia jolts me out of my trance. "What?"

"She wants us all to be on guard for any evidence of Singers. But we shouldn't mention it to the villagers. Last time we had a Burning Rain, well… You know what happened." She throws me a look of sympathy mixed with disgust.

Yes. Of course I know. Mom happened. Swine of Sefella. Did she have to point it out?

"Did she say who to watch?" I ask, hoping my voice is steady. The magic is buzzing, angry that I am ignoring it.

Maisy shakes her head. "No, not really." She snorts. "But we all know to watch your sister by now."

My stomach flips. "My sister?"

"We all know she's different. And your mother, well. If the Burning Rain is going to affect anyone, it's going to be Loxy, if you ask me."

The buzzing fear is morphing to anger. Our family has been a model family for years, ever since Mom left. Yet they still insist on judging our every move, spreading rumors and gossip like the latest disease.

I grit my teeth. "I didn't."

She pauses. "What?"

I grab the herbs out of her hand and drop them in the pot before the oil burns. "I didn't ask you. There's nothing wrong with Loxy."

I am struggling to keep the anger from my voice, and the magic buzzes approvingly. For years, I've had to listen to everyone in the village say these kinds of things about Loxy, about our entire family, no matter how hard I've worked to make our family respectable again.

I'm tired of it.

The rain strikes the window in a sudden flurry. Maisy glances outside, stepping back from the bench. I grab the mortar and pestle from her and keep grinding the herbs, my movements jerky and fueled by anger.

"I... Did you see that?" she says, her eyes on the window.

I don't answer, my mind consumed with defending my family. "Loxy is sweet and kind and smart, and I don't understand why everyone insists on picking on her so much." I grind the herbs harder, releasing their heady scent into the air. I don't know who I'm trying to convince with my words. She is all of the things I just said, but she is also everything the village fears.

"It's not like she's ever done anything to deserve it. If anything, we should be asking her for her help. But instead, we fear anything different and try to silence those who would help us most!"

Bright One, I'm starting to sound like my sister.

Maisy hasn't responded, and I look up at her. Her eyes are on the mortar, so wide I can see all the way around her green irises, and she takes a small step back from me. She points a trembling finger at my hands, and I finally look down.

As I grind, sparks are shooting from my hand into the mortar. They strike the herbs, singeing them so they brown and curl, releasing tiny tendrils of pungent black smoke.

The mortar and pestle drop to the bench with a clatter, and I step away, raising my hands. "I...I have no idea...what..."

I look at Maisy pleadingly, take a step toward her even, but every step I take forward, she takes back. She is trembling.

"What is this?" she whispers. "You're one of them?"

I take another step. "Please…"

I don't say the words I should say, don't remind her of the years we studied together, the games we played as children, the rituals we attended as apprentices.

I don't get the chance. She spins on her heel and bolts from the room.

I start to stumble after her, my breath hitching in my chest and my heart thrumming so fast I feel dizzy.

This is bad, this is really bad. Maisy is probably halfway to High Priestess Cydia's chambers by now. What are they going to do with me?

I already know the answer.

Run, a voice whispers in my ear, the same voice that has been calling my name for days. *Run!*

I can't control the magic pulsing in my veins, not anymore, not after *that*. I glance at the broken mortar, the scattered herbs, and heed the voice.

I run.

I fly down the stairs to the main hall, not pausing to pay my respects at the shrine. I feel sick as I run past it, my head now pounding in rhythm with my heart. Maybe I'm not a faithful servant of Ivlene after all if I can't even pause to pay respect in my moment of greatest fear.

I blink back hot tears, bolting past my oilskin hanging in the entrance, even though the rain is falling in opaque sheets outside. The sea between the steps of the temple and the floating walk boils with energy unlike anything I have ever seen.

Well, no. I did see the sea this upset once before.

The water climbs up to my knees, and I slog through it. It writhes as if it is alive with the force of the storm, and I barely make it to the walk. The planks buck and sway, and I nearly lose my footing several times.

If I can just get home, get to my room, then…what?

Loxy. I need Loxy. If anyone can help me, it's her.

I bolt for our house, all the way on the other side of the village. I knock shoulders with someone, nearly brush a person into the roiling waves, but my mind isn't coherent enough to care, and I don't bother with an apology. I just continue my blind sprint for home, the rain like needles against my cold skin as panic rises within me and buzzes as loudly as the hum of magic.

My body is alive with the power under my skin. It arcs and buzzes between my fingers, it races from neck to toes, and the wind howls around me, speeding my feet forward.

Thunder rumbles again.

I finally slide to a stop in front of the house and throw the door open, but the house is dark and empty, cold without the presence of humans or light.

"Loxy!" I call, desperate, my voice cracking on her name.

There is no answer except the ticking of the clock on the far wall, no indication of movement.

"Sefella take me!" I curse.

Where is she?

But I know the answer, even before I ask myself the question. The apiary.

I slam the door closed and turn toward the apiary, wiping the streaming water away from my eyes. The sky grows darker with every step I take, the wind more violent, the storm more alive and out of control. It runs with me, hastening my steps, boiling in my chest. The magic weaves throughout it, like gold threads in a fine tunic, sparkling against the black of the clouds. The blackness I feel in my very soul.

My bare feet slap against the wooden boards, shaking the entire walkway. If any splinters catch in my soles, I don't feel them. There is nothing to feel but the blind panic, the race to find Loxy.

I round the bend to the apiary, feeling the buzz of the slumbering bees in their hives radiate through the air around me and in the soil underfoot. Loxy isn't by the hives, leaving only the office.

I cross the dry, dead grass and throw open the office door. I am on the edge now, barely holding myself together, barely keeping back the raging magic inside me. I know I will lose control any second, and I can only hope Loxy will be there to stop it before something horrible happens, to help me explain it away to the priestesses like I explained away her magic so many times.

I need my sister. I need her to help me like she did yesterday.

I feel more than see the energy arcing off of me into the dim interior, illuminating a mop and pail, two pairs of shoes against the wall. I see Loxy. I see Audrey. I see them locked together, arms holding each other close, foreheads touching. They jump back as the door hits the wall.

I shouldn't be here, shouldn't interrupt their time together. But I am desperate. I need Loxy.

My mind spins, trying to process what to do, what to say. There is a great surge of energy as my fear finally overtakes me, and I cry out, grabbing my head as it pounds like the rain outside.

And then I know nothing more.

Eight

LOXY

Sefella still roams the world, devouring those she can in retaliation for her fall from grace. She raises the outcasts to dangerous positions, grants them power over evil and darkness that no follower of Ivlene will allow. You will know them by the Mark of Sefella and by the Singing they wield like a sword.

Excerpt from *The Records of Bright*

The door to the office flies open, and Audrey and I jump back, breaking away from each other reluctantly. El stands in the doorway, water streaming off her body in sheets, her eyes as panicked as a deer's in the light of a lantern. Electricity crackles around her, thunder following her from outside. The sky is so dark now that I can barely make out Audrey's form standing next to me.

"Bright One protect us," Audrey breathes.

El's empty eyes jerk to Audrey, and my stomach drops, heart fluttering in true fear now. I watch as if in slow motion as a bright blue bolt of lightning arcs into the office, bending and breaking as it seeks a target, finally landing on Audrey with a boom. She slams into the back wall and collapses to the floor, shaking the entire office and nearly driving me to my knees.

I turn my gaze back to El, horror filling me, then turn and run toward Audrey. She is still, so still…

The floor rumbles underfoot, and the glass windows, whatever are left after the Burning Rain, shatter in their frames. I throw a hand up to protect myself, but the shards still slice my skin as they fly like bees through the air. The walls shake, rattling the jars of honey on the shelves.

El is going to bring the roof down on all three of us.

I stop my dash toward Audrey and turn to face my sister. Her eyes are nothing more than puddles of white light, the magic obliterating the normal seafoam color of her eyes, the human-ness of them. Her arms are raised as lightning and wind spin in a dance around them, around her torso, her legs. Stray bits of dirt and paper join in the dance as they whirl faster and faster.

I have to stop this. Stop *her*.

I raise my own hands, feel the call of crystal, the resonance in the air around us, the sea air so heavy and rich with salt and other minerals.

I call it forth.

Crystals burst up under El's feet from the sea beneath the planks, climbing her like a lattice, trapping and encasing and immobilizing. My heart aches with every creeping crystal, every force I send at her.

But I can't stop. Stopping would be worse for both of us.

Still, the wind and lightning dance across her skin. It's not enough. My power is not enough, is no match for her Atmosinging.

I glance back at Audrey. She hasn't moved. How badly is she hurt? Curse Elodie for keeping me from learning the healing she hoarded for herself!

I turn back to El. "Elodie!" I yell over the howl of her magic. "You have to stop! Please!"

Tears sting my eyes, stream down my face, but El's eyes remain blank. It's like whatever makes her Elodie is gone, replaced with nothing but raw, unfiltered magic.

I blink back the tears. "Remember that first time? Come back to me, just like that! There's no need to be afraid!"

She doesn't respond to my words, and a sob escapes me. A memory rises, unbidden, of another woman. A face with silvery eyes, much like the white ones staring sightlessly at me now. A human torch, with flames of violet, rose, and white.

Our mother.

My crystals begin to glow, and their Song grows faster, warmer, full of energy they cannot contain. They shatter explosively before the tongues of flame, exactly like those in a memory I don't remember forming.

Elodie looks like Mom.

I freeze and stare, unable to respond to her shattering my crystals or to Audrey on the ground. I am a statue, vulnerable to the wind and rain and sea.

And lightning.

Lightning arcs toward me, illuminating the office in blue, and I instinctively throw a hand up to protect myself. A shield of crystal forms across my forearm, deflecting the hot light into the wall before it, too, shatters. The walls shake with the impact, and jars hit the ground, breaking into unsalvageable fragments. I can't catch my breath, can't tear my eyes away from the destruction around me.

"Elodie Shayde," comes a voice, familiar and terrible, from outside the office. "Leave them alone and come face us!"

Elodie pauses and turns, distracted, in the doorway.

I seize the opportunity and grab Audrey under the arms, hauling her into the warehouse at the back of the office. I put my fingers to her neck, feeling for a pulse. It's there, but barely. Her eyelids don't even flutter at my touch. My heart breaks as I stare at her pale face, one that should be full of life. One that was full of love.

For me.

I tuck a burlap bag around her, trying to keep her from going into shock, though I'm not sure she hasn't already. How does one treat a lightning injury? What am I supposed to do?

I lay a hand over her heart, reaching for a bit of almost forgotten magic. I haven't used this more than once, and I had hoped to never use it again. That day is all too clear in my mind, how the house had rocked with the impact of the explosion on the other side of the village, how Dad stumbled home alone, covered in blood. I remember knowing somehow, instinctively, what I had to do. I remember laying hands on his head, absorbing the concussion like a sponge absorbs water. The headache had become mine, the cuts mine.

The look of horror from Dad also mine.

I shrug off the memory and try to recall the magic. It tingles under my fingers. I pull the injury from Audrey, but it's too much. I can only take a piece of it, and it weakens me, stealing my breath and strength. My heart pounds as the shock enters my system, and I fall back to the dusty floor.

Loxy...

I drop my hand. I can't do any more, or it may kill me. I have to leave it at this, to hope it is enough to keep her alive until Priestess Illume can see to her. But from the pale cast to her skin, she already looks dead.

Ivlene, preserve her. Ivlene, heal her. Ivlene, save her.

It's all the prayer I have time for.

I dash as quickly as I can back to the warehouse door, my heart straining with the effort, my breathing labored. I peer into the dim light of the office, but El is gone, leaving the doorway clear and the door hanging crookedly off broken hinges.

Now is my chance. To escape, to find help, to save Audrey.

I toss Audrey one more anxious look, then bolt through the office.

Outside is a battleground of magic and steel. Rain falls in sheets, obscuring everything farther than the next block over. Five priestesses stand on one side of the apiary. I recognize the high priestess, the herbalist, and El's friends. All but High Priestess Cydia stand in crouched, defensive positions, holding curved blades in each hand, standing between the village and the danger they see.

And opposite them, just outside the office, only feet in front of me, stands Elodie. Her feet hover inches off the ground, limp, her toes not quite brushing the soaked brown grass. Wind swirls about her, and she faces them with her arms outstretched. She looks completely broken, like a doll held up by strings.

Is this how it had been when Mom was afflicted? When they drove her out?

I don't dare turn my back on the scene before me, so I sidestep along the wall of the office toward the walkway. Priestess Illume's eyes follow me. As soon as my feet touch the planks, I let out a breath of relief. They haven't attacked me.

Yet.

I turn toward the priestesses and try to recapture Priestess Illume's attention. I wave my hand, and she turns her head.

"Audrey is inside!" I call. "She needs help!"

She stares at me a moment too long, then nods before returning her attention to my sister.

"Elodie," High Priestess Cydia calls, her voice clear and bright in the rain, "have you harmed Audrey?"

Elodie's puppet-head tilts to one side, regarding the priestess with that blank stare.

"If you have harmed her," the woman continues, her voice shaking in the wind, "your life here is over."

My stomach drops, and I nearly fall to my knees.

They're going to banish her. I'm the one who's had magic my entire life, yet the day El gains such power, they want to banish her.

It should be me, not her.

But then my mind flashes back to Audrey, and a stab enters my heart like a wound from one of my own crystals. Elodie did that. Audrey could die. Does my sister know? Does she realize what she's done?

I will lose my entire world today.

A flurry of motion erupts in the garden, and my head snaps back to attention. Priestesses charge toward Elodie, deflecting what they can with their crescent blades. They distract my sister, and Priestess Illume rushes past them into the office.

El sends everything she has at her friends. And they fight back with equal viciousness, like feral cats left to fend for themselves in the wilderness. I can't see Elodie behind her silvery eyes, but I can see the hate filling her friends' faces.

A priestess sends her blade singing through the air toward El's head.

Goddess! Do they hate her so much now?

El throws an arm up to block, and wind pushes the other woman back. The distraction is enough for two other priestesses to move in, swinging their own blades toward my sister. One blade nearly connects with El's forearm, but El throws a hand up just before it hits, a whorl of fire spinning away from her hand toward her friend. The fire twirls around her, setting the ends of her hair and gown ablaze. She cries out, dropping her blade to the ground with a clatter, and jumps back. Her hands are over her face, and her shrieks of pain echo across the tempest-tossed sea.

The remaining priestess glances back toward Priestess Cydia, but the woman's face is stone, her eyes fixed on Elodie. She lowers her blade slightly and steps back. She kneels in the grass, holding the fallen woman's shoulders as they shake with sobs.

Elodie looks toward them, in line with High Priestess Cydia, and holds up her hand, stretched out toward them as if in supplication.

But no. The blank look has not left her eyes, and I see the building charge of electricity before the priestesses do. It's an orange glow surrounding her arm as the energy builds, and I see the bones under her flesh glowing red.

"No!" I cry, hurling myself toward the garden.

I won't let my sister hurt anyone else. I won't let her give them more reason to cast her out. Perhaps this can still be salvaged.

I throw my arms out in front of me, and crystals rip up through the wood planks underfoot, displacing the pebbles and soil of the garden. The spires grow and twirl. The wood cracks and splits. Rocks spray in every direction as the sea rushes up through the cracks.

The first crystal strikes Elodie. It lands on her jaw like a right hook, and I see the unearthly light flicker from her eyes, revealing the familiar green of my sister's. Her eyelids flutter, and she collapses to the ground. As she falls, the intensity of the rain lessens, and the wind ceases its earnest howl.

The crystals begin to spear up in a line toward the priestesses. Desperately, I call them back, try to halt them. The last crystal nearly strikes Priestess Cydia, but she merely quirks a single eyebrow at me, her eyes like steel. Cold, unforgiving steel.

The priestesses, and the crowd that has gathered to watch from around the corners of buildings, stare at me. Not a sound echoes across the space, nothing to disrupt the misting rain surrounding us. Not a breath.

Priestess Illume appears in the office door, carrying Audrey's limp form. Her face is grim, and she stops and stares from the safety of the doorway.

I shake off their stares and approach Elodie defiantly, my steps carrying a confidence I don't feel. I kneel beside her, place my fingers against her neck.

"Loxy Shayde."

I try to ignore the voice. I don't want to hear the words that I know will follow my name.

"Loxy, you will look at me."

I raise my eyes to High Priestess Cydia. She stands before me, only a few steps away. I didn't even hear her approach. Her chin is tilted skyward as she glares down at us, her arms crossed in front of her body. I blink up at her form towering over me.

"I can help her," I say, pleading in my voice. "We can both help the village."

"Loxy and Elodie Shayde, it is clear you are a danger to this community." She ignores me, gesturing to the broken walkway. My crystals. The priestess's ruined face.

Audrey.

This isn't what I wanted. My heart races as I take in the destruction. I never meant... It was never supposed to...

I am shaking my head, though I barely realize it. "No, it was only an accident!"

But she is not listening. A numbness, like the coldest rains, the frigid Sea, creeps over me with every word she speaks, and I can't make myself plead anymore.

"You have been infected with the darkness of Sefella."

No.

No, we haven't. We are good. Clean. Haven't we always done everything they've asked of us? Would they really send us away now?

One glance at Cydia's eyes confirms our fate.

Ivlene, have mercy on us.

"This infection will not be tolerated among our people."

Ivlene, protect us.

"You and your sister are hereby banished from Limutria. Take her and go. Before we change the sentence to fit the real danger you pose to this world. May the light of the Bright One shine favorably upon your corrupted souls."

I glance back at the crowd. Dad is crumpled on the ground, his body wracked with sobs. My heart breaks, and I can practically hear the crack. I feel hot tears coursing down my cheeks, but I don't know when I started crying.

They don't care about the good we could do. All they see is Elodie's destruction. *My* destruction. I won't get a chance to help Audrey or Dad.

I won't get to say goodbye.

"Go!" Priestess Cydia commands, this time with more force, and I flinch away from her.

I gather up Elodie and support her limp body as best I can. At least she is light. I turn toward the expanse of the sea, almost calm in the aftermath of Elodie's storm. I spare one more glance for Audrey, sending a prayer to Ivlene that she isn't dead, that she won't die, that we'll be together again. That we will find Dad again. That we can still, somehow, have a family after this.

I look out at the sea, and I drag my sister's limp form into the water, letting the sea soak me to my knees as my bare feet sink into the soft silt and salt. The water is cold, so cold, but I am too numb to care. There's nothing I can do about that. I feel the eyes of the village following us with every step I take, and bumps rise along my skin with the hatred in the stares. They might as well have killed us. The Sea will probably do that for them, though; it is unlikely we will survive long enough to reach somewhere safe.

I carry my sister into the sea's embrace, into our future, into our banishment. Probably toward our death.

Ivlene save us.

Part Two

DROWNED

Nine

LOXY

I hold the broken, I bandage their wounds.

Excerpt from *The Ballads of Sefella*

I don't look back as I walk away, though every fiber of my being screams to. I can feel every stare and glare piercing my back with invisible knives as cold as ice. Instead, I slog forward through the restless sea, pelted by the wind and rain and burdened by the near-unbearable weight of my sister and the hollow hole in my chest. I don't see where we are going or the direction I've taken. I see nothing but the sea splashing around my legs, the rain striking the water.

The Sea is as it always has been: knee-deep in the rainy season, only subsiding to an inch deep when the rains start to dry up. Our village rests on the surface of the evanescent sea, and there has always been water around us, beneath us.

And now I walk through it, no shelter, nothing but silt and salt underfoot.

There is nowhere to go except forward. No safety in the storm. And so I keep moving, dragging my sister along with me. There are no thoughts in my head except to keep moving, to get as far away from Limutria as we can, to get out of the Sea and find solid ground.

I walk for hours, numb in body and spirit, until Limutria is a shadow in the distance, until I am soaked through and shaking with cold and fatigue.

My feet finally slow, then stop, and I finally feel the burning in my thighs and calves, the aching in my arms and back. I glance at Elodie. She has been showing signs of waking on and off throughout the walk, but she still drifts in-between. Despite my anger and fear over the circumstances of our banishment, over Audrey, over Dad, I am starting to worry that she hasn't regained consciousness. I could try to heal her, like I tried to heal Audrey, but I am too weak now. Did I hit her that hard? Is it the magic keeping her under?

Is she turning into Mom?

And no matter how angry I am with her, how despondent over our predicament…she is still my sister. I still care about her.

Sefella take me.

So much for her priestess friends. The moment she becomes something different, they drive her out. Abandon her. Just like I always knew they would. Just like they've always been. I wish she could have seen it before.

I shake her lightly where she rests on my shoulder. "El?"

She moans but shows no other sign of life.

I glance up at the sky. Rain strikes me, cold against my numb face. I can't be any wetter at this point, but if we stay in the rain with our feet in the sea, we will doubtless fall ill. The Sea and the sky will finish what Limutria did not.

I spin in a slow circle and look around. To the south, an endless expanse of water stretches all the way to Nasmarya's border and beyond, into lands unfamiliar and dangerous to outsiders. Limutria is a barely visible speck against the eastern horizon. Somewhere to the north stands Aeglora, the capital, but it is too far to see, at least a week's journey if not more. Truthfully, I don't really know how long it would take. But on foot, it seems an impossibility, even though it would be a safe place, since they are unlikely to have heard about the troubles of a village as small as ours. And in truth, the priestesses will likely hide knowledge of our existence just like they hid Mom's. Wherever we go, we will be unknown.

I'm too tired and cold and numb to even consider the possibilities that could present. To see a potential bright side. After all, I've already lost everything I've ever known. Why should I look at any bright sides?

There is nothing to the east beyond Limutria except the Wood, Brightval Flats, and—if the rumors are true—the gate to the Halls of Sefella. I shudder at the thought, feeling the cold fingers of Sefella reaching toward me through the wind and rain, the magic buzzing under my skin.

Does magic actually come from Sefella? Were the priestesses right all along? Am I as terrible, as evil, as they've let me believe my entire life?

I shake myself out of my anxious thoughts. There is no time to dwell on them now.

I turn to the west, where I can just see the smudge of the mountains on the horizon. The mountains are our best hope, at least to make it out of the sea and to shelter, but the light of today is already fading, and I have no strength left to continue carrying my sister. Even if part of me *does* want to simply drop her in the sea and leave her there, I can't do it. She's my sister, and…she's the only thing I have left now. And I still love her, despite everything.

Ivlene help me.

I sigh, running through the possibilities in my mind. Obviously there is no shelter out here. The sea is unbroken all around except for the ripples from the falling rain, no structures or rocks for miles. When I told El I wanted to relocate, to start fresh somewhere else, this is not what I had in mind.

I shiver, examining the Sea around us. Limutrian folk tales always warn us not to stray too far from the village. They claim that restless spirits live here, the souls of those long gone, lost in the time before Ivlene took control of the world. Those who were never given proper funeral fires, whose bodies remained to decay instead of burning to ash.

I don't want to be in the open like this when the daylight fades.

The soft Song of a dissolved crystal weaves around my feet. Perhaps I can use that, create a shelter for us.

But am I capable of magic on that scale? I've never been able to fully test my ability, to really let my magic loose.

I think I can.

I shift El on my shoulder, readjusting her weight to free my left arm while still supporting her. She seems to have gained a hundred pounds since we left. I reach an arm forward and close my eyes.

Dancing in the sea, buried in the ground, I can feel the minerals, the crystals, the Songs. I call them, I Sing to them, and they Sing back.

The sea flows around my legs, tugging at my tired muscles, pulling my dress, washing over us as the crystals rise and part the water. It begins with a brightening of the sea as rock rises to the surface. Then, there is a rush of the water toward us, away from the rock, as the platform I coax into existence rises out into the rain. I flick my wrist, call up the columns that will support a roof, fill in the sides to give us some shelter from the storm.

And then it stands before us, rosy pink and almost glowing against the gray palette of the world around us. The sky and the sea match my mood, but this little bit of magic I create—its brilliant color a symbol of the little bit of joy magic gives me in a world not made for me.

I yank my hand upward as I take a step toward the shelter, and steps appear beneath my feet, carrying me into our home for the night.

I drop El on the floor none too gently, only being sure I don't bang her head against the crystal. I think perhaps I am too harsh, too rough, until I remember Audrey, limp and lifeless on the floor.

Does she live? Why couldn't El just let me train at the temple? I would have known what to do to heal Audrey if it wasn't for Elodie.

She wouldn't have *needed* healing if not for Elodie.

My mind is exhausted. I crawl to one corner of the shelter and drop to the floor, my body spent, occupying my hands with small exercises to control the crystal while my mind spins in circles. It's an unconscious motion, one I used years ago to calm myself down until Elodie yelled at me to hide it when she finally caught me. But out here, it's like an old friend, something normal, something that takes so little effort that it soothes me. I stare out into the misty Sea, where the water melds with the clouds and rain. For a moment, I think I see the form of a person glimmering against the watercolor sky, knee-deep in the salt like we were.

But with a blink, the vision is gone. No matter how much I stare, it is as if nothing was ever there.

Eventually, my eyes blur, and my mind loses the war against fatigue. I slump over into blessed oblivion.

Ten

ELODIE

Give us water, for the Sea is high. Give us shelter, for the rains are falling. Give us hope, for we are hopeless.

Excerpt from *Sefella's Prayer of the Lost*

My head pounds like hammers at the blacksmith. I can feel it even before I open my eyes. It is the pain that wakes me, throbbing like a drumbeat, stabbing like a pebble in my shoe.

And once I am awake, I feel *everything*.

My body, soaked through and shaking with cold, feels torn and used, like I have just come out of a sparring match with Menna. That girl always did throw a mean punch.

But that's not right. I haven't sparred in months. Priestess Illume has been too focused on completing my herbalism lessons.

The rain hits something hard overhead, but none of it touches me.

So why am I wet? I try to move, but the hard surface on which I rest presses into my bones. I moan in pain.

"Finally awake?" comes a voice. An irritated, angry voice.

I force my eyes open. Loxy sits nearby, separate from me. We are both bathed in soft rosy light.

"Where are we?" I manage, my voice barely a croak. "What happened?"

Loxy rubs her eyes and sits up straighter. She must have been asleep, too. There are dark shadows cradling her eyes, and the bottom half of her legs are bright red, either with cold or abrasion.

But then she narrows those sleep-filled eyes at me, anger still lacing her every word. "We've been banished."

I shove myself up to sitting, and my head swims, stomach roiling. "Banished?"

No.

No, no, no. This can't be.

"Yes. Banished. Because of you. And now we may never see Dad or…or Audrey…again." Her voice breaks, and she blinks rapidly.

The rock underneath me trembles, and I flinch against the heat in her voice as my heart cracks. My stomach does a somersault, and my last meal pushes against my mouth. I try to force back the bile. I don't know if it's from the head injury I've probably sustained or the shock of our predicament.

One that I somehow caused. I always thought it would be Loxy that would lead us into this sort of trouble. Not me.

"What did I do?"

"That's what I'd like to know!" She jumps to her feet, all traces of sleepiness gone, and props her hands against the pink rock ceiling as if bracing herself. "Why did your magic go crazy, Elodie?"

The blood drains from my face. I can't remember any of it, but something terrible, something horrifying, must have happened. "What did I do?" I repeat.

"Well, for starters, you maimed Maisy, and you may have killed Audrey."

Audrey. It comes flooding back to me. My fear, my shock, my confusion. The darkness that followed. I don't remember hurting Audrey *or* Maisy.

But Loxy isn't finished. "And you probably ruined any chance that the people in Limutria will accept our magic. Will let us contribute to the village. Will accept *us*. I told you we needed to start over somewhere. Now we have no choice."

I feel my blood run cold at the words. She's right. She kept herself safe all these years, and I ruined it in a day. I *hurt* people.

I press a hand to my mouth, sure now that I will be sick. I've broken both people and dreams this day, and the shame churns like bad fish. I scramble to my feet and rush to the edge of whatever platform we rest on, making it just in time to lose the contents of my stomach into the sea.

I stand there a few more moments, letting the rain strike my back as I double over, stomach heaving. Finally, I run a shaking hand across my mouth and straighten. I turn back toward Loxy, needing her not to be angry with me, but the sight of our shelter nearly causes me to tumble back into the waves.

Loxy created a shelter. Out of crystal. I had no idea she could do something like this.

I can't tell what kind; I'm not a Halosinger. Or rather a Crystallosinger, I should say. It is protected on three sides and rises up out of the sea to keep us from sleeping in the water. And the roof protects enough area that we can both fit comfortably.

The entire structure glows with soft pink light, either the fading light of day or what daylight makes it through the rain.

"How long was I out?" I breathe. I rejoin Loxy in the shelter, forcing brightness into my voice. "Lox, this is amazing! Why didn't you tell me you could do this?"

She stares at me with those hard eyes a few moments longer. "I didn't know. Besides, you were a little busy attacking people."

She drops her hands from the ceiling and crouches on the floor by a wall, alternately clenching and unclenching her fist. A small pile of dust solidifies into a cube of pinkish-white, then crumbles back into dust with every flick of her fingers.

I catch my breath and settle down next to her, careful not to jar my battered brain too much. She flinches away from me, but I wrap an arm across her shoulders anyway. Her hurt, her pain, radiates from her in a palpable wave.

I lean my head against hers. "I'm sorry, Lox. I don't know what happened. I'm so sorry."

Tears run down her face, and I know they're running down mine as well. But we've been banished. I think we deserve to cry.

She opens her mouth, then closes it again. For several long moments she says nothing, then she finally croaks through her tears, "What are we going to do?"

I catch my breath at her broken voice. I don't have an answer. I wish I did, but I am just as lost as her. And it's my fault. It's all my fault.

But I'm still her big sister. I still have to take care of her, even if she hates me. Even if she had to take care of me first. Even if all I can do now is hold her and share our sorrow.

I rub Loxy's shoulder with my cold hand, and together we cry.

The sun rises behind the clouds, and my stomach grumbles, yanking me out of a nightmare filled with lightning and fire. In it, I watched Audrey fall countless times, saw the lightning leave my hand, saw the horror on Loxy's face. I don't actually remember doing any of it, but my dreams seem to remember.

I push myself up from where Loxy and I had fallen asleep the night before and wipe the crust of dried tears from my cheeks. It is still raining beyond the walls of the shelter, and the sea is restless, slapping against the sides of the platform. Everything about the day, about yesterday, tells me to go back to sleep.

But we need to eat. Or Loxy needs to eat, at least. I'm not much hungry after that dream.

I shake my head, trying to dislodge the dream images that still linger, and rise to my feet. I wander to the edge of the shelter, just so I can see into the water without re-drenching my clothing. After yesterday, it is stiff with salt and smells of the sea, but at least it's finally dry.

For now. But the Bright One knows we can't stay here.

All I can feel where I stand is a light mist from the falling rain, splashing off the shelter just over my head and from the restless surface of the sea. The mist is cool on my skin, chilling me even more as the wind lifts my hair away from my face and neck. I try to pull my hair back, tie it with a strip of fabric barely hanging onto my sleeve. It only takes one tug to rip it the rest of the way free, then a couple more tugs and my hair is secured.

I cup my hands around my eyes, trying to cut down the glare so I can see below the surface of the water, but it doesn't help much. Not with how rough the sea is right now. If I could only see, I might be able to see something worth eating, a fish or plant or *something*.

I let out a huff and drop my hands. Some small corner of my mind tells me to try the magic, to use it. After all, we have already been banished. They can't do much else to us, especially out here. Yet, I feel sick at the mere thought. What if I can't control it? What if I hurt Loxy?

And even if the priestesses can't see it, the Bright One can. Priestess Cydia taught me that using magic would be a violation, a corruption of morality. And all my life, I've dedicated everything to worshipping Ivlene.

But what does that mean for Loxy?

I lean back from the water and stare out to where the mist melds with the sky. For a moment, it almost seems like someone is standing out there.

But that's crazy. We're in the middle of nowhere.

There is a scuffing sound behind me, and I turn to see my sister standing next to me.

She wraps her arms around herself, dark, salt-crusted curls blowing in the breeze. "What are you doing?" Her voice is flat, hollow.

I gesture toward the sea, forcing brightness into my voice. "We need something to eat."

She kneels down on the edge of the crystal floor and leans toward the sea until her nose is almost touching the water. The rain pours down over her, and her long, curly hair falls, floating along the tops of the waves. I'm sure it is enough to scare away any fish. And with it, our chances at food.

Eventually, she stands back up, brushing salt from her wet hands. "I can see a few minnows in the shadow of the shelter, but they're small."

I nod and turn back to the dry interior of the shelter.

"If you isolate the water—" she begins, gesturing toward the sea.

I interrupt her before she can finish the thought. "I can't do that."

She takes a step toward me, eyes sparking with irritation and something else. Excitement? "Why not? Atmosingers can control all elements, including water. You could catch us a fish. Probably a bigger one than these minnows."

"I already thought of that." I flinch, keeping my face angled away from her. Even if I could control the magic, that still doesn't mean I'd be able to catch a fish with it.

My sister has way too much faith in my ability, especially after yesterday's debacle.

"Why won't you, then?" she glares at me, anger written in every line of her face, every turn of her body. The anger is out of proportion to the fishing discussion, but I suppose I deserve it.

"I can't. If I couldn't keep it under control in the village, what makes you think I can do it now?" I slump down in the corner.

"It's not that hard." Loxy scoffs and turns back toward the sea.

She drops into a crouch and holds her hands over the water. I watch as she turns her hands and flicks her wrists quickly, her eyes boring into me the entire time. A small, thin needle of crystal shoots from the water, a tiny, wriggling silver fish impaled on the end of it.

Just as it always has, the Sea provides. Ivlene provides.

Loxy laughs hollowly and plucks the fish from the crystal. She pulls her hand up next to her, creating a crystal bowl out of the shelter's floor. Rain immediately begins to pool inside, and she drops the minnow into the clear water. She continues to repeat the dance of spear, grab, plop until her bowl is filled with minnows.

She stands and shoves her hand down, pushing the spears back into the water until they disappear. For a moment, I am envious of her power, her control, but I push it away. I shouldn't envy something so dangerous.

Loxy brings the bowl back into the shelter and shoves it at me. "Breakfast."

I look at the silver slivers and have to catch my breath as my stomach turns. I should have been the one figuring it out, finding us food. "They're raw."

"They're food," she retorts.

My stomach turns again. "I don't think I can eat that. But you should."

She wrinkles her nose at me and raises an eyebrow, a look of derision I remember all too well from the times I tried to force toddler Loxy to eat her vegetables. "You have to eat, too. We're stuck out here until we can figure out a solution or walk ourselves out. I can purify water, but I can't make food appear out of thin air. It may not be to your liking, but at least it's something."

I push the extended bowl away from me. "It's raw." I try not to look, but the silver shine of the scales draws my eye again, and my stomach heaves.

I wince as Loxy throws up her hands and shouts, "Then cook it!"

"With what?" My voice rises to match hers.

She grabs my wrist and shakes my hand in the air. "You can control fire! When are you going to get that through your thick head? If you want it cooked, then cook it!"

"I can't control anything, Loxy! How about you get that through *your* thick head?"

I pull my hand away from her and hug my arms to my chest. She shakes her head at me and turns away with the bowl.

I curl into myself. She doesn't understand. She's had power her whole life. Sure, she's had to hide it. But it was harmless.

Almost nothing.

But this? Atmosinging? Power over fire? It is a curse. I can't control it, can't hide it, and because of me, people were hurt.

I'm dangerous. I am everything Ivlene told us to fear.

Eleven

LOXY

Ivlene holds the world, but Sefella holds the records of the world and what comes after.

Excerpt from *The Ballads of Sefella*

El refuses to use her magic. Worse, she can't even see how it might be a blessing, especially out here. I almost can't believe it, but this is Elodie, after all. Stubborn, high-strung Elodie, always afraid of the magic that could keep us alive. All I wanted her to do was cook the stupid fish! But even that is too much for her.

And then, while I glare daggers at my sister, Audrey drifts back into my mind like a ghost.

Elodie hurt her. Elodie did this—got us banished. If she had listened to me in the first place, agreed that Limutria had no future for us, maybe none of this would have happened.

I turn away from her with the bowl, and my stomach churns at the sight of the raw fish. I can't eat this, either. I shove the bowl away, water sloshing over the side. The Sea gives us everything we could need to survive, but why does it have to take so much effort from me?

I turn back to her. "What's our plan?"

"What?" She looks up at me, eyes glazed.

Sefella take her! We have to focus on our survival now. She can't fall apart.

I'm not. And maybe more than anyone, I think I have a right to fall apart. But I'm not.

"What do we do now?" I say again, more slowly this time. I can't keep the bite of irritation from my voice.

El sighs. "Well, we can't very well stay here, can we?"

I want to hit her again. Of course not.

I look out across the barren, choppy sea. "So where do we go? I can see the mountains from here. That was my plan yesterday."

She rises to her feet and strides to the edge of the shelter, looking in every direction. "We could go to Aeglora. Or the Wood."

I shake my head. "Aeglora is too far. We don't have the supplies. And the Wood is no better. It's so close to Brightval." Brightval Flats was a whole lot of nothing, other than toxic gas and mud pits. "Besides, have you ever even seen a forest?"

El hesitates. "No. But I'm sure we'd figure it out."

"Not without supplies," I say again.

She lets out a frustrated huff. "Then what do you suggest?"

I blink. "The mountains. They're closer than Aeglora and safer than the Wood. They are more familiar to us. I'm sure we can find supplies and decide where to go from there."

"And then what?" There is heat and frustration in her voice.

"Does it matter?" I fire back. Hopelessness sits like a weight in my chest.

Her question hangs in the air, though. What indeed? I drop to the ground and prop my head in my hands, elbows on my knees where I sit. What I really want is to go back, see Audrey, make sure she's alive. I have no idea, and she was so pale, so still. I need to see with my own eyes.

My heart clenches in my chest, and I squeeze my eyes closed against the burning tears. My entire body aches with the pain of it. All I want is Audrey. *My* Audrey.

I hold my breath, the only thing keeping me from dissolving into sobs.

I can't go back. I can't see if Audrey is okay. And it's El's fault. The anger builds like a fire in my belly, releasing the vise of pain around my chest. It's just like what happened with Mom.

Mom. The only other person who could possibly know what we're going through now. The only person who might be able to help.

"We should find Mom." My words hang in the air just as long as El's question. If we're going to fix this, who better to help than the one person who's already been through it? If we had her, she could teach El how to control her magic, and then maybe we'd stand a chance at changing how the world sees Singers.

Maybe we could have that fresh start someplace new. We could be a family again, and I wouldn't have to be afraid all the time. We could go back and get Dad—and hopefully Audrey. Elodie could transfer her apprenticeship. I could become a healer, like I'd always wanted. I have a life ahead of me, with Audrey, with her bees.

The possibilities are endless.

Eventually, El responds, but her voice is cold. "Mom? Why do you even think she's still alive?"

My heart lurches, her words only fueling my anger. "She is. She has to be. What else are we going to do?"

The more I think about it, the more excited I become. Our banishment is a terrifying and uncertain future that could end our lives, but Mom?

This could not only be a chance to learn how to deal with having magic in a world that hates magic, but it could also be our chance to find her. To find out what really happened all those years ago.

To be a real family again. To change everything.

"She has to be?" El cuts in. "If she's alive, why didn't she ever come back to us?"

My thoughts freeze. Why? There could be a million reasons. She could have gotten lost, or maybe she was trying to build a new home for us before she came back. Maybe she couldn't come back and is waiting for us to find her, somewhere out there.

Or maybe she abandoned us.

I shake the thought from my head. No. She's alive, and if she could have come back, she would have. And if she can't come to us, then we need to go to her.

"It doesn't matter. We have to find her," I say.

"Just how are we supposed to find her?" El says with an exasperated sigh. "She could be anywhere!"

I glare at her. "So we at least try." I rise to my feet. "I'm going to the mountains, whether you come or not."

Indecision flits across her face like a nervous bat.

I pull out words I know will break through her guilt, break *her*. "You owe me this much."

Pain flashes in her eyes like lightning, and she nods. She stands and joins me next to the sea.

"Then let's go," she says, though she doesn't look happy about it.

She extends a hand toward me, but I pretend I don't see it and take a step into the water, into the fine mist that isn't really rain.

We've been walking for hours, and the mountains seem just as far away as when we started. Every so often, we take a break, and I desalinate some water for us to drink. But neither of us has eaten since yesterday before the banishment.

I try to ignore the weakness behind my steps, the pain in my stomach, but I know it won't be long until we are forced to eat fish after all. Hopefully, by then, El will get over herself and just cook them.

Anger grows in my chest, and I welcome it, embrace it. At least if I'm mad, I'm not numb like yesterday. The glimmer of salt fills my vision, dances in my wake. And I have so many things to be angry about. With every step, I name one of them in my head.

I made it twenty years without betraying us. I did *my* part.

El got us banished in a day.

Mom never came back for us.

I never asked El to be Mom.

I'm so hungry.

Elodie could cook us a decent meal. But she won't.

I've had to look out for us since we left.

El's been so self-absorbed, it's like she can't even see me.

Why can't she trust me?

Why can't she use her magic?

Why can't she let me be who I am?

"So what's your plan for finding Mom?" El says, sloshing along behind me. There is no inflection in her tone.

I blink the rain out of my eyes, surprised by her intrusion into my anger. "Get out of the Sea. Find someone who might have seen her."

El's steps slow behind me, then double to catch back up. "Lox, it's been twenty years. I mean, we do need to get out of the Sea. But she left us. And she never came back. Why *should* we find her? And what are the chances someone even remembers Mom?"

Why does she have to say it again?

"We don't know they won't," I retort.

El huffs out an irritated breath. "Where will we look?"

"We can figure that out once we get to shore."

I wish I still had Mom's portrait.

"We may never find her," El continues, oblivious to my furious thoughts.

"So what? We don't even try?" I hurl the words over my shoulder. "We stay a broken family? Dad ignoring me and loving you? You so busy with your ambitions that you barely notice us breaking apart? The whole village so afraid that I can't even make more than one friend?"

El doesn't answer for a moment, and when I glance at her, her mouth is pressed into a thin line. "We're not broken, Loxy. And I do notice you. I wanted to help you for years."

"Help me? How? By selling me out to the temple so they could do goddess knows what to me?"

"I could have done something."

"You're right," I bite. "You could have cared enough about my dreams to help me reach them. You could have helped me show them the truth. Instead of pushing me to hide, feeding my fear and theirs."

"That's not fair," she snaps.

"Isn't it?" I clench my teeth. "All of this is your fault. If you'd really tried to help me, if you'd really been on my side, maybe the village wouldn't have hated me. Maybe they wouldn't have exiled us when you lost control. The only friend I've ever had, the only person who's ever accepted my magic—you probably killed her!"

My voice breaks on the last word, tears pooling in my eyes. But they are invisible in the rain, and I bite my lip, turning away from my sister.

Audrey was the only one who ever truly loved me for me. Even after she knew everything.

"Lox," El says softly, laying a hand on my shoulder.

I shake it off. "No. Don't. You're so afraid of your magic that you won't accept my help. You won't even try. You've always had everything. And now you have the most powerful kind of Singing, amazing power, an amazing gift—"

I break off again as the realization hits me: I'm jealous of Elodie.

For several long moments, I can't speak, and for once, El stays quiet, though I hear her sniffling behind me.

When I speak again, my voice is so small, so quiet, that I feel the warmth radiating from her body as she leans in to listen. "You were always the favorite. You took Mom's place for me. Or you tried. Even when Dad couldn't stand the sight of me."

"That's not true," she says softly.

I look at her now, hating how the hot tears run down my face along with the rain. "Yes, it is. You were Elodie, the model child, loved by everyone and destined for great things, while I was the awkward outcast, the cursed-by-Sefella freak. Or so Dad told me, not that you cared. All I was to Limutria was a nuisance destined to either fade into obscurity or implode in a great cataclysm, like Mom."

El stops walking. "Dad said that?"

My steps slow, and I turn to face her. "How could you not know?"

She blinks at me, her expression stunned. "Really, Loxy. I promise...I never heard him say anything like that. If I had..."

"What? What would you have done? Let it slide like you always do? Since I'm such a *freak*?"

She winces, and I know I struck a nerve. I swipe at my tears, hoping she thinks it's just the rain. I hate that I'm crying in front of her, showing her how much Dad's words and how little she did about it affects me.

"I should never have said that." Her voice is so soft that I'm not sure I hear her correctly. "Especially when Dad has been so awful to you." Her gaze drifts up to mine. "I swear, I've only ever wanted to protect you."

I turn slightly away, looking out into the rain. I don't want her to see the pain anymore. She doesn't deserve it. But I can barely breathe, it hurts so much.

"It wasn't easy for me, either, you know," she says. "Losing Mom like that...she left us all, but she left me to take care of all of you." She throws her hands to her sides. "I was *five*, Loxy. I was five, and I was trying to take care of a sister who could have been taken from us at any moment, just like Mom was. And Dad? He may not have said anything like that to me. But that's because he barely said anything at all."

I bite my lip, fresh tears spilling over my eyes. "We could have helped each other, Elodie. Actually been there for each other.

What are we, really?" I finally turn back toward her. I'm still angry, I can feel it in my bones, but my next words are pleading. "You're my sister, El. You're supposed to be my first and best friend. My truest ally. All I ever wanted was to be like you. For you to like me. You're my sister."

The truth burns in my chest as I release it, those words I've kept myself from saying all these years. Because, yes. I've been jealous of her. Of her poise. The way she handles the world and our family. She's never had to worry about what the world would do to her like I have.

Well, until recently.

El watches me for several long moments, her lips still pressed in that thin line. I wonder if, beneath all the rain, she is crying, too.

Finally, she says, "You're right." Her voice is strained, her expression pained. "I'm a horrible sister. You needed me to stand with you against Dad, and I never even noticed." She looks away. "You deserved so much better."

I press a hand over my mouth, simply staring at her. I can't believe she said any of that. A small sob escapes, my chest still tight with the force of holding back my emotions. I've never heard her admit that she could have done better by me. But…maybe she actually heard me, for the first time in our lives.

And for her part, I guess I never stopped to think about how Mom's exile affected her, either.

She meets my eyes again. "I'll try, Loxy. I'll try to do better. I promise. And maybe… Maybe we can find Mom."

She reaches for my hand, and this time I let her take it. Anger still churns in my chest, burning where my hand touches hers, but together we turn back to the endless waves and the mountains at the edge of the sea.

El takes a step, then suddenly jumps back, pulling her hand away from me. She lifts her foot from the water, rubbing at her bare toes, moaning through clenched teeth. She stubbed her toe on something, maybe a crystal. I kind of wish it was one of mine. I can't help but smile a little, but I'm glad I didn't cause it.

If she's willing to try, then maybe I can try, too.

And maybe together we can survive.

Twelve

ELODIE

Ivlene, save me from the depths of the Underworld, for in my brokenness, I have broken others.

Excerpt from *Ivlene's Prayer of Redemption*

O ww," I moan through clenched teeth, rubbing at my foot. I can barely feel it through the numb cold, but it was enough to send a spike of pain shooting up my leg.

Loxy covers her mouth with her hand, and I know she's smiling. But I suppose I deserve that. What she said was true, all of it. I am a terrible big sister.

I bend down and dig through the soft dirt of the seabed until my fingers graze something solid. I wrap my hand around an object the size of my fist and pull it free. It is much heavier than I expect for something so small, and I have to readjust my grip before pulling it out of the water.

It's a piece of black rock with slashes of silver at every angle, no two streaks headed in the same direction. The silver catches the light with every turn of my wrist, and the surface is polished smooth.

"What is this?" I finally say, holding out the stone for my sister to examine.

She takes it and turns it over in her hand, examining it like I had for several moments. "It has a Song I don't recognize. I can't even begin to understand it."

The wind whistles across my ear, and for a moment I think I hear my name, just like during the Burning Rain. I turn in the direction of the sound, but, of course, the Sea is empty.

Elodie.

I whip my head back in the other direction. Loxy looks up from the stone and follows my gaze before looking back at me.

"Do you hear something?" she says.

Elodieeee.

"It sounds like someone is calling me," I finally respond.

Loxy tilts her head, listening to the wind. Her eyes narrow, then grow wide. "I hear it, too, but calling *me*."

We listen a few moments longer, but there is nothing around us that could be calling to us, that could sound different to each of us. I shiver, spooked that there may be a spirit nearby.

However, when nothing appears, we continue onward, Loxy gripping the rock tightly in her hand.

Within ten minutes, we come upon something large and black protruding from the sea. It shines with the same silver streaks as the small rock, only this rock is the size of the kitchen at home. It has large, flattened facets, all polished like the smaller stone.

Elodieee.

I walk closer to the boulder, and my reflection appears in its mirrored surface. I almost jump away, surprised to see the dirt and paint smudged over my face, the dark shadows under my eyes, the hollows between my bones. My hair is matted, the lavender color subdued and sickly.

What I wouldn't give for a good brush. And maybe some soap.

Something shifts in my reflection, and my eyes flick back to the image. My familiar face shifts to another familiar one, only for the briefest of seconds, as if my vision twitched. But I can't place the face, at least not in my current state.

"What was that?" Loxy snaps her head to the left, in the direction behind the massive rock.

I lean around, following her gaze, but I see nothing. I shake my head and shrug when she looks my way.

Movement in my periphery catches my attention, and I spin to face the rock. For a second, the blurred figure of a person seems to be perched atop the stone. But again, just like with my reflection, it's gone before I've really even seen it.

Loxy shivers. "I don't like it here."

An image fills my mind, the vision of Mom on fire, Mom surrounded by wind, Mom made of crystal. And behind her, a figure I'd only seen in temple depictions: Sefella, feeding power to her.

The image expands, Sefella reaching a hand toward me, offering me…something.

I rub my arms, trying to brush away the raised bumps on my skin as I shake the images from my mind. "Me either."

The longer we stand near this strange, shining rock, the more a chill seeps into my bones, a feeling like eyes are following our every move. My eyes dart across the landscape, but there are no flickers of life. Nevertheless, anxiety causes a spark to jump from my finger to the surface of the water.

Though I promised Loxy I'd work on control, I push it away, stuff it down. I can't deal with it now. Not yet.

"Let's get out of here," I say.

But before we can go, a splash breaks the still water behind us.

Thirteen

LOXY

Pursue the lost, raise them up and return them to life.

Excerpt from *The Ballads of Sefella*

W hat was that?" Elodie says.

I freeze, my mind half on the voice that had been calling me only a moment ago. The only sound now is the *shhh* of the rain hitting the water and the sloshing of the sea around our legs.

Then I hear it. The splash behind us, toward the mountains. I turn away from the boulder to face the sound, barely locking eyes with El. She follows my gaze.

The sea behind us is broken only by the falling rain. It is gray, stretching on for infinity in our wake, almost melting into the sky on the horizon. Nothing out of the ordinary appears present, nothing that would have produced such a splash.

We turn back toward the distant mountains, no choice but to continue. But just a few minutes later, there is another splash, this time much closer.

"You're hearing this, too, right?" I turn toward the sound again.

Before El can respond, something leaps out of the water next to me, striking my torso with the force of a punch and knocking me back a few steps. I barely catch a glimpse of a creature half my size and clear as glass before it falls back into the water.

Why didn't the crystals warn me of this?

I crouch low, peering beyond the ripples into the shallow water, trying to see a creature that should be obvious with its size. Every gasp is shallow, my breath knocked out of me by the impact.

Something brushes my leg, but I see nothing, just a current of water passing around me. I can feel the water moving around my bare legs, and I shiver in revulsion. I listen for the Singing of the crystals suspended in the water, but they don't say anything different from what they've said all day. They simply Sing their Song of drifting on the endless sea.

There is another splash, this time in El's direction. I whirl toward her, my hair slapping me in the face. I shove it away, blinking water out of my eyes. I manage to clear my vision enough to see the same creature that had slammed into me, only this time I get a better glimpse of it.

It's bigger than I expected, twice as long as El is tall, but narrow and flat like a ribbon. It is mostly transparent, like a creature carved from crystal. But crystal can't move with those undulations, and it has no Song I can hear. Instead, it's more like water given life. A line of glowing white runs along the center of its body from the creature's nose to its tail fin, waving like the undulating fin along its back.

It slams El with the length of its body, knocking her off her feet before disappearing back into the water.

But now I know what I'm looking for. A Water Dragon.

Water Dragons are rarely sighted, and never near Limutria. They are generally shy, but they are also predators, seeking out the largest prey in an area.

Which, unfortunately for us, is two humans recently exiled from their home.

I scan the water again, looking for the ribbon of light along its body. This ribbon is the actual creature, not the surrounding flesh made of water, though all Water Dragons have the same aqueous form.

Light dances around my ankles, and I call forth crystal spikes. They shoot up from the sea floor in an explosion of silt, narrowly missing the graceful bends of the Water Dragon.

The light vanishes beneath a bright refraction of the dim daylight, and I lose track of it. For several minutes, the water is still, nothing but the rain pounding on its surface. My heart pounds in time, and I feel the crystal in the water tremble with me.

Then, the sea breaks to my left. I try to dodge, to summon a crystal to my defense, but my reflexes are too slow. Hunger has gnawed away my speed.

The Dragon flies through the air, mouth open and whiskers undulating with the leap. The water teeth gape at me, and fear courses through me as they strike my arm, sinking deep into my flesh. I cry out and fall to my knees, my mind unable to think clearly enough to summon crystals.

El runs up to me through the waves and begins pounding her fists on the Water Dragon's body. Her action is enough to pull me back to the moment, and I create a spike from the salt in the water, driving it straight through the pulsing, beating heart in the head of the Dragon, the bulge at the end of the light ribbon.

The Dragon releases me and collapses, the water body dissolving back into the sea and leaving a slimy, gelatinous ribbon floating on the surface. The light slowly fades as the creature dies.

The current carries the body away from us, and I clasp my hand over my arm. El wraps a piece of her gown around the wound, staunching the bleeding, at least for now.

"Impressive."

As one, we whirl toward the voice breaking the silence. My heart pounds in my chest, adrenaline pulsing through my body. My eyes search the misty sea, but it only takes a moment to find the person perched on the top of the strange boulder, legs crossed beneath a long tunic that shimmers like salt left to dry in the sun. The face is familiar somehow, but I can't place it.

I glance at Elodie, but she seems just as confused as I am. Just as fearful. How much did the newcomer see? How much does she know about us?

The person slides off the boulder effortlessly, her feet not even making a splash in the rippling waves, and approaches us. "I knew the two of you had potential." She looks up at the clouds, raising her voice. "And I got here first!"

"The...two of us?" El says, voice shocked.

"First?" I echo.

"Sure," the stranger says. "Though, it would have been better if you'd fought a little more, Elodie. Your Singing is a gift."

Elodie presses her lips together, narrowing her eyes at the stranger. But I can't tear my eyes away from her feet—and how they seem to be gliding through the water without disturbing it, like she's not really there, at least not in a physical sense. Like a spirit or a goddess.

"Who are you?" I force through frozen lips. Stars speckle my vision, and I just want to get away from this place, away from the pain.

She shakes her head. "Not important. Not right now. But what *is* important—I think we can help each other."

I exchange a look with El again, but she seems just as confused as me.

"What do you mean?" she says.

The stranger lifts one shoulder. "You have power. I need power. You need help. I can help."

"You can help?"

She nods. "You want direction, right?" Turning slightly, she extends a finger toward the mountains. "That's the way to go."

El nods slowly, then begins walking that direction, taking a wide berth around the stranger and grabbing my elbow to pull me along behind her.

The person—or spirit—follows only a few paces behind. "There's more."

El stops and drops my elbow. "More?"

"If you'll let me come with you, I promise it will all become clearer. But for now, will you let me join you? Don't worry, I can fend for myself."

I look at El. There's really nothing we can do to stop her, not out here with nowhere to go, nowhere to hide. If she wants to follow, she will, no matter what we say.

Yet, somehow, as I look into the stranger's warm eyes, I see something glimmer. Something like…understanding? Compassion? Or maybe even…love?

I glance over at El, but her face is nearly impassive, nothing but that telltale twitch she gets in her jaw when something has made her uncomfortable.

"What do we do?" I whisper to El, reaching for her hand.

El grinds her jaw again, but she wraps her cold fingers around mine. The small gesture gives me a bit of comfort. Whatever happens, at least neither of us is alone. "If she's a spirit, we don't have much choice."

I shudder. I don't like that idea, that we could be haunted now, but I'm already haunted by memories. Maybe it won't make much difference. Besides, neither of us has ever met a spirit. Maybe the stories are scarier than reality.

I hope.

El glances at me again, her expression cracking just enough to let me see her unease, then nods curtly to the stranger. "Fine."

The spirit smiles and take a few steps closer, looking at me. "I'm sorry I cannot heal your arm right now. I would if I could."

I give her a confused look, but before I can respond, El says, "You can come with us, but keep some distance. We don't know you."

She smiles again, wider. "Oh, I believe you do. But I can wait. Just call for Sef." Her body fades back into the mists, nearly disappearing in the rain. The water doesn't shift around her like it does around us, and she seems to have faded so much that I'm barely sure I even saw her in the first place. Neither of us says a word as we hurry away from the boulder and the toxic goo of the Water Dragon, ahead of the newcomer.

Away from the one who says we know her. The being following us through the Sea.

The one I strongly suspect is a ghost, if not something much, much worse.

Fourteen

ELODIE

The Underworld pushes at the hold of the Bright One. Be vigilant, dear children. Do not allow yourselves to be overcome.

Excerpt from *The Records of Bright*

It's hours before we are forced to stop again, the night approaching fast through the watery clouds. We settle into the shadows of Loxy's new shelter, again made of the pinkest quartz, and maintain the silent walls between us. Every time the wind howls, I find myself listening for my name, but I don't hear it.

I examine Loxy's arm again, but it is warm, too warm, and streaked with angry red slashes. I wish I could smother it in a salve, but for obvious reasons, I can't. Instead, I re-wrap it and say a prayer to Ivlene that the bite won't kill her.

And the spirit, Sef, is no help, keeping her distance without a word. At times, she falls back so far we can almost forget we are being followed. Then, just as I begin to breathe a little easier, she returns. Occasionally, I think I see a glimmer of concern when she looks at Loxy.

Who is she, and why is she intent on following us?

I sniffle, my nose running. These past days of walking in the sea, soaked to the bone, are taking their toll, not to mention the stress of having to survive out here. With Sef.

With Loxy.

I glance over at her on the opposite end of the shelter, her knees pulled up to her chest, her body shivering with cold. It's not only her arm that's too warm.

I scoot to the edge of the shelter, my back to her, and rub at my blistered feet. Skin peels off my heels in sheets. Not blisters, then. I am simply waterlogged.

My stomach growls, reminding me that it's been too long since we've eaten. I wish we had thought to sneak back that first night and take anything that could have helped us survive. That *I* had done it.

I could have gotten supplies…and found out whether Audrey still lived.

Though I cling more than ever to the Bright One herself, my faith in the priestesses is faltering. I never noticed the way they treat those they deem something less than themselves. I had been accepted among them, at least tentatively, and so I had been exempt and blind to it.

But when the magic manifested, that all changed. How could my friends abandon me so easily?

Were they ever friends at all?

The weight of my thoughts drags me closer to the ground, heart squeezing in my chest.

"Hey, dummy," says Loxy, bending over to look into my eyes. My face is pressed against the wet crystal floor, my thoughts crushing me. "It's time to eat."

"I'm not hungry," I say, even as my stomach growls in defiance.

"Oh yes, you are. And so am I. And guess what else? You're going to cook our meal this time. I want to eat, and I'm not eating raw fish when you're perfectly capable of dealing with that."

I groan and push myself up. "It's not going to work," I insist.

"And I told you I don't care what you think. Keep holding it in and it's going to go crazy again."

When I don't answer, her voice turns pleading. "You promised. You promised you would try."

I did promise. But my mind drifts, unable to hold onto that promise.

Why would the Bright One curse me with magic when all I've ever done is serve her? Even now, cast out from the village, I maintain my prayers and meditations.

Loxy flicks me on the forehead, and I blink, bringing my thoughts back to the present.

"See, this is exactly why we need to eat." She thrusts another bowl of fish at me. When did she catch those? "Now. Cook. Please."

The fish gleam silver in the dim light. More minnows. I assume Loxy has already adjusted the water to an appropriate salinity for a fish stew, and I can only guess that the plants are seaweed.

Another growl roars from my belly, and I close my eyes against the pangs. My own body has failed me. When hungry enough, a person will eat anything, do anything.

And I am hungry enough.

I accept the bowl from her, holding it like one would hold a newborn kitten. I try to imagine the fire again, but the buzz under my skin must be as tired as my body.

Nothing happens. I am not sure whether I am relieved or disappointed, but I keep trying anyway, glaring at the bowl.

I stare for several long minutes before I drop it to the ground and shove myself to my feet.

"This is ridiculous. I told you it wouldn't work!" I pace in a small space at the edge of the platform.

Loxy snatches up the bowl, then grabs my shoulder and spins me to face her. "You barely even tried."

"It's hard."

"Yes, it is." She narrows her eyes at me.

We glare at each other for a full minute. Eventually, she lowers the bowl and holds it between us, her glare still firmly locked with mine.

"Light a fire, Elodie."

I hold my glare for several more moments. After all, fear or no, hunger or no, I am still the older sister. I can't let her best me at a glaring contest.

Then, when I'm sure she understands, I drop my eyes back to the soup, letting the angry stare drop with it. I don't want to live my life in fear, but I wish I didn't have to accept that this is my life now, either.

But what if she's right, that if I don't use the magic, it will overwhelm me again? Is that why I couldn't control it in Limutria? Is that why I killed—

No, I can't let myself think about that again. We don't know. Not really.

Maybe Audrey is even now recovering.

I hold one hand out, and Loxy deposits the bowl into my palm. I stare at the floating bits of fish and seaweed again and swallow back bile. I have to try.

Loxy is counting on me.

I close my eyes. I think of the cookfires at home and try not to fall into bittersweet memory. I think of my passion for the Bright One in my veins, imagine it like fire. I pretend that all of that heat and fire pulses through me, toward my hand, into my fingers, into the stew.

You can do this, I coach myself.

And I feel warmth in my fingers, that grease coating my skin, the buzzing underneath.

I open my eyes and stare down at my hand. It begins to glow from within, a bright orange filling my flesh as my bones are illuminated in dark red. Fire spreads from my palm up the sides of the crystal bowl, and as I watch, the liquid inside begins to boil.

I glance up at Loxy, and she smirks. "Told you."

I return my attention to the bowl and watch, transfixed, as the soup boils down and the fish cook. My mouth waters at the smell of cooking food on the air. Then Loxy gestures at the ground, and I set the bowl down.

But my hand is still on fire.

My heart flops in my chest before it takes off in a sprint, fear replacing pride. I try to imagine dousing my hand with water, imagine the flames going out, but it doesn't seem to work. Instead, the flames burn hotter, brighter.

I turn panicked eyes to my sister. "How do I stop it?"

The fire is starting to hurt. It didn't hurt me before.

"You have to calm down," Loxy says, her voice low and even, her smirk gone.

But I can't calm down. I can hear her anger behind her words, I can feel the pain I have inflicted on others, and the heat morphs into that searing pain. I can't hold back a cry. My world is narrowing to the burning of my body, the intense pain it causes. Tears stream from my eyes, and a sob breaks from my lips.

Loxy grabs my hand and shoves it into the Sea. Steam hisses and writhes upward, enveloping us in a cloud, and the heat leaves my hand.

The fire is out.

I remove my hand from the water and examine it, tears leaking down my cheeks. Blisters cover the red skin, and it still feels as if it burns, though there is no trace of fire.

"What happened?" Loxy says, pulling on my fingers to examine my hand.

"I…I don't know," I whimper, my voice shaking. "I couldn't make it stop."

Loxy grunts. "So you need practice." She glances up and stabs a finger toward me. "And don't you dare try to use this as an excuse to stop!"

I look at the ground. Easy for her to say; she's had years to learn something she expects me to master in only a few days.

I examine the blisters. If I had my herbalism kit, I could treat the burn. But out here it may become infected.

Loxy grabs my hand and squeezes it flat between her palms. I cry in pain, and she shushes me roughly, nodding at the hands. As I clench my teeth at her touch, the pain fades.

She releases me, and I look at my hand. The skin is pink, as if newly healed, and I look back up at her, startled. "What was that?"

She grunts again and rubs her hands against the fabric covering her legs as if wiping away grime. When she moves them again, I see blisters on one, the skin puckered and raw—the same hand that I had burned.

"Loxy, what did you do?"

For a moment, I think she won't answer me. She begins to eat the cooked fish and seaweed. And then she finally speaks. "I have a bit of empathy in my magic. It's some kind of fluke or side effect or something."

"But...why didn't you ever tell me?"

She levels an incredulous look at me, and there is something else behind her stare, some haunting memory I can't know. "When everyone thinks Singing is just a curse? Would anyone think healing was a blessing? Or would it just be another excuse to ostracize me?"

I drop my eyes, hearing the truth of her words. Empathy would be even more likely to land her a banishment than her Halosinging. A Singer with power over injury or disease? Sefella-marked. Is this why she'd always begged to serve her apprenticeship with the healers?

And I always said no. Or, like the last time she'd tried to take the test, actively sabotaged her chances.

I really am an awful sister.

And now her expression gnaws at me. There is more here than I could see before, that much is becoming abundantly clear. "Loxy, what happened?"

She takes another bite of fish and chews for several long moments. "I healed Dad once."

My heart flops. "Dad knew about this?"

She nods, her voice bitter. "And I'm sure he still has nightmares."

I can feel the pity transforming my face. I can't help it. I'm suddenly hit with a weight of disgust that we could make her feel like such a monster. "Loxy, I'm so sorry. I had no idea."

"Yes, you did." She takes another bite, refusing to meet my eyes.

I blink at her blunt words, stunned for a moment. I don't want to admit it, but despite all the pretty words…

She's right.

I sigh. "Yes, I did. I guess I just never realized…" I trail off, unsure how to finish. "I never wanted to upset Dad. And sometimes…defending you felt like putting us all in danger. I'm sorry. I really am."

She just shrugs. As she chews her next bite, she rubs her hand on her thigh again.

"What about your hands?" I say. Without being too obvious, I try to see the blisters she is hiding from me. "How does it work?"

"I take on your pain, but it heals more quickly than if it were my own." She holds her palm out toward me, and I see the blisters already shrinking. "They'll be gone in an hour or two."

"Why didn't you heal the bite? From the Water Dragon?"

"It doesn't work that way. I can't heal myself."

I lean back and try to process this. Does her ability mean I can heal, too? Why didn't Loxy try to heal Audrey?

My stomach drops, and guilt rises to my throat again like bile. Maybe she did.

"Did…Audrey…" My voice breaks as I utter her name. I feel as if I am violating something sacred by daring to mention the name of my sister's love, the name of a person I may have killed. But a part of me needs to know. I need to know if Loxy healed her, too.

Loxy's face grows cold and distant. "My power isn't that strong."

I blink, unsure what to say, my chest constricting. My sister, the strongest person I know, couldn't help Audrey. I almost reach a hand to her, wishing I could comfort her. But then I blink back my own tears.

I caused this. I broke the only person who made my sister happy, and there was nothing she could do to stop me. I'm worse than a bad sister.

Maybe I'm the monster.

Fifteen

LOXY

The man's very nature had eroded away to almost nothing, but with his last human thought, he pleaded to Sefella. "Return myself to me, and I will give you whatever you desire!"

"Fool," Sefella responded. "I gave you everything. Now when it no longer suits you, you dare throw it back in my face?"

Excerpt from "The Foolish Beggar," a Limutrian folk tale

It's been five days. My feet drag through the Sea, and I can't find warmth, even at night when Elodie lies close. I can finally see the mountains within our reach, but I fear we will never make it. I curse the priestesses for leaving us out here without a raft, without hope—without even shoes on our feet—but I yearn to feel the hard, dry earth underfoot. Both mine and El's feet are peeling from the constant submersion in the saltwater, red and sore and prone to infection. I'd heal her, but it wouldn't do either of us any good; I would just be worse off than before.

My wound from the Water Dragon is red and puffy, and there is an ache in my joints. There is nothing we can do out here to fight it.

And the stranger, Sef? We haven't seen her in days. Maybe she changed her mind after all. Maybe we lost her. I am relieved to no longer be haunted by a wandering spirit in this wasteland Sea, but a bit sad she's gone. Whatever she is, she was company.

By the end of the fifth day, the Sea grows shallower. Instead of rising to our knees, it is now only ankle deep. The mountains loom before us, only miles away by the time darkness falls. Without a word, we both agree to keep walking, to end this wandering in the endless Sea.

El's control over her magic, or at least her fire, has grown over the past few days. After that first mishap, she learned to quench the flames without harming herself and without me having to drench her, so now she feels no fear cooking. At least, no fear she deigns to share with me. She is unbearably quiet at times, and I can see sadness emanating from her like a cloud.

"You need to keep practicing," I say, breaking the silence of the evening.

She doesn't answer, and I feel my anger stir like an animal, heat rushing into my face, my neck.

"We aren't safe just because you can cook now."

"Save it, Loxy," she finally says, but her voice lacks heat.

I glare her way, but I am too tired and my body hurts too much to keep up the argument this time. My anger is tempered by exhaustion, by the tedium of placing one foot in front of the other.

With her newfound control, El summons a flame to her hand, just large enough to act as a torch in the night. We walk for another hour in the forbidding darkness, the only sounds the sputtering of the flame in her hand and the sloshing of our feet through the sea. The orange light dances across the water, reflecting across our bodies. But the light goes no farther, lost in the void of night that surrounds us. There is no other sound to break our stubborn trek other than the occasional fish jumping, and we keep our silence. On previous nights, we've stopped and made shelter at sundown, but tonight we just keep plodding along, the mountains feeling close and far at the same time, an unspoken hope that maybe if we walk a little longer we'll escape the water.

An hour and a half after the sun sets, I lift my foot from the sea and plant it on dirt. Actual dirt. It doesn't submerge into water or silt, though the ground is still wet from the small waves lapping against the shore. For a moment, I am stunned, frozen in place, blinking at the lack of water beneath me.

We made it.

I run forward, unable to stop the grin splitting my face, the pain from my wound and the saltwater trek momentarily forgotten, and dance in the starlight. The moon is hidden behind the clouds in the distance, but even Sefella couldn't stop the stars over the mountains from shining, from celebrating with me.

I hear more than see El run forward beside me. She drops the flame, and we drop our grief and our anger for one blessed moment. We grab each other's hands and dance together, spinning in circles, laughing with glee.

We made it.

Eventually, we are too tired to continue our dance, too exhausted and ravenous.

I turn to my sister. "What do you think? Should we find shelter, or should I make one again?"

El glances around us at the barren shoreline. The lapping waves along the sand are gentle, almost peaceful in the quiet night. I can just barely make her out in the darkness.

"Is there enough mineral for you to work with here?" she asks.

I close my eyes and listen for a Song. And what I hear takes my breath away.

There isn't just enough crystal here for a shelter. There is enough for a palace. A city. A country! Miles upon miles of crystal in the mountains, spreading north and south, extending deep into the earth like roots. We stand on a land more plentiful than any I could have imagined, any I could have dreamed.

I sense the strongest Singing coming from the west, deeper into the mountains, out of range of tonight's hike. I tuck the information away for tomorrow. I will find what Sings so loudly, so strongly, so beautifully.

For now, though, I erect my most beautiful shelter yet.

It is a mix of rose and crystal quartz, selenite, and halite. And it holds more than just the crystals in the sea of our home. I can summon marine crystals like calcite, anhydrite, sylvite, and countless minerals whose names I do not yet know.

The world is growing, bright and new, even in the midst of our endless night. As the last spire forms under my direction, I am filled with a boundless energy I cannot contain.

I lower my chin from where it had been lifted to the heavens, open my eyes to admire my handiwork. I can't keep from smiling. I can barely keep myself from squealing from the sheer joy and excitement of it all.

Impressive, comes the voice, the one from the village. I've barely heard it lately, but for some reason, it is a comfort, a joy, to hear it now.

Elodie walks into the shelter. Her clothes are wrinkled, wet, and dirty after five days in the sea, and she appears dingy against the gleaming walls of crystal. And suddenly, the reality of where we are, what happened to us, crashes back down on me.

I didn't create this for art. I created it for survival.

My feet are now solidly on the ground. I am still filled with energy, light and fluid, but my head no longer swims and Sings with the resonance that surrounds me.

"Why don't I see if I can find something to build a fire with?" I say. I can't stand to look at the dirt against my pristine structure, let alone the sister that got us into this mess.

Without waiting for a response, I turn on my heel and stalk into the dry reeds that line the beach. Their roots are crusted with salt, but this type of reed doesn't mind the salinity; it thrives on it. In fact, these are the same reeds grown in Limutria for everything from sleeping mats and mattresses to rugs and shoes. Their tough fibers make them durable and resistant to wear. I would recognize them anywhere, especially since they are grown along the edges of the apiary gardens.

The thought of the apiary draws me up short, and I allow myself to slouch down into the muck of the reeds. Motion above me catches my eye, and I look up to see stars streaking across the sky in blurs of silver against the velvet black night. I look away quickly, shuddering at the memory of the Burning Rain. I feel weak, as if now that we have made it to shore I can finally let myself worry and mourn and fret. One nightmare ended, that of the endless void of water, but the real nightmare is still only beginning.

A life cast out from the village. Without Dad. Without Audrey. A life with Elodie.

Up until now, we'd stayed together out of necessity. If we left each other, neither of us would survive.

But now that our feet are on solid ground again…do I really want to stay with her? After everything she's done?

Can I bear it?

And yet, there is still a feeling of duty, like I can't just abandon her now. At least not without saying something first. No matter my feelings, she's family. And she has taken care of me since Mom was exiled. I at least owe her a goodbye.

I collapse into myself and let the tears flow, shoulders shaking, breathing in gasps, too tired to decide anything, wanting only Audrey…and peace.

Part Three

BLIND

Sixteen

ELODIE

The Sea is life. It is food and material and trade. It is our most valuable resource. And yet, the Sea is also death.

Excerpt from *Ivlene's Early Childhood Primer: Limutria*

I wait nearly an hour for Loxy to return, my knees pulled up tight against my chest. I am huddled in the corner of the shelter, jumping at every scrape across the ground, every howl of the wind around the corners of the stone. It isn't raining, but this land is alien. I've never been beyond Limutria's borders, let alone on dry, stable ground. The lack of movement is too solid, too steady, and my body still feels like it swims in the sea.

A wolf howls in the distance, toward the mountains. Its call is long and mournful, and I can relate. I feel the same way.

Another wolf answers it, and I shudder, hugging my knees tighter. Wolves are pack animals. I know that from lessons, though

I've never seen one near the village, even during the dry seasons when they venture into the Sea.

The wolves finish their song, and the silence of night descends. Insects buzz and chirp in the distance, frogs and toads croak in the marshy reeds, and the waves of the sea lap steadily against the shore. My eyes begin to drift closed, and I struggle to stay awake. I want to give Loxy her space, but I can't let myself sleep until she comes back.

Footsteps thud on the ground outside the shelter, deep and hollow on the packed soil, soft on the wet earth. My eyes snap open, and I tighten my grip around my knees.

Are we near a village? What will people do if they find us? Loxy spent her whole life hiding her magic, but I blew our secrets in one day. Will they know when they look at us?

Will they kill us?

How many reports did I hear back in the temple about cleansings in the remote villages? Too many. And not cleansings like I tried to get for Loxy. These cleansings were murder.

I have even more reason to worry now.

I can't wait here without knowing. I can't sit around and welcome a possible violent death.

I can't leave Loxy like that.

The footsteps thud ever closer. I unfold myself and crawl toward the door. Keeping as much of myself hidden as possible, I peer into the darkness.

A dark shape suddenly materializes out of the blackness, and my heart leaps. I jump back against the wall, looking around for anything I can use to defend myself. Somewhere in the back of my mind, I know I myself am a weapon, but I can't reach for that power, can't embrace it.

The shadow grows closer, and I scold myself. It's probably Loxy. Yet, I can't quite make myself call her name, instead pressing myself deeper into a corner.

The night clears as the form steps into the doorway, and Loxy's face appears. I breathe out a great sigh, welcoming air back into my lungs.

Her arms are full of long sticks and reeds. She drops them to the ground inside the shelter, tossing a few herbs toward me, and begins sorting. But her movements are slow, and a flush paints her cheeks.

"We should make some shoes before we set out again," she says, laying another reed on her pile. She doesn't look directly at me, and the closer she is, the more I can see her puffy face and glassy eyes.

Has Loxy been...crying?

But Loxy never cries. She barely even cried as a toddler.

My heart lurches, but I don't know what to say, what to do. I can imagine the pain she's feeling, similar to what I felt when Mom was banished, but I also know she wanted to keep it to herself enough to run off and cry without me.

I'm not sure I can blame her.

At a loss, I look over the herbs she gave me. She must listen to me after all; in my hand, I hold Moonwort, a plant that flowers only at night and can be made into a poultice for most infections and wounds.

I scoot across the ground toward Loxy and begin helping her sort. Guilt stabs my chest. I sat here, hidden in the shelter, while my baby sister ventured into the unknown to find us what we need.

Some sister I am.

I shove the thought aside and turn to arrange driftwood into a pile for a fire. I leave plenty of gaps between sticks so that air will have access to the fire and allow it to feed, then I hold my hand out toward the pile and let a single orange flame jump from my skin to the wood. The wood cracks and pops as the fire dries it out and burrows into it. After a few minutes, a cheerful fire blazes in the center of the shelter floor.

I grab two flat rocks and crush the buds of the Moonwort, releasing a sharp herby scent into the air. Then, I lay them next to the fire.

I return my attention to Loxy. She must have left again while I was working on the fire, for she now holds two quartz bowls filled with seawater. She sets them down between us and begins dropping bits of onion and shellfish into one. I peer into the depths and breathe a sigh of relief when I see no minnows in the water.

I have had enough of those to last me a lifetime.

She slides the other bowl across the ground toward me, and I drop the Moonwort in, mixing it around with my finger until it forms a paste.

Once our dinner, and her treatment, are boiling in the fire, Loxy sits back and looks at me with her big, liquid eyes. "So where do you think Mom would have gone?"

I shrug uneasily. "I told you, Lox. I don't know that Mom is still…" I can't bring myself to finish the thought, not with her eyes staring at me so intently. "I don't know."

Loxy leans back against the shelter wall and looks toward the ceiling. "Was Mom always a Crystallosinger?"

My breath catches, and I can't keep the irritation from my voice. "She was born a Halosinger. You know that. We assumed that was why you are a Halosinger, too."

Even as I say it, I question myself. After what happened at the Burning Rain, I'm not so sure the first one isn't what changed Loxy, giving her the magic Mom had in the beginning.

The Burning Rain is change. *As a priestess-hopeful, you should know this.*

The voice from the village. It's back. I grit my teeth, trying to push it away again.

She nods. "But she was a Crystallosinger later?"

"Does it really matter?" I'm so tired I can barely focus on her, let alone answer all her questions about Mom. Thinking about Mom just makes me ten times more tired.

We fall into silence. I'm not sure if she's thinking or angry. I'm hoping she's just thinking. I know she has every right to be mad at me now—Ivlene knows I'm mad enough at myself—but we're still family. We've never fought for long. I can't bear the idea that I've made a mistake so large we can never recover from it.

I should answer her, tired as I am. "Yes, Mom was a Crystallosinger. She went through more than one Burning Rain, and it seemed like the second one gave her more Singing than ever." I look at her. "Kind of like you."

"Like Atmosinging," she says, flushing, her eyes narrowing like she's angry. "Which *you* have. Not me."

"True." Is she mad that I have more powerful Singing than her?

I wait for her to say more, but resentment sits in the air like a shroud I'm afraid to part. If I poke at her feelings, will she just hate me more?

I watch her for a few moments, then break the silence and change the topic. "I think tomorrow we should look for supplies and head for Aeglora. It's closer than Salitas, and even though we made it to shore, there's nothing else here."

She looks at me. "Closer doesn't mean better. And there *is* something over here."

I blink. "What?"

She hesitates. "I heard it. Something that would have called to any Crystallosinger. And I'm going to find it."

Her proclamation is so final, that for a moment I can't even think of a response.

You owe her, the voice cuts in. I tap my fingers against my forehead, irritated at the intrusion, but it's not wrong.

I owe her so much.

"Fine," I say. "Tomorrow. But if we don't find anything, I'm going to Aeglora. And you're coming with me."

She opens her mouth to respond, anger glinting in her eyes, but is interrupted by a fit of hacking coughs. I don't like the sound of those coughs, but I am relieved it keeps her from responding. Keeps her anger at bay, at least for now.

Keeps our relationship safe.

I slide closer to her, stifling a cough of my own, and grab the bowl off the fire. I unwrap her arm and bite back a hiss at the angry red skin, puffy and puckered around the teeth punctures. I glance at her, then press my hand over the wound. I hear her sharp intake of breath, but she must know what I'm trying to do.

Trying to heal. Like her.

"Listen for the pain," she says through clenched teeth. "Call it away."

I do as she says, but nothing speaks to me. I keep trying for nearly ten minutes, trying to find the healing magic Loxy has, but it seems that is a gift that did not transfer. My heart sinks with every passing minute, and for the first time, I find that I am jealous of my sister. I have years of training in the ways of healing, yet she can merely touch a person and heal their hurts.

I release her arm and slather poultice over the wound. I re-wrap it, hoping it's not too late for it to work, then let her go.

I sit back and take up some of the reeds she brought back. Without waiting for help or another comment, I begin tearing strips of reeds to weave into shoes. She doesn't speak, either, but joins me by the fire.

We must have drifted off sometime during the night. We had traveled halfway through to midnight, then kept ourselves up for hours weaving, so it was no surprise.

I sit up and rub at the grit in my eyes. My throat is sore, as if someone took all the lava salt from the deepest pits of the great ocean and ground it against my insides.

Loxy is already up and tying her crude shoes to her feet, the same kind we made as children just learning to weave. Without a word, I join her, tying my own shoes tight and then draping the rough reed cloak over my shoulders. She glances at me with an odd expression, like she wasn't expecting me to join her, and I flash her a shaky smile.

The light of day, clouded and rainy though it is, chases away my fear of the night before, and I find that I want nothing more than to take charge of my situation for the first time since we left.

There's something else I need.

"Can you make me a mortar and pestle?" I ask.

She nods, still not speaking, then drops to her knees and holds her hands over the earth. I watch, fascinated, as she closes her eyes and hums, barely audible over the crackling of the fire. The ground under her hands trembles, and spires of crystal thrust up from below the surface. She begins weaving her hands as gracefully and skillfully as she had been weaving the reeds, and I am mesmerized as the crystal obeys her command and coalesces into a tiny pink mortar and pestle set.

She sits back and hands me both pieces. "Here."

I nod, speechless, and take the object from her. Even at temple, we never had tools as beautiful as these.

"Beautiful," comes another voice.

"Sef," I say, turning to face the stranger at the door. "You made it."

She nods once, solemnly. "So did you." Her eyes travel from the shelter around us to the mortar and pestle in my hands. "Wonderful work, really."

I narrow my eyes. "Where did you disappear to?"

She smiles, the expression small and mysterious, betraying nothing. "I told you I could keep to myself. That you didn't need to worry about me. But I will fulfill my promise. I can lead you to great places." Her eyes turn to Loxy. "I believe you already know, though."

Loxy doesn't respond, but understanding fills her eyes. I can see her determination double, and I groan inwardly.

"Fine. Let's go, then. Before I change my mind."

I kick dirt over the fire and strap together the mortar and pestle and more reeds to continue weaving later, and Loxy raises her hands to erase the shelter, staring at it forlornly for several long moments, a distant look in her eyes as if she is listening to some far-off song.

"Maybe we should leave it," she says.

"Why?" I say.

"For other travelers? I don't know. It's just…this is the most beautiful thing I've ever created."

Sef rubs her chin. "It is a marvelous structure. A real testament to your power. It would be a shame to destroy it." She walks a few steps away, attention focused on the mountains and our path ahead.

I take a step back and look at the shelter again. And it's true. It has twists and designs in the spires and walls that Loxy never bothered to create in our other shelters. Every turn, every curve, screams out the joy we felt last night, finally on dry land.

But it's still crystal of the sea. "Won't it just erode in the rain anyway?" I say. "Most of the crystal around here dissolves in water."

She shrugs. "Some of it is quartz. Maybe enough will stay."

I shrug back at her, then turn toward the mountains. "Whatever you're going to do, just do it and let's be on our way. I don't want to be soaked before we're three steps from camp."

Loxy drops her hands and looks at the shelter for another moment, then she steps in front of me and turns inland, following Sef. I glance back at the shelter, still standing, rain dancing off its bright walls and roof. I smile, somehow proud and happy in this moment, a feeling I didn't expect to feel for a long time. Happy that my sister is proud of something for once.

For now, it feels like we will be okay.

But the happiness fades quickly as we begin our trek surrounded by the elements. Rain falls harder than it has in days. It's the kind of day when staying indoors with a book and a hot drink would be best, but we don't have that luxury anymore. We walk past the field of reeds and toward the edge of a meadow. The grasses here are thinner, dry, and speckled with yellow and white flowers. As I approach, I can even see nizeo, a grassy plant with tiny pink flowers that is useful for curing fever.

I wish I had a bag.

As we walk, I scour the meadow for whatever herbs I recognize, whichever ones we might need now or later. Some of them require mixing or special preparation for use, and if we have them on hand, at least we will be ready. I pick some of the nizeo, then I continue with the yellow flowers of a pengu bush, stalks of herby brixawan, blades of peppergrass. Some of the plants are edible, but most are so tough and fibrous that they wouldn't be anyone's first choice for dinner. Sef watches, slowing her pace for me, interested but silent. As in the Sea, her body does not seem to disturb anything around her, the plants not even shifting as she passes.

Definitely a spirit.

The rain hounds our every step. We are drier now that the reeds help protect us, but even they are not enough to keep the water from streaming down our necks, drenching our backs until it is almost as if we don't have the cloaks at all. Our feet in their new protective coverings suck into the mud, nearly remaining in the muck several times, and only the strong knots with which we tied the reed-shoes keep them secured. At least our feet hurt less now that we are not barefoot and constantly submerged in saltwater.

The Sea disappears behind the scrub, and then rocks begin to rise up from the ground and block the rest of the view back home. No, no longer home. But the place that once held all my dreams for my life. Dreams now broken.

Like me.

I catch Sef's eyes on me, and I flush, turning away quickly. It's as if she can hear my thoughts, knows exactly how I feel. I am too cold and miserable to think of a response to her.

The rock grows taller, towering over us and offering a partial shelter from the falling rain. The mountains rise up around this narrow pass, fencing us in, enclosing us in a way I've never been enclosed.

Ivlene, have mercy on us.

My heart begins to pound, and not from the exertion. The mountains are closing in around us. Perhaps it is their magnitude, their solid, unwavering stone. In Limutria, all stone is temporary, easily dissolved. Even the ground is not constant as it is here, instead rising and falling with the shifting of the seasons, always in motion.

There is nothing quite like this unmoving ground, these immovable stones. Does Loxy feel as I do, this fear? This closed-in feeling?

But no. She looks from one peak to another, awe on her face, joy. Why it does not bother her, I don't know. Sef also seems undeterred.

We turn a corner in the narrow pass, and suddenly our feet are on smooth white stone, slick with water. I look out at the valley before us. Stacked against the mountains here are terraces of white-walled pools filled with brilliant blue water. Steam rises above the pools, and the white stone looks as if it is flowing down the mountainside to the valley where we stand. And on the far side of the valley, past the steam and stone and water, towers a gleaming white mountain.

"What is this place?" I say, breathless.

"I don't know," Loxy says, equally breathless. She steps forward, turning in circles to take in our surroundings, eyes wide and sparkling. "I could feel it, though. All the way from the sea."

So that explains her desire to come this way. Her questions about Mom. Just like Mom, she could hear the crystals. And, somehow, I can't fault her for wanting to see this. I can see notes of Loxy everywhere, mixed in with scents of minerals and the heavy, humid air.

And I can see Mom in everything, too. She's in the scattered piles of broken crystals and salts, in the mineral pools. So much of what I've always associated with Loxy is like Mom used to be, too.

I shudder and wrap my arms around myself.

Loxy runs ahead, feet slipping on slick white flowstone. She touches everything, resting her hands on the warm walls of pools, dipping her fingers in the mineral-rich water, inhaling the steam.

I'm not sure I've ever seen her happier.

Seventeen

LOXY

Everywhere Ivlene created beauty, Sefella was sure to follow with logic and with meaning. And in so doing, Sefella gave that beauty depth and clarity.

Excerpt from *The Ballads of Sefella*

I close my eyes and allow the steam to encase me. I can hear the minerals Singing in the swirling vapors, in the cerulean pools, in the ground under my feet.

I snap my eyes open and bend down, untying the knots on my improvised shoes. I am overcome, heart pounding and full, compelled to immerse myself in the minerals, the richness, the luxury of magic all around us. How could I not? I climb a few of the oddly terraced flat white rocks, then sit on the edge of a pool, on the only wall that rises above the surface. The rest of the water sits like a mirror up to the very lip of its container.

"There is something here," I hear Sef say through the ringing of the crystals. "I am going to scout ahead."

Her footsteps—something I can hear, for once—grow quieter as she walks off, and I turn my attention fully to the Song of the water's crystals, listen for their energy. Somehow, I know the water will be a relief, without danger, without scalding. They tell me so, with their seductive embrace of Song.

I plunge my hand into a pool, and Elodie screams, running up behind me. She stumbles, slides across the flowstone. As she approaches, terrified by my impulsive action, I let the minerals slide over my skin like a balm.

"Calm down," I snap, my voice scratchy, raw, and irritated. "How's your cough?" My eyes are on my fingers in the slick water.

In answer, the cough covers her words. I wince, but I can't help her with my magic. I am just as sick. But…

"What herbs do you have?" I say.

Her face is puzzled, and I reach a hand down. She passes me a small bundle, and I drop it into the water. The herbs break away from the bundle and join the chorus of crystals in the pool, spreading their floral scent amid the sulfur of the steam, the calcite of the stone, the silica in the clay at the bottom of the pool. The small yellow blossoms drift on invisible currents, bright as sunshine on a cloudless day.

And then there is no stopping me.

I strip out of my outer dress, down to the cloth that covers my chest and my lowest layer of gown. They are still wet; I'm not sure they've dried at all over the days since our exile. I swing my legs over the wall of the pool and slide in, finding another terraced ledge just inside and allowing my body to sink onto it like a chair.

The heat floods my bones with a warmth I haven't felt since home. The mineral-rich pool cradles my wounded arm, soothing the last bits of pain and infection. It eases the salt crusting my body, the raw places where the sea chafed away skin. I close my eyes and lean my head back, letting the rich water hold me, letting the healing in the herb-rich steam fill my lungs. There is a splash next to me, and I smile as drops of warm water rain down on my face along with the cool rain of the storm above.

El reaches out to me, brushing my hand with her fingers, and I open my eyes a crack. Her expression is full of awe and pleading.

I squeeze her hand before pulling it back again. There is a warmth in my belly, not the same as the fire of anger, but more like the warm glow of comfort. I slide a little closer to her, resting my head on her shoulder like I used to. The hole in my heart feels a little bit smaller.

I had woken up at least an hour before her this morning, fully intending to leave without her. Yet, for some reason, I found myself moving slowly, putting off that first step out into the rain, putting off the separation.

I'm not even sure why.

But there was a part of me that just couldn't leave her. That wanted to give her another chance. After everything she's said since we've been out here, I'm starting to wonder if maybe that's all she's ever needed: a chance to show me how much I mean to her as her sister, not just an obligation since Mom left.

I want to give this another try. I know that now. I *want* to be around my sister, to go through this together. To have someone to share this journey with.

But underneath it all, I can still feel the bitter fire of my pain. Audrey's name pulses in my chest like my heart, and a pang of longing for Dad's arms fills me.

I should have stopped this. If only I'd known how strong El's magic was.

I slide away from her, feeling the cold creep back into me. I won't leave, not yet at least, but right now I need a little distance. I can't let myself forgive her that easily. Not after everything she's done over the last week.

No, the last twenty years.

Instead, I focus on the Songs around me and let them cradle my broken soul. I feel myself drifting at the edge of sleep, my mind growing slack and then snapping back. I can barely feel the cool rain on my face over the steam of the pool now, but its gentle patter and the calm and peace of the valley wrap me in security.

"Who in Ivlene's great sky are you?"

I jump up, spluttering water, heart pounding. I don't know how long we've been dozing, unaware, vulnerable, but it was long enough for a small, fiery boy about my age to approach unnoticed.

The crystals—not to mention Sef—didn't warn me there were other people here, and I feel a twinge of betrayal. But the Song fades as I focus on the boy.

I cross my arms over my chest instinctively and see El do the same out of the corner of my eye.

"Who are you?" El says. The muscle in her jaw twitches as she grinds her teeth in irritation. I am all too familiar with that expression. At least this time it isn't directed at me.

The boy stamps one foot and props his hands on his hips. "I'm pretty sure I asked you that already. Who are you, and what are you doing here?"

I exchange a look with El. Do we tell him anything? If we say we've been banished from our home, will he shun us, too?

El speaks before my brain can make a decision. "I'm Elodie, and this is my sister, Loxy. We're…travelers."

He glares at her. "And why are you *here*?"

She looks around the valley. "We needed rest. This is a good place for that."

He lets out a huff of exasperation. "Yes, I know. That's why people usually hire a *guide* or a *healer* to get here. No one knows the way except a few. And you are certainly not among those few!"

I cut in. "We were simply walking through the mountains and stumbled upon this valley."

He turns acidic eyes to me. "That seems awfully unlikely. There are only two ways to access this valley, and no one travels through the mountains anymore."

"Soltan, there is no need for this hostility." Another man, perhaps in his forties, steps up behind the boy, supporting his weight on an intricately carved quartz cane. "The pools are for healing. For everyone."

Soltan steps aside and crosses his arms, unrepentant.

The man takes a step closer, then his eyes dart between us and widen. He turns away quickly. "Perhaps you should dress before we talk."

El flushes, and we both climb out of the pool and wrap ourselves back up in our already-wet dresses. At a word from El, the man and Soltan turn back to face us. The man's face is kind, peaceful, while the boy's is indignant and disgruntled.

"My name is Iarann. Soltan is my apprentice. We run the springs, but I have never seen someone able to find them on their own. Well…at least not in a great long while." His face is puzzled, but then he sweeps the appraising, evaluating look of a physician over us. His eyes rest slightly longer on my swollen arm. "You are injured. And you both appear a bit worse for wear. Perhaps we can discuss this back in the village?"

I glance at El, but she is watching the strangers, so I look back to them. Do we trust them? Iarann seems safe enough, but Soltan…I don't want my back to him. And where did Sef get off to? El glances at the men again, evaluating them with her calculating thoughts, just like she evaluates everything, and then she nods.

We really could use some help. And it would be nice to have real shelter and food again. Besides, we can still run if we need to.

"We did have another companion, but I'm not sure where they got off to," El says.

Iarann nods. "Well, there are regular patrols, so I'm sure one of them will find your companion. In the meantime, let's get you both back to shelter."

The men turn and lead us toward the towering white mountain. I have to trust that he's right, that Sef will be fine. This isn't very different from the Sea. Sef will find her way back eventually, if she still wishes to haunt us.

As we make our way through the valley, I can't help the smile that tugs at my lips as I listen to the mountain Sing. I've never seen such a large creation of salt before!

About halfway through the valley, a mound of white stone rises up next to the poorly defined path. It's made of the same material as the flowstone, and I bend to examine it. I can hear the signature of Singing in it, magic carving the stone rather than tools. Hands delicately completing the cairn.

"Pretty, isn't it?" Iarann says, appearing at my side. "The only other person I've ever seen find this valley alone created it."

Soltan snorted, crossing his arms. "About the only good thing she ever did."

"She?" I say, my pulse rising. Could it be…Mom? Was that why the Singing signature called to me so strongly from the carving? "When was this visitor?"

Iarann smiles, and there is fatigue in the lines of his face. "Long ago. But the day is short, and we should continue before night falls. The mountains, even here, can be dangerous after dark."

Reluctantly, I step away from the cairn and rejoin El behind our guides. I glance at her, trying to get her attention, trying to tell her without words what I heard. But her face is stern, disgruntled, and she ignores my attempts. With a sigh, I give up and turn my attention ahead of us.

As we grow closer, my steps slow. I can't believe the magnitude of the Song I hear. It's not only a mountain of salt. It's a vast network of caves and caverns. And, as promised, a village on the far side of the mountain. A normal person would never be able to navigate it alone, not without an escort familiar with the layout of the tunnels. And even though I can hear the crystals Sing, I can't distinguish the layout just from the Songs. There are far too many, all layered until it's one large harmony.

I could be lost in this labyrinth for centuries. I shiver. Somehow, that both thrills and terrifies me.

The light grows dimmer as we enter the shadow of the mountain. The Song is now so loud in my head, I can barely hear my companions' footfalls. We step under the protection of the mountain, into the mouth of the cave, and the rain stops striking us like daggers.

"What is this place?" I breathe, my gaze riveted to the bright white, glittering stalactites of salt overhead.

Iarann glances back over his shoulder, smiling. He takes another limping step into the mountain. "This is Montalo."

"Is it… Is it salt?" El asks, touching a piece of wall to her left.

"Mostly, yes. At least here. Some calcium as well, though. Long ago, this was all covered by the sea, but as the world's climate changed and ice developed to the north and south, the ocean fell away. It layered the salt here, and then the rains carved the caverns. We stand in a place almost as old as the world itself." Iarann takes a globe-shaped lantern off a hook just inside the mouth of the cave and turns a key. A blue-white light inside the globe grows bright, and he steps into the bowels of the earth.

Into a land forged by Sefella herself, perhaps even a gate to the Underworld.

No one speaks as we trek deeper. I don't know why El is silent, but I am too overwhelmed with the grandeur of the caves to say a word. Water drips from the ceiling into saltwater pools of bright blue, the splashes echoing around the cavernous halls. Salt crystals encrust the stalactites and stalagmites, sparkling with every movement of Iarann's lantern. The light strikes even more facets of crystal all around us, casting diamonds of blue light from one end of the cave to another.

We continue along a path worn smooth by countless feet, the salt and calcite slick with water dripping from overhead. A drop hits my nose, and I jerk back at the sudden cold, startled.

Iarann glances over his shoulder and chuckles as I wipe my nose. "Don't worry, that's good luck."

We walk deeper, so deep that the daylight fades completely and all that remains is the lantern light. Here, I can almost feel the cold touch of Sefella, the thin border between our realm and that of the Underworld. The blue pools are bright within the glow of the lantern, but they quickly fade into a black darker than any night outside the edges of Iarann's ring of light. I shiver, my skin crawling. Even the crystals, still too numerous for me to understand, fail to tell me what lies beyond the light. Several times I think I hear movement, a scuffing of feet or snuffling of breath, but I never see the source.

The ground begins to curve upward, flowstone of calcite covering the walls as they close in to a path barely wide enough for one person. I don't know how Iarann navigates with the cane, but he is the most sure-footed of the group. I wonder how many years he has spent tending the springs and guiding their visitors.

We turn a bend in the path, and daylight reflects off the stone ahead, the sounds of life greeting our ears and breaking the monotony of dripping water. Children laugh and scream, a hammer rings on metal, and voices are deep in conversation. The scent of woodsmoke drifts down to us, and we suddenly exit the blue glow of the salt cave to find ourselves standing in the center of a town.

Iarann glances over his shoulder as he extinguishes the light and hangs it on another hook. "Welcome to Ryth Hollows."

We are in a valley, the ground churned to mud by the rain and feet of the townspeople. The mountains rise up all around, but a break on one side shows a vast plain of white sand I've never seen before and the bright blue glimmer of water on the horizon. The ocean, perhaps? I've never seen anything other than our own sea, and my breath catches at the sight of something far bigger, far deeper, than anywhere I've been. On the far side of the valley, green crops wave in the breeze while women and children tend to them. Men stand in open-air stalls working forges or performing other skilled trades. If I close my eyes, it almost feels like Limutria.

And it turns my stomach.

But one thing separates Ryth Hollows from Limutria: these people appear to have electricity, lights blazing through windows with a steady yellow glow, music blaring over small radios. Limutria is so far behind this, and our…their…hydroelectricity has not yet been perfected. There, oil lamps light the way and batteries power only our most necessary devices, like the water purifiers.

I don't expect the jealousy that strikes me, and I do my best to shove it away. Limutria isn't even our home anymore; does it really matter that they don't have the same luxuries as the rest of the country?

Iarann and Soltan turn toward a small building just to the left of Montalo's gaping entrance. It reminds me of the apiary office, but this office is connected to the side of a home.

They lead us through the door of the office into a sitting area, and I look around, almost expecting to see Audrey at her desk. But instead, a larger desk lined with shelves and cupboards is built into one side while the far wall is rock—the solid, white stone of the mountain. Two cots line this wall, and I can almost smell the salt in the air, concentrated over the sleeping area. Across from the desk, a door covered in bright white fabric must lead to the main house.

Iarann wastes no time and crosses the room to an armoire. Inside are linens and boxes of supplies. The heady scent of herbs and spices drift from the closet, and I close my eyes appreciatively. He removes two fluffy towels and two simple white dresses.

"We usually give these to paying customers, but I can't have you catching cold in my establishment. I am, after all, a physician." He limps back toward us, handing each of us a towel and dress. "You can change through the door there. We'll get your clothes cleaned and get you back on your way."

"Thank you," El says. "This is very kind. It will be remembered by the priest—we will remember your kindness."

His eyes flicker with something at her words, but he simply nods. We leave the room to change, hearing the low voices of our hosts following us out.

Eighteen

ELODIE

Invite all weary travelers to share in your meal. Cover their heads in the rain. But be wary for those followers of Sefella who would see you destroyed.

Excerpt from *The Records of Bright*

Loxy and I retreat to the main house, still tracking water across the floor. I shiver and let the curtain fall behind us. On the other side, we find ourselves standing in a small foyer; stairs ascend to the left, and a single room holding a kitchen, dining space, and living area take up the rest of the floor.

I glance at Loxy, then venture farther into the house, turning left around the stairs into a small alcove. An overstuffed armchair sits under a portrait of a happy family. I glance around furtively, making sure I haven't missed anyone in the room, but the house seems empty.

I shuck off my wet clothes and rub my skin down with the towel, relishing the warmth the friction provides. Beside me, Loxy does the same. Bumps rise along my arms, and my skin holds that sting of tenderness I always feel when I'm sick.

The medicine is wearing off.

"Where do you think Sef went?" Loxy whispers.

Sef. Right. Our ghostly companion. "I'm sure she's fine. We can always go back out after we warm up and try to find her."

Loxy chews her lip. "Maybe she doesn't want to be found?"

I pause for a moment, startled. Could that be it? Could Sef be an outlaw? Or maybe she's just hiding Singing, like Lox and I.

We really don't know much about her. Maybe it's for the best she didn't follow us here. But I keep that thought to myself and simply shrug at Loxy.

We throw the frocks over our heads, then gather our belongings to return to Iarann and Soltan. I'm not sure we can trust the boy, but Iarann seems kind. He did, after all, provide us with dry clothes and a roof between us and the rain. Like any good physician of Ivlene.

I take the towel from Loxy and hand both to our host. "Thank you so much for your kindness."

Iarann takes the towels and places them in a cloth bin near the door. "Has not Ivlene declared it so?"

His words are a comfort, a balm to my bleeding soul, and I blink back tears. He is truly a physician if he follows Ivlene's healing teachings so closely. Limutria was never large enough to attract one of them, having instead the healers of the temple, but both physicians and healers follow the same teachings.

Teachings that I'm not so sure the priestesses of Limutria actually follow. The words they taught me to say, the way we were told to accept and protect all, feel hollow now, as drenched as we have been since leaving, as brittle as dry towers of salt.

"Yes," I finally say, my throat thick. I can't stop the small, genuine smile I give him, tears still burning my eyes.

He reaches a hand out for the clothes, and we pass them over. Soltan takes them from his master and hangs them along a line now strung across the room. While we were gone, someone also started a roaring fire in a small iron stove in the corner and placed a kettle on top of its hot surface. The fancy electric lamp glows on the desk, sending soft, artificial light to chase away the gloom of the rainy season. I lay the mortar and pestle from Loxy on the small table in the sitting area, next to a large wooden box emblazoned with the symbol of the Bright One.

"Please, sit," Iarann says, dropping himself into one of the armchairs. "Soltan will fetch food from the community kitchen. Rest, tell me your stories."

Soltan nods sullenly and escapes the office as Loxy and I join Iarann in the chairs. He beckons Loxy closer and holds out his hand toward her arm. She glances at me, and I nod. Somehow, I trust this man. And her injuries may be beyond my ability to heal.

He gingerly takes her arm and turns it back and forth in the light, examining the now-clean punctures. "This looks nasty. What kind of beast makes a bite like this?"

I lean forward on my knees, my leg bouncing. I can feel the anxiety beginning to build in my chest, a tightness, a tingling. I take deep breaths, willing the magic to stay in check. I can't let him find out. If he does, we will lose what courtesy we have been shown, and Loxy will have no care for her injury.

Neither of us answers him, and he doesn't pry. Instead, he flips open the box on the table and lays out a number of bottles and small piles of gauze. He busies himself treating and wrapping the arm. "Where did you say you are traveling from?"

Loxy glances at me, then turns her attention back to Iarann's gentle ministrations. She is completely absorbed in every motion he makes, in every tool and its use. When had her fascination with medicine become so strong?

My heart lurches. How much I have missed. Or rather, how much have I been willingly blind to when it comes to Loxy?

"Limutria." Loxy's eyes are locked on the rag he drenches with something yellow-brown in color, barely even wincing as he begins dragging it over the punctures.

A look of understanding washes over his face. "That explains how you found the springs. The only other path, besides through Montalo, is from the east. Where did you leave your raft?" He tightens the bandage, fastening it with a small crystal pin.

"No raft," Loxy says before I can respond.

He looks stunned, his hands pausing in their work. For a moment, he doesn't say anything. Then, "How did you cross the sea?"

Loxy glances at me, her eyes now full of worry, and I clench my jaw. She shouldn't have said anything. She should have let me deal with this. That's her problem—she never thinks things through!

I smile at him, teeth clenched tightly. "With a lot of willpower and perseverance."

He nods, though his expression is still clouded. He releases Loxy's newly bandaged arm and repacks the box. No one says a word for several minutes, although it feels like an eternity. Then, he sits back and rubs at his chin, gazing into space.

Loxy leans forward. She opens her mouth, about to spew something else that will get us in trouble, I'm sure. I reach out and grab her uninjured arm, any attempt to silence her, and her mouth snaps closed as she leans back in the chair.

"I think we are both too tired right now. Our words aren't making much sense. Would you mind postponing this conversation until tomorrow?" I smile at him again, hoping it will be enough.

His expression doesn't clear, but he nods. "Very well." He stands and takes his cane from where it is propped against the wall. "We can discuss tomorrow."

"Thank you," I say, rising with him. "Your hospitality be blessed."

He points his cane toward the stove. The kettle is steaming and releasing an herbal scent into the room. "There is tea in that kettle. I want you both to drink the entire thing. It will help with your fevers and any infection you picked up that might be causing it."

I can smell the nizeo mixed with another herb I don't recognize. I incline my head at him. He nods back to me and limps through the fabric curtain into the main house.

I sit back in the chair and look over at Loxy. "You almost blew it."

She scowls. "What are you talking about?"

"We've been gone a week. How do you know they haven't heard from Limutria?"

"Do you really think our people are talking to outsiders about their shameful secrets?"

My stomach drops, and heat flames my face. But she has a point. Why would High Priestess Cydia share our…weakness…with the rest of the world?

But that wasn't the only problem. "What about telling him we didn't use a raft? Isn't that kind of suspicious?"

She throws her hands up in exasperation. "What's he going to do?"

"I don't know, kick us out?" My voice is rising with every word, with my temper. The redness of my skin is no longer shame; it is anger. "Pry until he knows too much? Remember those stories about remote villages killing Singers?"

Loxy's face pales. "Or maybe this is our chance to show people that Singers are *good*. That we can help them. Or perhaps this is a place we could settle after we find Mom. Didn't you see that cairn? It had to have been her. And if not her, then definitely a Crystallosinger."

Mom. Here we go again. She just won't let it go, won't let the past stay in the past!

She doesn't remember what it was like, watching Mom change, watching the way she and Dad fought all the time toward the end, the fear after that Burning Rain, the one that gave Loxy Halosinging and ripped Mom from us.

She doesn't remember how we both stared out into the Sea for weeks, hoping to see some glimmer of her returning.

She never let go of hope, while I had to be the practical one. I had to be the one to accept the fact that Mom was never coming back, that maybe she was gone for good, that she had given up on us by not even trying.

My anger and irritation build with each thought, like the rising of the Sea during the rainy season.

The door slams open against the wall, and I jump, the anger quickly receding as Soltan appears carrying a loaded tray covered with a towel. The towel is dotted with dark spots of rain, and the hiss of a downpour follows him inside.

He drops the tray on the low table between us and then himself into the opposite seat, leaning forward on his knees and pinning us with a glare.

"What have you been talking about in here?" he demands. "Where is Iarann?"

Loxy jumps to her feet, expression solid as the mountains. "It's not your business what we discuss."

I take a breath, trying to calm myself before I say something we will all regret. "I assume he turned in for the night, as we would like to do."

He rises, matching Loxy's energy and anger stride for stride. "You may have my master fooled, but not me. Outsiders can't be trusted."

He spins on his heel and storms out the door. As it slams behind him, I nearly scream in frustration, and static crackles the air around me. Over on the desk, the electric lamp flickers. Between Soltan and Loxy, I may lose my mind.

Loxy laughs bitterly. "Good thing you waited until *after* our hosts left to lose it."

I snap my head around to glare at her, but my irritation at her words—and Soltan—can't hold up to the expression on her face. She looks absolutely pitiful, all wrung out and still as wet as a drowned deer, and I am sure I look the same. The tight anger and frustration that had been clenching my chest releases, and suddenly I laugh.

Loxy glares at me, but it isn't long before she is laughing, too.

After a hearty, silent meal of barley stew, dense bread, and the hot tea from the kettle, we pile the dishes back on the tray and collapse into the cots on the other side of the room. It only took a few minutes for me to recognize the other herb in the tea, a mild sedative the priestesses use to help anxious patients sleep. Part of me is alarmed, but part of me is also grateful.

As soon as my head hits the pillow, I close my eyes in bliss, relaxing into the sweet embrace of the clean, crisp sheets and the fresh scent of soap filling my lungs. I tug the blanket tight around me, relishing the warmth of a real bed.

I am nearly asleep when Loxy speaks, her voice slow and heavy with the sedative.

"Do you think Dad's okay?" Her voice is small, and I can hear the medicine fighting her for control.

I feel every big sister instinct rear up as I prepare to tell her yes and not to worry. But then I remember how broken he was after Mom was exiled. How he changed. I'm not sure he isn't broken all over again, and for once, I can't make myself gloss over the truth just to make her feel better.

If we are to make it through this together, maybe I need to start being more honest. For both of us.

Instead of a lie, I say, "I'm sure the village is taking care of him." Which I am. Sort of. Unless the priestesses are keeping them away.

Loxy pushes herself up on one elbow and shifts to face me. "Are you? I think they'd hold us against him. Three of his family corrupted? His *entire* family?"

I wince. "There's nothing we can do."

"We can find Mom," she says quickly, hope still in her voice. "We can get Dad. Start over, finally."

"Maybe."

"We could ask Iarann tomorrow."

"Ask him what?" The sedative is heavy in my blood now.

"If he knows where Mom is."

I don't answer, instead letting the silence stretch on. It was twenty years ago. And she never once tried to come back. Never tried to contact us. Never cared how we were doing. Just let Limutria kick her out and gave up.

My eyes burn again with tears, and now I am too tired to hold them back. They slip down my cheeks, hot and quick.

And what if asking about her makes them more suspicious of us? Soltan already doesn't trust us, and perhaps his fear of outsiders is shared by the village. What reason would they have to answer our questions?

I do not want to become one of the dead Singers in the news.

I look over at Loxy, at the hope in her eyes. How can I take that from her when I've already taken so much?

"We can ask," I finally say, just before I drift off into the dreamless sleep of the tea. "If it's safe."

The next morning, rain is pounding against the window panes. I don't notice it until the office door opens and Soltan enters, letting in a blast of cold air. I blink at the sudden daylight, gloomy as it is, and watch him drop wood in the firebox next to the stove. In the house on the other side of the curtain, I hear footsteps, uneven and slow, creaking on the stairs. I squeeze my eyes closed and pretend to sleep, unwilling to leave my cocoon of warmth.

As I listen to the sounds of morning, I take stock of my own body. My bones do not ache today as they have for the last week, and I do not feel that same sensitivity to touch as I did last night. My fever must have broken, and I can only hope the sickness has been pushed from my body.

I crack open one eye to watch Soltan moving about on the far side of the room, stoking the fire back to life and turning the switches on the lamps. I watch this with particular interest, fascinated by the power of the electric bulbs, jealous of Ryth Hollows for having something we never did.

The curtain to the house whooshes, and uneven steps enter the office. "Soltan, will you join me in preparing breakfast?" Iarann whispers.

I sit up. "May I help?"

Iarann glances at Loxy, who snores lightly in her cot. She's always been a heavy sleeper, and the trials since our exile have earned her the right to sleep as much as she wants now.

He turns back to me and nods, stepping to the side and beckoning me into the house.

I rise, smoothing the blanket quickly, and follow Iarann and Soltan to the kitchen. Soltan immediately begins stoking the fire in the oven, and Iarann pulls jars from open shelves.

"Do you know how to bake bread?" he asks, holding a large jar of flour.

"Yes," I respond, taking the flour from him.

I smile at this menial, normal task and begin measuring ingredients into the bowl. Just like herbalism, baking is a precise science. I wait for the yeast to bloom, using the time to lay out the other measuring cups and ingredients. Ryth Hollows has running water, just like Limutria, so there is no need to find a water pump or well. After the yeast blooms, I dump all the ingredients into the bowl and begin mixing it when Iarann appears at my elbow, holding one more jar.

"What's this?" I say breathlessly. Dense bread is hard to mix.

"Elderflower honey," he says with a smile. He pops the lid and hands me the jar, and I freeze.

The sickeningly sweet scent of the honey assaults me, and for a moment I fear I will be ill. I see the same bolt of lightning as in my dream, striking Audrey, a girl as sweet as honey, my sister's beloved.

Did I kill her?

"What is it?" Iarann asks, concern on his face.

I shake myself out of memory. "Nothing. It just…reminds me of someone."

Iarann eyes me as if he knows there is more, but he doesn't pry. Soltan, on the other hand…

"What did you do?" he blurts, whipping eggs in a bowl with more vigor than necessary.

I blink, my eyes burning, unsure whether or not to answer. Then, I find myself speaking to these people, these strangers. "I don't completely remember what happened. I…I hurt someone. An accident. Someone my sister loved. Loves."

I can't let myself fall into that trap of believing she's dead. If I do, Loxy may never forgive me. I may never forgive myself.

"It was my own fault," I continue. "I was careless. Afraid of myself."

A snort comes from the doorway, and I look over to see Loxy. Her hair is knotted and tangled, dress wrinkled with sleep. She doesn't meet my eyes, hugging herself tightly. The pain around her is palpable.

"You *were* careless. You should have asked for help," she says, her voice tight.

I glance at the two men next to me. Soltan is glaring at the two of us. "I don't think this is the place to discuss this."

"I'd like to hear what happened," Soltan says. "After all, it's our safety we're risking."

"Soltan, she said it was an accident," Iarann cuts in. "Let it go."

"But—"

"Enough. Finish the eggs."

Soltan looks stormy, but he obeys, turning as far from us as possible. Loxy sits on a stool at the kitchen island, just beyond my bread. She remains silent, picking at the skin around her nails until she draws blood. I used to scold her for that, but is that really my right anymore?

Iarann shoves a bowl of fruit toward Loxy, breaking the serious, silent atmosphere of the kitchen. "Would you mind cutting this, please?"

Loxy nods and takes up a knife, and I can almost imagine us back in the kitchen at home, working together to make dinner.

But everything is different now.

As she cuts, she says, "Any sign of our companion?"

Iarann shakes his head slowly. "I'm afraid not."

I am almost ashamed of the relief I feel. There is something more to Sef that I can't quite figure out.

Loxy plunges on after a moment's hesitation. Is she actually worried about Sef? "Iarann, can you tell us more about the mountain?"

I lean toward them as I mix, interested in the answer.

Iarann smiles, expression distant. "Some say the caves were carved by Sefella, the first gate to the Underworld after Ivlene cast Sefella from the heavens. It was a place for all the outcasts, those in pain, in sickness. The springs were born, and if the springs weren't enough to cleanse the pilgrims who came, Sefella would carry them to the Underworld through the crystal caverns. The journey was meant to be of peace and acceptance, a journey into the change that comes to all."

His words grate on my nerves, too close to blasphemy, if I go by what the priestesses teach. Yet, at the same time, the words catch at me like a burr in my clothes. Like there's something more to what I was taught—or not taught.

"But Sefella is death. How could they find peace with her?" I blurt, my hands pausing in their work as I push my discomfort back.

I hear a hiss in my head, then, *Isn't Death peace just as much as the Light of the Bright Ones?*

Iarann's smile fades. "Sefella wasn't always held in such low regard. The priestesses would do well to remember that, lest they fall to sickness and be prevented from entering into the presence of the Bright Ones."

Bright Ones. Plural, just like the voice only a moment ago. Does Iarann follow the Old Records? The Ballads of Sefella?

I focus on the bread under my hands. Bile rises in my throat. Would Ryth Hollows' own priestesses come after him for speaking this way? They would have in Limutria.

Neither of us responds for a moment, then Loxy says, "How extensive are the caves?"

"The caves have not all been explored," he responds, "but they seem to lead toward the south. Some of the townsfolk wonder if those caves are unnatural, created by the priests in the south as a way to travel easily from their temple to the springs."

I perk up at the mention of priests. All the clerics in Limutria are female; to hear of a temple of priests is new. "What is this temple?"

"Oh, we aren't even sure it still exists. No one has heard from them in a number of years. It may be completely gone by now. But it was said that these priests knew all and could heal any ailment. And if they couldn't, then they could tell petitioners where to go for answers."

My mind jumps to my magic. I have made an uneasy peace with some of the magic in my blood, but is it possible I don't have to keep it? That these priests could heal me? Cleanse me? Could Loxy and I be whole again, accepted back into Limutria? I could return to the temple, and Loxy...

Loxy could return to Audrey.

My heart flutters at the possibilities, at the hope Iarann's words spark within me. At the chance for things to go back to normal, for me to atone for what I've done.

To be whole again.

Iarann takes the bowl. "Let's get that bread in the oven."

Nineteen

LOXY

Beware the followers of Ivlene who weave beautiful lies. Test all things. Keep only what is true.

Excerpt from *The Ballads of Sefella*

After breakfast, Iarann leads us to the temple. I don't really want to go, but El seems to need some chapel time. I believe in the goddesses. And I believe in Ivlene's ability to protect us, in her immense power.

At least…I did, once. Now? I'm not sure she really cares about the outcasts. And if I'm honest, I haven't believed that in years.

And no matter my feelings on Ivlene, I do not believe in her people.

I barely trusted them before, and now…now I have nothing left to give them. But out here, we are observed and followed, and any suspicious activity could put us in danger. So, even though

I'd rather not go, I act the part of the dutiful sister and devout follower and tag along to the temple.

The town teems with activity this early in the morning as people run to jobs and errands and children play and learn and work alongside their parents. The town seems to be full of farmers, many of them growing medicinal herbs I recognize from El's bag back home. This really must be a healing community, between the medicinal fields and Iarann's task of leading the sick to the springs. In fact, he spends half the walk to the temple telling us about the economy of the healing springs and the medicines Ryth Hollows offers to the outside world. El nods along, engaged in the conversation, but I feel like an outsider…not a healer, not a priestess, not even "normal."

I tune out their words after a few minutes and just take in the scenery and rare spots of sun. I don't know how long the rain will hold off, so I drink in the golden rays and allow Ivlene to touch me with light and a feeling of peace, of rightness.

Ivlene isn't the only one who comforts, comes the voice. But this time it sounds almost…angry?

The feeling of peace flees, and I return my attention to the town. Anger aside, the voice is right. Ivlene has never been the one to grant me peace. I thought so, years ago, but even if she is everything I've been taught, her people…well, her people certainly don't act like she would want. They act more like they say the followers of Sefella once acted. And none of Sefella's followers remain to argue.

We cross the small valley, approaching the tall mountains opposite the salt mountain, where a simple wood structure set with shining, Singing-carved rose quartz stands defiant to the wilderness. It is not as large or grand as the gleaming pink temple back in Limutria, but it is warm and welcoming where Limutria's temple is arrogant and imposing.

As we approach, a strange expression washes across El's face, and I struggle to read it. Usually I can tell right away what my sister is feeling, but this…this is more complicated. It starts as a reverence, a peace and calm I've rarely seen from her, but it morphs into something more like fear. She stops just outside the door, not following Iarann inside.

I stop next to her, my heart fluttering. El has always been the one in control, the confident one.

"What's wrong?" I whisper.

She looks up at the carved quartz relief over the heavy doors, her eyes wide and shining. "Do you think Ivlene still accepts me?"

I feel a flash of irritation, both at her words and my own doubt. "Why would you even question that? The Bright One accepts all. Of all people, you should know that."

I say the words because they're what she thinks she needs to hear. Whether they're true or not. She wouldn't listen to anything else.

"But I'm not the same. I'm…tainted."

Does she mean Singing? The same magic I've had as long as I can remember? Anger rises in my gut, heat rushing to my face, salt sparkling and dancing on the edges of my vision.

But before I can respond, she takes the few remaining steps separating her from the temple. I follow as the anger pulses with my heartbeat.

How could she still say something so hurtful after everything we've discussed since the Rain? She knows how I've been treated, how I view Singing. So if she still thinks she's tainted…

Then she still thinks there's something wrong with *me*, too.

And then I step into Ryth Hollows' version of a sanctuary, which is really much more like a simple chapel than a temple. Rose quartz, which is commonly used to represent the Bright One, covers many of the windows, filling the room with soft, diffused pink light and granting the space warmth. Pews line the sides of the room, facing a shrine at the front dedicated to Ivlene. It is simpler than the shrine at Limutria's temple, but it still has all the same elements, the same symbols. A door stands to the right of the shrine, I assume leading to the priestesses' quarters, study rooms, or work spaces. A few people sit in the pews, their whispered prayers sounding like the casting of an eerie spell.

But I can't get over El's words. Tainted? Is that really what she thinks of me, too? I've spent my entire life attending services, worshipping at the shrine. Why would she suddenly think she's unworthy of setting foot here?

The doubt prickles again, and my stomach churns. The skin around my left wrist begins to grow tight, and I look down to see salt crusting over me, settling and blooming from the salt dancing in my vision. I brush at it, but as soon as I knock one crystal loose, another blossoms.

This is all El's fault, too. If she could just accept things, I wouldn't be so angry. I should be in control. I've been in control for years.

So why is the salt defying me?

I tug my sleeve closer to my hand to cover the salt and stalk to one of the pews, throwing myself down as my heart pounds with fear that someone will see my magic, fear I haven't had so viscerally since I was young. I pull a prayer book from the seat in front of me and look for the Song of Serenity. If I ever needed it, it's now.

Twenty

ELODIE

*The fires of Sefella burn bright, and we need hope now more than
ever. Grant us acceptance, grant us peace, grant us serenity.*

Excerpt from *The Song of Serenity*

My stomach churns as I step through the doors. It's the
first time I've been in a holy place since the…exile. I
can barely even force myself to think that cursed word.

Iarann walks ahead of us, toward the pews on one side of the
chapel, and Loxy breaks off from behind me, dropping herself
noisily into a pew and grabbing a prayer book. I cast her a puzzled
look, but she doesn't notice.

I turn my attention back to the shrine at the front and
approach it reverently. As is customary for a priestess, or even a
lowly apprentice like me, I dip my fingers in a bowl of holy water.
The water is cool against my skin, like a gentle rain in the dry

season. I touch my cleansed fingers to my forehead, lips, and heart, cleansing each of them in turn, then bow my head and begin a liturgy of prayers.

The prayers flow like they haven't in a week, maybe even my entire life. I hadn't realized the stopper that was sealing them inside me, clogging my head and my heart with words unsaid, emotions unfelt.

I feel my lips move with the liturgies, though no sound escapes to disturb the peace of the chapel.

"Ivlene, forgive me. I have sinned. I have injured those around me with my careless actions.

"Ivlene, grant me grace, that I may be a grace to others.

"Ivlene, have mercy on me, so I may have mercy on those who need it most."

The words aren't one of the sanctified prayers printed in a prayer book, but in this moment, it doesn't matter. No one hears me but the Bright One. The roiling of my stomach calms as I feel her peace settle over me like a blanket. I feel lighter than air, no longer weighed down by a rock in my chest. How could I have ever thought otherwise, that she would suddenly no longer accept me, hear me? She is mercy, she is acceptance. Even if I live out my days in this exile, even if I can never forgive myself for the pain I've caused, the lives I've ruined, at least I know she has accepted and forgiven me.

Then why can't you accept the change that has been brought to you? My heart lurches at the truth in the voice. And suddenly, the peace I thought had settled over me feels more like a mask.

Maybe Ivlene doesn't hear me after all. The prayer I thought I'd sent to the Celestial Temple now seems to simply fall back to the ground. The weight returns, the reprieve so brief I must have imagined the peace, that sense of rightness.

"Priestess, we welcome you to Ryth Hollows."

I jump, my eyes flying open as I turn to face a small older man behind my elbow. He wears the long robes of a senior cleric, likely the high priest of this shrine. It still throws me to see a priest rather than a priestess, but Limutria seems to be the exception, or so I am finding.

I bow slightly. "Forgive me, Priest, but I am no priestess."

He smiles, his eyes flicking to my head. "You have the hair of one. An apprentice, then?"

I flush at the compliment, at the awareness that others still see me as holy. "Not anymore, I'm afraid."

He must see the shadow I feel pass over me, because his brow furrows and he extends a hand toward me. "You seem as though you carry a great weight. Would you care to unburden yourself?"

I clasp his hand to buy myself time to think. Do I dare? Do I tell my worries to this priest? This stranger?

I glance back and see Iarann deep in prayer, cane propped on the arm of the pew next to him. Loxy sits hunched in her own pew, paging through the prayer book as her lips move. I feel warmth blossoming in my gut to see my sister in practice of our faith.

Will I violate her rights to privacy by telling my secrets? *Our* secrets? I look back toward the priest and drop his hand. "I am afraid my burdens cannot be shared."

He nods as if he understands, though I know he cannot. "Then perhaps we can simply talk. Join me in the study?"

He gestures toward the door on the left, and I find myself nodding, though my anxiety has begun to build again. Talking wouldn't violate our secrets, but it will create opportunity for mistakes. I breathe another prayer to Ivlene before following him, willing myself to be wise.

And still, again, it feels as though my prayer falls back to the ground, never reaching her ears. I wince and follow behind the priest, trying to ignore the unpleasant, unfamiliar pressure in my chest.

While the chapel was quiet with reverence and penance, the halls beyond are quiet with the simple peace of reflection, just as I always felt in Limutria's temple beyond the shrine's corridor. Except now, instead of only peace, the silence feels weighted with the dread of something coming, something terrible approaching, though I don't know what that would be. The priest leads me to a small study at the end of the hall, leaving the door open behind us. He gestures toward a plush blue chair on one side of a desk, and he settles into another chair on the other side, then pours two glasses of cold honey wine.

I blush with embarrassment at my last memory of honey wine, at my drunkenness, at Loxy finding me in such a state in our home, but I accept the proffered glass anyway.

The priest takes a sip of the wine before addressing me. His eyes drift closed in bliss as he savors the sweet concoction, but all I can taste is the tart bitterness of the alcohol. My stomach rolls at the taste, tainted with the bad memory.

"You know, I used to have dreams of running my father's vineyard," he says, setting the glass on the desk.

"Oh?" I say, unsure how to respond. "What happened?"

"It burned down. Government took everything that was left."

"So what did you do?"

"Moved to Ryth Hollows and took up the priesthood."

I watch him over the rim of my cup. "Why are you telling me this?"

For a moment, he simply watches me, too. Then he says, "That was the greatest upheaval in my life. I had never felt less grounded or sure of where the Bright Ones were taking me." He studies me again, and it is as if he sees beyond the carefully curated mask of my appearance. That he sees my loss, my shame. His next words prove it. "I sense you have recently had your own upheaval."

My heart flips in my chest, and I set the cup on the desk, stomach churning again.

He nods to himself. "I thought as much. Young lady, I have been a priest a great many years. I can spot a soul in turmoil miles away. And you, my dear, are most certainly in turmoil. So what really brings you here? Penance? Absolution? Wisdom?"

The words run circles through my head as I try to find a response that keeps Loxy and me safe, that doesn't betray too much but is enough to grant me peace.

"We…" How much can I say? How much *should* I say? "That is, my sister and I…we are on a journey together."

"Family can be the best company on a journey. Or the worst." He smiles.

I can't help but smile back, agreeing. Even now, with Loxy withdrawing herself from me, holding back everything but her anger. The Bright One knows I haven't even begun to forgive myself, so why should she?

But there's also no one I'd rather be exiled with.

The unexpectedness of the thought surprises me. In Limutria, I did all I could to keep my distance from her in public, to hide her from my fellow apprentices. But things feel different out here, beyond the rules and expectations of the priestesses.

"My sister and I are not quite like other Nasmaryans," I finally say.

The priest chuckles and takes another sip from his glass. "Oh, child. If I had a coin for every time someone walked into my office and said that, well…I could go back and build that vineyard! We are never quite as unique as we tell ourselves. You'd be surprised."

I duck my head, warmth spreading across my cheeks. I bristle at the implication that I am still a child—Loxy and I haven't been children in years. And not as unique as I think? Is that an insult? A truth I should heed?

Does he have any idea what we're capable of? What if he knew we are Sefella-marked?

"So what else is there?" he says, pulling my attention back to him. "Why did you start this journey?"

I feel as if I am about to burst, wishing to express all the things I told the Bright One in the chapel, to have a real, living, breathing human answer my fears in real, audible words. Because for one of the first times in my life, I don't think Ivlene heard me, and the uneasiness of that feeling sits like a stone in my stomach.

And as a priest, he is bound to confidentiality. I want to trust him. But I also remember how the priestesses in Limutria gossiped.

Which kind of cleric is he?

"It wasn't by choice," I begin hesitantly, skin tingling with the magic in the air.

"Few great journeys are." And he looks at me with such understanding, such kindness, that I know he is a priest to be trusted.

My story comes spilling out like the tears spilling down my face. Something in me pushes me to talk, to tell him every good, every bad, every terrifying thing leading up to and past our exile, up until the moment Iarann found us yesterday. His expression never flinches, never darkens, never wavers from the kind eyes of a true listener. He waits patiently for me to finish my story before speaking.

I have never had anyone's attention like this. Even among the priestesses, real, true listening is a lost art.

When I finish, I feel deflated, spent. All the pressure has been lifted off my shoulders. Could this listening, this unburdening, be what the Bright One intended of the priesthood? And if so, why did the temple in Limutria never teach us anything like this?

Then my lightness is replaced by fear—of what the priest will do now that he knows I have been corrupted. Tainted.

Instead of censure, he repeats what he said before. "I stand by my words, Elodie." He speaks my name, and I do not know how he knows it. I did not tell him. And I have yet to learn his. "You are not as unique as you believe."

"Why would you say this? Are you telling me our country is poisoned? Corrupted by more people like me and my sister?"

Now his face shows a glimmer of anger, and I snap my mouth shut, flinching back.

"Do you truly believe this of yourselves? How dare you question the will of the Bright Ones!" Bright Ones. Plural. Was he saying that earlier, too? "They allowed this power to come to you and your sister. Your magic is a powerful gift, not a curse to be cured away like a rash! And after a Burning Rain, no less, when Sefella's hold on this world grows stronger. I know not many in my profession would say this, but those who disagree with me are small, narrow-minded people who do not truly believe the messages they preach."

I hug myself, trying to stop the trembling in my limbs. Sefella? Sefella has a hold on the world?

"Tell me, girl," he continues, heedless of my thoughts, "does your sister believe as you do?"

I only need to think for a moment. "No. She believes our magic is a great power, a blessing. She is…jealous of me. Angry at me."

"And I would say she is justified. Especially if you utter the things to her that you just said to me, that her magic is a curse and a dark mark on her soul. Any true priest of the Bright Ones will agree with her, not you. Your magic is a gift."

I flinch and duck my head again, shame running hot across my skin. But my confusion at his pluralization of Bright One remains.

"Magic is a rare gift," he continues, "yet our people have tried to remove every trace of it. Out of their own jealousy. Their fear. Even here, the townspeople would not respond as I do. Because they are afraid. As you are."

I blink, speechless for a moment as I digest what he says. It's true that many of the priests and priestesses I have met don't act like this man, don't care about people the way clerics are called to care.

I have never heard a cleric speak like this man.

"What makes you different?" I finally manage, tears brimming in my eyes. "Why don't you condemn us, drive us out into the wilderness like our own people did?"

He refills our glasses, though I've barely touched mine. "My dear, not all agree with the way this country has turned from magic. The temple where I studied many years ago was one of the greatest beacons to the world, at least for Ivlene's followers. They called Singers from all over, helping those who needed it, training those in need of training. And, on occasion, releasing Singers from their gifts, if they were a danger to themselves or those around them."

I lower my chin, rubbing at it in thought. Could this be the same place Iarann referenced this morning? Could this be a place where Singing can be cleansed?

"I pray you will embrace the gifts you have been given," the priest says, breaking my thoughts again. "The power of Ivlene does not exist without the power of Sefella. And maybe you will learn that on this great journey."

I glance back up at him, seeing nothing but compassion—pity—in his gaze as he sips his wine. "Will you tell us how to get to this temple?"

I am not sure what he sees in my eyes or if it's simply what I said earlier about Singing, but suspicion clouds his eyes at the question. "Why do you want to know?"

"So that I may seek the truth. And how do you know my plan, my desire, isn't their will as well?" I use his pluralization of the Bright Ones, hoping it will soften his response.

He pauses, wine halfway to his lips. "I suppose I don't."

"Then will you tell me? Please."

He studies me for another moment, then sighs with a nod. "I will tell you. I forget that all young ones must make their own way, their own mistakes."

I flinch again. Every word from this kind man carries the weight of mountains, and I can't explain why. There are things he isn't saying, important things. Things I feel like I should know but still somehow elude me.

"But remember this, even if you go to the temple," he continues. "I am not like most of the priesthood. Not like most of the citizens of our poor country. Not all who see your magic will simply exile you."

I swallow, afraid of his next words, knowing what he is about to say.

"Most will kill you."

Twenty-One

LOXY

There will come a time when truth must be revealed, when change must be accepted. And in that time, know that Sefella will be with you.

Excerpt from *The Ballads of Sefella*

Someone settles into the pew next to me, and I stop my liturgy, turning to see Iarann.

"How are you faring?" he asks softly.

I put my hand over the salt crust on my arm, hoping he doesn't notice. Instead of answering, I shrug.

He offers a small smile. "I can't imagine what has brought you to us, but I have to believe it isn't by accident. You don't need to tell me, but know that I only wish the best for you and your sister."

My mind drifts back to his tale of the springs, how Sefella formed them to heal. "Do you really believe the stories? About the springs?"

He takes a deep breath. "Yes, I do. I know many would call me a heretic for believing that Sefella ever had something good to contribute to us mortals, but as a physician, you learn quickly that death cannot be escaped. And even disease has its place in this world. Why shouldn't the goddess of Death comfort those near to the Underworld? And why shouldn't that be a comfort to the rest of us?"

Death and disease are seasons of change, the voice adds. *Change isn't bad. Don't you know this by now, Daughter of Songs?*

Something resonates within me, a hum in concert with my empathy.

"There is something within you that tells me you have a natural gift for healing. Don't let your circumstances kill the compassion, the empathy you've been gifted."

I wince at the word 'empathy,' but pride wells in me nonetheless. A physician thinks I could have a gift for healing?

Will I ever get the chance to prove it?

Thankfully, I am rescued from responding by El's sudden reappearance.

She returns from behind the shrine, her face red and splotchy, as if she's been crying. I close the prayer book and tuck it into the pocket on the back of the pew, then rise and meet her at the door, my heart stuttering with fear and—unexpectedly—a protectiveness I'm not sure I've ever felt before.

Why was she crying?

"What happened back there?" I ask quietly, trying my best to keep Iarann from overhearing. He's gone back to his prayers, either unable to hear us or polite enough to pretend. The crystals surrounding my wrist have shrunk to a thin band, like a bracelet, but I can feel the skin around it tingle with my fear.

Oh, hounds of Sefella.

El shakes her head as if bewildered. "I found a kindred spirit. And a plan for our next stop."

We walk outside, away from the silence of the chapel, from the potential for eavesdropping ears. I feel hope blooming in my chest that she is accepting our exile as something more, a chance at new beginnings. A chance for better. The fear dissipates, overtaken by this hope.

"Where do you want to go?" I say, watching as people hurry by, giving us a wide berth. Even here, the people can tell something isn't quite normal about us.

"There used to be a temple to the south. It might still be there. In the mountains." Her eyes rove the mountain peaks around us as if she can see it from here. "Cliffreach."

"Would Mom have gone there?"

She doesn't answer for a moment. "I think Iarann mentioned it this morning, and the priest told me about it today. It's supposed to have been a mecca of sorts for those who can Sing, or at least it used to be. So it's possible."

"Such a thing exists?" I say, dumbfounded.

El shrugs. "It did at one time. It may not even be there anymore. But what have we got to lose?"

I shrug, too, knowing the answer. We've already lost everything—what else can there be?

It's not like we have any other hints for finding Mom, either. The cairn doesn't say much, and after Soltan's outburst this morning, I am afraid of asking the villagers.

Plus, a mecca for Singers sounds like a wonderful place to go.

"Then I suppose we should figure out how to supply ourselves," I say.

Her next words surprise me. "All we need to do is tell Iarann. The priest I spoke with arranged the rest. We will be much better off than when we left home."

I am stunned, barely able to move, let alone think. The people here will supply us? We will be able to continue our journey, our search, fully prepared.

We will have real shoes again!

But more than anything, excitement fills me that El and I are finally on the same page. The hope growing in me pulses that maybe this means she is finally accepting her gifts. *Our* gifts.

It's almost enough to make me forgive her for getting us exiled.

For Audrey.

Almost.

"When do we leave?" I say.

"First thing tomorrow."

Early the next morning, long before the sun provides any light to the day, rain is pounding on the roof so hard that it's like a constant roar of screaming. For a few minutes upon waking, I forget the soft cot and sheets, I forget the exile.

I am back in Limutria, and the Burning Rain falls around us as people scream and run for their lives.

And then Audrey is in front of me, reaching for me. I start to run to her, fear tightening my chest until I can barely breathe, heart pounding harder than the rain and choking me. I reach toward her, desperate to draw her toward me, to protect her, to save her, just as a bolt of blue lightning strikes her square in the chest. She screams.

I only realize I am also screaming when El appears at my side, grabbing my shoulders and shaking me gently until I wake.

She settles onto the cot next to me, pulling me close. "Just a dream," she murmurs into my tangled hair. "Just a dream."

But this dream is *her* fault. *Everything* is her fault!

I shove her away and press my wet face into the pillow. For a few moments, as I cry into it, she stands by my bed, and I can only imagine the heartbreak on her face.

But I don't want to see it. She deserves it.

And I am so frustrated with myself. One minute I'm ready to forgive her, and the next Audrey's ghost haunts me from my dreams, reminding me of my sister's greatest sin.

I want to be comforted, but it still feels wrong to let Elodie do the comforting. I can't. Not yet. Maybe ever. And I'm irritated that I can't decide how to feel about her—torn between what's happened and what I wish could be between the two of us.

Reconciliation. Love. A real relationship.

Eventually, I hear her return to her bed, though I don't hear any indication that she has fallen back asleep. The room is dim with reflected light of the electric street lamps outside. Soltan won't be here for several hours yet.

But I'm awake now. There will be no more sleep for me; it's as afraid of the past week as I am. And so I spend the rest of the night staring at the ceiling, watching all of my most horrible memories replay over and over before my eyes, given new life by the nightmare.

When the sky finally brightens from soot black to dirty gray, the rain is still falling in sheets and roaring on the roof. It clicks against the panes of glass in the windows like the nervous tapping of fingernails, reflecting my own nerves about the coming day.

Today, we will leave this place, venture back into the wilderness full of unknowns.

And yet we both continue to lie in our borrowed cots, both pretending the morning hasn't come. If morning comes, reality must return. At least under the guise of sleep, the world can hold no trouble, no sorrow.

But the protective blanket of the night is pulled away when Iarann limps into the room. He doesn't speak, but it is still enough to break the illusion of peace.

I turn onto my side and watch him shuffle about the office, arranging papers on the desk, straightening pillows in the sitting area. He doesn't seem to notice I am awake, or, if he does, he doesn't acknowledge me.

El sits up in her bed and rubs a hand over her eyes. I can imagine the grit she feels in them, the same grit I feel in mine. By now, we must have been awake for nearly three hours.

I take my cue from El and shake the sheets away from my body. I regret it immediately as the cool air of the room invades the warmth of my bed, and I shiver.

Iarann finally looks over at us. "Good morning, ladies. Sorry for the chill. The weather took a turn last night. Soltan will be by shortly to stoke the fire."

I drag myself from the cot as if lead weights are strapped to my limbs and force myself through the motions of re-making the bed.

"Oh, don't worry about that, Loxy," Iarann says, tapping a stack of papers on the desk. "After you are on your way, we must change them for the next visitors."

I smooth my hand over the fabric one more time anyway, then straighten and turn to face him. El comes to stand beside me, trying to wrap her arms around me. But the nightmare of Audrey is still fresh in my mind.

I shake her off and stalk to the seating area. El sits across from me, and we wait for Soltan in heavy silence. If Iarann notices this heaviness, he remains blessedly silent.

I tug at the laces of the tall leather boots, then let my dress fall back into place and lean back on the bench, turning my foot side to side and admiring the shine on the boot's toes. There is a sheen in the leather, a rosy sparkle, that tells me they come from the hide of Ivlene's cows. Inexpensive, but sturdy. They are fitted but not tight, despite my thicker-than-average calves, but my favorite part of them is that my feet are no longer exposed to sharp stones and cold earth.

Beside me, El stands in her own shiny new boots, another generous gift of the priest she met in the temple, and adjusts the straps of her pack. Besides the boots, we have been equipped with warmer clothes, waterproofed oilskins, and provisions to last us for at least part of our journey to the south. El was even given a medicine kit and special pack to hold all her herbs, a personal gift from Iarann.

Iarann seems to have taken a liking to us, despite Soltan's mistrust.

I look around again, almost expecting to see Sef materialize out of nowhere, but with no word from her the whole time we've been here, I have to wonder if she's decided to leave us for good. If she's changed her mind about us helping each other somehow.

My gaze travels to El. Even though I could easily make another, she carefully packs the mortar and pestle I made for her of rose quartz. My heart lurches with the compliment, with the pain of her love. Despite Sef's disappearance, maybe I have all I need. Maybe I just need my sister on this journey. Even if I am still trying to find it in my heart to forgive her.

Maybe trying is enough. Or maybe one day it will be.

But uneasiness sits like a rock in my stomach nonetheless; I am anxious to leave this place. The people of Ryth Hollows know little of us, of where we go or who we are, but the priest…he knows far too much. Just what did El tell him yesterday? Unlike our own people, he treated us like daughters.

As if summoned by my thoughts, he appears at the door, and my suspicion billows to the surface.

"Do you have everything you need?" he says.

"I believe so," El responds. "Thank you. For your kindness."

He nods, glancing between us. For a moment, he hesitates. "You know I believe your…abilities…are a gift. But the others here will not agree. I would advise you to keep them hidden until you are out of sight and well on your way."

So she told him *everything*.

El presses her lips together and nods. The fire of anger churns in my stomach. It's not just her secret; it's mine, too.

The priest steps forward and hands her a rolled piece of paper. "A map. It's not much, and it's not as extensive as you will probably need, but at least it's something."

"Thank you," she says, accepting the gift. "You've been too kind."

"Yes," I cut in, rising to my feet. "You have. Why are you helping us? Why give us so much?"

He glances at his shoes, again hesitating before responding. "As I told Elodie, I can understand the difficulty of such great changes in the direction of your life."

But it doesn't make sense. He doesn't know us, doesn't know anything about us except what El told him.

"Cut the sediment," I snap. "What's the real reason?"

He looks at me, and there is a new light there, as if he sees something he hadn't before. El seems to sense it, too, and she steps closer to him.

"What do you know?" she says.

He smiles sadly. "You both look so much like her."

We glance at each other, eyes wide.

"Who?" I demand.

"Volta. You are Shaydes, yes? You must be related."

My heart stutters. "Volta Shayde is our mother." I step up next to El. Excitement and hope push out the anger. "What do you know of her?"

I want to scream and break and cry all in that moment. No one in our lives has heard from or seen Mom in over a decade. The reports stopped trickling in quickly, like Cydia was trying to hide she had ever existed, had ever been a part of our village. Of our family.

Like she was erasing Mom from the world.

But now, hearing someone say her name…

"Volta visited us, much as you did," the priest says, unaware of the explosions going off in my head. "The mountains called to her, and she found us. We helped her. Or we tried to. You probably saw the cairn she built in the springs. Her way to lament what had happened to her. And to her family."

I *knew* she regretted leaving us. We have to find her, figure out why she couldn't come back.

"Why did you leave this out yesterday?" El demands.

He shrugs. "Volta became special to our town. And I wasn't sure if she was a part of your family. But I can't deny how much you both look like her. Carry yourselves like her." He stops talking, thoughtful.

"Then what?" I say, impatient.

He gives me that sad smile again. "She had been trying to hide her Singing, as you do now, but she couldn't suppress her true nature. At first, she seemed in harmony with herself. But then, she changed. Completely. As if she was suddenly two different people. Then, one day, her magic exploded with a violence this town hasn't seen before or since. Many people died, and Volta ran off, through the mountain."

We stare at him in stunned silence. Many people died? It sounds like her exile did nothing but worsen her control of her magic. We need to find her, to find help for her, to bring her back.

Will that be our future, as well? My mind drifts to the salt yesterday, the crust on my arm I couldn't control, couldn't stop for hours.

No. It can't be.

Maybe El is right to think she's dead. And if she is, Limutria is what killed her, not her magic. If she had never been exiled, if our people had just accepted her…

"Do you think she was heading for the temple?" El's voice is small.

The priest sighs. "I don't know. I wish I did. But there is nothing else to the south. And after something like that… I spent months getting to know your mother. She would never have chosen to hurt anyone. I can't imagine what the guilt would drive her to do, if she was even still lucid. As I said, something…drastic…changed about her. Before…well."

There is the scuff of a boot on the floor, and we turn to see Soltan staring at us with wide eyes. The surprise and horror on his face shifts to something darker, more dangerous. Contempt. Revulsion.

"Your *mother*?" he practically spits.

"Soltan—" El begins, already trying to mend the situation.

But Soltan doesn't wait for her to finish. He turns on his heel and bolts from the storehouse, yelling as he runs about witches and death descending on Ryth Hollows.

"I think you should go now," the priest says, eyes still fixed on the open door of the storehouse.

No kidding.

We gather up the supplies we have been gifted and draw our new oilskins up over our hair and packs.

"Ready?" I say, casting a look at El.

She seems shaky, uncertain, but she still nods.

And we step outside.

A bell begins ringing in the temple, as if our step triggers it. The priest waves a hand at us, then runs toward the temple, waving his arms and yelling for people to calm down.

But his words fall on deaf ears.

The people remember Mom, her scars of death and pain. She left holes in their community. And the people are out for blood.

But we are not our mother, and we don't deserve their ire. We hold our heads high and walk as calmly as we can manage toward Montalo, ignoring the screams and taunts of people filling the street. As we walk, salt floats around me, and I hope they cannot see it as my heart races faster than our steps.

We are almost to the mountain when a rotten apple hits my jaw with enough force to knock me back a step.

I rub at the spot that will almost definitely bruise, fury building in my chest and salt speckling my vision in its glittering dance.

The magic prickles at my fingertips, begging to be released, to hunt down the thrower of the apple.

But I can't release it. Not after all these people have been through. It would confirm everything they think we are.

El lifts her hand as if to touch my shoulder, then thinks the better of it. I can feel the rage radiating from me, and I don't blame her caution. I have more control of my Singing than she does of hers, but she still doesn't trust me. After all, I'm just her misfit little sister.

I glare into the crowd and then turn back toward Montalo. Its dark mouth gapes in stark contrast to the bright white salt that makes up the mountain, calling for us, beckoning us to safety. The rain hits my face and somehow finds its way past the hood of my oilskin and down my neck, chilling my skin.

That's when Soltan yells to the crowd again, "Are we just going to let them walk free? After what their family did to our families?"

I glance at him in alarm. His eyes are bright with unshed tears.

He's been hurt dearly, comes the voice, filled with pain and compassion.

Well, that hurt has morphed into violent rage.

What is rage but pain unhealed?

I won't take responsibility, won't feel remorse for something I didn't choose. Isn't that what I've been doing my whole life already? And where did that get me? Exiled and run out of town. This makes twice, now.

His rallying cry has its desired effect. A group of young men bolt from the crowd, each holding a different tool. One even carries a sword, though it is rusted and dull with age.

I grab El's arm and take off toward the cave. If we can just get there, we may be safe, at least for a time.

And then I feel something that makes my heart flip in my chest with fear after my loss of control yesterday. I feel crystals building under my feet, leaving spires in my footsteps, crunching on the ground as I run. A man cries out in pain behind me, and I wince.

Control! They need me to be in control!

I push the panic away, grasp for the threads of control I'd built up my entire life, barely managing to weave them back together as we reach the entrance to the cave. We slide across the ground slick with mud and stumble into the protection of Montalo. The men keep pursuing, now only a few steps behind us.

And I do the only thing I can think to do, though it pains me to cut Iarann off from the springs.

I call forth the crystals, and they heed my command, falling to block the entrance to the caves. The cave descends into darkness, and we stand alone in the sudden creeping chill of the earth.

I swear I can feel the voice smile.

Twenty-Two

ELODIE

And so Sefella was given the Underworld as her domain. The spirits of the dead were passed to her and judged for their final placement.

Excerpt from *The Records of Bright*

Tears cool on my cheeks, or perhaps it is just rain from our sprint to the cave. The shouts from the townspeople are muffled behind Loxy's wall of salt, and now the earth calls up to us in dripping water and whispering wind from deep below.

The rain outside is falling harder than it had been when we arrived in Ryth Hollows, and it passes through the salt and crystal of Montalo more quickly. The dripping today is frantic, hurried, more of a faucet turned on than the gentle drip it had been.

I hope nothing flooded with the deluge, or we may be trapped.

There are only a few cracks in the fallen crystal, allowing small pinpricks of diluted daylight to filter down to us. I walk over toward the side of the wall where Iarann had left the lantern. I pat my hands over the rough surface of the rock, feeling for the cold metal in the dark. Finally, my fingers brush the smooth surface, feel the small turnkey that ignites whatever it is that powers the lamp's light. I pull it off the hook and feel again for the key, my fingers shaking so hard that Mom's ring clicks against the lantern's glass globe. The magic buzzes in my fingers, and I whisper lullabies to it, willing it to remain in check. I turn the key, waiting for the cool glow of light we had seen when Iarann held it.

Nothing happens.

I suppress a sob, but Loxy must hear it.

"What's wrong?" she says from somewhere to my right. Her voice is tight, high-pitched.

"The lantern is broken," I say. It takes me a full minute to find the hook again, then I replace the lantern.

I hear a thud and the rustle of fabric, the clanging of metal, a click. Moments later, the entrance to the cave is filled with a soft blue glow, and I can see Loxy's face. She must have had a lantern in her pack. She seems calm, collected, other than that single muscle that always twitches in her jaw when she's anxious.

Aren't I supposed to be the calm and collected one? Yet here I am half-panicking in the dark. Some big sister I am.

"What's all this?" comes a voice.

My sister and I turn as one to see Sef standing just a bit deeper in the cave.

"Sef," Loxy says, her voice soft as a breath. "You're back."

She sounds…relieved.

Sef nods. "Yes, sorry about that. I wasn't completely gone, though. Are you all right?"

I raise an eyebrow at the cryptic words, but I'm too focused on calming down to respond. Loxy nods as she re-packs her bag, and I close my eyes, concentrating on slowing my breathing and raging pulse. After a count to one hundred, I finally feel my equilibrium returning, and I open my eyes. Even the shouting on the other side of the rock has faded.

But then I hear something that sends my pulse soaring. Metal striking stone.

Loxy swings her pack over her shoulder. "Time to go." She bends to pick up the lantern and turns toward the all-consuming dark.

I cast a glance over my shoulder at the rock covering the cave's entrance, watching the shadows dance along the brilliant white salt as Loxy carries the lantern away. Sef doesn't hesitate, just follows her into the dark.

I turn and hurry to catch up with my sister, afraid to be left behind, alone.

The dark didn't seem quite so pressing, so endless, when we had an experienced guide. Now, we have no such luxury, just a rough map drawn by the priest.

I never did get his name, not that it matters now. We will probably never see him again.

"You probably shouldn't wander off in here," I say, glancing at our mysterious companion.

But her face is calm, almost at peace. "There is no need to worry about me, as I've said before. I will always be nearby."

I evaluate her, looking for any hints as to who she is—or *what* she is—but she seems as impassive as always. So I bluntly ask the question that has pressed on my mind since we met her. "Are you a ghost?"

Sef looks sincerely startled at that. "What? No, of course not."

I bite my lip. "How do you keep disappearing, then reappearing right when we think you've gone for good?"

Loxy's steps slow, her head cocked slightly as she listens.

A smile tugs at Sef's lips. "I have always been such. I come and go as I am needed. Where I am needed."

"But where do you *go*?" I want a real answer, not sidestepping.

Sef actually laughs now. "I'll explain in due time."

"When?"

"When the time is right."

"And it's not now?"

The smile fades, and she sighs. Sef pauses, turning to face me. For a moment, I almost expect her to put her hands on my shoulders, but they remain firmly clasped in front of her. "Listen, Elodie. I know you have many questions. I have answered few. You are cautious and stable and steady."

I swallow as she lists off the qualities I'd always liked about myself.

"But for once, I ask you to be less logical. To trust. Trust the…" She pauses, eyes flicking up to the sparkling rock overhead. "The Bright Ones. I do not ask you to trust me, not yet. But perhaps there is a little voice inside you that can guide you. Tell you the truth."

I narrow my eyes at her. A little voice? Surely she can't mean the voice I've been hearing on and off, could she?

But Sef says nothing more, merely turning back to follow Loxy's trailblazing. I keep close on Loxy's heels, trying to hold the map in the shaking light of the lantern as we walk. So far, there is no real need for the map, as there is only a single small tunnel leading away from the townspeople. But then the map indicates we should turn down a side tunnel away from the springs where we first met Iarann and Soltan.

We follow this other, even smaller tunnel for nearly half an hour. With every step, the ceiling drops lower and the salt mixes with other minerals and bits of rock so that it is no longer the bright, pristine white we had seen on the way to Ryth Hollows. Now, everything is a dingy gray illuminated by the cold blue light of the lantern.

It is far too much like every picture of the Underworld I've ever seen, and I shudder as we walk, expecting a spirit around every corner. And even if Sef says she isn't a spirit, this place makes that hard to believe.

The ceiling drops lower, and I find myself hunching over behind Loxy and Sef. My heart races at the thought of becoming stuck and unable to move. It is enough to strike cold terror into my steps, and I walk faster, pushing Loxy ahead of me.

And then the cramped tunnel opens up around us. The light from the lantern doesn't even reach the edges of the walls or ceiling before it is swallowed up by the earth's night.

But the floor sparkles underfoot with halite crystals, which are a mix of that brilliant white we saw on the path to Ryth Hollows and a rainbow of other colors. Pools of crystal-clear water sit scattered across the uneven floor as far as the light reaches, filling every dip and hollow. Every few seconds, drops splatter on my head or face, chilling my already cool skin, and around me, that same dripping echoes, telling me we are in a massive cavern.

"How long do you think we'll be down here?"

Loxy shrugs, but I can see the wrinkles between her brows. "I hope not long. I don't like this darkness. It's too…enclosed."

At least I'm not alone in my fears.

I hold the map up to the light, trying to parse out our location. "I think we're in a room called The Star Court," I say.

It's easy to see how this glittering room of darkness got that name. Out of the direct reach of lantern light, sparkles from the crystal facets lining every exposed surface remind me of stars on a clear night. It's exactly the kind of place I would expect stars to hold court.

I look back to the map. "There's a traveler's stop on the other side of this room."

"You want to stop already?" Loxy snaps.

I grit my teeth. "It's still early, but we can stop for a few minutes, maybe have a meal and plan out the next part of the route."

Loxy doesn't answer, and we resume our trek. Sef does not wait, already several paces ahead of us.

The fragile salt crystals on the floor of the room break underfoot as we walk. The crunching echoes like eerie movements of ghosts unseen, and I am reminded again of Sefella's realm. I am grateful for the thick soles of the boots; I can't imagine the number of cuts and bruises these crystals would leave on my feet without them. I splash into one of the many clear brine pools along the floor, but the boots are weatherproofed and my feet stay dry.

There is a sound like the croak of a frog nearby, and I jump. I look toward the noise, but whatever made it is too far outside the lantern's light, and nothing but sparkling salt meets my eye. Sef has also faded into the darkness.

Cautiously, Loxy and I turn back in the direction of the traveler's stop. But we have only taken a few more crunching steps when there is the slap of something wet into a brine pool, and we both jump.

"What is that?" Loxy whispers, her voice loud in the silence of the deep earth.

"I don't know," I say, voice shaking.

We stand in silence, huddled together in the light of the lantern, and listen.

Nothing.

We take another few steps into the dark, only to freeze again when there is a splash right next to us. I squeak and slap a hand over my mouth, reaching for Loxy's arm in the dark. This time, she swings the lantern toward the sound. The blue light ripples across the shining water and salt spikes, but nothing else stirs.

Until the water begins to move.

Something from the center of the brine pool leaps straight toward my face. I jerk away from this thing I cannot see, but it strikes the edge of my jaw before falling into the pool on my other side with another splash. It's like I've been slapped with something wet and shapeless, like a dish rag or handful of mud. I lift my fingers to wipe at the wetness clinging to my face, and my hand comes away trailing strings of slime.

The burning pain starts moments later, on every piece of skin in contact with the slime.

I scream, unable to bite back the pain as the slime sears into my face, my fingers. Loxy sets the lantern on the floor and reaches toward my face, and I step back.

"Don't touch me!" I manage. It will hurt her just as much as it's hurting me.

My foot shifts across the ground as crystals break, and I fall into the pool, whimpering and crying.

I flinch at several more splashes around me as I fall. Loxy grabs the lantern from the floor and swings it around, searching.

A wet slap next to her foot draws both of our attentions to the body of a frog the size of my fist, its skin perfectly clear like glass. Under its skin, I can see the outline of organs, ranging from clear to white to pink in the light of the lantern.

No wonder we couldn't see it in the water. It reminds me of the Water Dragons, how they are almost impossible to spot.

Until they attack.

Sef appears from the shadows moments later, face concerned. "What happened?"

Slimy secretions stretch along the edges of crystals behind the frog, trailing from its body to the pool in which I sit.

I look down at the pool and have to cut off another scream. It is filled to the brim with salt frogs. And every single one of them watches me with glowing green eyes.

I scramble to my feet, hand on my jaw, and stumble away from the pool. I am no longer screaming, no longer making any sound at all.

We need to get away from these things.

"Run!" I whimper.

Loxy snatches up the map from where it had fallen, and we all hurry away from the frog-filled pools and toward the traveler's stop indicated on the map. Hopefully, it is protected.

There are more thuds and slaps in the darkness around us, speeding our flight through The Star Court. A few minutes later, something brown and shadowed catches the light of the lantern. We dash for it as fast as we dare amid the rubble of fallen rocks and brine pools, sliding on broken crystals, crunching through salt spikes.

Finally, we duck under the tarp. We freeze, listening for frogs, but all we hear is water dripping onto the canvas overhead. We do a quick sweep of the camp, looking for any frogs, but there doesn't appear to be a single one within the perimeter. The spicy, musty scent of old peppergrass fills my nose, and I wonder in some corner of my mind if it is a deterrent.

I drop to a reed mat on the ground, still clutching my face, trying to stifle the sobs of pain. My skin feels as if someone has run a hot iron across it, pulsing with intense heat. I wipe at the slime, trying to peel it away from my skin. Sef simply stands back, wringing her hands, looking more helpless than I've ever seen her, body almost transparent.

Loxy falls to her knees, holding a canteen up by my face, and I tear my eyes away from Sef. "Let me help, El!"

She grabs my wrist and pulls my arm away, pushing me toward the edge of the camp. She pours the fresh cool water over the slime, letting it fall to the crystal over the edge of the tarp, keeping the traveler's stop free of this noxious slime.

But the slime sticks, undeterred by the stream of water. She tears a piece of cloth from the bottom of her skirt and begins to wipe at it. I can feel it peeling away from my skin, barely, but as she removes it, the pain lessens to a throb. Once my face is clean, she moves on to my fingers, tending to them with the same gentle care.

She would have made a great healer. The thought stabs at me, piercing me with guilt. How much, how long have I held her back from her calling?

I shake it off and half-smile through the throbbing. "How do I look?"

I say it as a joke, but I want to know how badly I'm injured. My fingers are red as a beet and twice their normal size already, and tiny pinpricks cover the inflamed skin like the body of the frog had been covered in invisible spikes.

She tilts her head and raises an eyebrow. "Like you fell in a fire," she says.

"That bad, huh?"

At least the slime is off, and now I will heal. I hope that the water cleansed enough to avoid any long-term effects. There's no guarantee that the slime doesn't have some kind of acid or toxin, but this is the best we can do now.

Loxy raises her hand toward my face. I can see the look she's given me before, the one I now know is associated with her empathic magic. But I can't let her use it on me, not for a toxin like this. She might end up just as bad off, maybe even worse. I have no idea how magic will affect it. Or how it will affect magic.

I slap her hand away. "No!"

She opens her mouth, the look on her face promising a fight, but I glare at her and she snaps it closed again. She closes her hand and drops it back into her lap, her eyes distant and sad.

I sigh and look around at the traveler's stop. I don't want to hurt her feelings or push her away, but if one of us needs to feel this pain, I'd rather it be me and me alone.

The stop doesn't have much beyond the frayed reed mats that make up the tarps overhead and underfoot. There is a small table in the corner with an empty crate set up like a chair. The tarp stretches overhead between four wooden posts, each sunk into the floor of the cave. There is no way to tell how deep the posts go, but they have been here long enough that the bottom of each one is covered by a crust of salt.

But that's it. No water. No food. No beds.

At least the ground beneath the mats is flat and smooth and dry. It must have been graded when the stop was set up to create an even surface.

Suddenly, Sef cries out like I have never heard her before. She looks over her shoulder, as if seeing something I cannot.

And then she seems to vanish.

Loxy and I shoot to our feet, staring after her into the darkness. The pain merges with my sense of unease, and I wonder again at the nature of the stranger. She claimed not to be a ghost, but…

Where has she gone now?

We stare uneasily for several long moments before finally sitting back down, huddled together. My fear is somehow even greater now that Sef is missing. But what are we to do? She didn't run off, didn't fall over, just…disappeared.

Loxy hands me the canteen with the remains of the water, pulling me from my shock. She seems to have recovered from her surprise much quicker, returning to her concern, thinking of me.

Like a healer would.

"Drink." She pushes the canteen into my palm again.

I take it, swallowing in deep gulps. She has already removed the other canteen and is drinking her share. At this rate, she will definitely have to purify more water for us before we get out of the cave.

We sit together for a few more minutes, listening for frogs and examining the map as if nothing else happened. We are at the far end of The Star Court, near the next tunnel.

I shudder as I read the name of the next room: the Hall of Sefella. I'm not dead yet, and I don't want to find myself stuck in a place where I will be doomed to wander as a spirit. Even though Sefella isn't really evil and the Underworld is the natural end of life, I am not ready to leave.

"Ready to keep going?" Loxy says, distracting me from my fear. Her voice is softer than before, as if she is afraid of waking something—or hurt by my refusal of her help. Perhaps both.

Probably both.

I wish she'd just understand I want what's best for her.

But then guilt twinges in my gut again. Do I really?

Or have I always just wanted what was best for *me*, like Loxy said days ago?

Uneasy at this new thought, I nod and push myself up from the ground. She takes the lantern from the center of camp, and we turn back to the room. Keeping the visible wall on our right, we continue toward the far end of the room and then along the far wall when we reach it, looking for the opening in the layers of salt. We finally find it and duck under a low-hanging rock into the tunnel.

The world closes back in around us, no longer the wide-open blackness of the previous chamber, and I find I am relieved for the closeness. Now, we can see every turn and niche in the rock except for the tunnel stretching on in front and behind. Loxy takes the lead, holding the lantern out in front of us, and I keep an ear behind for any lingering frogs.

Twenty-Three

LOXY

We cannot lose hope, we cannot lose heart, and, most of all, we cannot give up this fight.

Excerpt from *Singers in Solitude* by Orella the Singer, who
died during the Great Culling

The tunnel between The Star Court and the Hall of Sefella stretches on for hours, time in which we keep silent, allowing my thoughts to drift to the scream of pain caused by my crystals in Ryth Hollows. Did I hurt that man? Where is he now?

Why did I lose control?

El walks quietly behind me, and I can almost feel the pain radiating from her. Even my Water Dragon bite from days ago aches in the damp chill of the caverns, and her wound is much fresher. I worry that there is something toxic in the frog slime, something that will make her sick or—worse—kill her, but I don't give voice to those concerns. If I do, they will be too real. And sometimes, calling attention to a thing draws it near, like death or illness. And with the Hall of Sefella before us, I don't need the goddess of the Underworld seeking my sister.

Unless that wouldn't be such a bad thing? Isn't Sefella also the one who heals, who comforts? At least, that's how it used to be. Before Ivlene cast her from the heavens for reasons she didn't deign to share with humanity.

I stumble, surprised at my own thought. Even though it's been years since I agreed with the temple about Ivlene, this feels like a step too far. I feel chilled as if I will never be warm again, that there may never be light again. It weighs on me like a burial shroud, and I trip several times as my feet begin to drag.

And yet, for a moment, I can't help but wonder what the thought means, why the attention of Sefella might not be dangerous.

I sniffle, my nose cold, the sound breaking the tomb-like silence around us. Even the dripping fades as we travel into the tunnel. The ground is drying out beneath us, leaving the crystals tall and untouched, though they still break off whenever we step on them. Crystals like these, so common in the salt flat that is the Sea of Broken Glass, dissolve well in water, so they tend to be fragile when they form. As we walk, the salt crystals are slowly replaced with heartier crystals like quartz, and the salt walls turn to ancient stone marked with the carved symbols of a language I recognize as long dead, a language from people who came long before us.

Then a new sound greets our ears: rushing water.

We pause and look at the map. There is no indication of running water anywhere along this corridor, and El and I trade confused looks. Cautiously, we step forward, searching for the source of the roar of water.

The roar builds with every step, and the ground gradually falls away into dark holes as the path widens. The rock surrounding one of these holes is wet and slick, and as I watch, splashes of water leap upward.

"A river?" I say.

El shrugs and shakes her head, pointing at one ear. She says something, but I cannot hear it, and I realize how loud the river really is.

We step around the hole and take a few steps farther. Talking is impossible as the water rages beneath the stone floor.

And then we turn the final bend in the tunnel to the Hall of Sefella.

The room is narrower and the ceiling lower than in The Star Court. The walls on either side of us are illuminated by the lantern, but the light cannot reach the far side of the room. Large columns of calcite and limestone line the left and right, and enormous crystals of gypsum twice as wide around as I am tall crisscross over the path of broken stones, obviously having been here a long time. The ceiling above is made of the same rock as the floor, but stalactites run in ribbons as far as the light touches, and everything here glistens with the sheen of moisture like what we saw above. It's like the whole place was made for a king.

Or a goddess.

Some of these fallen stones are stable underfoot, but many shift with every step we take. Several times we are forced to sidestep gaping holes.

Bright One, don't let us die here.

I kick a stone with my next step, and it tumbles through the nearest hole, plunging into the night where the lantern light can't reach.

El turns toward me, and I can see the puffiness of her jaw and a distinct red streak where the slime stuck to her skin. That wasn't there earlier. My heart lurches, and I step closer to her.

A large crack echoes over the water's roar, a vibration tickles my feet, and I flinch. The ground dissolves under El's feet, and she falls into the black.

"El!" I scream.

I lunge toward her and slide across the last foot of ground, but her hand slips through my grasp.

"No!"

She is falling, away from the surface, away from me, her form shrinking into the darkness below. Water leaps up to splash me as she hits the river, and without thinking, I shove the map into my bag, throw my legs over the side, and leap after her, one hand clutching my alexandrite necklace.

I hit the water, the cold shocking my system as I plunge beneath the rapids.

This was a mistake.

I struggle toward what I think is the surface, but the water dunks me again and again. Every time my face hits the cool cave air, another rapid pushes me under. My limbs are pulled and yanked in the torrent, and I am unable to control even a bit of my movement.

I can't get enough air, not like this. I gasp and splutter, trying to catch a breath, but instead I catch more water down my throat. Somehow, I keep my hold on the lantern, its strange light still glowing inside the glass, casting the water into every shade of aqua and silver imaginable. The bubbles from the rapids tickle my skin as they flow around me on the current, dancing for their effervescent lives. I imagine them carrying me up, higher, to El, to safety, but they're too small to fight the river.

Just like me.

My vision begins to turn gray, then black, around the edges. I am going to die here, drown in this river where no one will ever find my body. My heart pounds with my terror, stealing more precious oxygen from my lungs, oxygen I can't spare.

And then I slam through a wall of water and fall forward on my hands, through air, onto hard-packed…something. The lantern spins away from me, throwing unsteady light around a vast bubble of air. Halfway up the bubble, water surrounds me as if it is a wall, and above that, the rapids rage and churn around the outside of this sphere.

I cough and rub at my eyes, trying to clear them. After a moment, a dark figure comes into focus, dripping. Every drop returns to the river underfoot, disappearing out of the bubble and into the torrent. The figure holds up her arms, shaking, her eyes so wide that they gleam bright white through the darkness.

"El!" I breathe, as much awed by finding her as by this bubble she created around us. She did it! She used her magic!

I grab up the lantern and run to her, wrapping my arms around her sodden middle. I sob in relief, in pride at her. She says something, but I still can't hear her over the roar of the river, so I step back and simply stare at her.

Her chest rises and falls in a sigh I know too well, and she nods her head toward my right, taking a step toward where I can just barely see what might be a shoreline.

Right. We're not safe yet. The thought ratchets my heart rate up again with fear, but at least this time I can breathe. Together, we step in that direction, El shifting the bubble along with us until our feet hit solid rock and we scramble to the shore.

El drops the bubble of air, and we collapse together on the rocks, breathing heavily, recovering from our near deaths. She doesn't speak, but she reaches a hand toward me, brushing her fingers lightly against my skin. I reach back toward her, shaking with relief and surprised at myself, at my need to touch her.

We're alive. We're both alive!

After a few minutes, I sit up and dig through my now-soaked bag. Delicately, I extract the map. Its paper is nearly ruined from the river, and my stomach sinks. I turn wide eyes up to El, and she gazes back at me with the same horrified expression.

Without the map, we'll never get out of here.

El reaches her hands out, and I hold it out to her. As delicately as when she is creating a poultice or tincture, she smooths it out onto a flat rock next to us, one that is mostly dry and safe from the spray of the river.

There is no way we are ever getting that paper back off the rock in one piece. But before I can do anything, El holds her palms over it, and a warmth starts filling the air around the map. The cool light of the lantern wavers in the heat emanating from her palms, and I watch, utterly transfixed and amazed.

My sister is a powerful Singer.

Before my eyes, the paper begins to dry out, the dark wet splotches lightening until they are damp and then completely dry. The ink barely ran, only bled slightly onto the surrounding fibers of the paper, creating a soft, dreamy look the map didn't have before. Hope flares in my chest at her actions, pride still wavering along the edges of my emotions.

I can't believe she is doing this after how afraid she was of her magic only a few days ago. A week ago. How afraid she probably still is.

But she's doing it, finally, and my eyes prick with tears. Only this time, it's not fear. It's joy. I wish I could tell her so, but the river roars so loudly in our ears it drowns any attempts at talking.

The corner of the paper whuffs into flame, and El snaps her hands closed. My stomach lurches in sudden fear again, reminding me how dangerous our situation is, how precarious. We both leap forward, knocking heads in our haste to pat the fire out. We manage to stop it quickly, losing only the bottom right corner of the map, and then we both lean back and rub at our heads.

Ow.

I blink back tears of pain, and we rise to our feet. I take up the lantern again, and El holds the now dry map up to the light, her hands shaking and her face pale. Fear flutters in my stomach again, like a swarm of bees.

What did it cost her to use so much magic? Especially with her injuries?

I hesitate a moment, then reach out for her hand. She doesn't look at me, doesn't acknowledge me. Instead, she grabs my hand with more strength than I thought she had left, and even in the dim light I can see the tears in her eyes. She holds me as if I am an anchor, a tether to the ground, and I hold her back with just as much urgency.

We retrace our steps upstream as far as we can, trying to find the hole where we fell, but we soon realize such a feat is impossible. There are so many holes in the ceiling here that there is no way to tell which leads back to the path.

Hot tears of frustration fill my eyes. "What are we going to do?" I yell over the rush of the river. How will we ever find our way out now, even with the map?

El places a hand on my shoulder and smiles at me. I stare at her, hoping she doesn't notice my tears, angry spots of salt glimmering in my vision. I wave my hands and shrug. What in Sefella's dark Underworld is she smiling about?

El grabs my necklace and holds it up, then points back at the map. For several long moments, I can't decipher what she is trying to tell me, no matter how many emphatic gestures she makes between the two objects.

And then I hear a strain of faint Singing, and I know.

I can hear Montalo still. I can hear all the crystals from where we have already been.

I can get us out of here.

The anger softens out of my face, and I smile back, nodding emphatically. I listen again and take a step upriver toward the Song. And another. And another. Until we stand beneath the hole where I recognize the bits of Song from before we fell.

I point up. El nods, then steps toward the river. She pushes her hands away from her and then pulls them back in. For several minutes, nothing happens.

And then the water begins to spiral up toward the opening, and El takes a step onto the flowing surface.

She is standing on the water.

As I gape at her, she extends a hand down to me, and I grab it to follow her up. The ceiling is relatively low, and it only takes us a minute to make it back to the Hall of Sefella.

We made it.

Well, sort of.

We laugh, the sound absorbed by the river's roar underfoot, and sag against each other in relief, clutching at one another like a lifeline.

I release her and bend forward, propping my hands on my knees as I breathe the sweet air here. The river is behind us, and even with the towering crystals around us and the threat of Sefella, I almost feel safe.

Almost.

Finally, I straighten again and look at El. "We should get going." I'm not sure she can hear me, but she still seems to understand.

She nods, and her face is full of the same relief as I feel, the same eagerness to be on our way. We carefully pick our way through the Hall of Sefella until the river's roaring fades into the distance. The dripping of the water through limestone echoes around us again, and as we walk, I hear another sound that sends chills across my skin.

In the highest and farthest reaches of the cavern, faint howls and moans swirl around the formations.

El stops behind me. "Do you hear that?"

I pause and glance over my shoulder at her. "Yes."

"Do you think there are actually souls here?"

I hesitate before answering. The sound is probably wind and likely why this room was named for Sefella, but that doesn't mean it isn't also connected to the Underworld. Who knows how many unlucky travelers never made it out of the caves? The thought makes me shudder, unease settling into my bones.

"I don't know," I respond.

Her lips move silently, and she touches her forehead, lips, and heart as if her actions can cleanse not only herself but also this place. Her hands shake as she makes the movements, and I wonder if she is afraid of spirits. We listen to the howling for a few more moments, but when nothing happens, we press on, wary for changes in our surroundings.

Eventually, we make it to the far end of the room. The howling has grown louder with every step, and as we approach the exit to the next tunnel, it seems to crescendo.

The lantern light flashes on something bright white, almost like the salt crystals but without their shine or Song. I swing the lantern closer and jump, startled, when a skull grins back at me, small jet-black and blood-red crystals sprouting from the bone.

Maybe the howling is a soul after all.

El says a short prayer as we pass, one meant to guide a lost spirit onward, and I pray along silently, hopeful that if the poor traveler's soul is trapped here, we are helping it to escape. I'm not afraid, not really. If something is here, I just wish it peace; the possibility of spirits doesn't scare me.

After all, spirits have never hurt me the way flesh and blood people have.

As we move into the next passage, I think I see the blue glow of a spirit over my shoulder, but when I turn toward it, I see nothing but crystal.

We have been traveling for hours, but without the sun or a chronometer, I have no idea just how many hours it's been. My only gauge is the ache in my feet and the fatigue in my bones. We have both been ignoring Sef's disappearance, like nothing happened. Is El as disconcerted as I am?

"You know, I've heard stories about people getting trapped in caves and losing their minds," El says, breaking the silence.

"I could see how," I say, my unease sitting like a stone in my stomach. Even now, after such a short time, I can feel the dark pressing in on every side.

"Do you think we should find a place to stop for the night?"

"How do you know it's night?"

"Okay, well, somewhere to rest, then."

I glance over her shoulder at the map in her hands. "There should be another traveler's camp coming up soon. Just one more room ahead."

El nods, and we press on. We continue for a while longer before finding the place marked on the map. It is a camp much like the one in The Star Court, a simple tarp spread over a section of cave with mats on the ground, and it stands just inside the door to another room, on the edge of a long, crystal clear lake. The ceiling here is low, forcing us to hunch over as we walk, and the tarp droops with the water it has collected. Hopefully, it won't burst while we sleep.

I take the lantern to the edge of the lake and look down. The water refracts the light in every direction, illuminating the lake's rubble-lined bed, every stone a uniform gray. There may even be a layer of silt, though it is hard to see from the shore. I can't judge the depth of the lake, either, not with how clear it is. It could be a couple feet or a couple hundred feet.

I move my gaze out over the lake and squint into the darkness. The water ripples with dripping from the ceiling, and several stalactites dip through the water toward the bed below. The ceiling drops as the distance from shore increases until it meets the surface of the lake and the water disappears farther underground.

"Lox, you have to see this!" comes El's voice. She sounds excited.

I turn back toward the camp, wondering what has captured her attention. She sits at the edge of the tarp, gazing at something on a stone shelf.

"What is it?" I drop down next to her and set the lantern on the shelf.

She just points, and my breath catches as the light hits four gleaming figures of pure crystal quartz. There is a man and a woman and two girls, one smaller than the other. The girls hold hands, and the woman gazes at the man with such love I can feel it through the stone.

"Mom was here." I brush a finger across the woman's hair as if I can reach through time to feel her again. "I know it."

"You think it was her?" El says. I'd been expecting resentment in her voice, but this time I hear only awe.

"Definitely. The carvings have the same low notes as the cairn in Ryth Hollows."

"What?" She hands me a packet of bread and fish jerky.

I wrinkle my nose at the jerky. More fish. "Carvings seem to have bits of Singing unique to their Singer. I didn't realize it until I found some made by someone not me. Mom."

She nods and sits back. "She was an artist you know. Just like you."

Warmth blossoms in my chest, a newfound joy at this discovery. So it wasn't just the magic that made me like her. I also got some of her skill, her passions.

El hesitates a moment before continuing. "And…and perhaps I was wrong to keep you from the temple apprenticeship."

She doesn't say anything else, but I'm not sure how to respond anyway. I feel the pull to learn healing more with each passing day. And I feel my jealousy mount, too. El always got everything. She even got an herbalist's apprenticeship, while she told me it was too dangerous for me to join the temple and have one myself. To a point, I understand why she was afraid, but…haven't I proven myself? Didn't I hide my magic my entire life? How could she not only keep me from it but also take it for herself?

And now… Now she's admitting that she was wrong? I bite my lip, my feelings at war with each other yet again. It seems like El is growing, changing into someone I actually like. And yet, sticking by her side, giving up my anger, feels like a betrayal to our past, to what I've been through.

And to Audrey.

"Sleep here tonight?" El says, pulling me out of my thoughts, out of the mounting anger and confusion.

"I guess. The next camp is hours away. I wish we had a chronometer." I set the packet aside and hum gently to the four figures. They separate themselves from the rock shelf, and I hold them together, encouraging them to fuse into a single sculpture. I already lost my portrait of Mom, so I'm not leaving this. Not when it's so much better than a picture someone else drew.

"I know. I never thought I'd miss that hunk of junk next to the hearth. But I'd even take that one now."

I laugh, pushing my last threads of jealousy away, at least until I can figure out what exactly I'm feeling, and turn back to her, grabbing the food packet but not letting go of the statue. "Do you remember the time it stopped running and Dad was confused for hours?"

El laughs, too. "Yes! He thought time was just passing so slowly because he was doing the books! He was so angry when it was midday for four hours!"

We laugh together and munch on our rations, basking in the warm memory. Letting ourselves just exist as sisters. As…friends?

She finishes chewing a bite of bread. "What about the time the bell didn't sound and we all overslept for the temple service?"

I chuckle, remembering how frantic we were when one of El's apprentice friends showed up at the door. "We ran around like the powers of Ivlene were after us."

"Well, they could have been. We were late for service!"

I finish my last bite and lick my fingers clean of crumbs, hugging the statue close to me. I almost can't believe I'm uttering my next words, but it's impossible not to let reality make its way through the warm memories. "I'd trade anything to get back there."

El's face grows cloudy. "Me, too."

"I miss Dad."

"I do, too."

"And Audrey." Saying her name is like a barb into my heart, but it hurts more to keep from saying it. She deserves to have me talk about her. Say how much I care about her. I should have said it to her when I had the chance.

Now, I may never see her again.

El doesn't respond for a moment, and I think the conversation is over. But then she says, "You really liked her, didn't you?"

"I've never liked anyone more." A pang of loneliness, of worry—and again, that nagging sense that I'm betraying her—shoots through me, a feeling that is becoming all too familiar when I think of Audrey.

El looks thoughtful, as if remembering something. But I know she never had interest in anyone, never expressed a desire for a long-term relationship.

"I'm glad you had her," she says. "I know living in Limutria wasn't easy for you."

I try to ignore the past tense in her words and find my thoughts drifting back to all the hateful comments and exclusions I endured in our home. The pain raises a fresh burst of anger and hurt. At her, at the village, at Ivlene…and at me, for not standing up for myself. But how could I?

It *was* hard. She's right.

But I don't say that. Instead, I snort. "I'm sure it wasn't easy for the sister of the town freak, either."

She waves her hand. "Please. You're not a freak."

It's been so long since she's said anything like that. For a moment, I'm stunned into silence, unshed tears burning my eyes. El stopped defending me years ago, and Audrey took her place. It's a bittersweet memory.

I think that was when I started loving Audrey.

"I'm glad you had her," El says after a moment of silence.

"And I'm glad you had the temple," I say.

She hesitates, her face changing in a way I can't quite read. Not wistfulness, not joy at the memory. It's almost like she is conflicted about something, too.

"Me, too. You know that's always been my dream." El says. The words sound sure, but her expression looks uncertain. She pauses, as if unsure how to say whatever she's thinking. Instead of sharing, she turns the conversation back to me. "But what about you? Were you ever happy? Did you ever find a path for yourself?"

I blink at her. "You know what I want."

She shakes her head. Is that shame on her face now? Guilt? "For what it's worth, I'd give anything to take back what I did. I'm really sorry, Lox."

I want to forgive her. But I just can't seem to let go of the embers of anger. And now that she's called attention to how she's held me back, to what led us here, I feel even more lost.

"It still happened," I say, not meeting her eyes.

She nods as if expecting that response.

I shove my canteen back into my pack and carefully tuck the crystal between the softest packets I can find, since the blankets are already out.

"Ready for bed?" El shakes out her blanket. "I'm not sure how well I'll sleep in this cold, though. And my clothes are still damp from the river."

I spread my oilskin on the floor and pull my own blanket from my pack, but I can't bring myself to answer.

She nods as if to herself and lays down on the mat. I reach for the lantern and turn the key, gradually reducing the light around us.

El bolts back upright, and I pause, hand on the key.

"Are you sure we should do that?" she says.

"Do you want to risk running out of light before we get out of here?" I snap.

She lays back down, unconvinced, but I finish turning the key anyway. I tuck the lantern next to my pack, in easy reach, then lay down next to El. She doesn't say anything else, but she slides just a little closer to me, and I can feel her warmth radiating from her body, especially along her jawline.

I could fix that, if she'd let me. She'd already held me back from learning at the temple, but I can still do this much. I bite my tongue in irritation. I could have done so much more, *been* more, if she'd let me.

But I have a chance now to do something. And not only for me, but for her. To help her, to take care of her. Because no matter how I feel, I know that's also part of our past, our truth: that she's taken care of me when Mom couldn't for all those years.

It's my turn.

I wait until her breathing eases, then raise my hand to her jaw, feeling for her face in the dark. Eyes open or closed, it makes no difference in this cave, so I leave them open and reach for the poison I felt in her blood earlier.

If she doesn't want me to heal her, I'll just have to try while she's not paying attention.

She's my sister.

The poison begins its transfer from her to me, and I have to bite my tongue to keep from crying out as my jaw begins to burn. How could she have hidden this pain all day?

There is a surge of magic as the pain causes my hand to shake, and this time I can't keep from crying out. I curl into a ball, shaking and crying.

El sits up beside me, feeling for me in the dark. "Loxy? Are you okay?"

"Y-yes," I stutter between chattering teeth.

She doesn't speak, doesn't move, for several long moments. "You tried to heal my face, didn't you?"

"Yes." There's no use lying.

"I told you not to! We have no idea what the magical effects of this toxin are! You could die!"

"But I had to t-try."

"Why?"

My mind flashes to everything I'd thought while she was falling asleep: the desire to be a healer, the innate power I have to heal, the way she'd taken care of me for so long…

"Because you're my s-sister."

That seems to draw the words away from her, and she lies down next to me and pulls me into an embrace. "Why can't you just trust my judgement once in a while?"

I can't help the defiant twitch of my mouth into a bratty half smile. "Because I'm your sister."

The pain is finally easing, and I stretch myself out next to her again. I reach up to touch my own jaw. It feels tender, but there are no raised welts or divots in my skin, so the healing must not have been complete. But maybe it is enough to keep El from scarring.

Although anger—or is it confusion?—fills me, at our situation and most of all at El, for Audrey, for her stubborn refusal of my help all day, I lean my head against her shoulder while the dark echoes around us.

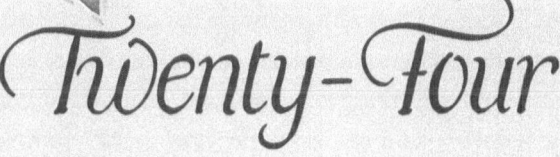

Twenty-Four

ELODIE

Do not grow complacent; do not be fooled. The Hounds of Sefella stalk the souls of the world. To drop one's guard is to succumb.

Excerpt from *The Records of Bright*

I smile a little when Loxy rests her head on my shoulder, but I keep still because any movement might scare her off. I know she's still mad, but if she's willing to be this close to me, gaining her forgiveness can't be hopeless. Within a few minutes, I can hear her breathing smooth out, long and slow, punctuated by an occasional snore.

But I'm too keyed up to sleep. I hadn't expected Loxy to turn out the lantern, and it hadn't occurred to me that its light might not even last us all the way through the caverns.

What if we get lost? What if we never find our way out?

My skin heats with my fear, like the tingling magic that causes storms when I'm afraid or upset.

Magic. Why am I so afraid when I have my own magic? When I can create light for us?

The thought eases some of my fear, but there is still the darkness beyond the lantern light, beyond what my fire could show us. Darkness filled with unknown danger. I flick my thumb against my fingers, igniting a small, candle-like flame on the tip, as I lay next to Loxy, trying to drive back the darkness she created.

But it doesn't do much good, not now that I remind myself of what could lie in the dark, and I let the flame die, huddling closer to Loxy instead. My mind is running in circles around the territory we covered today. The frogs. The Hall of Sefella. The plunge into the river.

Goddess, that river. I could have died. We both could have. But the power, the Singing…it popped up as if it were always meant to save me.

Could that old priest be right after all? Could the Bright One have granted me this power as a gift, not a curse?

Is this what I was meant for all along?

My stomach sinks again as my mind returns to the priestesses. If this is what I was meant for, why does this "gift" ostracize us? Is the problem me…or them?

Or is it Ivlene herself?

I try to shove the thought aside, but it's persistent, coming back just like it bit at my heels earlier, following our steps, never leaving me in peace.

Maybe the priestesses are wrong. Maybe *I* have been wrong. What if everything I've been taught is a lie?

I try to force my mind away from the thought again, listening for the sounds of the cave. Water drips onto the surface of the lake next to us, and I jump nearly every time a drop falls. In the blacker-than-night room, my eyes play tricks on me, and I think I see the orbs of spirits dancing like fireflies over the lake's surface. But the caverns are utterly silent, without even the howls of the Hall of Sefella. I can only hope our prayers were enough to release the spirit of the traveler, but I can't tell if what I'm seeing is real or not.

And now, I'm not so sure those prayers even mattered.

My eyes are still open, I think, but even on the blackest of nights, I've never experienced a darkness so complete. I hold a hand up to my face, trying to ignore the dancing lights, but I can't see the movement, can't see the outline, and somehow the darkness of the cave feels like a heavy blanket over me.

I let my hand fall back to my stomach and slide just a bit closer to Loxy until I am practically on top of her. She stirs, barely, but falls back to sleep as if nothing happened.

Eventually, I must drift off, my mind too tired to keep running in fearful circles. The world takes on that haziness, the dizzy, drowsy feeling between wakefulness and deep sleep. Figures dance in an eternal parade before my eyes—figures of the townspeople and frogs. They join the dance of spirits over the lake, each orb taking on a face and a figure. My face throbs and burns, but I can't tell if even that is real or dreamed.

A loud splash jolts me from my half sleep, but I don't move, my limbs heavy. I feel the sensation of waking and sleeping so many times that I can't tell when I am truly awake.

Someone shakes my shoulder, pulling me further from sleep, and I try to blink away the fog in my mind. The darkness is still too deep to see anything; not even the spirits or dancing figures remain. I feel myself beginning to spin in the dark. My heart is pounding now, and sweat drips down my back.

Then Loxy turns the key on the lantern. My fear subsides as the light grows, and I blink rapidly as my eyes adjust to the dim light and the spinning sensation slows to a stop. Now that there is light, I remember I could have created a flame, but it is still an afterthought, a power I'm not used to having, especially with the grip sleep just had on me.

"What's going on?" I manage.

She puts her finger to her lips. "Did you hear that splashing?"

My heart flutters. "Frogs?"

"Bigger."

I shudder. I open my mouth to respond, but something splashes again in the lake. Loxy and I turn toward the sound, but all we can see are the ripples on the surface, tiny waves lapping at the shore.

We stand and loop our packs on our backs, ready to run. Loxy picks up the lantern and steps toward the waves, holding the light ahead of her like a talisman.

Something lunges out of the water toward her. She screams and jumps back, barely out of the reach of long, sharp teeth. The creature, eel-like and as long as five men, falls to the ground with a heavy slap, splashing water at us. Its flesh is transparent like the salt frogs, but no organs are visible, only stark white bones glowing in the lantern light. Its head alone is as tall as Loxy. Worst of all, its hideous face, full of those sharp, dripping teeth, holds no eyes yet still seems to peer directly into us.

It hisses and rights itself on the ground, turning its massive head toward her. My chest clenches in panic, and I'm barely able to pull in oxygen to yell to Loxy.

"Run!"

Loxy jumps back toward me, and we sprint for the door back into the tunnels. Maybe it won't follow. Maybe it won't fit through the doorway.

As we slide across the loose gravel into the tunnel, we hear the beast slithering behind us. I glance over my shoulder, heart in my throat, only to see it sliding out behind us. Wide nostrils flare as it scents the air, then it turns toward us and covers half the distance with one great lunge of its body.

I push Loxy forward, trying to make her run faster. We plunge ahead into the night, no time to consult the map or choose the direction that will lead us closer to the surface. If we falter or hesitate for even a moment, it will be upon us, tearing us to pieces. I can barely breathe through my terror, my heart pounding so hard, so fast that it drives the breath from my lungs.

A wall looms in front of us, appearing out of the dark into the lantern light so suddenly that we almost collide with it.

A dead end.

We whirl about to face the creature. Loxy holds the lantern in one hand, clenching her other fist around her necklace's alexandrite. I hope she can find crystals in this part of the caverns to use as weapons.

But I needn't have worried. The alexandrite around her neck lengthens to a dagger-like point.

I turn to face the tunnel, listening as the beast slams closer and closer. The ground rumbles, and rocks crack and scatter in its path. I raise my hands to protect us, but I'm not sure what I'll do with them.

The next few moments happen in flashes and stutters. The beast lunges around the bend in the tunnel, flopping and slithering toward us. It snaps its great jaws at Loxy, catching the lantern with one sharp tooth. The lantern falls to the floor, and the fragile glass globe strikes a dark gray rock.

The light goes out, plunging us all into black. My mind stutters again, and I forget anything of use as fear sweeps over me.

Loxy screams, and I hear rock shift, strike flesh.

"Loxy!" I yell, heart pounding.

"Fight!" she screams back.

I can't see her, but I follow her voice with my blinded eyes anyway. A snap of the beast's jaws confirms its location, and I raise one hand toward it, feeling for the tingle of magic. I pull the tingle into my fist, feel the fire burning just under the skin. Before my eyes, fire builds in my hand, compressed into an orb full of energy and heat. With a shout, I hurl it toward the beast.

I watch the fireball fly through the air, watch it strike the beast full in the face, splattering out from its point of impact like a splash of water. A flash of white light follows the impact, spreading down the length of the beast's body. It screams, and I call more fire.

I rain fireball after fireball down on it. The wind builds around me, whipping my hair across my face. With each impact, I can see the beast falling back, the flashes of white light dimmer with each blow. And on its other side, Loxy pummels it with slashing crystals, so many more than I'd ever seen her summon before.

But I am weakening, too. I can't hold up this pace, can't call the magic fast enough. My arms are shaking, my wounds burn, and I struggle to catch a breath in the heat of my fire.

Despite the fatigue, I feel power like never before, power that overtakes the fear, at least for the moment. For the first time, I think I might be able to control this, to use it for something good.

Maybe Loxy had the right idea all along. I wish she'd gotten the chance to talk to that priest, too. Beyond her suspicious questions.

The beast lets loose a blood-curdling scream, collapsing onto the stone floor of the tunnel. I hold a fireball ready in my hand, using its flickering light to watch its unmoving body. The tunnel is suddenly quiet, so quiet my ears roar, the only sounds remaining the crackling of my fire and our heavy breaths.

I approach cautiously, kicking at it. There is no reaction, not even the wave of light.

It's dead.

I let the fire die and collapse to my knees, no longer able to hold myself up. The dark closes back in around us.

"El?" comes Loxy's voice, startling me. There is a tremor in her words, her voice high with fear. "Where are you?"

"Here," I say, still panting with the exertion. Tiny spots of white are dancing in my vision against the velvety black night of the underground, and I gently rub the wound across my jaw. "Are you okay?"

"Yeah. You?"

My muscles shake, and my breath is still desperate gasping. I hate this darkness. I need light.

I hold up a hand, try to summon a flame to me, but nothing comes. I try again, but still nothing. Panic swells in my chest, my gasps becoming wheezing.

"Loxy?"

"Yeah?" She makes it to my side and drops down next to me. I can hear her breathing just as heavily as I am, just as strained and panicked.

"We don't have a backup lantern, do we?" I say.

She hesitates. "No."

"I can't call the fire."

She places a hand on my shoulder, so gently as if it were a bee alighting on a flower, and is silent for several moments. Is she testing me? Probing my body for answers?

"You used up too much energy fighting that thing," she finally says. "Your magic is exhausted."

My heart flips in my chest. "Will it come back?"

There is another pause before she answers. "Eventually. Maybe."

Maybe? A glimmer of something like fear fills me, different from my terror of the dark around us. I thought I wanted to be rid of the power, but now that I might not have it anymore…

I'm so scared.

I reach out for her, pull her close to me. I push away thoughts of the magic, forcing myself back to our more immediate problem. "How are we going to get out of here with no light?"

Though she resists my hold at first, she relaxes after a moment instead of pulling away. "I don't know. Maybe if we rest long enough, your fire will return."

"Maybe," I say, unconvinced.

I actually miss that hum of magic under my skin.

I can't say how long we sit there, surrounded by dark that presses in like a sentient monster. We shake with cold, with fear. Several times, I curse Sef for leaving us here, for not providing the help she promised.

But, despite how little I know her, I also worry. Where is she? What happened to her? Is she all right?

I try several more times to give us light, but there is nothing, no well from which to draw. Hopefully, there aren't more of those things.

Eventually, we rise to our feet, still gripping each other as if letting go means losing the other. And honestly, with how dark the caverns are, it's a very real possibility. We have no idea where we are or where we need to go, and we certainly can't look at the map to orient ourselves.

But one thing is certain: if we stay here, unmoving, we will most assuredly die, just like the traveler in the Hall of Sefella.

I extend my free hand in front of us, bumping against Loxy's free hand as we both feel for the walls to avoid crashing into them. As we approach where I think the door is, I stumble over the soft, cold body of the beast. I shudder, half expecting it to rise up and attack again, but it stays where it is, motionless.

For a moment, I think I can see its outline, like the light it generated when I struck it, but it's gone almost as soon as I see it. Just a trick of the dark.

We are truly alone now.

I pull my attention away from the beast as my hand slides past the wall and falls through the air.

The door.

As we step into the tunnels, Loxy says, "Do you think we passed many branches?"

Maybe? Probably? There were hundreds not marked on the map, some only knee-high and some twice our height.

"It's hard to say."

"So which way should we go?"

My disoriented and blind brain is telling me we came from the left. But can I really trust it? There were so many twists and turns in our run from the lake. Left is probably wrong.

"Right. I feel like that's the correct way."

We turn right, and I reach for the wall to my left, still clutching Loxy's arm with such ferocity that I'm sure I'm hurting her, but she doesn't say a word. We stumble so often that our progress seems to take eons. Since we are still holding each other tightly, when one of us falls, we both hit the ground. Hard. By tomorrow, we will be covered in cuts and bruises.

Whether we will be able to see them, though, is another matter entirely.

We keep wandering forward, hoping for another room, an exit from the caverns, just a modicum of light, but nothing appears. Hours pass, I think, and the pack digs into my shoulders, like the bite of a wild animal. My back aches and groans with every step. My eyes are gritty and burning. I think I have been forgetting to blink. It's hard to remember such a thing when I can't tell if my eyes are open or closed. I am exhausted from lack of sleep, and my jaw still burns from the frogs.

When Loxy begins to wheeze, I pull her to a stop. "Let's take a break and try to get some rest," I say.

She sinks to her knees almost immediately. I hear her pack hit the ground, and I follow suit, dropping my straps and rolling my aching shoulders. I switch my grip on Loxy, still afraid to release her in the dark even though we are no longer moving.

I lean back against the tunnel wall and clench and unclench my free hand, hoping to see even the faintest spark of fire, but it's no use.

I pull a blanket out of my pack, after much shuffling in the dark, and drape it over us. Loxy holds it close to her, leaning into me, and I'm glad we had one in the packs, since we were forced to leave the other one behind.

My ears ring with the quiet now that we are no longer crushing crystals and knocking over stones with our steps. Instead, the tunnels are filled with our loud breathing. Perhaps we should be quieter, more alert for potential threats, but this darkness is maddening, and I just want to be rid of it. I only allow us to rest here for Loxy's sake, since we have no idea when or if we'll see light again.

We rest for only a few moments, my panic just below the surface, and then we rise again, turning back to face the dark.

Twenty-Five

LOXY

There are many who are lost; those who wish to be found must seek the light of Sefella in the darkness.

Excerpt from *The Ballads of Sefella*

When we can't put one foot in front of the other, we take another break, but my instinct just wants us to find daylight and escape this place. Every step feels the same, and the world has been reduced to placing one foot in front of the other and trying not to panic at the eternal night surrounding us. I know El is also struggling, and we didn't manage to get a full night's sleep amid our two days of walking through the caverns. It may even have been longer than that.

I dig in my pack for the canteen, but it is difficult to find without light. I wish El could make a fire for us, but her magic is still burned out. Mine feels weak, too, something I've never experienced before. Hopefully, whatever is depleting our energy subsides soon. Hopefully, there's nothing else out there in the dark. I don't think we can survive another attack.

The darkness seems to have a more insidious effect than just the disorientation, though. As we sit, I can feel hopelessness descending on me.

Does El feel it, too?

I do my best to try to remember the map, but our flight twisted and turned so many times I can't re-orient myself even though our life depends on it.

But we will keep trying. We will search for the light. We may die of starvation or thirst or the maddening dark, but we will try.

A light pressure at my side tells me El is settling in next to me. She loops an arm across my shoulders and draws me close, again. How many times has she tried to comfort me since we've been out here? We've been angry and scared and alone, but she's not once abandoned me, never suggested that we couldn't make it through this.

As if sensing my thoughts, she says, "Don't worry, Lox. We'll get out of here."

My stomach drops, as if her words make the reality of our plight more real. Again, my guilt and conflicting feelings about my sister bubble to the surface.

"But what if we don't?"

"Then we will journey together to see the…the Bright One."

El is silent for a few moments, as if unsure whether to say anything more. Something wet plops onto my head from her face above me. "But I'm sure she will lead us out of here."

"And how are you so sure?"

I hear her hand opening and closing, her fingers slapping against her palm in the dark. Is she trying to summon a flame again?

"I don't know why she would bring us here, after so much, after letting us be infec—after granting us Singing, only to let us die now," she says.

I don't miss her correction. She was about to call Singing an impurity, something to be healed, cleansed.

But something stopped her. I don't know what, but perhaps she is starting to see the gift of Singing as a blessing and not only a curse.

A warmth expands in my chest, and I can't help but wrap my arms around her and squeeze her tight. "Thank you," I say into her hair, unwashed and greasy, still smelling of lavender, of Elodie.

"For what?" she says, returning the embrace.

I shrug. "For being my sister."

We stay that way, clutching each other, until we fall asleep.

The next hours or days or eons pass in a blur of stumbling and intermittent sleep. There is no telling how far we have come, how far is left to travel, or how long we have been here. I lose count of the periods of rest after the second, and when I ask El, she doesn't know either. Our food and water are starting to run low, and there is little water in this section of cave. And no crystals. I am as blind as ever, unguided, uncertain, ungrounded. My body is sore from constant falling, and my joints ache from resting against the cold rock floor. I begin to feel as if we are too close to the arms of Sefella to argue anymore.

One rest, after I have been asleep for some time, there is some small change, a shift in the air of the cavern, a flash behind my closed eyelids, and I wake from restless sleep. The air smells musty in a way it hadn't before I fell asleep. I blink into the black, adjusting my eyes to a sight I haven't seen in what feels like several eternities.

Light.

It blooms and blossoms around me in fuzzy clusters of blue and green, my eyes barely able to discern them from the background black of the cavern.

It's light!

I shake El's shoulder roughly. "Wake up!"

She groans, then straightens from where she had slumped against the wall. She blinks in the light. I see it happen. Just barely, but I *see* it!

She squeezes her eyes shut again, open and closed, as if trying to clear them. "What's going on?"

I point at the wall, able to see the outline of my arm against the background of dark rock. "Light!"

She sits up straighter, so suddenly that I lose my balance from where I had been leaning against her. She follows my finger with her eyes, not even realizing she can see it.

But I know the moment she does. Her eyes grow wide and glossy with unshed tears. She clamps a hand over her mouth, dipping her head as the tears start to fall.

"Oh, Bright One be praised!" she chokes out.

We stand together, and she pulls me into an embrace. We laugh and jump in excitement like we did the day we finally walked out of the Sea.

After a few minutes, we calm ourselves. El pulls out the map, holding it inches from her nose to try to distinguish the markings in the dark, while I take a closer look at whatever is lighting the tunnel.

The musty smell intensifies as I approach one of the spots of light, and I see a small creature—plant or animal, I can't be sure. It is made of tiny feather-like fronds surrounding a round body like one of the salt urchins at Limutria's docks. It's even the same size as those urchins, about half the size of my fist. And the best part is that every bit of the frond and body is infused with a gentle blue-green glow.

But the glow doesn't just exist as a single, unwavering characteristic. The patterns cross its body, filling its fronds. Tiny streaks of pink make up the backbones of the fronds while brighter blue-white dots speckle the round body.

I take a step back, allowing the magnificence of the colony to wash over me. For there isn't just one of these glowing creatures.

There are hundreds. Thousands.

They cover the wall like a tapestry of light, of hope, leaving trails of glowing speckles on the wall around them where they have crawled. I have no idea what they are—I've never heard of such creatures—but right now they are the most beautiful things I've ever seen.

I rush back to my pack, watching my step as I cross the treacherous, jagged rock of the tunnel floor. I wish I had been cognizant enough to grab the lantern before we left, but there has to be something else we can use to hold one of these creatures. I start rummaging around in my pack for anything I can use so neither of us has to touch one of these creatures. After what happened with the frogs, I don't trust these things not to hurt us, pretty as they are.

I freeze mid-rummage. I'm a Crystallosinger. I can make a vessel. That is, if there is finally crystal here again.

I laugh to myself and sit back on my heels. I look around. The tunnels here are mostly rock, but I can hear some quartz veins Singing beneath us. That's luck, since I haven't heard a crystal in several sleeps. I close my eyes and call them up, call them to me, Sing them into the shape of a globe.

The Song ends, and I open my eyes and take up the globe. It's the size of both my fists together, with a lid I can twist closed and a handle for carrying it on the side, like a candlestick. The crystal itself is a mix between opaque and clear, depending on whether the quartz on that section is composed of crystal quartz or milky quartz.

I stand and take up a small, flat stone from the ground, then approach the creatures again.

El steps up next to me. "What are you doing?"

"Making us a new lantern," I say, mouth twitching with a smile at my excitement and relief.

I twist the lid off the crystal jar and hand it to her, then hold the jar below one of the creatures. Using the flat rock, I try to push it into the jar, but it clings to the wall.

I use a little more force, and the creature falls into the jar with a small bit of stone. I flash El a smile, then add a few more creatures. Once it is mostly full and giving off a healthy blue-green glow, I drop the flat rock and replace the lid, holding the improvised lantern up triumphantly.

El smiles at me. "Nice work!"

An unexpected warmth floods me, a happiness at the compliment. Instead of thanking her, I nod at the map in her hand. "Any luck figuring out where we are? Or where we need to go?"

Her smile fades, and worry seeps back into her face. "No. There's no way to tell where we are. Between running from that lake beast and stumbling through the dark, we've lost all landmarks."

My stomach sinks. Right.

"So what do we do?"

I can't think of any way the light will help us now, other than help us keep wandering into oblivion. At least we will be lucid when we die.

Neither of us speaks for several minutes. El continues to study the map, occasionally looking up at the tunnel or wandering a few feet in a random direction. I contemplate the creatures. Why are they here, so far below ground and in the dark? Where did they come from? Do they really move around, or are they sedentary? What do they eat? Rock?

What *are* these things?

El walks a few steps deeper into the tunnel, around a bend. She gasps, and I run, my heart in my throat. Did another beast find us?

I slide around the curve and echo her gasp. The creatures line the wall all the way down the tunnel in a breathtaking display. There aren't thousands; there are millions.

"Should we follow them?" I say.

"What else are we going to do?" she responds, eyes alight with their glow.

What else indeed. But more than that…something tugs at my heart as I take in the colony flowing down the tunnel. There has to be a reason they're here. Hope blossoms anew, fragile and small, but hope nonetheless. Maybe these creatures are a sign.

We retrieve our packs and follow a trail of stars.

We follow the creatures for nearly an hour, no end to their stream in sight, when El speaks.

"How many do you think there are?" she says. She finally rolls up the useless map and shoves it into her pack.

"Thousands, at least," I say. "Millions." I clutch my lantern closer to me, even though we don't really need it now. At least until their trail ends. Wherever it is they're leading us. My heart flops at the thought, but I'm not sure if I'm more excited or afraid of what lies ahead, of yet another unknown.

I study the creatures in the globe. I have been watching them as we walk, and now it's clear that they do, in fact, move. And they eat rock. The pieces of rock that fell into the globe with them disappeared with a few loud crunches early on, and I've been slowly adding pebbles to their tank as we go. The walls around us practically vibrate with the crunching of their multitude.

"What should we call them?" I say, still examining my captures.

El glances at the walls, at the lantern in my hands. "Fuzzy lights?"

"Boring," I retort. Then, as if planted there by a goddess, since we are surrounded by the Halls of Sefella still, the name comes to me. "Stars of Sefella."

El shudders, then smiles, her face bathed in their soft glow. "A little creepy, but I like it."

"Me, too," comes a familiar voice.

Spinning around, we come face to face with Sef.

I blink. "Where did you go?"

My eyes scan her form, and even in the darkness, I see the tired look in her eye, the way she seems just a little less solid than before. Maybe El was right. Maybe Sef is some kind of ghost. Even if she denies it, that doesn't make it wrong.

A new sound meets our ears, and we freeze.

"It can't be," El breathes.

But I hear it, too. The chirp of a songbird.

We exchange a look and hasten our steps toward the sound, still following the trail of cave stars. The swish of Sef's steps follows close behind. We round a turn, not bothering to watch our steps, not caring about tripping on loose rock, and are greeted with the most wonderful sight of all: daylight.

We plunge on ahead amid a chorus of birdsong, following the twists and turns of the tunnels until we break into a shallow room that opens into the brightest and most beautiful meadow I've ever seen in my life.

Granted, I haven't seen many meadows out in the middle of the Sea of Broken Glass. But still.

We blink rapidly in the bright sunlight and cry, tears of joy mingling with tears from the light.

We're not going to die! At least, not underground.

I sniffle and carry my Stars of Sefella back into the tunnels, unlatching the globe's lid as I walk.

"Thank you, little friends," I whisper, voice hoarse as I hold it up to the wall. My chest is tight with gratitude for their light, for the path that led us back to the world above.

They climb out, funny little balls of fuzz with no visible legs, and I laugh as they latch back onto the stone next to their colony.

I turn away from the dark, the despair, the hopeless, endless night, and join Elodie at the end of the caverns, that small blossom of hope blooming into a vibrant new flower.

Part Four

LOST

Twenty-Six

ELODIE

Praise Ivlene, from whom all good things flow. Carry these souls safely to the arms of Sefella.

From traditional Nasmaryan funeral rites

I sink to my knees in the thick grass outside the mouth of the cave, watching the bright red sun sink in a rosy sky, closer to the tops of the mountains to the west. Birds sing and hop around me, bright white creatures with not a hint of color, even in their eyes. I suspect they're blind, both from the milky tone of their eyes and the way they move their heads, but they don't seem to mind. They've adapted to their condition.

We would never have adapted to the darkness below.

I close my eyes and drink in the sun, feeling the wind caress my face. I thought I'd never feel these things again, but the Bright One is with us.

We are saved.

I raise my hand to touch the three points again, forehead, lips, and heart, and mutter the liturgy of thanks, and then the one of blessing, and then the one of guidance. All three feel needed in a way they never did before.

Could Ivlene be the one communicating with us? Has she been close to me all this time?

I catch Sef eying me with something like sadness, then she wanders several steps away, surveying the land in front of us. In the light of day, she looks even more ethereal, more vaporous.

More like the pictures of Sefella in the temple.

I'm not sure I believe she isn't a ghost, or at the very least, a spirit of some sort. And there is another part of me—a large part—that believes Sef is really Sefella, walking among us.

I shake my head quickly, discomfort filling me at the idea we are traveling with the enemy of Ivlene. How can that even be? Why would Sefella be here, seeking *our* help?

And, more importantly, if we help Sefella, will we doom ourselves in the eyes of Ivlene? And…does that even bother me anymore, after everything the priestesses have done to us?

My head hurts with the contrary thoughts, the teachings of the temple at war with what I am learning out here in the real world.

The ground shifts beside me, the crunching of pebbles and crackling of dry grass, and Loxy sits next to me, interrupting my troubled thoughts. She sits with what I assume is the same look I have, one of wonder, of gratitude, of bliss, even some conflicting emotions below the surface, and her lips move in her own silent prayers.

We journeyed through the Underworld together, and we made it out alive.

We watch the sun set before either of us moves again, and for the moment, Sef does not join us. The temperature drops rapidly after the sun is gone, reminding us that the rainy season has not yet ended and we will freeze without a source of warmth.

I open my hand in front of me, feeling the buzz of magic returning. A small spark jumps to life in my palm, barely there, but enough to tell me it's not gone. Loxy points at it, smiling, and I smile back. She was right—I just needed rest. Or time. Or hope. Either way, I have fire in my blood again.

Loxy stands, brushes off her dress, and walks over near the mouth of the cave to collect bits of dried grass and twigs. I watch her for a minute before digging into the packs and searching out something to eat. The night will be cold, but at least it will be bearable next to a fire with food in our bellies.

And at least it won't be spent underground.

Once the fire is built, Sef finally returns to us, settling into the space around the fire companionably, as if she didn't disappear when we were in the most danger. As if she didn't reappear like nothing had happened.

The aloof attitude, the contrived mystique, is beginning to chafe as badly as dried salt.

It is time for answers.

I turn my stare to her, and she looks right back with a gaze that is somehow like the night sky—dark, endless, and glimmering. "Is the time right now?"

She almost smiles, but it is tired, distracted, like she has been since the cave with the frogs. "Perhaps. Perhaps a bit."

She looks away, up toward the darkening sky, silent for several long moments. I do not move, focusing on her. Even Loxy stills beside me, pausing in her quest to prepare something to eat.

"You are…almost right when you call me a ghost," she finally says. "But I was never quite one of you."

I exchange a puzzled look with Loxy, but neither of us responds. Even if she *is* Sefella, why would we be almost right by calling her a ghost?

"All will become clear in time, but what you should know now is that I am on your side. You might say… I am the source of Singing."

I catch my breath. The source of Singing? What does that even mean?

As if to illustrate her point, she holds up one hand, igniting a small flame. The fire dances in her eyes, illuminating that night sky in flickering orange. "I was cast out by my sister years ago. My twin. She rules while I am forgotten. Feared, even." She snaps her hand closed, eyes locking back on mine. "No longer. I wanted to return, to reclaim my place. To provide a home for those who had none. The Singers. The cast out. Like you. But I want to welcome all again. To be what I was always supposed to be."

I lower my eyebrows, unsure what to make of Sef's words. At the same time, I feel something I hadn't associated with Sef before: welcoming. Warmth. Belonging.

Love like a mother.

Does Loxy feel it, too? One glance at her is all I need to confirm it. She does.

"It is difficult for me to stay in this world," Sef continues, "so I have need of a vessel. And I had found one, a woman with great power who had undergone much suffering. I rescued her, restored her, gave her a home and shared a body with her." Sef's face darkens. "And then my twin decided I could not have even that." She turns her gaze back to us. "Which is where the two of you come in. This is what I've needed you for. To help me reclaim what is mine."

"What do you mean?" I ask. I'm not sure if I actually don't understand…or if I don't want to admit yet that I *do* understand.

Sef stands and crosses the distance between us. She reaches a hand toward me.

"Take it," she says.

I dust off my hands, then reach for Sef. But as my fingers touch what should have been hers, they pass straight through, and I fall back, startled.

"I want to help you," Sef says, "but I meant it when I said I needed you. With my twin taking everything from me, I don't have much power here. And the longer she stays like this, draining me, the weaker I get. Eventually, there will be nothing left to keep me here, which I'm sure is exactly what she wants. So I can't touch you. Which means I can't fight for you. But I will help you, as best as I can."

Understanding fills me, and I turn back to fire.

"And us?" Loxy says. "What do we get from this?"

Sef smiles. "You know already, daughter. You get a home. Family. Acceptance. And…" She pauses. "I will help you find your mother."

Loxy beams back at her. "I'm in."

Both of them turn back to me, waiting. My heart beats furiously, fluttering helplessly in my chest. Do I even want to find Mom?

I look at Loxy, at the hope in her eyes. The longing. How can I say no now, after we've come so far, after she's given up so much our whole lives?

But does she realize what I have realized? That Sef is Sefella, and if we help her…we will make ourselves enemies of Ivlene, irrevocably?

I glance back at Sef. I don't want to have this conversation with my sister in front of a goddess. And I'm not sure I want to help her, even if I'm not sure about Ivlene anymore, either.

For now, even though I still don't know what to do, even though my stomach churns with unease, I nod slowly. "Okay."

Something rustles in the grasses, and I jerk awake, my heart pounding. Could it be another creature like the lake beast?

I open my eyes and stare up into the darkness, listening. A wolf howls somewhere nearby, answered by another. Fear rises in my throat like bile.

I roll onto my side and shake Loxy's shoulder, eyes fixed on the meadow toward the howling. Loxy shifts. I wince at the crackling of the grass beneath her.

"What is it?" she mumbles, still half asleep, her voice peevish.

Nice to see she's back to her cheerful self.

A wolf howls again, closer, responding for me. Loxy's eyes blink wider, and I know she is truly awake now.

Magic begins to buzz under my skin, stronger than it's been since the beast. Much stronger. I can feel a tingle in the air, smell the sharp scent that comes before a storm. I can feel the pull of power beckoning to me, a sweet song instead of screaming nightmares.

Sef—Sefella—appears from the night around us, locking eyes with me, as if she senses my thoughts. There is almost pride in the stare, and I shiver, still unsure how I feel about her.

Loxy leans forward and scatters dirt over the embers of the fire, not that it will help much. The wolves must know we are here by now, considering how close they are. From what I've heard, they have excellent senses of smell, and the wind is blowing directly toward them from our campsite.

We rise to our feet, slowly, quietly, trembling with fear and anticipation. I allow power to build in me, and clouds begin to form overhead, spinning in a lazy whirl as they come together. I still don't know that I can control it, but I'm not sure I could stop the power building if I wanted to. I'm too scared.

Loxy glances up, then over at me, her eyes concerned. But I nod to her, trying to communicate that I'm fine, that I want this. We have no other way to protect ourselves, and I'm certainly not about to let a pack of wolves eat us. Not when we're finally free.

A rock falls from above the cavern mouth, triggering a small cascade of pebbles and dirt. We both whirl about to face the disturbance.

And come face to face with a wolf.

It stands on the ledge of rock over the cave's entrance, serene, graceful, gazing at us with bright eyes. But the most amazing sight of all is the glittering of its coat against the moonlight. It appears to be made almost entirely of crystal.

Twenty-Seven

LOXY

When the land is covered with the sea, when the wolves close in, then night shall fall as Sefella roams the world.

Excerpt from Itano's 152nd Prophecy

I blink at the sight before us, disbelieving. No creature should be able to live as this one does, yet it seems the wolf is made almost entirely of crystal spikes and spires, all diamond-like and rosy and lavender. I can even hear it Singing, a Song different from any I've ever heard, yet one I can recognize. It has the Song of crystals, but it's also woven with a Song of healing I can only hear when trying to heal.

The wolf turns its nose up to the sky and sings a different song, a vocal one, one meant to be heard by all. It is mournful and deep, full of longing.

Full of hunger.

My pulse quickens, and I involuntarily take a step back as the grasses rustle behind me, my awe mingling with spiking fear.

I turn slightly as I pull my necklace from around my neck, afraid to put my back to the crystal wolf. Three more wolves stalk out from the meadow only ten paces away. Terror steals my breath, but I hold up my hands, preparing to fight, the alexandrite necklace extended into a dagger.

The wolf on the cave ledge barks sharply, and the three new wolves lower their heads and peel back their crystalline lips in a snarl. Deep growls emanate from their throats, and they crouch low to the ground as they stalk toward us, the sound of crystals tinkling with every movement.

I take another step back, colliding with El so we stand back-to-back, her facing the lone wolf and me facing the three newcomers.

The lone wolf howls again, then drops its head to glare at us with malice.

The three other wolves lunge forward, as if the howl is a signal. I hear El's feet sweep the ground behind me, feel the muscles in her back tense and relax as she waves her hands, gathering magic. The air is abuzz around us with the electricity of her Singing, and the hair on my arms stands up with the static.

I jump out of the way as one of the wolves leaps for my throat, and I throw up my arm in front of me, summoning a shield of crystal. The wolf smashes into my shield, then bounces back to land hard on the ground. It pushes itself up, shakes its head and glares right at me.

"You started it!" I say, feeling an odd need to explain myself.

It blinks with surreal teal eyes and snarls. This close, I can see threads of white fur weaving through its crystal coat. It is an odd blend of organic and crystalline.

The lead wolf jumps down from the ledge and joins one of the others in attacking El. She runs toward the ledge, pulling herself up the side of the mountain, the two wolves snapping at her heels.

The other two wolves stalk toward me, teeth bared.

I take a deep breath and listen for their Song. It's uncomfortable to hear a Song of life so intertwined with the Song of crystal, though it's similar to what I can hear when I heal.

I call to the Song, Sing back my own.

The two wolves pause, but they continue to stare, snarling. I keep Singing, calling them with crystal notes on the night air, trying to entrance them, to see me as a friend. *Know me*, I Sing. My breathing is shallow, my heart pounding as I hope they recognize what I'm trying to say.

The snarling fades, and they cock their heads to the side like house dogs.

I glance back at El. It's all the wolves need to free themselves of the spell I am weaving, and they lunge for me. I throw my hands up and raise a spiked wall of crystal before me, but it slips out of my control and extends an extra five feet, barely missing me. One wolf slams into it with such force that the crystals crack. I hear—and feel—the crystals in its body crack as well, and it drops to the ground, panting and whining.

The other wolf catches a spiked point, and I wince as my wall plunges into the beast's shoulder. It tears through muscle, glances off bone. The wolf yelps and cries, trying to free itself of my crystals.

I drop them, horrified at the extent of the gore and the pain I caused. I hadn't meant…I didn't want…why did this happen?

"It was an accident!" Sef says, as if hearing my thoughts.

Sefella. I know that now, and though it should fill me with terror to have the attention of Death, it doesn't.

Has El put this together yet? What will she do when she realizes who is following us?

I'd think a goddess would be able to help us now, actually protect us from this danger. Yet Sef stands back, not helping, not fighting, nothing. She paces along the side of the fight, as if incapable of doing anything. And, after what she said last night, she probably is. "Accidents happen as you grow," she adds reassuringly.

As soon as my crystals disappear back into the ground, leaving a line of blood in the dirt, the bloodied wolf lopes off into the meadow, tail between its legs. The other wolf lies on the ground, panting, eyes closed, and my heart squeezes in my chest.

I turn back to El. She stands at the top of the ledge now, hands stretched up to the sky. The two wolves pursuing her are close behind, but a crack rings out so loudly that my ears ring, all sound deadened for several moments. A bolt of blue lightning strikes the ground in front of the wolves, between them and El, scattering blackened rocks and leaving a crater in the mountainside.

The wolves yelp in surprise, in fear, and then they are running after the wolf I injured. All that remains is the one wolf with the broken crystals.

"Are you okay?" El says.

I can't help smiling at her, though it is shaky. She's finally using her power, and more than that, it seems she's embracing it. "That was amazing! When did you get so strong?"

She smiles back. "I don't know. But it felt…good?"

The wolf on the ground whines, and my stomach flips. I can't bear to hear it in pain, especially pain I caused. I turn away from El and approach the wolf carefully, slowly, so as not to startle it.

"Shh," I murmur, sinking down next to it. I hold my hands over its body, listening to the broken Songs of the crystal, of the life connected to the crystal.

Sef kneels beside me, eyes earnest, pleading. "You have so much power. Harness it. Use it."

The wolf isn't hurt badly, but there is a painful crack across where the crystal and flesh have fused. The two are inseparable, each a part of the other.

I am beginning to think of El and I the same way, how we are so different from each other but still a piece of the same thing, still somehow dependent on each other. Inseparable.

The wolf snaps at me, and I jump back, startled. But I won't stay away. I won't leave it like this.

I close my eyes and begin humming the Song I send toward it. *I don't want to hurt you*, I Sing. *Let me help*.

For a moment, I think I hear two other voices Singing along, one canine, the other the voice that has been speaking to me since the Burning Rain.

A voice like Sef's.

No. Sefella's voice. I know now it is, in truth, hers.

I open my eyes and look at the wolf's face. It looks up at me with its bright eye full of pain and full of intelligence. Slowly, I lay my hands on its heaving sides.

I can feel where the crystal is broken, where the wolf is hurt, and I focus on it. I don't have the same advantage I have with humans, that of a shared anatomy, so it takes me longer to knit together the pieces. But the crystals hear my Song, and they respond quickly. The wolf's panting grows deeper, and its eyes drift closed as I work. By the time I am done, I am exhausted, the wolf asleep. But we are both whole.

I sit back in the dirt and stare at the wolf. The warmth of a fire drapes across my shoulders. Elodie must have rekindled it while I worked. I hadn't noticed, my focus absorbed in healing. Empathy takes so much energy.

I spin around in the dirt, crossing my legs. El sits nearby, cooking something over the fire. Her eyes dart between the cookfire and Sef, and I can practically touch the tension in the air.

"Why didn't you help us?" El finally says. Her words are an accusation.

Sef smiles sadly. "I wish I could."

"Nothing?" she spits. "There's really *nothing* you could have done?"

Sef's smile remains fixed, an expression full of sadness and pity. "Not yet. But soon, I hope. If you both keep helping me."

El's face grows several shades paler. She *must* know who Sef is. It's hard not to.

But why is the goddess still pretending?

El does not respond, merely turning back to the fire, and I am too tired to fight for more answers, chilled with the understanding that everything I was taught was a lie, that I have an opportunity to change things.

Or an obligation… Sefella hasn't made it clear what happens if we refuse. But at the same time, I find I'm not afraid. Instead, I feel as if a lost part of me has returned.

Soon, the heavy, warm scent of yeast greets me, and El passes me jerky shoved between two slices of toasted bread. A few herby greens poke out from inside. I take a bite, and together we watch the sun rise.

Sometime after dawn, we fall back into a restless sleep. I wake before El, hearing the sizzling of rain falling into the embers of her fire. The wolf is gone, but there is no sign of any of them returning.

I stand quietly so I don't wake her, then make my way toward a small outcropping of rocks near the center of the meadow that will provide me with some privacy. My eyes scan the grasses, and I listen for any hint of the wolves, but there is no sound beyond the gentle falling rain and whispering of the grass.

I am turning back toward camp when something deeper in the meadow catches my eye. There is something gray poking out of the light-green grass and brilliant yellow flowers. It could be another rock. After all, we are in the mountains. But I've never seen a rock naturally shaped like a faceted pillar, at least not one with a Song like this.

Curiosity overcomes me, and I approach as quietly as possible in the high grass. The monolith gradually rises above me as I step closer. It's much taller than I thought, and farther from the camp. But as I reach it, it becomes clear that this isn't just a manmade marker.

It's a grave.

I look around me, starting to count the half-sunken, crooked grave markers, some taller than me, some shorter than the grass, but I stop when the number quickly climbs over one hundred. There must be thousands in this field. And the dates are all on the same day.

The Great Culling. The one time the government tried to eliminate Singers by force, rather than by making it undesirable to marry someone with magic, ensuring Singing would eventually be diluted out of Nasmarya's blood.

A chill floods my veins, and not from the cool morning air. Just like when I'd learned about it in school, horror punches me in the stomach, leaving me breathless.

If I'd been born a thousand years earlier, before the shape of our country changed, back when it was teeming with commerce and full of life…I'd be in one of these graves.

And it wasn't until after that great wave of violence that our people scattered to the hills and flats, our population so low we became entirely dependent on trade agreements with the countries around us.

I laugh to myself, a hollow, joyless sound. They thought removing the Singers would improve life. But it didn't. It destroyed this country, and I'm not sure we'll ever recover, not unless they embrace people like me. Like Elodie.

Like Audrey did.

Audrey. The thought of her stabs me again, the guilt and the confusion between my desire to forgive and my feeling of betrayal.

Yet, I don't think Audrey would fault Elodie if she were here, would she? Audrey, who accepted and protected me, knowing what I am, even through the bad days and times I myself lost control as a child.

And Elodie didn't have the time I did to grow and learn before the most powerful magic of all was thrust upon her. Audrey would have understood.

Would have forgiven.

Would forgive me for letting it go. For letting *her* go.

The remaining guilt lifts like fog, leaving only a great sadness. After all, this is a place of mourning. Is it time for me to mourn Audrey?

Do I let her go?

Do I let El put this into our past?

I lower myself to the ground next to a grave that shares my name. Loxy Callow. Born and died one thousand years ago. And she was my exact age at her death. I mutter the Song of Mercy, praying for the girl's murdered soul.

But here, in this place of death in the name of Ivlene, a prayer to Ivlene doesn't feel right.

If I'm honest, they haven't felt right for a while.

The wind rustles through a bush next to the gray-and-glass quartz, and my eyes are drawn to the plant's bright white fruit. Grave peppers. Forbidden to pick, used as memorials to guide spirits to Sefella.

Sefella, the goddess walking with us. The Source of Singing. A power so much bigger than Death, than change.

I reach a hand out, touch one of the shining peppers, ghostly in the mist and rain. There is nothing wrong with this pepper. Nothing at all. We need food, and these people don't. They haven't for ten centuries.

Besides, it would piss El off. My mouth quirks in a half smile despite my sadness. My anger has fizzled, but it still seems like great fun to annoy my big sister.

Before doubt can overwhelm me, I pick several of them, holding the small peppers in my hands, and rise to my feet. I look out over the field of the dead, seeing the edge of their fallen city at the bottom of the hill, spilling down into the valley and shoved up against the sides of the mountains all around. The city is so wide, miles maybe, that we won't be able to simply go around it.

I head back to camp. The sadness at the fate of these people so like me hovers like a cloud, and I imagine the ghosts we will walk beside on our way south.

Twenty-Eight

ELODIE

But most of all, let no Atmosinger live unto tomorrow, lest we all die.

Excerpt from the *Proclamation of the Singer Threat* on the
eve of Korilia's Great Culling

I am woken by the fragrant and spicy scent of food. I look around, still deep in a haze of sleep, and take in Loxy by the fire, cooking something in one of the crystal bowls she made last night.

Wordlessly, she spoons something into a smaller bowl and hands it over to me. I lower my nose to the steam above it and inhale appreciatively, my eyes already watering with whatever spicy plant is floating amongst the jerky. Peppergrass? No, that would have an herbier smell. And then I recognize the scent and see a flash of white amid the deep brown broth.

It can't be.

My heart stutters. "Are those grave peppers?"

Loxy finishes chewing something. "Yeah. I found them while you were still sleeping."

"And you picked them?"

She shrugs. "Who says I can't?"

Everyone! "You'll bring a curse on us. You know that!"

"You only believe that because Cydia said it. They're just peppers. The Bright Ones created them as much as any other pepper. I think they'd want us to eat them."

I blink. I can't even form a word to respond. Did she say 'Bright Ones,' as in more than one? Just like the priest. Did she notice?

And…maybe she's right. That I believe it because Cydia said it. How many things do I believe just because the priestesses told me to?

How many of those things are wrong?

"Loxy is right," Sef says from where she sits looking out over the valley. "The dead do not care if you eat the peppers."

"Besides," Loxy continues. "We need food. And they don't in the afterlife."

"They?"

Her face shifts, and she stops chewing, as if a weight is suddenly draped over the top of us. "The meadow is a graveyard. Thousands, maybe millions, all struck down in the Great Culling."

I feel as if she punched me in the gut. The Great Culling— perhaps the worst event in Nasmaryan history, just after the great prophet Itano had a vision of what destruction the Singers would bring down on us. No one has seen one of these graveyards in hundreds of years. They were assumed lost, buried by time. The last physical reminders of what our nation brought on itself with its panic.

I hesitate, my mind wandering to what I've heard of the crippled state of our country. Even in Aeglora, the most advanced and prosperous city in the country, they feel the loss the Culling brought. Nasmarya used to be a respected power with a booming economy and lush fields.

But after the prophecy, that all changed. Sixty percent of the population killed in one day, one thousand years ago. Brother turned on brother, neighbor on neighbor. The country burned.

It's never recovered, and even before I had Singing, when I still though I was only protecting Loxy, it made me sick. It *still* makes me sick. Tears prick my eyes at the hatred around that day, even though I never lived it.

But I feel it, now more than ever.

I look at Loxy, the very thing they feared all those years ago. I'm one of them now, too. But now I can't help but wonder…perhaps what Itano actually saw in his prophecy was the Great Culling itself. A genocide of Singers, rather than destruction wrought by the Singers.

The people were wrong then. Just like they were wrong to cast us out.

Right?

"We have to go that way. You'll see it," Loxy says. After a moment's hesitation, she adds, "Those people were just like us."

I nod, my stomach churning still at the thought of so much death. Of that time when people started seeing Singing as a corruption. A plague.

The killing had mostly stopped after the Culling, but it had been replaced by banishment and selective breeding.

For the first time, I feel as if I understand a fraction of what Loxy has been experiencing her entire life. Not only the shame society heaps on our heads. But also the pride, the heritage.

The anger.

This is what I am now. And for the first time, I'm not sure I want to go back to how I was before.

I look over at Loxy, and a surge of strength fills me. We will find answers for her, even if Mom is gone. And we will find a life for ourselves.

We only have each other.

I take a big bite of pepper, and Sefella smiles. My veins turn to ice at the look, but I don't stop.

Loxy hadn't been exaggerating.

The hillside is covered in graves as numerous as the stars in the sky. I've read about it in the history books, but to see it in person… Books can't express what we see here, what we feel.

The meadow is eerily quiet, only the rain falling on our oilskins, the crunch of grass underfoot, and the wind whispering through the field. Fog lies low, drifting between graves like a cloud of spirits.

This place is either holy or cursed.

We don't speak as we make our way slowly, quietly, through the sea of crystalline graves. The field is so large that it takes us over an hour to pass the final marker, and that is in spite of us cutting through the narrowest part of the graveyard. Had we tried to walk from one end to the other, I suspect it would have taken the better part of the day.

Sefella glides through as if she is one of the spirits, but now I know why. She *is* practically a spirit. Though I still don't understand exactly what it all means, I am beginning to see a bigger picture. One where Sefella isn't what I always thought, what I was taught.

And neither is Ivlene.

I glance back over my shoulder at the graves and make the cleansing sign, offering up a prayer for all the souls we have passed. I don't know what is appropriate in this situation. It's hard to believe any priest or priestess could have been in this position before, but someone must have dug all these graves. Though I don't know how to respond, the sorrow draws me to a prayer of mourning, and I set the words free. It is an old prayer, one I learned at the temple. But I don't direct it toward Ivlene like I used to. Honestly, I'm not sure who I'm praying to right now, just hoping the words reach the right ears.

Did Sefella welcome these people to a good afterlife? I want to ask, but something keeps me from speaking, perhaps the reverent quiet around us, the sorrow of so many lost in one place. I glance over at our companion, hoping her face will give me a hint, but it is nearly impassive, nothing but a stern determination piercing through.

Just as I say the closing words to my prayers, something with more substance than a spirit rustles in the grass behind one of the gravestones. I jump, startled at the sudden change, and my heart gives one great bound against my chest.

As one, Loxy and I turn to face the sound, but nothing except the waving sea of grass and graves meets our stare.

I look at Loxy, and she holds a finger to her lips. Whatever it is, she can sense it.

And then I know why.

A delicate sparkle, dull in the overcast rain, parts the grass to my left, followed by the elegant lines of a wolf's face.

My heart leaps to my throat, but the wolf does not advance. It glances at Loxy, frozen in place, one paw in the air. Then it glances at me.

I look over at Loxy, but she appears unconcerned. She turns back toward the city and takes a step. Cautiously, my breathing shallow with fear, I follow, looking over my shoulder every few steps to see the grass swaying behind us or the tip of a crystalline ear.

But it never attacks.

We head toward the city, always wary of the creature at our heels, one slow step at a time. The city is ruined, just as monolithic and sepulchral as the meadow had been, and the air feels just as heavy as we take our first steps into the streets.

The street is eerie, as quiet as the graves through which we just passed. The only sound is the light whistling of the wind around the corners of the buildings surrounding us, those stark, gray witnesses to the carnage a millennium ago. Somehow the buildings are still well-preserved, even after all this time. Paint along the walls is vibrantly colored, and the images in advertisements are still sharp and clear. Murals cover walls on at least one building of every street we visit, telling the story of a city booming with trade and life and culture.

Yet, nowhere do we find an explanation for who buried the thousands on the hillside. I would've expected a mass grave, not the individual, carefully plotted graves we saw.

Loxy digs in her pack as we walk, dropping bits of jerky on the ground behind us without looking back. I can hear the wolf's padded steps, but I dare not turn. Instead, I pin Loxy with a glare, afraid to speak but wishing she would stop feeding this creature.

Either she doesn't understand or she ignores me. Probably the latter. I sigh.

We stalk deeper into the city, and the silence grows heavier as even the wind dies. No bird calls here, no rodent darts between buildings, no wild dog, other than our wolf stalker, roams the streets. The city is truly dead, nothing left but the wind to sing funeral songs.

We turn a corner and find ourselves face-to-face with a breathtaking structure: a great shining temple constructed entirely of crystal quartz. Its clear facets distort the reflection of the city, catching what little light there is on this rainy day and transforming it to the most beautiful glow I've ever seen.

I know where we are now. The Glass City. Korilia.

This city has been lost to time for centuries, remembered only in somber histories, a footnote in most texts. Texts that only the priestesses are allowed to see. Texts that explain how the city declined in the year following the Culling before being abandoned entirely, the people scattering and forgetting about their past here.

But now I know who buried these people. And I have to see that temple.

I glance at Loxy, her face enraptured by the crystal. I assume the Song is unlike anything she's heard before, but I have no way of knowing.

"El," she says, her voice hushed, "what is this place?"

I lead the way toward the temple steps. When I speak, my voice is as hushed as hers, as the wind. It feels wrong to break the silence. "For a long time, this was considered the pinnacle of religious society. A mecca for priests and priestesses. Before…before the Culling."

Loxy drops another scrap of jerky, and I fight not to grab her hand. "What happened?"

I take a breath, trying to ignore the wolf pacing behind us. "After the Singers died in the Culling, the city was emptied. The economy slumped. People began to doubt the religious powers, question whether they were truly connected to the Bright Ones.

They even began fearing priests and priestesses and the return of the spirits of the Singers they had killed. There's a theory that's why the fear of the Singers continued, that it began with the prophecies prior to the Culling and grew when the people feared retribution from angry ghosts."

Loxy is silent for several long minutes. The wind gusts between the buildings around us, louder than my voice. I stay quiet, allowing the wind to speak. Are the spirits of the dead in it?

When it dies down, Loxy says, "Why haven't I ever heard of this?"

I sigh. I questioned Priestess Illume on this myself, but her answer was just as unsatisfactory as the one I am forced to give my sister. "The priestesses didn't want to upset the people. They wanted to let the citizens worry about daily life, let us worry about the histories."

Loxy's brows draw together, her lips pressed into a thin line. "I see." I can feel the anger emanating from her. "So the priestesses have just been…hiding part of our past from us? Like we're children? Or like we're stupid?"

I glance at her, stomach clenching. My first instinct is to defend the choices of the church, but it doesn't feel right anymore, and I'm done hiding things for them. Especially to my sister.

Instead, I say, "There is a lot the general population doesn't know. The priestesses hide anything they don't think the people can handle, and they leave the rest of the histories for the theologians to study. I got to read some of it in my studies at the temple, but even I don't know everything."

Loxy nods, but it is still full of anger. "So they hid an entire city from us? We already knew about the Culling. Why would they hide the knowledge of this place?"

I wince. She asks the very question I have been avoiding. "They wouldn't tell me more than what I just told you. But… I'm starting to think they just didn't want people to question Ivlene. Or the priestesses. How better to maintain control than to hide important things, to not trust people to come to their own decisions?"

Sefella half laughs, and I look over at her sharply. "What?"

She shakes her head. "You, Daughter. You're a long way from Limutria."

I stare at her for a few steps. What does she mean? That we've literally come a long way from our home?

Or that I'm not who I was a few weeks ago?

But she doesn't give me a chance to ask, returning her attention to our surroundings.

"I have never forgotten even one of these people," says Sefella, voice hushed as ours are.

I nod, though I am cold at the reminder that we walk with Death herself—but I am oddly comforted by her words at the same time—and we pass by a silent, still fountain in the center of the street before the temple.

"Why did the city empty?" Loxy says, obviously not done with our previous discussion.

I glance back at her as she drops another bit of meat. "There was a plague. It started only a few days after the Culling, dragging more people to Sefella. They buried the Singers, gave them proper graves and end-of-life rites. They were hoping this would allow the spirits to rest and no one else would die."

"But it didn't work, did it?"

I shake my head. "No. It didn't. Whoever was left eventually scattered when the city became too empty to support the survivors.

The people in Ryth Hollows probably emigrated from here. Maybe even our own ancestors."

Maybe one of my ancestors was a priest or priestess, maybe one of them founded the temple in Limutria. Maybe I was always destined to be a priestess.

But I was cast out. And I'm not sure if I'm angry about it anymore.

We make it to the bottom of the shining, glasslike steps. Now that we're closer, I can see the veins of gray smoke running through the quartz. Inside, past the glassy walls, I see a glint of gold that must be the shrine, somehow untouched after all these years.

Even grave robbers know not to tread through a cursed city and steal from the Bright One.

I climb the steps, scarcely noticing whether my companions follow me or not. It feels like returning to the temple in Limutria, only not, and I can't decide if I am excited and happy to see part of our history, horrified at what that history means, or angry and hurt again at losing the place I had called home. The mix of conflicting emotions churns together in my stomach, making me feel sick, and I press a hand over my navel and swallow past the lump in my throat.

I pass through the arched doorway, forcing myself to take a step even though fear is beginning to surround me like a blanket.

I catch my breath as the crystal structure opens up around me.

Spreading out on either side of me is a hall much grander than the one in Limutria, even with Limutria's beautiful rose stone. Or at least it had been grander at one time. But now, a coating of dust covers everything, dulling the bright shine that must have once been here. A few of the columns and walls have collapsed to time, but the bulk of the structure seems intact.

The layout sends a pang of nostalgia through me. It is nearly identical to the temple in Limutria. We enter the main hall, and at the far end stands a shrine to Ivlene. This shrine is bright crystal quartz and gold leaf, but the symbols and carvings are different, more complicated. An extra symbol—the symbol of Sefella, partially obscured as if someone tried to destroy it—stands along with the symbol of Ivlene. Also like the temple at home, rooms shoot off the main hall on each side.

I shove thoughts of home out of my mind and approach the shrine, pausing to leave my customary liturgies for Ivlene, though they now feel hollow, then walk straight past it to the door on the left, the door that should have once been the quarters of the High Priest or Priestess. Though I know it is unlikely, I'm hoping to find something, a piece of hope or part of the story of this place, something I can hold on to.

Something that will finally tell me a truth not obscured by prejudice and hidden agendas. By a hunger for power.

Nausea rolls in my stomach again at what I am discovering about my beliefs, about everything I once held true.

I push through the crystal door, climbing a few stairs into the room behind the shrine. But with every step, my stomach sinks.

There is nothing here. No tapestries, no murals, no artifacts.

Nothing to tell me what is real.

I find myself blinking back tears. This is the most important temple in Nasmarya's history, and I hear nothing from the past. Nothing from the Bright One.

She isn't here anymore. Just like she isn't with me.

I don't know if I'm more saddened or relieved.

Nails click on the crystal floor behind me, and I turn to see Loxy and, peering around a corner, the wolf. It stays back, not attacking, not venturing closer. But still it follows. Sefella stopped at the bottom of the steps outside, and I can just barely see her across the gleaming distance.

I keep an eye on the wolf but turn my attention back to Loxy. "There's nothing here."

She shakes her head. "There's history here. That's not nothing."

I nod. She's right, of course. If I'm ever allowed home, I should share this place. People could find it again, understand how the priestesses have hidden our history from them. They could know the truth.

I turn back toward the stairs, trying to ignore my feelings, my sudden burning desire for everyone to see our world for what it is. "Let's keep moving."

As I approach, the wolf turns and runs toward the entrance, its claws clicking and paws sliding across the smooth, slick floor. It's out the door and gone before we even make it halfway.

But as we walk, something wedged against one of the broken columns to my right catches my eye. I kneel and pick up a small pendant, the chain tarnished but unbroken. A talisman from a priest or priestess long dead. An amulet with the dual symbol of the Bright Ones—Ivlene and Sefella.

So it's true. At one time, we really did follow both Ivlene and Sefella together.

I trace my thumb over the familiar raised sun, the bright rosy crystal in the center. And a twin to the bright crystal set next to it, a stone of deep, sparkling blue shaped like a crescent moon. It's a beautiful piece of history.

I blink tears out of my eyes again, feeling the presence of the Bright Ones—yes, a dual nature—near, covering us, protecting us, as it was supposed to be. Balance in the world. I straighten, pretending not to see Loxy staring at me, at the amulet, her eyes full of awe. Impulsively, I loop the pendant over my head, and it settles next to my own simpler, less expensive symbol from Limutria. A pendant without the moon of Sefella. It feels…right. A warmth spreads through me, and I mutter a prayer of gratitude before we continue out the door, my fingers lingering on the new symbol I now hold, a truth I can't deny.

The sun, peeking through gaps in the clouds, is low on the horizon now, setting the crystal temple on fire with its light. It won't be long before we need to find a place for the night.

But I only have one thought as I take in the glowing temple.

And the priest had said, there is more than only Ivlene.

The Bright Ones are still here.

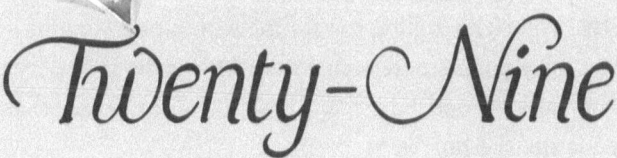

Twenty-Nine

LOXY

I tell you, there are worse things in this world than death.

Excerpt from a letter written one day before Korilia's Great
Culling

O nce we leave the temple, we find a nearby building that
isn't too damaged to shelter us for the night. We are so
tired, so emotionally spent, that we fall into a deep sleep
quickly, despite a hole in the ceiling, despite the rain that continues
to fall on and off. The night is quiet, almost too quiet, and I don't
move for hours.

Then, something warm, furry, and spiky drops itself next to me,
startling me awake. It nestles into the curve of my body, and I blink
my eyes open to see the wolf, the one I have been feeding, curled up
in the dirt and grass with me, breathing slow and deep already.

The same wolf I hurt. And then healed.

Cautiously, I raise a hand, reaching toward it.

Its white fur is coarse and thick, punctuated by spires of pink and gray crystal. The crystals are warm with the body heat of the wolf.

"Does this mean you're staying?" I say softly.

The wolf sighs, rolling toward me without opening its eyes. It must have understood what I said. Or maybe it understood the language of food I'd offered it all day. Or the fact that I'd healed it after I'd hurt it.

I drape an arm across its body, enjoying its warmth and companionship.

I saved this wolf. I'd lost control and nearly killed it. But I saved it, too.

My mind drifts to the healers in Limutria, then to Iarann back in Ryth Hollows. What would life be like if I could use my magic to heal for a living? My mind sifts through this question as my body floats back to sleep.

The rain starts again, drawing me out of sleep a second time. El is protected under the overhanging roof, but my head is under a hole in the ceiling, one we must have missed in the fading light of day. I sit up and pull my oilskin up over my hair, scooting back away from the hole. The wolf raises its head, blinks up at the sky, then scoots closer to El.

"Thanks," I say. "Leave me out here in the rain."

My ears detect something outside, and for a moment, I think I see a blue light coming from the street. But as quickly as I see it, it's gone. My body is so exhausted that I fall back into sleep immediately.

Thirty

ELODIE

This is the end. Sefella has found us after all.

Final words of Korilian mayor, two weeks after the Great
Culling

Sunlight falls across my eyes, and I blink awake. Something warm is nestled up against me. But Loxy sits on the other side of the shelter, picking through her pack, and Sefella stands over her, watching.

I turn my head, taking in the wolf asleep next to me. My heart stutters, but the animal doesn't move. Obviously if it wanted us dead, we wouldn't be awake now.

I grunt and sit up. The wolf blinks its bright teal eyes and yawns, breathing rancid morning breath in my direction. I wave my hand, and a small breeze blows it away.

Oops.

"What are we going to call him?" I say, eyes on the wolf. I am still uneasy, but it doesn't seem aggressive like it had before. I think Sefella would have warned us if it was a danger, since it spent the night sleeping by my side. "I assume he's staying."

It shifts, and its crystals ring together like bells in the wind.

"Her." Loxy smiles, also watching the wolf. "I think Teklari, like the tinkling of chimes. It fits."

I nod. It does fit. Loxy has a real gift for naming.

She hands me a packet of food, and I unwrap it. Next to me, Teklari licks her lips, and Loxy tosses a chunk of fish jerky her way.

"How much food do we have left?" I say.

She peers into her bag. "Enough. For now."

I nod, and we dig into the packet, splitting it between the two of us before breaking down our campsite and venturing back outside. Now that I know Sefella is not corporeal, I do not bother offering her food.

We walk for hours. The ruins are extensive, as labyrinthine as the caves we left just yesterday morning. Several times, we find we have walked in a circle, finding the same crumbled mural or ancient business sign broken in the dust that we had passed hours before.

The sun is starting its descent in the sky again when we turn a corner to find ourselves in a plaza we have somehow wandered back into three times already this evening. I huff out an annoyed breath, and Loxy throws herself to the ground. Teklari's tail is low, half tucked between her legs at our irritation.

"How did we end up here *again*?" Loxy cries, throwing a pebble across the square to bounce off one of the walls on the other side of the street.

I stalk to the fountain in the middle of the plaza and drop myself onto the broken stone wall, looking into the stagnant water overgrown with reeds and algae. I can't even see my reflection through all the grime. I retrace our steps in my head, trying to fix my mental image of the city, but we have gotten lost so many times in the last few hours that I can't reconcile it. Even Sefella looks confused, her form fainter in the fading light of day.

The sun dips below the mountain peaks to the west, and the shadows grow ten times, stretching long claws toward us.

"Maybe we should make camp for the night," I say, watching the shadows of the fountain's broken statue of some long forgotten hero reach toward the buildings in the east.

Loxy sighs. "I really thought we'd make it past the city by now."

I drop my pack from my shoulders and start peeking into the doors of the buildings that appear mostly intact. There aren't many of them in this part of the city, but I'm just looking for one with enough remaining roof to keep us dry, like last night. I can smell rain on the air, and clouds have been building in the east for hours.

The first few buildings are nothing more than storefronts, their rear walls and ceilings completely collapsed into themselves to form great piles of rubble. But the third building I search is remarkably intact. All the walls still stand, though there are some cracks here and there in the mortar and stone. The ceiling is also mostly intact. Hopefully it can remain that way for one more night.

But just to be safe…

"Loxy, can you reinforce the building? This seems like a good campsite." I start walking toward the fountain, picking dry reeds and small branches from the trees that have grown through the pavement.

Loxy stands and walks toward the building. She lays her hand on the empty frame of the door, and pillars of dark crystal rise up from the ground and interweave with the remains of the building. A few pieces of mortar fall from the ceiling, but when she removes her hand and steps inside, everything else stays in place.

I pick up my pack and drag it along to the building, dropping it next to Loxy. Then I take my firewood and tinder to the corner of the small room, under the only hole in the ceiling, a smaller hole than last night's campsite, and build up a small stack of wood. I snap my fingers, igniting a spark at the heart of my pile of reeds and cattail fluff.

My magic has come so far. And calling the magic, controlling its energy, has become easier since I stopped fighting it at every turn.

I feed the fire more energy and wait for the wet fuel to catch. Soon, a tendril of white smoke drifts up from the pile, and I feed it larger fuel until a cheery blaze is burning.

I turn around to see Loxy digging through her pack, but Teklari is nowhere in sight.

My heart lurches. "Where is the wolf?"

Loxy points out the door, seemingly unconcerned, then hands me a small parcel of fish jerky.

Great. Just what I wanted.

Just as I lean back against the wall, resigned to my meager, fishy dinner, Teklari appears in the doorway, a large rabbit between her shining teeth. I can't help but smile. Finally something other than fish!

"Where did you find that?" Loxy says, accepting the gift from the wolf. She looks into its eyes, and I swear it understands her, though I don't know how.

Loxy smiles at Teklari, then brings the rabbit to the fire. Using some of the firewood, she erects a small frame to hold the rabbit.

As she starts cleaning the kill, preparing it to cook, I walk to the doorway and look out into the square. I can almost see the ghosts of people walking around, living normal lives like they had years ago.

The skies choose that moment to open, dumping rain on us so hard and fast that I can barely see the buildings on the far side of the square. The downpour kills any remaining daylight, and Sefella fades away into the shadows. I feel suddenly bereft at her departure, like I've lost Mom all over again, and I blink, surprised at myself, my heart clenching in my chest.

I turn away, trying to ignore the vanishing act and the unexpected feeling of abandonment.

But then I see something I never expected to see in my life, at least not this definitively, and it drives back the feeling—and the questions—that Sefella's disappearance brought me.

As I watch the rain fall, as the rabbit begins to cook and spread its mouthwatering fragrance, columns of dim, translucent lights begin to appear and disappear before my eyes. The constant rush of the rain is now punctuated by the howl of the wind…except I don't feel any wind.

Loxy appears next to me. "What's that?"

She must have seen my muscles tense, seen me staring intently into the rain. "I'm not quite sure."

We both watch the streets, watch the columns of light. As night falls, the columns grow brighter, more distinct, the air punctuated by green and blue orbs of varying sizes floating between the columns.

And then suddenly we see a face in a column, and I know for sure what this is.

The parade of the dead.

I know the moment Loxy sees the face. Her skin goes white, and she stands straighter, creeping closer to me and taking my arm.

"Maybe the spirits really were restless," she says.

"Maybe," I respond, thinking of the voices I thought I heard on the wind earlier in the day.

The spirits move about the streets as if unaware they are dead, as if they continue to live their lives without interruption. The orbs, maybe weaker spirits unable to hold a shape, follow the same patterns of movement. But they all ignore us, not looking in our direction or approaching. Either they don't know we're here, or they don't care.

A drop of fat falls from the rabbit into the fire, hissing loudly against the backdrop of rain and invisible wind. We jump and turn back inside the building. Teklari remains at the door, looking out, her strange teal eyes filled with the light of the dead.

Loxy strides across the room to check the rabbit, and I sink down in the doorway, looping my arm over Teklari's shoulder and watching the parade.

Our fire is reduced to a smolder, barely burning, and the night is late when I am pulled from sleep. I hadn't wanted to sleep; I wanted to watch the spirits. Yet I find myself slumped over next to the wolf.

But it isn't Teklari that wakes me. Instead, I feel a chill, see a light build on the other side of my closed eyelids. I open my eyes and push myself up, blinking at the bright light within the building. My eyes go wide, and I glance at the fire where Loxy is asleep. She doesn't stir, unaware of the spirit. Even Teklari still sleeps next to me.

I return my gaze to the spirit as it walks past me through the door, toward our dim fire. My breath puffs white, and bumps rise along my arms as the temperature drops. This spirit is nearly fully formed, only missing the clear distinction of its lower legs. It is a small girl, no more than seven years old, her hair flowing the palest white and her dress billowing away from her in an unfelt wind. Her eyes are as bright white as her hair. Her movements mimic a shopper, walking back and forth in straight lines, moving her head up and down as if looking at shelves full of goods, reaching her tiny hand toward something invisible.

And then she freezes in place. She tilts her head as if listening, but all I can hear is the falling of the rain outside and against the roof.

My heart pounds so loudly I can't hear anything except the pulsing blood in my ears. I wrack my brain, trying to remember everything I can about spirits. I know I had classes on them during my apprenticeship, but those lessons were early in my training. No spirits walk inside Limutria. And the spirits nearby, those hapless travelers lost out over the Sea of Broken Glass, were beyond my ability to help as an apprentice.

I swallow. We were very nearly one of those spirits.

But now one stands before me. Are they dangerous? Omens? Can they reveal the future?

One story filters into my mind, the story of a salt merchant who crossed paths with a spirit and failed to pay respect to its death. He was subsequently ripped to shreds.

I shiver. Will this spirit destroy us?

But then there is the story of a small boy lost in the sea a mile from Limutria. When he encountered a spirit, drawn by his cries as if remembering its role as a mother during life, it led him home.

So what kind of spirit is in our camp?

Slowly, I rise to my feet, trying not to offend or disturb the spirit. She watches me, her head tilted in that peculiar way, eyes alight. I shiver again and glance back at Loxy, but my sister—although she also shivers with the cold—does not wake.

I wonder if I should stoke the fire. I could do that from here, simply feed it more energy. But that could anger the ghost, make it think I'm trying to banish it. And we are far outnumbered by spirits in this city; I have no way of telling how those outside would react if this one attacked us.

Sefella appears next to me, staring, her face puzzled as if she recognizes something, as if maybe she's seen this girl before. "Could it be…"

The light of the spirit brightens, and I look back at the spirit. Her body shifts and grows, the straight lines of the child redrawn into the curves of a woman. When the light fades back to a brightness I can tolerate, I rub at my eyes, unable to accept the sight before me. I hope, especially for Loxy's sake, that it's a cruel trick.

Because I could swear where the girl had stood now stands—

"Mom?" Loxy says, sitting up and rubbing her eyes. "Is that really you?"

I whip my head toward my sister, and my heart sinks at the fear, the disbelief in Loxy's eyes. Does she realize this is a spirit? That a moment ago it was a small girl who looks nothing like us, like *her*?

The spirit glides toward the door, watching us silently. Sefella takes a step to follow, enraptured. It pauses at the threshold next to me, hovering just over the muddy ground. Behind it, the rain continues to fall steadily.

Loxy rises to her feet and takes a step toward it.

I hold up a hand. "Loxy, no. It's not Mom."

She looks between the spirit and me with a pained expression, as if unsure what to believe. She takes another step.

"Loxy, please, trust me!"

"But El, it's Mom!"

The spirit floats out the door and to the left, out of sight. Loxy runs up next to me and looks out into the rain. I follow her gaze, see the glow of the spirit turning into an alley next to us.

Sefella takes off into the deluge. "I knew it!"

"Come on!" Loxy says, running out into the rain without even her oilskin to protect her. Without even her boots.

"Sefella take her!" I curse, shoving my feet into my own boots and tossing my oilskin over my shoulders. The words I just used grate against my thoughts now that I have been traveling with Sefella, but I have no time to dissect that. I grab Loxy's boots and oilskin before following her out into the night, praying we won't lose ourselves in the city streets again, separated from all our supplies.

I glance at Teklari. The wolf is still asleep, somehow, but I don't have time to worry about it.

I run after my sister.

The rain is like daggers of ice wherever it hits my skin. I spend a second orienting myself, then take off toward the alley. I round the corner just in time to see Loxy disappear around the next corner after a blue-white glow reflecting off wet, ruined walls. I pursue, my mind spinning as I try to keep track of every twist and turn so we can find our way back, but it quickly becomes impossible as the spirit leads us so deep into the alleys that everything looks the same.

We dodge more spirits of every shape and size, and I do my best not to touch any of them. I am shaking with the cold, looking around and trying to orient myself again when I realize that we are lost.

"Sefella take her!" I yell again into the night as I run. "Stupid, stupid! Why couldn't she just listen to me for once?" The spirits ignore me.

I slide around another corner and almost knock Loxy to the ground. At this point in my anger, I wouldn't have minded if I did. But the sight in front of us quickly diverts my attention.

The spirit brought us to a small building, no more than a hole in the wall next to the other small buildings this deep in the alleys. This must have once housed the city's poorer population, as cramped as it is. And over this hole in the wall, a tattered bit of fabric flutters from a broken edge of masonry.

No fabric would have survived one thousand years in the elements.

The spirit hovers inside, still holding Mom's form, in the middle of what looks like an old abandoned camp. And, on the far wall, a shrine is built roughly of crystal points and burned bits of animal fat and wood.

Why did the spirit bring us here?

The spirit turns to us with a smile, pointing toward the shrine, and Loxy and I approach, careful not to touch the floating, icy light of the ghost. Sefella is already here, staring, a hand over her mouth.

"Yes, I remember now," she says softly, not to us. To herself.

Behind the crystal points and burned out wood, there is writing on the wall, but I can't make it out in the dim light of the night. I summon a small flame to my hand, and between that and the glow of the spirit, I can just barely make out a prayer written in fine Nasmaryan handwriting. Whoever left this prayer had good education and a caring hand.

"'Ivlene forgive me for what I have done'," I read aloud. "'I knew not what I was doing. Have mercy on my daughters. Protect them and raise them as I cannot. May my husband forgive me and move on. Save my soul from the death I carry with me. Sefella, bring me in peace into the Underworld.'"

My breath catches at the last line. I've never heard anyone offer a prayer to Sefella; usually, it's forbidden, an omen of illness or death. Almost unconsciously, I touch the symbol on the pendant, the one I picked up at the Korilian temple.

The symbol of Sefella.

Loxy leans in as I read, glancing over her shoulder at the spirit wearing Mom's image. "Do you think…this was Mom?"

I examine the handwriting, searching my childhood memories. She didn't leave behind much writing, at least not that Dad kept around the house, so it's a while before I answer.

"It could be."

"It is," Sefella says, her voice low. "This is where she called Sefella first. Once she knew." She blinks. "But it was already too late by then."

I look back at the shrine. I feel a hunger for more, something I never expected to feel. I thought the chapter of my life with Mom was over and that I had moved on. But I was wrong.

This prayer, and the pain and guilt behind the words breaks my heart. I touch the charcoal form of the letters gingerly, trying to reach through time to see her.

Part of me is glad to feel the guilt. She's the one who left us.

But then another thought occurs to me, chasing away my anger like the sun chasing away night. Maybe, like me, she hadn't been in control. Why else would she say she didn't know what she was doing?

There is a lurch of sympathy in my heart for this woman I only remember as the one who left me, who didn't come back.

"Look!" Loxy says. Something gold glints in her soot-blackened fingers. She must have been digging through the shrine's fire while I was deep in thought.

I take the item from her hand, instantly recognizing the ring that is the companion to the one I wear on my own finger. Mine is silver, where this one is gold and in every way the match to mine. Every curve of the metal is shaped to fit my ring, Mom's old ring. The stones are even the same color, the same kind.

"Mom's wedding ring," I breathe.

"I thought you had her wedding ring?" Loxy says, pointing to the glint of silver and aquamarine on my hand.

I shake my head. "No, this is her betrothal ring. Her wedding ring—she took that with her."

We both stare at it for a moment, then I grab Loxy's hand and shove the gold ring onto her finger. It mostly fits, only a little loose.

"There," I say. "Now we match. She was *our* mother, not just mine. It's only fitting that we divide the rings."

"Was?" Loxy says, her voice small.

We turn slowly back toward the spirit. It is still there, but the image of Mom is gone. The small girl once again floats in her place. Sef sinks down next to the shrine, touching the letters as I had only moments ago. The sorrow on her face matches what I see on Loxy's and what I am sure is on mine.

Tears slide down Loxy's cheeks. "She's not here."

"I tried to tell you," I say, wrapping my arm over her wet shoulders. My anger is gone, and instead I'm six years old again, watching Mom walk away from Limutria—from *us*—in a fury of uncontrolled magic. "It wasn't Mom."

Loxy collapses in sobs, and I hold her close while she cries, crying silently along with her. My tears are lost in her wet hair.

But even though my heart is shattered all over again, something is different this time. I look down at Loxy. The pain is there, yes, just like it was twenty years ago.

But this time I'm not facing it alone.

Fresh tears spill down my cheeks, and I hold my sister harder, grateful and broken and healing all at the same time.

Thirty-One

LOXY

Forgive us, Ivlene, for we have done great harm. Protect us, for only you can show us mercy now. Save us from those we have forsaken.

Prayer of the Korilian people, two weeks after the Great Culling

I don't know how long we sit, crying together at the shrine, watched by the spirit that isn't Mom. At first, Sefella stands aside, staring at the shrine and lost in her own thoughts, but eventually, she crouches down next to us, reaching toward us as if trying to comfort us.

As if she really does care about us, not just need us for her own ends. I don't know that for sure—who can tell with a goddess?—but the thought warms me in the wet night air. The ring burns cold at first from the chill in the air, only gradually warming from my skin.

I wipe my tears and sit up. The spirit disappears, and I didn't even thank her for this. We may not have found Mom, but we found her ring. Her camp. Her prayer. She never wanted to leave us, and my heart swells with warmth at the knowledge.

But then, why didn't she come back? Did this message, the lost ring, mean she gave up?

And then I look to Sefella. Sefella knew her. No wonder she said she can help us find her. But what did she mean "it was too late"?

I look at the ring on my finger, evidence Mom had given up hope of ever coming home. Or that something has been keeping her away all these years. But that only makes my conviction to find her that much stronger.

If she can't come to us, we will go to her.

I look at Sefella again. "How did you know her?"

Sefella blinks, as if my words pull her from a deep memory. "She…she was like you. Lost. Forsaken. Yet, she was my daughter as much as you are hers." Sefella blinks back tears, smiling sadly at us, looking from me to El with tenderness like what I've always imagined Mom to have. "As much as you are mine. I found her before she knew me.

"Then, my sister… Before your mother and I could seal our bond, my sister stole her. Took her from me." Sefella gestures at the wall, anger and pain overtaking the tenderness on her face. "Volta was to be *my* vessel, once she figured out who I was. But by the time she called me here, it was too late. My sister had already claimed her, had taken away her choice. She'd stolen her not only from me, but from Volta herself."

El stands and reaches a hand down to help me up. Neither of us can take our eyes off Sefella. I take El's hand, also accepting my boots and oilskin from her.

El stares at Sef with wide eyes, unbelieving. "How can you be sure?"

Sefella shakes her head. "I found her long ago. Fifteen years, maybe. It took…time to convince her. But in the end, she agreed to host me. We grew stronger together."

"Until your twin," I say, wiping at my nose.

Sefella nods. "Until my twin."

My heart races, newfound energy invigorating me. We are so close now, I can feel it. "So let's go! What are we waiting for?"

Sefella rises to her feet, eyes afire. "I know where we need to go next. The next place she went. Cliffreach."

Cliffreach. The very place El wants to go. Maybe it is destiny after all.

It's time to go. Except…except I stupidly ran out into the rain, away from camp, with no trail to follow back to all our supplies.

I glance at El. She is grinding her jaw, the way she always does when she is miffed but there's not much she can do about it, but she also seems almost as excited as me, bouncing on her feet like she's as ready to go as I am.

But it's my fault we're separated from camp, and I find myself waiting for an outburst from her, ducking my head to avoid her wrath.

I do my best to wipe the mud off my bare feet, hoping that cleaning myself up will reduce El's irritation, but it is an impossible task. The mud just smears, so I return to the pouring rain outside the hole in the wall and allow it to wash me clean as I shiver. Then El pulls me back in and holds a flame close to my feet, drying the rain and warming me before I shove my feet into the boots.

"I can't help with your clothes," she says, holding out the oilskin. "We'll have to find camp again and give you time to dry out."

I look outside. Our footprints are gone, erased by the rain.

"Sefella, can you lead us back?" El asks.

Sefella frowns. "I am sorry. I do not have enough power to find the way… It is seeping away from me every day."

I got us lost, running without thinking. And El followed. And now not even Sefella herself can help.

Stupid, stupid! The longer we are away from Limutria, the more idiotic, uncontrolled messes I create.

The man in Ryth Hollows. The loss of the lantern in the caves. The crystals that almost killed Teklari.

I freeze.

"Where's Teklari?" I ask.

El shrugs. "Last I saw, she hadn't woken up."

I close my eyes and reach out for the feeling of life and crystal that is unique to the crystal wolves. I hope Teklari is the only one nearby. I follow the trail back through the streets and alleys as surely as I could follow footprints in the mud.

And I sense her, huddled in the camp, surrounded by the supports I erected earlier. I open my eyes and look at my sister. "I know how to get back."

Still shivering, I lead her into the rainy night. As we walk, the number of spirits diminishes with the approaching dawn.

Eventually, we make it back to the camp. Teklari meets us at the door, pushing herself close to me until I stroke her head. I risk a look at my sister, and sure enough, the anger has faded.

I did something good. Maybe I don't *only* mess things up.

El stokes the fire, and we huddle next to it, falling back into a deep sleep.

Despite our long, depressing night, I wake feeling refreshed. My clothes are dry and warm from the fire, and my body temperature is back up. Teklari nudges her head under my arm as I start pulling out jerky and bread for breakfast, and I obligingly feed her a bit while we wait for El to wake.

It isn't long before she's up and bossing us around, pushing me to move faster to pack up the camp.

Neither of us is keen on staying in this haunted place any longer than necessary. Even Sefella seems anxious to be on the road. Though, if Mom really was supposed to be her vessel, of course she would be anxious to find her again.

Vessel. I'm not sure what that means, but I am beginning to suspect. If we do find Mom…will we also find ourselves in a war between goddesses?

Part of me is still confused, still trying to piece together what I wasn't told for so many years, what the priestesses hid from me. I haven't trusted them for a long time, but their betrayal of our people is so much bigger than I imagined.

And the magnitude of what they've hidden terrifies me.

We extinguish the fire, repack our bags, and head back into the city. This time, El hands me the cave map.

"You're the artist," she says. "Want to try cartography?"

I smile at her, though I still feel uneasy from last night's revelations. I also feel proud at her recognition of my ability. I turn over the cave map and draw out our route as we traverse the city. All I have is a tiny stump of charcoal leftover from the fire, but I'm used to drawing with charcoal anyway. Together, we decide what landmarks to include, and we don't get lost even once.

"How do you think the spirit knew Mom?" I say, sketching a thin line to mark an alley.

El is silent for a moment as we continue toward the margins of the city. Then, she says, "Spirits tend to remember the people they see. And that one was strong. When Mom came through, it probably saw her."

"Did it recognize us? Somehow know we were related?"

The sun is slowly sinking, but we press on through the mist and out past the last building into the valley.

El shrugs. "It's possible." Her eyes settle on my face, and for some reason, I feel myself blushing. "You do look just like her."

"You *are* just like her," Sefella says, though she doesn't look at me. It feels like something the voice would have said...except, I'm realizing I have not heard the voice from Limutria in days.

And that the voice from then sounded an awful lot like Sefella does.

I drop my head and roll up the map.

You are just like her.

I am warm at the compliment. Both of them think I'm like Mom, and that connection to a woman I've always wished to know fills me with joy.

The first day after the city, we make our way through grassland and patches of mud in the valley between the mountains, but the meadows slowly turn to rock and our path begins to ascend toward the mountains. And then, poking up through the grasses and gray stone of the valley, stand three pink quartz columns, all broken to different heights.

I stop next to them, examining a smooth foundation, the remains of walls, broken stone that may have once been a ceiling. And when I listen, I can hear a now-familiar tune.

I smile. "Mom," I say. "She was here. We're going the right way!"

El nods, her face clouded. I'm not quite sure how to read it, but it lacks the resentment that often accompanies conversations about Mom. We stop here to eat more of our food stores, which are starting to look thin, and then continue climbing. I make sure to leave a tiny sculpture of my own next to her crystal, one that looks like the statue I still carry in my bag. It won't ever mean anything to anyone other than me, but that small gesture makes me feel closer to her for a moment, like I really *am* like her the way Sefella and El said earlier.

We are near the top of a low ridge when a gentle chiming adds its sound to the falling rain. My steps slow, and I look around for the source of the bell-like ring. But there is nothing in sight except rocks and more grass.

I turn my head to ask El about it, but her eyes are wide already.

"Do you hear that?" she says.

"The bells?" I say.

Teklari pauses and looks back at us, her own crystals chiming softly.

"A little farther," Sefella says.

A little farther? Until what?

Then that odd Song, the one I couldn't recognize from that strange stone in the Sea, joins the chorus of bells. It has layers of familiarity, but with an overtone like the stone we found before, layered and full of a cold, smooth energy.

I reach out into the space around us, through the rain, through the chimes. I can hear quartz underground, semi-precious stones, and veins of minerals. Some of these crystals extend up into the mountains around us. And then, in the bottom of a crater, another strange stone.

"Up there," I say, pointing.

El nods, and we walk slowly toward the edge of the rise before us. As we crest the rise, something large, black, and shiny comes into view, surrounded by a pit of empty dirt and scorched plants pushed back away from it in an area as large as the entire village of Limutria. From here, I can't tell if this stone has the same silver streaks as the stone I carry in my pack; I can't see anything except shining jet.

I glance at El, and she nods. Slowly, we begin descending the crater toward the stone. With every step, the ringing grows louder. When we are only a few paces away, I can see the shiny silver streaks again, can hear the Song louder than ever.

El stops, but I advance, feeling a chill around me. The dark reflection of my face appears in the facet before me, and I reach out a hand to touch it. The surface is colder than the air, slick with rain.

My reflection flashes, and for a moment I think I see another, familiar face. But I can't quite place whose reflection I see, and then it is gone and my own reflection stares back at me.

"I can't believe we found another one," Sefella says, awe in her voice.

I drop my hand and walk around the stone. My reflection multiplies, jumping from facet to facet. One of three reflections halfway around the stone flashes again, back to that face. I stop and turn toward it. In each face, I see stars sparkling in the heavens, two of them brighter than the surrounding stars. Instead of silver-white, these stars are blue and gold, like the stones in El's new pendant. Somehow, I know this is the Celestial Temple—or at least what my mortal mind can perceive as the Temple.

"Wow," I breathe.

El steps up behind me, and I know she sees exactly what I do when she catches her breath. "Is it…?"

"Yes," Sefella answers softly. "This is how things used to be. How *I* used to be."

I turn from the stone to meet her sad gaze. "Do you miss it?"

She shrugs, then smiles. "Sometimes. But you humans are pretty wonderful creatures. It's almost better to be here, with you."

I warm at the words and glance at my sister. She gives me a small, guarded smile, reaching for my hand, and I let her take it. I can't read whatever thoughts are behind that smile, but her lips tremble. I don't know if what we've just seen changes anything or what kind of battle wages in her mind…though, I wish she would tell me.

El gives my hand a squeeze. "We should probably keep going."

El turns back the way we had been traveling, pulling me along behind her. I have to walk quickly to keep up with her, and I watch her carefully for any sign as to what thoughts are behind those carefully guarded eyes. My heart pounds with the anticipation of knowing, with the hope that maybe she understands what I've been trying to say for years, that maybe we can agree on another thing.

But she remains silent, keeping whatever she's thinking to herself. And each time I try to ask, she simply shrugs until I give up asking.

The rain doesn't let up all day, and we are forced to erect a shelter when night comes. I pull crystal from the side of a cliff's base, giving us some measure of protection against the wind and driving rain, and we huddle in for another cold, wet night. We don't say anything, though I keep looking to El to see if she'll finally share what's on her mind. But still, nothing.

I sigh. Maybe she needs a little processing time. I can give her that. At least until we reach the temple.

That night, I dream of Mom, consumed by magic, attacking us as we try to save her.

I only manage a few hours of sleep.

When morning comes, Sefella is nowhere to be seen, and El looks almost forlorn. As we pack up camp, I try again to break through the wall she's put up between us. This distance, after all the things we've been through and the way I thought we'd grown closer, is starting to hurt. Like maybe I was wrong to allow this to happen in the first place.

"El?" I say. "Are you okay? You haven't seemed like yourself since…well, since that stone."

She barely glances at me. "Fine, Lox. I'm fine."

I glance at the mountains ahead of us, their peaks covered in a brilliant layer of white. "Are you? Did you…did you know Sef is Sefella? Before the stone, I mean. You didn't seem surprised is all, and I thought…"

"You thought I'd throw a tantrum?" She looks at me now, her expression tortured.

My heart twists. I've never seen her look this way, like something is physically hurting her. Whatever she told me, she is *not* fine. I don't answer her, merely pressing my lips together, watching her.

She sighs. "I figured it out. Back around the caves. And if I'm honest… I'm starting to change my mind about…about the priestesses."

"I could have guessed that much," I say, "after what you told me in the city. You seemed angry at what they'd hidden from me. From us."

She blinks rapidly, looking down at the remains of the campfire. "Okay, not just the priestesses, then. Maybe...maybe I'm starting to doubt...that Ivlene..."

She stops there, as if unable to make herself finish the thought. But I can guess.

Like me, she's losing her faith in Ivlene.

My eyes burn with unshed tears, and my heart lurches again with the pain of what she's going through, of remembered pain at what I went through years ago with this same revelation: Ivlene is not who we were told.

I rush forward, grabbing her in a hug, and she hugs me back. I close my eyes, trying to let my touch tell her how much I value her, how grateful I am for what she shared with me.

Finally, we pull apart and finish breaking down camp. It's time to be on our way. There is a fragility around El that keeps me watching her, that makes me want to pull her back to me and protect her from what's hurting her, but she needs to figure things out for herself.

It doesn't matter how many times you tell a person something; they still have to figure it out on their own.

I stick close by El as we continue toward the mountains. The rain is nothing but mist, just enough to keep a chill in the air. The rocky terrain begins ascending the mountains, and we draw our oilskins tightly around our shoulders, hoping they will offer some protection from the dropping temperature as well as the rains. Sefella has been nowhere to be seen all morning, and I wonder if she is giving us time to think, to adjust, to accept who and what she is. The magnitude of what we are doing with her, of helping her.

The rain shifts to light, feathery flakes of snow as the day passes, something we only rarely saw in Limutria, and we find ourselves building the next night's camp quickly just to keep from freezing to death after the day's exertion. The cold doesn't seem to bother Teklari much, but I can feel how hot her blood runs in her veins.

The next day, I spot straight lines and squares jutting from the top of one of the mountain peaks ahead of us. Buildings.

"Look!" I say, pointing.

El follows my finger, and a smile spreads across her face. "We made it. It's here. It's real!"

I eye the path up the mountain, a narrow and steep trail covered in loose gravel and ice. "We haven't made it yet."

We cast one last look at the mountaintop temple, then turn around the edge of the cliffs and step onto the trail.

The side of the mountain falls away quickly to our right, dropping down to jagged rocks and small pools of water. Snow flies in our faces, more intense than it had been yesterday, and frost forms on our hair and eyelashes. But at least we don't have the rain to soak us through anymore. Just cold.

Such deep cold.

I slide on a patch of ice, and gravel skitters across the ground to fall down the cliff next to us. I slip along with it, until Teklari's teeth and El's hands catch my elbows. My heart is in my throat, pounding with fear at my near death as I pull myself back to my feet and glance over my shoulder down the side of the mountain.

I can't even hear the rocks hit the ground.

I take a deep breath, relieved Teklari and El caught me, and re-center myself before following El up the path.

The closer we come to the ridge connecting this peak to the peak holding the temple, the narrower the path becomes until we must walk in a line like ducklings. The path leaves the safety of the mountain, and the wall drops off so that we walk on a bridge of land. Snow swirls about us on a stiff wind, and that same wind pushes us, threatening to throw us off the mountain. Several times, I think I see Sefella in front of us now, leading the way without really leading us.

The path now is at least apparent. Impossible to miss.

The path eventually becomes razor thin, but El pushes forward seemingly without fear, arms stretching out to her sides.

"I'm going to try to subdue the wind!" she yells over the gusts.

I nod. She closes her eyes, arms stretched wide as if inviting the wind for an embrace. It dances and twirls about her, and I can see sparks of magic flying from her skin into the air. I pray to Sefella that El can do this. I don't relish the thought of crossing the path before us with the wind trying to drag us to our deaths.

The wind pushes out away from El, and I feel the edge of it pass through me, behind me, until the three of us stand in a bubble of still air.

She did it!

I am relieved and proud and excited for her all at once, and I can't help smiling in her direction. She catches it and sends a small, shaky smile back.

I am still terrified by the drop-off on either side. I try not to look, heart pounding, and force my attention to remain on El. My long, curly hair drops over my face and into my eyes, suddenly released by the wind, and I shove it back behind my ears. El's gauzy dress stills around her, and she brings her arms in, lowering her chin and turning to face me.

"I can hold it for a bit," she says, "but I don't know how long. Go!"

Without waiting for an answer, she turns to the path and takes her first step out onto the knife's edge of the trail. Shaking, I follow. I feel Teklari on my heels, and I send the wolf feelings of gratitude, of calm, of determination, urging her to follow my steps.

We are going to make it.

My courage wavers the farther we venture out over the path. It seems to stretch on forever in front of us, and behind us already seems just as far. One small step to the left or right and we fall. If El loses control of the wind, we fall. One stumble—we fall.

I swallow, blinking back my fear, and focus on placing one foot in front of the other.

Then, El's foot slips on a loose rock. The rock careens down the side of the mountain, and El follows it, sliding and scraping along. The wind returns with full force, much stronger than it had been on the other end of this land bridge, and I drop to the ground reflexively.

A shower of rocks accompanies El as she plunges. I grope about with my Singing, searching for something to grab, to pull, to stop her descent to death. But the mountain is loose and hard to catch.

There!

A vein of quartz. I grab it with my Song, and it thrusts out of the side of the mountain to form a ledge beneath El. She slams into it and tumbles along the glittering ledge.

And rolls off.

My heart flutters into my throat, panic filling me. I grasp for another vein, a bit of foothold, anything, and come up with bits of fluorite. I call them, and small spires of pink and green crystal shoot out and catch El's feet.

She stops, and we both breathe a momentary sigh of relief. She's still not safe, but at least she isn't falling anymore.

I check the integrity of the fluorite, worried that her weight will crack it, but it seems intact. For now. I can't let her fall. I won't lose her, not after everything. I can't lose my sister. Even the thought sends red-hot bolts of fear through me, overpowering the love I feel for her, love that has grown stronger with each passing day.

Pushed back to action by my fear, I cup a hand around my mouth, lying flat on the path and reaching my head over the edge. "Climb!"

She nods, fear dancing in her eyes, and I listen for more crystal I can use. One after another, I create ledges and footholds, and El follows my trail. Quartz, fluorite, selenite, minerals I know, minerals I've never heard of. And little by little, she makes her way back to me.

As soon as she's within arm's reach, Teklari and I haul her up.

We lay flat on the path for several minutes huffing and panting, Teklari between us. The wind whistles across our heaving bodies. Neither of us speaks for several long minutes until our breathing slows and our hearts calm from racing to a steady, strong pulse. My terror slowly subsides, and I reach for her, still exhausted. Her pinky curls around mine, and I let my eyes flutter closed for a moment, just grateful she's okay.

Finally, I lean up on one elbow and crane my neck to look at my sister. "Think you can do that again?"

She rolls onto her side and looks up at me. "What, fall?"

I almost laugh. I would have, if I wasn't still terrified of just that. "No, hold back the wind."

She closes her eyes and lets her head fall back onto the path, highlighting the hollows in her cheeks, the dark shadows under her eyes. Her face is pinched, and I realize I haven't seen her laugh in days. I can't even remember if I've seen a smile.

This exile has taken a huge toll on both of us, but I suddenly wonder just how difficult it has been for her in particular. A pang of guilt stabs my gut. Could I have stopped our exile, all our losses, if I'd just forced her to deal with her magic? Forced her to learn?

Could this be partly my fault, too?

After a few seconds of silence, she pushes herself to her knees. The wind whips past her, and she sways with the gusts. My heart somersaults as I watch her body move back and forth with the wind, waiting for the gust that pushes her back over.

But instead, she raises her arms again, and the same display of sparks and whorls fills my vision. The wind subsides, and she rises to her feet slowly, one foot and then the other. And just like that, El leads us across the land bridge to the other side.

The tension begins to melt from my muscles, fear loosening its grip on me. We sigh in relief and lean against the rock face of the far peak. We made it.

After sharing a triumphant look with El and scratching Teklari's ruff to comfort her, I turn to the path. It takes us about ten minutes to make it around the bend, but then the temple comes into full view.

Across only one more valley lies a bright white stone temple. It is divided into several large buildings, all situated at different levels on the mountain. Vast balconies stretch along the end of the cliff, looking out over the misty valleys below while snow swirls like glitter falling from fluffy steel clouds.

Over the valley between us and the temple stretches a wide stone bridge. We glance at each other and approach. It appears sturdy, though ancient, and is composed of gray and pink granite.

Two pillars flank the entrance to the bridge, made of tourmaline, and I catch my breath as I hear the Song.

Tourmaline is a rarity in Limutria; this is the first I've heard it Sing. The columns are hexagonal towers of transparent teal and purple as tall as I am, almost like the fluorite I called forth earlier. But unlike fluorite, tourmaline is sturdy, closer to quartz, and more suited to last over time.

Beyond the bridge, I hear more tourmaline, along with a chorus of other crystals and gems Singing from the temple. And somewhere across this bridge, Mom may be waiting.

El takes her first steps forward onto the carefully cut granite, and I step up next to her. Teklari joins us with a tinkling of her crystals, and we make our final approach.

Thirty-Two

ELODIE

In the evening, the world grows dark. But morning always rises, bringing the light and life of Ivlene.

Excerpt from *The Records of Bright*

I almost can't breathe, too full of awe as the details of the temple come into view.

Mom could be here. And after twenty years, my feelings are a jumble I didn't expect, a mix of excitement and apprehension, anger and hope.

Loxy can't keep her eyes off the beautiful crystal columns that stand guard on each end of the beautifully-engineered bridge, and the look of joy on her face—happiness I haven't seen since the mineral springs at Montalo—leads me to keep silent. Maybe it's all going to be okay now, once we cross into that temple.

Every step brings us closer to a place we weren't even sure still stood. I don't know if all the stories are true, if they really do accept magic, but looking at it, I can believe it. The white walls shine bright in the gloomy light of day, and the roof is a bright turquoise color I've never seen in buildings. As we approach, it becomes clearer that the white stone of the temple wall is actually a mix of granite, crystal, and alabaster, as well as white tiles with a rainbow sheen that shifts with every step. Carved reliefs run along the wall parallel to the ground, depicting legends of the Bright Ones and the history of Nasmarya in such artistic beauty that I trip on the temple's first marble step.

No, not the step. An array of crystals sprouting from the marble. Some of them are broken, some singed black. My heart stutters, body growing cold. Maybe it's just a natural formation, but the soot…what would cause that?

I glance over at Loxy as dread grows in my gut. Something isn't right here. She shrugs, but her eyebrows knit together as she examines the broken spires glimmering in the daylight.

At the top of the steps stands a pair of large wooden doors. There is no knocker, but crystal spire handles that match the columns on the bridge are set into the wood with brass. I wrap my hands around them, though they are so wide that my fingers are an inch from touching.

I take a breath, looking at my sister and the wolf again, then push the doors. When they don't budge, Loxy steps forward, and we both put our shoulders into it. The doors scrape along the marble floor, finally opening into an airy corridor overlooking an overgrown courtyard. Massive columns line the wide corridors and arched ceilings, but some of them are cracked or collapsed on the ground, more of the singed and broken crystals sprouting from the stone. A smell of abandonment, that musty odor of mold and dirt, permeates the corridor.

And it's so quiet. The wind sweeps through the emptiness, setting sparkling crystal chandeliers to ringing two stories above our heads. Though it is slightly warmer here than it had been on the other side of the doors, I rub at my arms to ward off the chill.

"What happened here?" I breathe, heart pounding.

Loxy doesn't answer, seemingly frozen in place while Teklari tucks herself against my sister's side, ears down and tail tucked between her legs.

I take a few hesitant steps deeper into Cliffreach…or what used to be Cliffreach. The wind whips against my gown, and I can almost hear the cries of more ghosts carried along with it. The dread that began on the steps continues to fill me as I take each step closer to the courtyard, then cross into the tall grass. It rustles against my steps. I'm not sure where I'm going, not sure what we are going to do if this place is as abandoned as it seems.

What had I really hoped to find here? Kindred spirits, all deep in their religious pursuits? Mom?

Whatever I expected doesn't matter now, though. It's too quiet, too empty, for anyone to still roam these halls. Did Mom ever come here at all?

Disappointment fills my chest, squeezing me tight amid the dread at what we've found. Maybe…maybe I *was* excited to see Mom again. And maybe I was excited to find people who might teach me more about this magic that I actually like having.

I blink in surprise at the thought, still not used to the joy and pride my Singing brings me.

What else will we find here, if it's abandoned now?

A silent fountain stands in the center of the courtyard, the Bright Ones—both Ivlene and Sefella—standing atop it in tarnished silver. I kick something and look down, peering through the stalks of grass and weeds, then gasp and stumble backwards until my legs strike the edge of the fountain. Two empty eye sockets stare up at me from the ground, crystals spiking across the top of the skull and along the dirt in a line, as if they'd sprouted there. The rest of the skeleton peeks through the dirt and overgrowth, splayed out behind the skull, more crystals poking through the bones.

My breaths turn to wheezing, heart pounding in my chest with blossoming fear and realization. The crystals outside, the ones here, none of it is natural.

It was Singing. The Singing that they embraced and welcomed into their temple, the Singers they accepted and helped. The very ones they protected turned on them, killed them, destroyed this place of peace and sanctuary.

This is what Singing did to these people. And Sefella is to blame, is she not?

I was right the first time: Singing is a curse, better gone and forgotten. Too dangerous to hold onto, too unpredictable to control.

How long will it be until Loxy or I lose control? Who will be around when it happens? Who will be the next to die?

Why couldn't the goddesses just leave us all alone, fight their fights without involving us, without inflicting us with such a curse as Singing?

My heart thrums within me, and I press a hand over it, my breath coming in gasps. I turn toward the fountain, trying to block out the destruction those crystals wrought on whoever that poor person had once been. But even the fountain can't save me from the sight; the water, though tinged green with algae, holds two more skeletons arrayed across the stones at the bottom. Large crystal spires poke through the surface of the water, disrupting the few lily pads and water flowers that had managed to grow despite the chill in the air.

I clap my hands over my mouth and stumble back toward Loxy, tears brimming in my eyes.

Cliffreach wasn't abandoned. It was attacked. There is no other explanation. If Mom ever came here, either she found the bones of a once-great temple, or…

Or she was the one who killed it.

And we know Sefella had at least some part in it, and probably Ivlene, too.

I turn my tear-filled eyes to Loxy, my sweet, determined sister. She will never accept that Mom could have done something like this, that Singing really is dangerous. The priestesses were right all along, that magic corrupts everything it touches. But Loxy will simply explain it away, try to protect the mother who abandoned us, who may not even be our mother anymore.

Whoever controls her now may be even worse.

"What is it?" Loxy says, stepping toward me. Teklari slinks after my sister.

I can only shake my head, my throat tight. The image of the crystals protruding from bones, of the empty eyes staring at me…it wasn't like this in the Glass City. There were no bodies there.

But here…how many dead will we find? How many destroyed?

"El?" Loxy says hesitantly.

Oh, goddesses. The crystals. What if Loxy is turning into a crystal monster? What if *I* am headed there, too? How many people will we destroy before someone finally kills us?

Peace, comes the voice—Sefella's.

Peace? How can I have peace in such a place, and from *Sefella*? After everything she's told us, after what's happened here because of her and her twin? I was supposed to be a priestess, entrusted with the care of all humanity. How can I have peace when so many have been lost in this place because of the goddess I once swore to serve?

Peace, she says again, voice laced with calm, with grace. Despite myself, my heart slows its gallop, and I let my eyes flutter closed as I struggle to breathe. Loxy's arms wrap around me, and, after a moment, I hug her back, letting her comfort me, drinking in the warmth of her.

She, at least, is alive.

For now.

After a few moments, my breath steadies and I pull back. I wrap my cloak more tightly about my shoulders and turn toward one of the branching corridors. "We should probably find somewhere to spend the night. Somewhere...somewhere untouched by death."

Loxy hesitates. "What do you mean?"

I chew my lip, taking a few steps forward, not slowing until I hear Loxy and Teklari behind me. "They're dead, Lox. That's why no one's heard from Cliffreach. They're all dead."

She hurries her steps until she walks next to me. "Dead? How?"

I step over part of a broken column, my breath hitching with apprehension, revulsion. Loxy isn't going to like this. "It looks like...Crystallosinging."

Her steps stutter, but she recovers quickly. "But this is supposed to be a haven for Singing. For Singers. How could something like that happen?"

I blink at the tears again, anger rising in my chest. Isn't this what we'd been warned about our entire lives? Isn't this the very reason the Bright One calls us to heal those afflicted?

I can't contain myself any longer. "I don't know, Lox. But I told you. Everyone warned us. Everyone. And yet here we are, and for all we know, we could be the next ones to destroy a village or a temple or a city! Just like all those others!"

Loxy follows me through the rubble, picking her way around the largest debris. She presses her lips together, avoiding looking at me for what seems like eons. Finally, she says, "Do you really still think that? After all this? All we've been through together, all we've accomplished? Do you really think you could be lost like whoever *might* have destroyed this place? I thought by now you had more faith in us."

My steps slow, and a tear trickles down my cheek. It's true I had been starting to accept this new part of myself, to understand the draw of the power.

But no one should have so much power. It's too dangerous, too much of a temptation. "I…"

She rests a hand on my shoulder gently, turning me toward her. "I know you don't think that, not anymore."

I swipe at my eyes and stride forward again, lifting my skirts over part of a fallen ceiling, refusing to answer her. She's not ready to hear the truth. So why try?

We pick our way through the rubble of the corridor, neither of us uttering another word, until we find an area of the temple apparently untouched by the violence that had erupted here. A light breeze sweeps through, carrying the clean mountain air somehow.

I take another deep breath, calming further as I breathe in the fresher air of this corridor.

Though coated in dust and frost at the edges, this part of the corridor is clear of debris, clear of death. Wood doors stand closed along our left side, the other wall full of open, arched windows overlooking the valley and snow-capped mountains. A few flurries still float in the sky, and the sun is nearly below the peaks now, though it is mostly hidden behind clearing clouds.

Loxy makes her way to the nearest door, reaching for the crystal knob. It sparkles in the fading daylight, on fire with the red sun. The door is made of simple wood planks, and they still seem largely intact, protected as they probably were this far into the temple. Loxy pushes the door open and steps inside, and cautiously, I follow her.

Please, Ivlene, if you still care anything about us… Do not let this room contain yet more death.

The room is so similar to the guest rooms in Limutria's temple that I almost start crying again. The walls are made of the same white stone and rainbow tile as outside, but they are softly draped with satin and organza, now torn and faded. A few tapestries, also faded, hang around the room, depicting various myths and religious stories, and every few feet, glass globes protrude from the stone. At one time, they were likely lamps, but now they hang cold and dark. Directly across from the door, a massive window looks out over the snowy mountain range. It is covered in glass, holding back the cold wind that howls through the rest of the temple.

Other than the elegantly decorated walls, the room is simple, designed to promote study and tranquility. Two wide beds draped with blue quilts mirror each other, set on either side of the window that has a small table beneath it. A short bookshelf stands next to the door, near a writing desk filled with enough parchment, ink, and pens to fill a thousand texts. An open door stands between the desk and the bed, and I peek in to see a washroom. Finally, a small table with two chairs sits in the center of the room, empty except for a dark lamp of what appears to be pink halite.

Does the lamp affect Loxy? Would it, if its glow were active?

I glance over at my sister. She is absorbed in studying the room, touching the lamps and fabric draping the walls, running her hand over the bedspread and leaving clean trails in the dirt coating everything.

We could sleep here. Just maybe not on those beds.

"This seems as good a place as any," I say.

Loxy shivers. "But it's so cold."

It's as if our voices, or perhaps our presence, triggers something in the room. A warm breeze begins drifting down from the ceiling, and I trace it back to vents. Dust comes out with the air at first, but at least it's warm.

And the lights. All the globes on the walls and the salt lamp on the table begin to glow with soft light.

Is this place itself magic? It would make sense, given its reputation as a haven for Singers. I bite my lip, staring at all the place magic seems to have touched. That *Singing* seems to have touched. Indications that magic was at least once used for something useful, something life-giving.

Perhaps Loxy has been partly right. Even I, a new Singer, can feel the buzz of the electricity buzzing through the lamps, can feel the prickle of magic against my skin.

I shudder and cross the room. I strip the quilt from one of the beds, sending up clouds of dirt. Surprisingly, underneath the quilt the mattress appears clean and intact. This room must have been sealed well enough to protect it from damage from the elements or pests.

Loxy copies me, throwing off the quilt on the other side and leaving it in a heap at the foot of the bed. Then, she sits on the mattress and pats the space next to her. Teklari only hesitates a moment before jumping up next to her with a tinkling like windchimes, turning in a few circles, then settling her head on her paws as if she's always lived here.

I walk across the room to the opposite bed and drop my pack on the floor next to Loxy's. Eyeing the lights, a thought drifts into my head. "I saw a tub in there. Do you think it works now? I mean, the lights are all on now. Maybe the water works the same?"

Loxy shrugs. "One way to find out."

She follows me to the washroom, and we turn the spigot on the tub. For a moment, nothing happens. Then, cool, clear water gushes from the spout, blasting at the grime on the stone basin. After a moment, the water warms just as the air in the room had.

I catch my breath. A bath. I could have a real bath!

Exhaustion falls on me suddenly, and I slump against the stone. Loxy walks back into the room, then reappears with a bar of soap and one of the cloths we had wrapped food in. Wordlessly, she begins scrubbing at the stone until it's as clean as a bar of soap can make it.

If I ever see the priest from Ryth Hollow again, I owe him so much.

Loxy stands, leaving the soap on the ledge of the tub, and gestures at the flowing water. "You first, sister dear. You stink."

The joke is just like old, before…everything. Yet, I see compassion in her eyes. She hadn't seen what I did in the courtyard, and she is giving me a chance to compose myself.

When did my little sister grow up so much?

I smile weakly up at her, the warmth of her compassion pushing back my heavy soul, my fear, my uncertainty over what to do now. "I'll be quick. Then you can have a turn."

She laughs. "I'll bathe after you, but I'd like to find something to eat anyway. Even if it is more jerky. Bright Ones, I'm tired of smelling like fish!"

I smile, a mischievous glint in my eye. I still feel heavy with sadness, but I try to match her banter, to keep my words light if nothing else. Like in Limutria on the rare times we actually got along...well, *mostly* got along. "You think now is the only time you smell?"

She laughs again, her expression clearing, though I can still see the wrinkles in her forehead that say she's worried underneath it. My own smile widens. I haven't seen her laugh so much, look so light, in a long time. Much longer than our exile, in fact.

Did she laugh this much with Audrey? I hope so.

She returns to the bedroom, closing the door behind her, and I strip off my dress and sink into a warm bath, hot enough to melt every last bit of my pain from me.

For now.

Thirty-Three

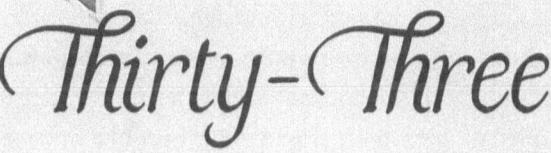

LOXY

The seas may dry, the rains may cease, but the salt always remains.

Nasmaryan proverb

I close the washroom door behind me softly, still unable to believe whatever facilities this place has are still working. Lights? Heat? And water? Amazing!

Yet, I can't relax, can't settle in for the night. El said everyone is dead, that a Crystallosinger—like me—killed them. But how can that possibly be?

I need to know. There's so much I needed to learn here, and now everyone is just…dead? How? Why?

My stomach is sick as I think of something else: what if Mom is among the bodies? Or, almost worse, what if she was the one who killed them all? I can't imagine El would ever just let something like that go. It's been hard enough simply getting her to search for Mom with me.

I have to know. I have to at least try to learn the truth, before El has a chance to make her judgement.

I hurry toward the corridor, keeping my steps light so El won't hear me. "Come on," I whisper to Teklari.

She jumps off the bed with a sigh, then pads after me. I slip into the hall, the wolf on my heels. We turn away from the entrance—and the bodies—and make our way deeper into the temple. We pass many closed doors, just like the one where we found the guest room. But there are also plenty of open doors, and I peer in as we make our way past each one. One looks like a dining room or cafeteria, a few are shrine rooms occasionally holding broken shrines, quiet study rooms, lounge areas. But then a large arched doorway rises before us, commanding my attention.

Through the doorway, towering shelves coated in dust hold thousands upon thousands of tomes and scrolls. A library? An archive?

I step through the door, one hand on Teklari's back as if I can keep her crystals silent by mere touch. It's so quiet here, almost too quiet. Even Teklari's soft tinkling seems too much. We glide inside, and I look around, though I'm not really sure what I'm looking for.

Where is Sefella now? I would love a little explanation from her.

The air is stale in here, like it was in the guest room, heavy with the scents of dust and mildew. Motes dance in the fading light, pouring in through narrow, towering windows on all sides. I walk to the nearest shelf, running my finger over the spines, taking in their subjects. It seems to be a section on the priesthood, each shelf holding a different discipline.

But there are so many more disciplines than what we had in Limutria. Bards, historians, astronomers. It just goes on and on.

My fingers leave trails in the dust, but I can't keep from touching the massive knowledge enshrined here. I am struck by the enormity of it all. And of how small Limutria is in comparison.

If these people were still alive now, what would they say? Would they agree with Cydia, that Singing is an abomination? Or were they truly as accepting as the priest in Ryth Hollows said? As accepting as the magic that fills this place seems to indicate?

I look out the towering windows again. There isn't much light left, certainly not enough to start looking at everything here. I would have to start fresh in the morning. Reluctantly, I turn from the stacks and shelves and tap my thigh to call Teklari.

"C'mon, girl," I say softly, leading her out into the corridor.

We continue away from the guest room, following the gentle curve of the hallway past the expanse of the library, past more closed rooms. Ahead, near the next turn, soft, fading daylight shimmers on the floor, catching bits of crystal quartz in the tiles. We round the curve, and I catch my breath.

Before us, the temple opens to a large field of swaying grasses. The field is entirely surrounded by the inner walls of the temple and smaller buildings and sheds. The air here is still warmer than what it had been outside, on the path here. There's not even a hint of the frost that rimed sections of the temple we'd already passed through. Could magic be keeping this all alive? Protecting it from the cold of the mountains?

But it's not the field itself, filled with flowers and statues and towering pillars of fluorite, that draws me up short. It's the water horses grazing peacefully. There's an entire band of them, each in varying shades of pale slate blue with misty white manes and tails. The wind shifts, and the sulfurous scent of the sea washes over me.

It's almost like being back at the stables at home. We had a few water horses there, mighty creatures with fierce spirits and strong constitutions. They are mostly used for carrying messages between Limutria and Aeglora, their feet as swift as a rainstorm. And of course, there are wild water horses roaming the sea.

How are they here? Why? Did the temple keep them for transportation?

The far side of the field is lower on the slope than this side of the temple, and something glimmers over the last mountains. I narrow my eyes against the glare, reluctantly pulling my gaze away from the horses.

It's the Sea.

The Sea we spent days—maybe more than a week—trekking through until we were constantly soaked, abandoned and alone, not even shoes to protect our feet. Where the Water Dragon hurt me. Where Audrey's loss was fresh.

Where our entire journey began, one filled with pain and strife and fear.

My heart hammers, and I take a step back, my peace shattered. The Sea was my home, but it also did its best to kill us. Am I afraid?

"This isn't what I wanted for Singers," Sefella says, suddenly appearing beside me. "To be feared. To lose themselves." She turns toward me. Tears glimmer in her eyes again. "I just want you all safe. Safe from each other. Safe from…from Ivlene."

She reaches a hand out, as if to touch my cheek, but I stumble backwards. Something crunches underfoot, and I shift my boot, peering into the grass. A broken pile of bones that was once a hand pokes up from the dirt. Just behind it, as if the hand sheltered its owner, a skull crusted in glittering scarlet crystals stares up at me.

I scream, and the horses bolt away from me.

Thirty-Four

ELODIE

A kind smile, a warm meal, and a night well spent are the blessings of the Bright Ones upon weary travelers.

Excerpt from *The Records of Bright*

The warm water is making me drowsy. It's taken at least half an hour for my thoughts to calm from their frantic circling into something I can work with, and the facts strut through my head now.

One: we made it to Cliffreach.

Two: Cliffreach is dead.

Three: a Singer destroyed the people here.

But now I am left to ponder who would have done such a thing. And if Mom came here all that time ago—really, it is impossible to say how long ago, other than within the last twenty years—did she escape?

The other possibility chills me despite the bath, and I shudder. If she did come here and if she did escape Cliffreach alive, it's only because she was the killer.

I sigh and sink deeper into the water. Loxy will not handle that idea well. We're finally getting along, finally a team, finally the sisters we were always meant to be. If I tell her my suspicions, it could ruin everything.

I don't want to screw it up. I've done enough of that to scar Loxy for the rest of her life.

My eyes are heavy, and they begin to drift closed. The water cradling me is too warm, too peaceful, after the stress and exertion of the road.

A scream pierces the air, echoing from down the hall, and I bolt upright in the tub. Water sloshes everywhere, but it doesn't matter.

That scream was Loxy. And she definitely is not in the bedroom anymore.

I pull myself up and out, slipping on the slick tile floor. I call a wind to blow the water off my body until I am merely damp, then throw my dress back over my head as I run from the guest room.

The hall is almost completely dark now, the daylight nearly gone. I glance back and forth, unsure which way she went. Teklari's bark echoes down the corridor from the left, away from the collapsed pillars and crystallized skeletons, and I spin on my toes, taking off after them.

I fly past so many doors, open and closed, past a large arched doorway, toward the screams, finally sliding onto a portico overlooking a vast field.

Loxy stands nearby, hand over her heart, eyes closed. Teklari growls toward the field, but all I see is a band of wild water horses in the distance.

"Loxy?" I gasp. "What's wrong? Are you hurt?"

She jumps, eyes darting toward me, but visibly begins to calm as she sees me. "I think I found more of what you saw."

"What?"

"Bodies in the field."

I nod and bend forward, resting my hands on my knees. She's fine. Everything's fine. As fine as it can be, staying here in a temple of the dead. I'm relieved she's fine, but angry, too, that she wandered off while I couldn't protect her.

That she found the very thing I have been trying to figure out how to talk to her about.

I straighten again, irritated at her, irritated at what I'm going to have to say soon. "Glad you're okay. Can you stop wandering off now? I'm tired, Lox."

She gives me a shaky smile. "Yeah. Let's get some rest."

"Just wait until you see it," Loxy says over her shoulder, leading me down the corridor from last night.

We haven't spoken much since then. I couldn't make myself bring up my suspicions to her, and she hasn't seemed to want to talk about it, either. I thought I saw Sefella with her last night, by the field, but she disappeared before I caught up to Loxy.

And now both of us are trying to pretend things are normal, that this is some big adventure to have instead of a killing field. At least for a little longer.

My stomach clenches in apprehension over the conversation I know is coming, but I'm not ready yet. Not ready to fight again, to risk the fragile relationship we've been rebuilding. So instead, when she said she found a library, I told her I wanted to see it.

Loxy's feigned excitement is contagious, and I hurry along beside her. We approach the large arched doorway, and my breath catches as the enormity of the collection comes into view.

She wasn't kidding. This is more than I ever could have hoped to find in my lifetime. Greater by far than Limutria's meager archives. And those archives are closed to all except the temple, so Loxy could never have hoped to snoop through them at home.

The shelves reach all the way to the ceiling, as far up as at the entrance to the temple. Ladders reach up to platforms between the two levels, situated on rollers to move along the shelves. There are tomes and scrolls filling every available space, dust dancing in the air around them. Study alcoves line the walls on either side of the door, and tinted windows, just dark enough to protect the contents of the room, span the far wall, letting the morning sun stream through and throw everything into golden light.

"Wow," I breathe.

"Right?" Loxy says, beaming.

She doesn't wait for me to answer. Teklari close on her heels, she hurries deep into the stacks, leaving me to find my own way.

What is she hoping to find here?

I sigh and turn to the right. Alcoves line my right side, shelves on my left, and I wander just to take it all in. I don't know what I'm looking for either. But surely this place holds the answers to countless mysteries.

I slow as another thought comes to mind. Maybe this place also holds the secrets of Sefella talking in my head. Maybe there's something here that can tell us the truth about the goddesses. I'm not sure if I can trust what Sefella says, especially with what's happened here, and I *don't* trust Ivlene anymore, not after how much the priestesses have decided to hide from everyone. I'm just not sure why it never bothered me this much before.

I leave Loxy to herself and take a renewed interest in my surroundings. The alcoves are mostly empty, other than stacks of books and towers of scrolls. The shelves are labeled by discipline, ranging from ancient history to medicine to philosophy.

A sharp, acrid scent suddenly hits my nose, and my steps falter. It is familiar, a singed scent of charcoal. Curious, apprehensive, I follow the smell, searching for its source past more shelves and alcoves.

I pass the wall separating two of the alcoves and slide to a sudden stop. This alcove isn't empty, not by a long shot. A crystallized skeleton slumps over the table, the wall and seat and table itself charred.

I am more prepared for it this time. Rather than scream, I merely catch my breath, steeling myself against the violent sight.

Something yellow-white pokes out from beneath the skeleton's arm, and I inch closer, trying to get a better look without touching the body. A book lies open on the table, neat Nasmaryan script filling the page.

With a glance at the empty eye sockets of the body, I reach for the corner of the book and pull it toward me. The skeleton rattles, the crystals chiming, and as the arm releases the book, the bones collapse with a clatter. I freeze for a moment, heart thudding.

"El?" Loxy calls from somewhere in the library. "You okay?"

"Yeah," I call back, eyes still on the book. "Just knocked something over."

She doesn't ask more, and I finish pulling the book free. A black quill flutters to the ground, landing amid the bones.

I take a deep breath and spin the book to face me, curious what the unfortunate priestess was studying when she met her untimely end. Her handwriting is easy to read, beautiful and flowing.

It does not disguise the ugly truths in the book.

I close the door softly behind me. Loxy is already making her way to her bed, as exhausted as I am, but for different reasons. She spent her day searching the stacks for Bright Ones knew what while I learned far more truth than I ever wanted to know.

My eyes are gritty, my bones ache with fatigue, and my body is cold. My fatigue, unlike hers, stems from the deep emotional turmoil raging inside me now. I should tell her, should share what I found. But I know she won't like it. She'll want to leave, to run after ghosts, after death.

And I am sure there are clues in that library to save us both, to cleanse the Singing from our bodies. The history of this place still leaves me cold. How can I keep this magic when this could be the end of it—death and destruction and hurting more people like Audrey?

I lower myself onto my bed opposite Loxy and start unlacing my boots. But eventually all the motions of preparing for bed are complete, and I have to either tell her now or commit to keeping secrets.

Which is more dangerous?

Truth is a weapon, comes Sefella's voice. *Or a medicine.*

I burrow into my blanket and turn on my side to look at her across the gap between beds. I don't want to hear Sefella's voice anymore. Not if this is the result.

Death.

Outside, flurries swirl through the air, their intensity increasing with my emotions. "Loxy, we need to talk."

She doesn't answer for a moment. When she does speak, her voice is strained with anxiety. "About what?"

Can she sense the devastating things I'm about to say?

"Our future. And…and our past, I suppose."

Worry passes across her face like clouds over the sun. "What about it?"

I pull the quilt up to my jaw, head engulfed by the fluffy pillow. "I found something while we were in the library today. It took me all day just to process what I'd read." It's my turn to hesitate. "I think…I think it would be best if we stopped searching for Mom. We could go to Aeglora now. It would be better, I promise. And you could even apprentice with a real healer, a physician. We could start over, just like you've always wanted."

She doesn't answer, as I'd hoped. It might be a low trick for me to play that card, to tempt her with her dreams. But even Aeglora, with its own dangers, would be better than pursuing Mom after what I'd read.

Better than dying for a fallen goddess.

Her jaw flexes in the dim snowy light as she clenches and unclenches her teeth. "Can't you just help me find Mom and then we can go to Aeglora?"

I sigh. She's as stubborn as ever. I shouldn't use what I'm about to say—it is certainly a weapon in my hands—but for once, Loxy needs to accept the truth. My voice is colder than I intend. "We don't know that we'll ever find her, Loxy. I found something out today. About Mom."

"What about her?" I can see the suspicion lighting Loxy's eyes now.

"I found a record. About the Burning Rains twenty years ago. Mom wasn't the only one to develop Singing, but she was unique."

"What do you mean?"

"Most of the other Singers, at least the ones who weren't killed right away, still had control of themselves. Mom—Volta Shayde—she wasn't like a person anymore. It was slow, progressive. When she arrived here—"

"When was that?" Loxy cut in.

"It didn't say. But she was unable to understand half of the conversations the priests and priestesses held with her. They didn't understand what was wrong. And it just kept getting worse, the Singing slowly taking over all her rational thought, worse than what Sefella said.

"And even worse, when she finally lost herself, they could see the mark of Sefella on her. And the book I found—"

"What book?"

"I found a priestess's journal. She was chronicling everything. Mom…Mom killed all these people, Lox. And if she's still out there, somewhere, I don't think we will ever really have her back. I think…I think Sefella had something to do with it. I think we may still have a chance though. I had a feeling there was something here that could cleanse us, make us normal again. We can find it. Fix ourselves. Then we can go. Forget the whole thing. We need to move on with our lives already, let Mom's memory stay a good one, and keep ourselves away from a war between literal *goddesses*."

The voice of Sefella doesn't intrude into my head, but I wonder what Loxy is hearing. I wonder if Sefella is listening to me now. I shiver, afraid of what a goddess could do to me.

But protecting Loxy is more important to me than a goddess's wrath.

Loxy stares at me, silently, her face blank and devoid of expression for a minute, before it slowly morphs into anger. Hatred.

"How dare you," she says, her voice barely above a whisper. "How dare you use Mom like this, just so you can get your own way. Is this why you really wanted to come here? To try *again* to 'cleanse' me? Us?"

I sigh, tired and resigned to this argument. "Loxy, I'm telling you the truth. There may be nothing left for us to find. Between what I read and what Sefella said…"

"We should at least try." Tears glimmer in her eyes. "We can always start over. Haven't we done that already? There's time for us. After we know for sure. My Singing isn't a curse, and I don't want to lose it."

"Are you so sure about that?" I feel my frustration rising now. "Loxy, you don't know whether we have time. I can't tell you, and you can't tell me. We have no way of knowing whether the power that claimed Mom is coming for us, too. What's the point? But if we search the library, give up this insane rescue mission… Maybe we can still be saved."

She doesn't answer, just stares at me with those tear-filled eyes. "Lox. Please."

Her voice is carefully controlled and calm when she answers. There is a bitterness underlying her words worse than anything she's said since we left Limutria. "You would just give up on her…on *us*…that quickly? You're so selfish! I thought you finally understood, finally realized that Singing is a gift. That Sefella isn't bad. That the priestesses have lied to us all these years."

"Loxy—"

"No, Elodie. You don't get to tell me what to do anymore. Sometimes, my opinion matters, too. But you never seem to care about that. It's always about you and what you want. What *you* think is best. Well, here's a thought: you're not always right."

"Loxy, please—"

"I'm tired, Elodie." She rolls over to face the wall. Teklari shifts next to her, snuggling into the shape of her body. "And I'm *not* going to Aeglora. I'm *not* giving up my magic. And I *will* find Mom."

"Loxy—"

"Good night, Elodie."

I sigh. "Good night, Loxy."

I stare at the shape of her on the other side of the room, my heart breaking and tears slipping from my cheeks to my pillow. Our delicate peace, our new relationship…Cliffreach has spoiled both.

Sefella has done this. Her and her war with her own sister.

All I want is for us to be safe, together. But Loxy can never make things easy, can never stop and think logically for even a minute!

I slowly turn over to face the opposite wall, my heartbreak festering to anger, to fear. If Loxy won't listen to reason, she could end up just like Mom.

And nothing I do can stop it. And for once, I'm not going to help.

I won't help her destroy herself.

Thirty-Five

LOXY

Do not allow the ties that bind you to be severed.

Excerpt from *The Ballads of Sefella*

I stare into the darkness for at least an hour, seething, simmering, unable to calm myself enough to sleep even as Teklari snores next to me, unaware. I hear El shifting around for a while, but eventually even she drops off to sleep.

How could she be so selfish? Why do only her dreams matter? Even if Mom is overcome by magic, stolen by Sefella's twin, shouldn't that just be more reason to find her? Shouldn't we do whatever we can to help her? To find out the truth? We've spent our whole lives following the rules, following Ivlene, but if what we are learning here is true, we've been terribly misled.

Besides, El already destroyed one of my dreams. I'll probably never see Audrey again. How could she steal my hope of finding

Mom, too? How could she *still* want me to give up my magic, the one thing that makes me feel like I mean something in this world?

I have to know what it was she read. Where Mom went. See it all for myself.

Glancing at El's sleeping form again, I disentangle myself from my blanket and tiptoe toward the table. She left a stack of books there, and surely one of them is The Book. Mostly, they appear to be tomes about different disciplines, but one stands out among the others, its cover blackened by fire.

As quietly as possible, I remove the book from the stack and begin flipping through pages. This is definitely it; Mom's name stares up at me over and over again.

I can't remember her, not really. But I remember the pictures around the house, can still see the one portrait I had of her as clearly as if I held it now, and the pictures of a once happy family. Mom was beautiful, her head full of lively black curls like mine, her eyes a piercing green like mine and El's. But I always looked more like her, while El takes after Dad. And the older I grew, the more apparent this became. I could see it in how Dad interacted with me, how he went to every single one of El's temple events and gatherings, how he could barely stand to even look at me.

That's when the pictures started disappearing. Whenever I asked Dad about one, he would simply give me an excuse. And then he started avoiding me.

I'm not sure what hurt worse: the loss of Mom's memory or Dad's affection.

He continued doting on El, and as we grew older, she became more ashamed of me, too. She stopped inviting me to go anywhere with her. She stopped introducing me to people. She started explaining away my behavior, and my existence, by telling everyone

I was just the poor little sister who barely knew her mother. That it had somehow *affected* me. Half the rumors about me had been started by her. Up until then, she had been my only friend, my teacher, what Mom should have been.

My eyes scan the page before me, but I'm not really seeing the words there. Instead, I see the day El stopped being my best friend.

It was the dry season, the middle of a long, hot day when I was twelve. The Sea of Broken Glass was true to its name; instead of the enormous polished mirror of water, it was down to only an inch deep, leaving rills of salt separating puddles into millions of small mirrors, like shards of glass. Looking back now, it seems appropriate that we were surrounded by shards. They were a symbol of how she shattered our relationship.

She was already a priestess initiate, the step before an apprentice, and she and her fellow initiates were on a gathering mission in the flats. During the dry season, certain sea herbs are accessible that aren't easy to find during the rainy season, so Cydia would send the initiates to gather them.

As every little sister does, I ran after her into the flats, just wanting to be close to her, wanting to be like her.

She tried to ignore me, pretend I wasn't there. I saw her roll her eyes at me to her friends, the whispers behind their hands. Everything she did to impress her new colleagues.

She had started doing it so long ago that I didn't realize this day would be any different, that it would do more than just hurt my feelings for a few hours.

I ran after them, just off the walkways for a minute, and one of her friends stuck her foot out. I remember seeing it, remember the helplessness of knowing there was nothing I could do to stop my fall. I threw my arms up, and the salt dissolved away from its hills, allowing the seawater to run into a pool under me, to catch my fall.

The initiates stared like I had a disease. I knew I'd made a mistake, that no one was supposed to know I could control the salt. But in that moment of fear, the Singing had taken over to protect me.

I picked myself up out of the puddle, dripping silt and seawater, my dress ruined with mud. I could hear El making excuses for me, covering up my magic like she always did when I messed up. Shooting daggers at me with her sideways glances the entire time.

But for the love of Ivlene… I was just a *kid*. Kids make mistakes. Kids can't control their Singing. Not like I can now.

Or like I had been able to, until the Burning Rain.

She shooed the others forward, saying she'd get rid of me and catch up. Then she bent down next to me and whispered in my ear, anger pushing her words through me like barbs.

"Why are you such a freak? Can't you ever just be normal? This is why no one likes you. You can't even act like a real person for one day. I'm sick of cleaning up your messes!"

I could feel the words crushing me, could feel my face flame hot as tears pooled in my eyes. But crying would only embarrass me more, bring more shame to me, to El.

"Go home, Loxy. No one wants you here."

She turned her back to me and hurried to catch up to her friends, already smiling and laughing, uncaring of the glass she left splintered in my heart. I stood in that puddle of mud another five minutes, trying to stop crying before facing the people in town.

But that was also the day I'd met Audrey. At least, that was the day she became my truest and only friend.

Five minutes after El left, when she was barely a speck on the horizon, someone jumped down into the puddle next to me.

"Are you okay?" she said. "Loxy, isn't it?"

"I'm fine," I said, not turning to face her. If I turned, she would see my tears. And just like El, she would either scold me or laugh.

Her hand landed on my shoulder, and she gently pulled me to face her. She wiped a tear from my cheek. "Are you sure? People don't usually cry when they're fine."

I nodded, unable to speak.

She didn't say anything for a moment, didn't demand anything, didn't do anything. She seemed troubled, lost in thought. It's the only time I've ever seen her at a loss for words.

Then, she said, "Have you seen the new flowers in the apiary?"

The day my sister killed our friendship was the day my relationship with Audrey was planted. An ending and a beginning. A curse with a blessing. How many times do the bad things bring the good?

Will the same prove true for this exile?

A fat tear smacks the page below me, drawing me out of my stupor of memory. I sniff and blink back the rest of the tears, wiping at my face and the drop on the page. At least these books aren't that old. A single teardrop won't harm them.

Mid-swipe, I freeze, a presence next to me. I turn to see Sef, face sad.

"Are you ready now?" she whispers.

I glance over my shoulder one more time, looking at the sleeping form of my sister. The anger wells up again, rage at her words, her deception, her lies. Then I turn back to Sefella—the goddess of the Underworld, the other half of the Bright Ones, the balance to Ivlene—and nod.

I'm going, whether Elodie comes or not.

Thirty-Six

ELODIE

Look kindly upon us as we travel into the night. Be our protection when the Hounds close in. May our eyes remain on you while the world watches us.

A traveler's prayer to Ivlene

E lodie."

Loxy's voice is soft, but it still pulls me out of sleep easily. After that fight, my sleep is light as a feather. I blink and sit up.

"I'm going to Brightval Flats." Loxy's voice is calm, too calm.

"There's nothing in Brightval Flats," I say warily. "Tenoch is the only habitable place there. And Mom did *not* go to Tenoch. We don't know where to even look. *And she killed all these people*."

Loxy presses her lips into a thin line. "Well, I'm going. Are you coming?"

I pull the blanket closer around my shoulders, shivering. "No, Loxy. And neither are you. We are going to Aeglora. After we deal with this stupid curse. It's time to end this futile quest."

She blinks at me. "No. Now, are you coming?"

I shake my head slowly, pulse throbbing in my ears with apprehension at what's about to happen, and she nods, as if she expected that.

She rises from where she had been seated at the table and makes her way to her pack. "Then maybe I'll see you in Aeglora."

"Loxy, please." I reach toward her, desperate for her to stay, for her to listen. For her to be safe, here with me.

She doesn't answer me. When she makes her way to the door, Teklari follows with barely a glance at me. There is still no sign of Sefella, though I think I feel her presence in the room. Or near the room.

I look out the window. The barest hints of rose tinge the horizon, still hours from daylight. "At least wait until the sun comes up."

Loxy pauses, her hand on the doorknob. "I've waited twenty years. I'm done waiting."

And then she is gone, leaving me alone.

I fall back onto the mattress, pressing my hands over my face, trying to stop the tears spilling to the surface. How could she just leave me like this? How could she ignore my warnings, after everything we've been through together?

How could she abandon me, just like Mom?

How could you leave her? Sefella's voice is cold.

"No," I say into the empty room. "*She's* leaving *me*. I followed her all the way from Limutria. Why can't she trust me once in a while?"

Why can't you trust the Bright Ones you claim to love? Why can't you trust me?

"You're not one of the Bright Ones!"

But I am here. Where is Ivlene?

I roll over as if that can push the voice away and blink back more tears. I can't quite suppress the sobs, though.

Sefella's voice is salt in the wound, reminding me of things I didn't want to acknowledge. Where *has* Ivlene been? Why did she let her priestesses treat us so? Weren't we still her children, Singing or not?

Ivlene's people will never accept you, Sefella says. I almost tell her to shut up. *She's already seen to that. But I will always accept you, Elodie. Singers are mine. Why do you think they fear you so?*

"Everyone fears Death."

I am not merely Death, Elodie. Death, disease, everything you have ever attributed to me—it is all change, a balance to life. Like you and Loxy balance each other. Need each other. It's scary, I know. But that doesn't mean it has to be bad.

I am too stunned to respond, but the words burrow themselves into me, spinning through my thoughts.

Elodie.

I shake my head. "No. She left me." I sob again. "She left me. I can't think."

Then take your time, she responds. Her next words feel heavy with words unsaid. *But not too much. Sisters like you need each other.*

I close my eyes, emotions wrung raw. If Loxy needed me so much, she would have listened to me.

Part Five

ALONE

Thirty-Seven

LOXY

Though I may leave, I will always return.

Excerpt from a Korilian love letter

I spend a little time before I leave collecting some of the precious stones littered around the temple compound, carefully avoiding the crystallized bones. I have never seen such rich deposits of gems, and I will need some way across the Sea. I hope I will find a place that rents or sells transportation.

I even gather extra crystals and tie them in a piece of cloth for El, draping it over the doorknob and pretending not to hear her sobs. Whether she decides to follow me or not, she will need money, too. I am angry, but I do still care.

Even if she does want to abandon me now, forsake our gifts, so close to the end of this quest.

Once currency is taken care of, I make my way with Sef and Teklari through the field, pausing to admire the water horses grazing nearby. The wet fur and seaweed smell surrounds me, reminding me of home and turning my stomach. The horses' fur is perpetually damp, a gray-blue coat with blue-green leaves of seaweed along the crest of their necks and trailing behind as a tail. Cliffreach must have purchased these horses from Limutria or caught them from one of the herds roaming the Sea.

Sefella leads me into the field, toward one of the smaller horses. She places a hand on its neck, and it blows a cold, wet breath in my direction. "You can ride her down the mountain. She wishes to return to the Sea."

I don't know how Sefella knows that, but I am not about to question a goddess giving me exactly what I need right now. I swing myself up onto the horse's bare back, breathing in the scent of brine as I turn her head toward the exit, toward a path that will lead us out of this tomb.

We begin our descent from the mountain to the Sea. Teklari jogs along next to me, her crystals tinkling with her movements. The snow turns to rain as we descend, but the rain is light and comes in fits and starts. The rainy season is nearing its end.

And then the Sea comes into full view, that great, shining mirror extending out to the horizon. And I feel something I never thought I would, something I just barely felt when we arrived and I caught a glimpse of these sparkling waves.

Fear.

Last time I was here, we were on the brink of dying. Barefoot, soaked to the bone, starving, uncertain of our survival. My mind may have moved on, but my body hasn't forgotten the Sea's punishment.

A vision clouds my view. I stand in the mud, the Sea around me mostly dry. Again, I see Mom's body, see who I now know is Sefella raise her up.

And then more. I see Sefella disappear into Mom's body like a spirit.

I see Mom changing.

As she walks along the barren shore, her steps grow lighter than air, her body shifting between elements until half of her is crystal and her skin like oil. And behind her eyes, flashes of Sefella. I can feel the power building under Mom's skin.

Is this why she never came back?

The Sea as it stands now comes back to view. And I have to wonder if this is the very shore where Mom…where Sefella found…

"Are you okay?" Sefella asks, standing next to me, hair flowing in the wind despite her nearly incorporeal form. Is she fading? How much time does she have left?

I nod. Mom needs me. I take a deep breath and push forward, hoping to find somewhere with a boat so Teklari doesn't have to walk through the water. I can ride this horse to Brightval Flats, but the wolf cannot.

As we draw nearer to the waves, a small blue house comes into view. It is raised up on pilings extending into the sea, a very different solution to the same problem of rising and falling sea levels that Limutria faces every season. Smoke curls from a chimney, filling the air with a cozy, woodsmoke smell like home, evoking warmth and sadness all at once. While I am still angry with El, I wish she were by my side. I was starting to grow used to having her near, starting to think she was accepting both herself and me.

I was wrong.

I make my way toward a small, free-standing pier on the other side of the house, floating on the waves. Several rafts and boats are moored to cleats along its length, and two men and a woman stand near a fire on the shore around the skeleton of another boat. Might these people be willing to rent me a raft?

"Good evening!" I call, raising my hand in a way I hope comes across as friendly.

One of the men breaks off from the group, the woman taking his place building the boat, and he approaches us as we enter the homestead. He raises a hand, and I stop in front of him. He appears unruffled by Teklari's presence, even going so far as to scratch her behind the ears. I soon see why, as a pack of three crystal wolves bolts from the pilings under the house and begins jumping around with Teklari. The wolves bark and yip in joy, and I can't help but smile.

"What can I do for you?" the man asks.

I tear my attention away from the wolves. "I am a traveler seeking transportation."

The man glances at me, his face uncertain. "Traveling alone?"

"No," I say. But when I look back, Sefella has hidden again. To cover my slip, I whistle, and Teklari comes running, sliding to a stop next to me and sitting with her tongue lolling out. "I have a traveling companion."

"The wolf?"

"Yes."

"Wolves don't like to travel over the sea," he says.

"This one will." I can already hear her Singing. She understands, and she's coming.

He sighs. "All right, then. Destination?"

"Brightval Flats."

He blinks at me, speechless, for several moments. "I'm sorry?"

"Brightval Flats," I repeat.

I can see his mind turning behind his eyes. "We don't do rental runs there."

"Okay."

"You'll have to buy a craft."

I curse under my breath, but I should have expected this. "I can trade. You can have the horse."

I step back from the horse while he examines the beast, then he steps back with a nod and leads me to the pier. At the very end, he stops next to a simple low boat, barely more than a platform of planks, with a flat bottom and sail.

"Have you ever sailed?" he asks.

"Enough," I say. I was never a sailor, but all Limutrian children can sail a boat.

He nods. "Do you need supplies? It will take three or four days, depending on the winds."

I curse El silently, wishing she were here to guarantee strong winds. But she made her choice, and it wasn't me.

I check in my bag and count the food packets I have remaining from Ryth Hollows. There aren't many, maybe enough for two more days, one with Teklari. "Yes, I suppose I do."

He nods and leads me back to the house, climbing the stairs and then reappearing a few minutes later with a shoulder bag, and I pass him a few of the stones I collected to barter with. The bag is heavy, full of food and water. I think for a moment to return the water, but any *normal* person would need it. Betraying I don't would be exposing the magic I've managed to keep mostly hidden my whole life, and even though things can't get much worse than they are now, I don't want to tempt my luck.

So I pay the extra money and stow the bags on the boat. I thank the boatman, call Teklari, and board. With one last look at shore and the descending sun, I untie the mooring ropes and push off.

One step closer to Mom.

Thirty-Eight

ELODIE

Do not be fooled; pride brings too many to the very arms of Sefella.

Excerpt from *The Records of Bright*

I jolt upright, breathing in pants and gasps, drenched in sweat. I glance over at the other bed, but of course it's empty. Loxy is gone. She left.

Selfish brat.

Is she?

"Shut up!" I snap at Sefella.

But this is the second time tonight that I've awoken in a cold sweat, unable to remember anything about my nightmares except that Loxy is in danger. That she needs me.

And that I can't help her.

I glare at Loxy's empty bed, then throw off the covers and stalk across the cool, empty room to the stack of books on the table. I grab the top one and slam it open. Maybe studying will calm my mind, at least until morning when I make my way out of the temple and toward Aeglora.

The book is full of descriptions of face paint markings. Many are familiar from my time at the temple. Some are unfamiliar.

And some are from a forbidden faith.

I slam the book shut, heart pounding as I remember my training at the temple, remember Ivlene. Remember what Sefella did.

But I still can't focus. I should have gone with Loxy. She's my baby sister. I'm supposed to protect her. We're supposed to protect each other. How can we survive apart?

Thunder claps outside, and I jump as lightning illuminates the room in harsh white light. Outside, snow falls in large, fluffy flakes mixed with sleet. I duck my head toward the open pages and try to drown out the guilt.

Loxy made her choice. And I am going to stick with mine.

Thirty-Nine

LOXY

Even when the storms rage, when the seas rise, when your companions abandon you, still do not allow your sight to be turned from the power and mercy of Sefella.

Excerpt from *The Ballads of Sefella*

Dark is fast approaching at the end of the third day, and as much as I don't want to stop, I drop the anchor. Better to lose a night to rest than to drift and be lost in the vast sea. The night is not forgiving to the reckless sailor.

Besides, the winds are dying, and my progress has slowed so much that I am forced to row. Though the winds were in my favor most of the day, they have been nearly dead for the past hour, and my arms ache with the strain of propelling us through the water. Sefella returned once we were out of sight of the shore, sitting primly at the bottom of the raft, but she is still unable to do anything to help me. I almost resent her, that all she can do is watch as I strain and suffer, but I remind myself that it is only with her help that I am finding Mom. That once she reclaims her vessel—Mom—she will have her power back.

My face feels tight and hot. Now that the rainy season is almost over, the sun is out for longer stretches, reflecting off the water to blind me and burn my skin. Anger flares again, and I clench my jaw. If Elodie were here, she could have given us wind, gotten us across the Sea, given me a little relief from this weather.

But no. She's decided to ignore my feelings, to assume that her way is the only right way. Again.

The stone anchor drops below the sea's surface with a splash, and we drift another several feet as the rope uncoils to its full length. We stop, jerking against the rope that tethers the boat, and drift slowly around the anchor as day fades into night.

Thunder rumbles in the distance, and I jump. Teklari shakes and cowers into me, trying to hide under my arms.

"Sefella take us," I mutter, watching the horizon for signs of lightning.

Sef half smiles where she sits. "I am."

I blink, startled somewhere between a shudder and a smile of my own. But then a bolt streaks across the sky far to the north, distracting me. I begin erecting the storm shelter between the mast and the gunwales. It is designed to allow wind to pass through while still providing enough shelter for the boat's occupants.

The waves shouldn't grow large enough to capsize such a stable craft as this, but the wind could break our anchor if I'm not careful. I roll the sails and tighten the last strap of the shelter, then I settle in to wait with Teklari in the dark.

We munch on jerky as the thunder grows louder and more frequent. My heart is racing, and I clutch at the wolf just as tightly as she hides against my side. We are the highest point in the sea, making us an ideal target for lightning. The boat may be safe from electrocution, but it is still vulnerable to fire.

For the hundredth time in the hours since we left shore, I curse El for abandoning me, for having the power I do not, power that could have protected us here.

The storm hits with all the fury of Sefella. Wind and waves toss the boat hard against the mooring rope, and I hear the lightning crackle through the air, striking the water with a pop and sizzle, leaving my ears ringing. Rain pours down in sheets, a constant static blocking out all other noise save the thunder.

Greatness is born of change. Change involves pain. You will be here soon.

I squeeze my eyes tight against Sefella's voice. While still in the boat with me, she is back to talking in my head rather than yelling over the wind.

Is this a hint that my time is here?

Is this what Mom went through? Is that why she couldn't come back?

I dig my fingers into Teklari's fur and crystal, tears streaming down my face, my breath coming in gasps. Rain sprinkles in through the gaps in the shelter walls. I bury my face in her neck as she whimpers and whines.

I can't protect her, protect *us*, not with Crystallosinging.

There is a crack so loud I lose all hearing for nearly a minute. I smell smoke curling around my nostrils and poke my head out of Teklari's fur in time to see the mast sparking with energy, glowing with fire in the blackened crack left by a lightning strike. The rain quickly extinguishes it, but the next bolt strikes the metal cleat to which the anchor is attached.

The rope snaps, though I can't hear it over the rush of the storm, and the wind catches our boat. It spins away on currents of wind, tossed by the waves, carrying us along at breakneck speed. A flap of the shelter tears open, revealing the boiling clouds and downpour of rain. Lightning flashes, and for a moment, I think I see the form of a woman in the sky.

Then the boat slams into something, and my head strikes the wood planks.

The world goes dark.

Forty

ELODIE

Do not ignore the visions that visit you. For many have done so before you, and their end was Death.

Excerpt from *The Records of Bright*

I stand in the Sea of Broken Glass, surrounded by unbroken water in every direction. The horizon melts into the sea like one large mirror, a swirl of white and blue and pink sky and clouds. I take a step, splashing in the shallow water, the only sound in the silence. The water doesn't even cover the top of my foot. It must be the dry season.

As if triggered by my thoughts, mounds of salt rise up to shatter the mirror, breaking the pink and blue into thousands, perhaps millions, of shards. The mounds are no taller than my ankle at their highest, but it is enough to destroy the illusion that I stand in another world.

"Loxy!" I call, my voice absorbed in the vast emptiness of the sea without even an echo.

I take another step, the salt grinding underfoot. I don't hear my sister respond, don't hear anything except my own breathing and the blowing of the wind past me. I shiver at its bite.

It's no wonder. My clothes are apprentice attire, that thin, gossamer gown of periwinkle matching the lavender of my hair. My hair is pulled back out of my face in a ceremonial headdress made of metal, crystal, and feathers that drape and weave around my head, tickling my forehead and neck with the bits of hair that have escaped the intricate twists of my hairstyle. I look down at my own reflection, and the face of a priestess stares back at me, the paint no longer the simple stripe of the apprentice but instead a detailed pattern in white and blue, like High Priestess Cydia's.

But I recognize this pattern now from my studies. I bear the pattern of Sefella on my face.

You are mine.

Thunder rumbles in the distance, and I snap my head up, away from my reflection. Gray clouds move in from the east, boiling with rage and energy, blocking out the pale pinks and blues of the sunset sky. The hairs on my arms prickle as the static in the air reaches me.

It feels so much like magic buzzing beneath my skin. The energy fills me at the reminder, humming in my ears, crackling in my muscles. It builds, and I feel powerful, unstoppable. The storm is at my command, the winds and rains and fires from the heavens.

And the magic hears my Song of power, the wind dancing around me and lifting me from the ground so my toes barely brush the mounds of salt. The lightning crackles around me, waiting for me to Sing it to life, while water swirls around my toes.

I am power. I am might. I am special. How could I ever have wanted to give this up?

Yes!

Lightning flashes, drawing my attention back to the angry sky. For a moment, I could swear I see the form of a woman in the clouds, but in the next moment, a bolt of lightning streaks toward me. I'm not fast enough to think, to react, to stop the bolt from striking me full in the chest. As if in slow motion, I am knocked out of the air, and I fall, my back hitting the ground hard.

The world changes around me the second my back touches the ground, things flashing into being that hadn't existed in this world of reflections and power.

I push myself to sitting, catching another glimpse of my reflection. The headdress is askew, the face paint smeared. Behind me, Limutria's temple rises up in glowing rosy hues, High Priestess Cydia standing on the threshold as the storm rages above us.

On my other side, Loxy screams.

I jump to my feet, and my first instinct is to summon the power, the might I had at my beck and call. What did I do before this? How did I ever protect my sister?

The answer is apparent as I turn to face her: I didn't protect her. I was one of her tormentors.

I see myself spewing venom in her ear while she drips with mud. I remember that day, the day she fell in front of the initiates, the day her magic slipped.

I had been so angry. But she had been a child. We both were.

How did I not remember until now?

I remember things feeling different after that day, but I thought we were just growing up. Was I that naïve, to believe the words I'd said in anger, in hate, in selfishness hadn't affected her?

Loxy's tears dry up as another girl slowly materializes before me. Audrey.

The girls separate, and I watch again as lightning strikes Audrey, and she falls. She is still, so still.

She vanishes, and Loxy is before me again, facing the storm to the east, the storm that is now overhead. A woman made of storm clouds and lightning descends from the sky, walking on air as if descending steps. Her face is familiar, but made of light and crystal, hard to read until she finally steps down into the sea.

Mom.

I see Loxy's face light up with a smile, see her reaching toward Mom, and I am four years old again and watching Mom rush away, cloaked in magic and violence.

Mom's face changes.

Ivlene.

"Loxy, no!" I cry, my mind obscured by the danger I sense.

My sister doesn't hear me, or chooses not to listen. She reaches for Mom, for Ivlene in Mom's form, and Mom reaches back. Lightning arcs between them, and Loxy falls to the ground.

I scream, and Mom-Ivlene turns eyes full of electricity to me. She takes a step toward me, and I see in her my own future.

The vision fades.

I blink against the suddenly harsh light of day streaming through the guest room's window, holding up a hand to block out the harsh glare. My head is clearer than it's been since Loxy left.

"Loxy needs me." I speak into the empty room.

Yes. Sefella sounds smug.

"I think I need to go after my sister," I say, almost afraid to admit it aloud.

I hurriedly throw everything into my pack and throw open the door. How long has it been? A full day? She's so far ahead of me...

I will help you.

I slam the door behind me, and something hits the ground. I turn to see a pouch, tied off with a bit of torn fabric. I pick it up, and the scent of fish drifts up to me. It must be from one of our food packets, which can only mean Loxy left it here for me.

But what could it be?

Gagging at the fishy scent, I open it. At least thirty gemstones of various shapes, sizes, and colors greet my eyes. Crystals. An exorbitant amount of crystals.

She left me money. Even angry with me, even on her way out of this place and away from me, she still thought of me enough to provide what I might need.

My throat is tight with unshed tears. I abandoned her so easily. After one measly fight. How many did we have over the years? And I couldn't weather one more? I couldn't give her closure?

I don't know what she'll—what *we* will—find, but I can't deny her closure. And I won't leave her alone.

I have to find her.

Another scent drifts down the corridor toward me, something wet and sulfurous like the Sea, and then a hollow clicking echoes through the empty halls. A moment later, one of the water horses steps around the corner, its eyes glowing red.

My heart leaps to my throat, and I take a step back, hand on the knob in case I need to hide. Why would a water horse venture indoors, and why would it come toward me? These horses have been wild for years, however long Cliffreach has been abandoned.

Fear not, Sefella says. *You need transportation. I have brought it to you.*

The horse stops in front of me, lowering his head and pushing his damp, velvety nose into my hand. His eyes glow with that unnatural red light, and he snorts, but he shows no signs of aggression.

Sefella brought him to me. And I think I can trust her. She is my only way of reaching my sister in time.

The horse—*Raiden*, Sefella calls him—kneels down, and I hesitate for only a moment before swinging up on his back, one hand gripping the slick, cold, seaweed-like strands of his mane. Once I am settled, he rises and makes his way down the hall carefully, toward a different exit than the doors through which we had entered. We cross that threshold, and the cold wind hits me full in the face, blowing my snarled hair back away from me.

I lean forward. "Like the wind," I whisper, heart in my throat. "Loxy needs us."

He tosses his head and lopes toward the mountain path leading back to the Sea.

Forty-One

LOXY

There must always be balance: life with death, light with dark, evil with good, the sister with her twin.

Excerpt from *The Ballads of Sefella*

I wake to Teklari's tongue tickling my face, her saliva mixing with a gentle rain falling from steel-gray clouds. I blink to clear the water from my eyes, rubbing at them until I can see again, and sit up. Teklari backs up a few steps, giving me room to sit, then plants her haunches on the bottom of the boat. My head is pounding, and my stomach rolls like the waves during the storm. I definitely hit my head hard.

I look around, taking stock of the boat. Portions of the low gunwales are cracked, but no water seems to be leaking in, at least not very quickly. The deck is at a slant sharp enough to send my bags and provisions tumbling to the bottom, suggesting we've run aground.

One look out of the shelter confirms this; stretching as far as the eye can see is wasteland, dark brown and flat and wet, a haze of steam and toxic gas hovering over the land. Lighter brown areas zigzag through the mud, drier areas with some solid ground, but even those seem precarious.

We've reached Brightval Flats.

Sef stands on a rock just above us, staring out over the wasteland. Her form is more ghost-like than ever, barely there. She appears to be concentrating on something, but I have no idea what.

I retrieve my bags from the boat and sling them across my body, then Teklari and I pull the boat up onto the shore, past the reach of the lapping waves. I'm panting by the time the heavy wooden boat is secure, my head throbbing with pain, but it had to be done. If I can't find Mom, I don't want to be stranded here with no escape.

My stomach lurches, and I lose my last meal of jerky into the edge of the sea. I drop to my knees, tears streaming down my cheeks, and close my eyes until the hammering in my skull subsides. Teklari nudges at my arm, licking my cheek again, and I loop an arm over her shoulders.

Eventually, the throbbing subsides, and I push myself to my feet slowly. Sef has rejoined me, expression concerned, but I can see straight through her now. She is losing her battle with her twin. I can feel it.

"Will you be all right to keep going?" she says.

I nod, wiping a hand across my mouth as I turn in a small circle, surveying my surroundings. There is no way to tell exactly where I landed, but a green smudge on the horizon to my left could be trees. I've heard they are large and green, much larger versions of the shrubs in Limutria's apiary. The sea stretches behind me, long and sparkling in the sun all the way out to the horizon.

And in front of me and to the right are the Flats, an expanse of bubbling mud and desolation. They seem to go on forever, unhindered by any attempt to tame them.

I look into my bag, suddenly anxious. I have maybe a week's worth of food in here, and I'm suddenly grateful I bought the water after all. There may be nothing beyond this shore.

I kneel in the sand next to the sea and filter the salts out of the water to refill my canteens. While my hands are busy, I try to remember back to my geography and survival lessons. What plants grow out here? Several shrubs and grasses might be able to grow in the hot, barren soil, having already adapted to sandy environments. Pengu, brixawan, and blackberries could be all over.

There may even be a tree or two. A few varieties have been known to grow in harsh climates.

Something with a yellow glow darts from behind a rock, almost immediately disappearing behind another. But I saw enough to know what it was: a sunglow rabbit. They are mostly known for their luminous pelts, often used for ceremonial garments, which I'll have no use for out here.

But at least I won't starve, if there are rabbits here. And, hopefully, I won't run out of water, either.

I tighten the cap on my canteen and turn to face the Flats, listening for any Songs I can hear. While they are faint within our immediate surroundings, there is definitely something strong deep in the Flats, far from the sea. We are so close.

Teklari howls, and Sef looks out at the wasteland again. She must feel how close we are, too.

I remove the shelter from the boat, wrapping it around three of the thin posts, and strap it to my back with a bit of frayed rope. Then, Teklari and I take our first steps into Mom's last known location.

How much of her is left? And could she really have killed all those people?

The sand quickly gives way to hard-packed earth, flat rock, and clay. A few wildflowers and dry grasses wave in the wind sweeping over the land, but the world here is mostly brown and gray.

We reach our first mudpot within forty-five minutes, a strange sight unlike anything I've seen before. A round depression in the ground is filled with dark-brown bubbling mud, heat rising off its surface and mud splattering onto the nearby ground every time a bubble pops. The air around the mudpot has a bite, burning my nose, and I pull a strip of cloth up to cover the bottom half of my face.

"Don't get too close," I say to Teklari, my voice muffled through the cloth.

She whimpers, her ears flat and head low, but she listens. We continue on our way, careful to give the splattering pools a wide berth.

The longer we walk, the more the landscape changes into something completely and utterly alien. The mudpots grow more numerous, some in the center of small mounts created by the oozing of the mud out of the ground, and the color of the mud begins to show more variation. White, gray, pink, and red pools dot the landscape just as frequently as brown, creating a colorful, toxic display.

I glance at Teklari, my heart in my throat. I hope the heat and fumes won't harm her. I have something to protect my breathing, but she does not. I send a prayer to Sefella to hold her close, to protect her as she protects me. After all I've learned, I can no longer pray to Ivlene.

"Teklari will be safe," Sef says, and my worry eases. I believe her. Now there's just the matter of Mom.

We walk until the sun sets and darkness makes travel impossible. Teklari wanders off as I set up camp, her nose to the ground. Probably tracking something. There is some wood nearby, or at least the woody stems of a pengu shrub, and I gather them up while there is still light enough to see. I also pocket all the fruit I find on the shrub, which isn't much. Then I quickly set up the shelter as best I can against a large boulder and stow my packs inside before returning to the fire with a tinderbox.

I curse El to the winds for leaving me to do this by hand, then sit down and spend nearly twenty minutes trying to catch a spark on the wood while Sef looks on helplessly.

Finally, after the sun has dipped below the hazy horizon and the shadows are deep and long, the small bits of grass beneath the wood catch, and I drop to the ground to blow on them gently, coaxing the fire to life. The fire grows, crackling and burning brighter with every bit of wood that catches.

When I'm certain it won't die while my back is turned, I return to the shelter to dig out a packet of food.

A warm yellow glow illuminates the rocks across from my fire, and I freeze, fingers poised above my pack. The glow disappears and reappears several times around the surrounding boulders, then I hear the scream of a rabbit.

Moments later, Teklari emerges from a cluster of boulders, glowing between her jaws. She jogs up to me, her chin high, and deposits the rabbit next to me.

I laugh and ruffle the fur behind her ears. "Good girl."

There will be no need to dig into my stores tonight, but I'm not sure I'll sleep. I'm too excited at what lies ahead, too worried about what I will find tomorrow. Or the next day. Or the next. Is there anything left of Mom? What has Ivlene done to her? What can Sefella do to help?

Will she remember me?

And then there's my fight with El. Angry as I was, I want her here now. She should be here when I find Mom. My heart aches with a longing for my sister, to share this with her like we always should have.

Maybe I should have stayed a little longer, tried harder to convince her. Listened.

But I had to go. Mom needs me. Sefella needs me. And I need them.

The excitement returns again, pushing my other emotions aside.

Mom could be just over the next hill.

Forty-Two

ELODIE

Do not let your differences separate you. Do not allow those you love to be lost.

Excerpt from *Singers in Solitude* by Orella the Singer, died during the Great Culling

Anxiety pushes me to ride Raiden hard down the mountain, and by the time we reach the fishers' homestead, he is lathered in sweat and seawater. I feel a pang of guilt, but my guilt over leaving Loxy and the fear lingering from my vision quickly eclipse it.

And then the sparkling Sea comes into view. I don't know what I expected, but the sight of that expanse of mirror-like water sends my heart racing. Sweat blooms across my face, and I swipe it away. My mind begins to play visions of our last time in the Sea, of the blistered feet, the hunger, the cold and rain. And then I see my vision again, over and over, the world of the sea and the woman of storms. Mom. Sefella.

Ivlene.

I do my best to shake off the feelings the sight of the Sea evokes in me and turn my attention to my mission. I know Loxy must have set out for Brightval Flats, though I don't know how she found a way across the Sea.

Trust me, Sefella says.

I shudder, both from her voice and from the idea of visiting that forsaken place. Visiting Brightval Flats, even landing on that cursed shore, is enough to set my heart racing. There is nothing there except the world in the process of eating itself and, if you believe the oldest teachings at the temple and reports from the east, the gate to the Underworld—not to mention the palace of Sefella—at the heart of the Flats.

And I do believe. But my love for Loxy outweighs my fear. Even the fear that Sefella has been right all along—Ivlene is not what I was led to believe.

I must press onward.

I push Raiden forward, trusting the water horse to find his footing in the rolling waves, and we head back into the Sea that rejected me.

The wind is in my favor for half the trip, and when it isn't, I command it to return and propel us onwards. Raiden's hooves dance across the water, and I can almost rejoice in his joy at returning home, feel it along with him. And calling on the Singing barely leaves that uncomfortable feeling in the pit of my stomach anymore. My lack of fear is what scares me now.

I could still end up like Mom. I'm dangerous.

You're powerful.

For the next three days, we ride twenty hours and rest four. When the Sea soaks me, I call the wind to dry me. As we approach the far shore, I begin to see bits of wood and rope floating on the gentle waves of the sea. My heart lurches, and I hope all I see is driftwood, unconnected to Loxy's boat.

I have to find her, or all my sacrifices, all we've been through together will have been in vain. And worse, I will have failed her, again.

I can't lose her now.

Finally, late on the third day, the shore of Brightval Flats comes into view. I am exhausted, fueled only by raw determination, and I can feel Raiden's matching exhaustion in each plodding step.

I will find Loxy. It's only a matter of when. I will protect her from whatever we find out here. And I know it won't really be Mom.

The winds carry me straight to a boat. But rather than a comfort, they hold the bite of a chill. I am about to go against everything I've ever believed.

We step up on the shore next to what I can only assume is Loxy's boat, confirmed by the mix of human and wolf prints in the sand and mud, not yet washed away or covered by rain and wind.

Good. Footprints mean she was alive when she arrived.

I jump down, allowing Raiden to rest for a moment, and turn to face the Flats. A shiver wracks my body. It is as if the icy grip of the Underworld itself has a hold on this place. The wind whistles between boulders and across the plains, a sad, plaintive sound. It is lonely and barren.

I take a deep breath and locate Loxy's footprints again. Then, Raiden and I follow them into the wasteland until the sun is low in the sky.

Forty-Three

LOXY

At the ends of the world, where life flees and the world itself boils in torment, there you will find the gates to the realms of Sefella.

Excerpt from *The Records of Bright*

The night is quiet other than the chorus of popping mud bubbles, the forlorn wind, and Teklari's snores. Sef is also quiet, letting me sleep or absorbed in her own thoughts, if she hasn't faded out again. The episodes of her fading away are growing more and more frequent as we venture deeper into the Flats.

She doesn't seem to have much time left. Ivlene is draining Sefella's foothold in this world.

My soul is unsettled, and I find myself staring up at stars I've only rarely seen for the past six months.

What will I discover when I find Mom? What has Ivlene done to her? What will Ivlene do to *me* for seeking Mom out, for trying to wrest her from the goddess's hold?

The fire has burned down low, and the night is cool, but I don't dare use more wood from my meager pile. Instead, I huddle closer to Teklari and let her keep me warm.

We have been out here for two full days now, at least. I'm not sure how much time I lost after the storm, but I know it's been almost a week since I left El.

I wish I hadn't. I wish she were here. Perhaps I was hasty, maybe I should have given her the time she wanted. We could have done this together, like we were always supposed to, like I always envisioned we would.

But could Mom have waited that long? How much has the magic eaten away at her like the sea chipping away at a mountain? Eventually, even mountains crumble. Eventually, Sefella wouldn't be able to stay anymore. Which seems to be Ivlene's exact plan.

Anxiety builds in my heart, urging me to press on, to continue, to forego sleep so I can be another night closer to my destination. But it would be foolhardy to navigate the mudpots in the darkness. We'd be lucky if we even survived the night.

I am finally starting to drift off when I see a glow on the horizon. Unlike the sunglow rabbits, the light isn't a warm yellow but a cool blue, much like the glow of the spirits back in the City of Glass.

I sit up, leaning toward the flapping length of canvas serving as the door of our shelter. Teklari doesn't move, still deep asleep. I draw my cloak tighter around my shoulders and stand, walking toward the glow while carefully avoiding the boiling vats all around us. I make my way to the next cluster of boulders, the largest ones about two times my height, and climb to the top. The rock is cold against my skin, and my fingers quickly grow numb despite the hot air drifting off the mudpots. As I reach the top, I readjust the cloth covering my face and turn to face the glow.

Few boulders obscure what I can see, and the sight makes my heart pound. Ahead of me, less than a day's walk, a building rises from the Flats. It is composed of spires and towers, minarets and arches, all glowing with that soft blue, and—most exciting of all—made entirely of crystal.

Between my camp and the palace, however, is a vast plain pockmarked by dark pits of boiling mud, chasms of broken stone, and fast shifting shadows of I know not what.

I am reinvigorated, thrilled to finally be so close after all these years. It has to be Mom. This is my chance to save her. To bring our family back together.

I am excited, yes…but also afraid. Tomorrow, I will know everything.

And tomorrow I will face Ivlene.

Resigned to wait for daylight, I climb back down and into the shelter, curl up with Teklari, and wait for morning.

The sun rises, but I am already awake, barely able to sleep the rest of the night with the possibility of Mom just over the next field of mud. Teklari rises with me, and we finish the rest of the rabbit and a few pieces of stale bread while I tear down the shelter. I rewrap the poles and the canvas with my salvaged bits of rope, string it onto my back, and kick dirt over the few remaining embers of the fire.

Sef takes the lead, and we set off in the direction of the glow, my heart beating at double our walking pace. This is it. Just a few more hours, and I'll finally see her. Meet her.

I'll finally know my mother.

Does she still look like her portrait?

I feel a pang in my chest. I wish I hadn't been forced to leave that behind. But at least I have her sculpture. It's even better than that old portrait.

What magic does she have now? What Singing? Does she love it?

Does she miss us?

Or has Ivlene stolen that from her, too?

Obviously she is a Crystallosinger; how else would the crystal palace exist? But does her Atmosinging still exist? Has it strengthened? Weakened?

Does she regret leaving?

Why didn't she come home?

I can't stop the questions from racing through my mind, both the ones fueled by curiosity and those fueled by anxiety. I barely notice huge spires of crystal sticking up out of the mud as we walk. Did Mom make those? They sparkle in the daylight, interspersed between boiling mudpots and blackened lightning strikes full of charcoal and glass. I can hear the lightning glass Singing, and I wonder if she created it to hear this new, beautiful Song.

Will she still love me?

My steps falter as the thought flits through my mind, and I stumble, knocking gravel into a bubbling pink pit to our right. The stones disappear beneath the viscous liquid slowly, sinking beneath the surface as I watch, transfixed.

A crack of thunder echoes across the plain, and I jump, yanking my attention to the horizon. Storm clouds are building, lightning flashing while thunder continues to roll like a low drum beating across the landscape.

"Come on, girl," I say to Teklari, resuming our trek forward.

We walk for another hour as the mudpots bubble and boil around us, growing larger and more numerous. The occasional mountain rises up out of the mudpots, larger than the hills closer to the sea. Here they are composed entirely of steaming clay left behind as the pools burst and writhe. The path narrows to weave between the boulders, mounds of mud, and crystal spires, and the horizon is obscured from view often.

With every step closer to the crystal palace, the sky churns gray, flashing with lightning almost constantly. We turn with the path, and the field opens up before us, a clear section of earth free of hazards and broken only by regularly-spaced spires of tourmaline. Even the toxic gases in the air seem to be clear here.

I pull the cloth off my nose and mouth tentatively, testing the air, but no foul odors or lightheadedness greet me, so I leave it draped around my neck loosely.

In the center of the cleared land is the building I saw last night. A tall minaret stretches toward the sky, attracting several bolts of lightning. Intricate buttresses and arches surround the main building below the tower, weaving in and out like the delicate threads of a spider web. The entire structure glows from within, a luminous blue that is not as bright as in the night but still luminous in the dim light of the stormy sky. It reminds me of a temple, the crystal an ode to Crystallosinging, the glow an ode to Atmosinging.

Perhaps Mom does still have both.

Sef's eyes are fixed on the structure. "I'm afraid I must leave you here."

I turn to her. "But how am I supposed to rescue Mom?"

Sef smiles sadly, already fading again. "This is why I needed you. I'm sorry, I cannot help more. I'm…I'm not strong enough to pass through those doors." Her voice turns bitter, and she looks to the structure. "Ivlene has seen to that."

And then she's gone.

"Well?" I say to Teklari with a sigh. "Shall we?"

Teklari slinks along behind me as we approach the large doors at the end of the crystal-lined path. Her fur tinkles softly amidst the wind and thunder howling around us. My dress blows against my legs with every step, my curls tickling my face where they escaped my tight plait. My heart pounds in time to my footsteps.

What if El was right about her? What if the Mom I find isn't Mom?

Why didn't she come home? I think.

The palace grows more intricate, more detailed, as we approach, each careful relief and carving resolving itself from the blur of distance. Large steps lead up to the door, and after only a moment's hesitation, I take the stairs to the foot of the door.

I raise my hand to grasp a crystal knocker, but I hesitate again.

This is it. I'm finally going to meet her.

And a thousand doubts flood my mind again, doubts about her, about our family, about how she will react.

Why didn't she come home?

I take a deep breath and let the crystal hit the door.

Forty-Four

ELODIE

Periods of lucidity mixed with longer, increasing periods of incoherence. Reports of possible Singing. Possible involvement with Sefella. Cast out from Cliffreach after physical appearance began to be consumed by her Singing. Judgement: no help available; to be expelled. No resistance is acceptable.

Excerpt from the final Cliffreach archive entry on Volta
Shayde

R aiden and I follow Loxy and Teklari's footprints deep into the Flats. There hasn't been any rain in the last couple of days, leaving the prints to solidify into mud casts, dark depressions in the earth easy to follow. I hope the sleep I have been skipping is giving me an advantage, allowing me to gain on them.

As I venture deeper into the Flats, the ground grows more treacherous, too soft in places and covered by broken rock in others, and the sky boils as angrily as the mudpots. I feel myself on edge, my heart palpitating, my breath shallow and my head light. Every sound is like the minions of Sefella—Ivlene?—coming to find me, to drag me to the Underworld, to separate me from life and family and the Bright Ones, though Sefella's voice claims nothing of the sort is happening. Why should it when I am coming to them freely?

I still don't know if trusting Sefella is the right thing to do, but after all we've been through, she is starting to seem more like home than Ivlene and the priestesses ever did.

I see no creatures and few plants as I travel, further convincing me that I am going straight to my own death.

I stop to rest for only one night when the exhaustion is beginning to take its toll, an eerie blue glow bright on the horizon, then continue onward, tracking my sister's footprints into the wastes as the air grows colder, the wind stronger. The deeper I go, the stronger the storm to the east appears to be. At times, it's like I can see the form of a woman fading in and out of the clouds, sometimes so clear it's as if she stands before me, sometimes nothing more than a suggestion.

It is far too similar to my vision, and I continue, my worry growing with every step.

I pass Loxy's camp, but she is already gone, her meager fire long cold and dead. The footprints lead off toward the glow I saw on the horizon last night. Could it be possible the gates to the Underworld really are there? Could that glow be the souls of the dead? It matches the light of the spirits in the Glass City.

Dread creeps into my belly as I imagine my sister dragged to the depths of the earth by the dark, shadowy Soul Hounds. As the sun begins its descent, casting long shadows between boulders and pits of mud, I feel as if I see the Hounds just out of focus in my periphery.

I need to stop imagining things before I drive myself mad.

I step around a boulder, and the most amazing, eerie sight opens up before me: a palace made entirely of crystal, glowing from within with that ethereal blue light, bright against the backdrop of the raging storm.

Maybe the stories were right.

And then I see the woman in the clouds separate herself from the storm, her features becoming more distinct and resolving into the face I remember from fifteen years ago, less cloudlike as she descends from the sky just as she had in my vision and shrinks to the size of a human. And on the steps of the palace stand a young woman and a wolf made of crystals.

The storm woman stops directly behind Loxy.

Forty-Five

LOXY

When all is lost and the world is at its end, remember those who love you, for they are the ones who will remain.

Excerpt from *Singers in Solitude* by Orella the Singer, died during the Great Culling

I hold my breath as I wait for some response to my knock. Thunder rumbles overhead, and then suddenly I feel a presence behind me. Slowly, carefully, I turn to face it.

A woman stands on the narrow path leading up to the palace, but she is unlike any person I have ever seen before. Her skin is a rainbow of hues, like an oil slick over the surface of the sea, shining and shifting with every small movement she makes. White paint covers her face in intricate lines like those of the priestesses, but hers do not match any of the lines I know. Instead, they make thin, blocky designs across her cheekbones and join in the center where another line runs from her hairline to her jawline, effectively bisecting her face. And along that line, white spikes of paint protrude to the sides. It seems to be a symbol for something, but of what, I have no idea.

I should never have come alone.

Besides the strange markings on her face, half of her body appears to be composed entirely of crystal while the rest of her body shifts between wind, water, and fire. The clouds themselves wrap around her, clothing her. She is utterly alien.

And yet completely familiar.

The lines of her face, the curls of the hair, the set of the eyes—in my mind, I can see the face from my portrait. I see those same lines in El's face, in my face every day.

Mom.

I blink back tears, unsure if I'm crying out of happiness or fear of what stands before me. "Mom?" I say.

The woman tilts her head at me like a bird, as if trying to understand my words. Lightning flashes behind her, shining through the parts of her body that are crystal and momentarily throwing the rest of her into shadow. Her face phases away into another face, the face from that strange boulder, but her own face is back so quickly that I think I must have imagined it.

I shudder, and my heart flutters in my chest.

"Loxy," Mom says, but her voice is strange, layered with the voice that's been in my head for so long.

I hesitate. "Ivlene?"

"We are one and the same, for now."

Mom's face flashes again, and now I know I saw Ivlene behind it. Sefella was telling the truth.

"Is this why she never came back for us?" I can't keep myself from saying. "You've been holding her hostage?"

Another thought makes my stomach drop: could Ivlene have already been in control when the people of Cliffreach were murdered? Would Ivlene destroy them for helping Singers? I hold back a shudder and meet the goddess's—my mother's—eyes.

Ivlene-Mom continues, undeterred. "You don't understand what you're seeing. Why don't you come in, and we can talk?" They step past me, raising a hand toward the crystal. The door slides open silently, and they step into a grand entry.

I glance at Teklari, whose ears are flat against her head. With a sigh, I follow and hear Teklari's claws clicking on the crystal of the floor behind me.

Ivlene-Mom leads us straight back, past two curved staircases that are mirror images of each other and through a carefully crafted arch between them. Through the arch lies a long hallway lined by crystal doors and glowing walls. We walk to the back of the palace and out into a courtyard lit by the light of the storm. The crystal underfoot is carved into images of great beasts like the Water Dragons of the Sea and that thing that attacked us in the caves.

I shudder.

Ivlene-Mom stands by a table set out with gleaming decanters of honey wine, bright green vegetables, and a perfectly braised sunglow rabbit, if my nose is correct.

How did they obtain all this rich food out here surrounded by toxic mud?

"Please, sit," they say, indicating a fine chair on the other side of the table from her.

I step forward and take the seat, Teklari cowering at my feet. Ivlene-Mom sits across from me and begins serving out the dishes.

"I imagine you have many questions," they say.

Understatement of the millennium. But where to even start? "How?" I find myself saying. "How is all this here? And Mom...?"

Ivlene-Mom smiles, their teeth bright white against the oil slick of their skin. "I know it's a lot to take in. Your mother belongs with me, though. I found her, and she is mine."

I can feel myself bristle at the comment. How can Mom belong to Ivlene? "As I recall, Sefella is the one who saved her. Not you."

Ivlene-Mom pauses at this, then finishes filling a teacup. "As for the rest of this, your mother's power created most of it, and I made sure to provide the rest."

I hear a howl in the distance, and an image of the Hounds of Sefella comes to mind. Do the Hounds bring them the food? Anything else they need here? Or did they, until Ivlene stole it?

I look at Ivlene-Mom, but they merely smile. How am I supposed to get Ivlene out of Mom's body? How am I supposed to do this alone?

"I want to talk to her," I say.

They pour honey wine into my glass, but my stomach flutters at the thought of food or drink. Of all the things I thought I might encounter here, a dinner of rabbit and wine with one of the Bright Ones inhabiting my mother's body wasn't one of them.

"Please, eat," Ivlene-Mom says. "Drink."

"My mom," I say again. "Please."

Ivlene-Mom puts the bottle back on the table, and the crystal around us seems to ring. They sigh. "In time. But first, you have had a long journey. Won't you just accept some peace from me?"

I merely glare at them.

They sigh again. "I see you aren't ready for that. How about we take a walk? See more of the palace? Then, if you still desire, you may speak with your mother."

A tour? What can the harm be in that? And if I can talk to Mom at the end of it, maybe get a clue how to reverse this, perhaps it will be worth the delay.

I nod, and Ivlene-Mom stands, leading me across the courtyard to a row of arches lining a covered walkway. I touch Teklari lightly on the head, reassuring myself that she's still with me.

We enter the open hall and make our way to a large, wide room filled with statues and reliefs covering walls. At first glance, the reliefs look similar to images I've seen my whole life in the temple, but upon closer look, they don't tell the same story.

"I have been working on this palace a long time," Ivlene-Mom says, voice heavily layered in chimes. "And many have come before you, living long, fulfilling lives in service to me. But the time is growing near that I make my next steps into the world."

"Next steps? But you stole all this. From Sefella."

They pause. "Ah, let me start at the beginning." They walk toward one of the closest reliefs, an image of orbs glowing with power much like what I had seen by the gleaming black-and-silver rock. "Sefella was like me, you know. Long ago. There were two of us, the Bright Ones. And Sefella wasn't always seen merely as Death. She was the cycle of life, of change. Rebirth. But the world forgot, and I chose humanity while Sefella chose the Singers."

I swallow, knowing where this is going. "You cast her out."

"Yes. She followed the Burning Rain here, trying to establish a new kingdom, to find those forgotten or rejected by the world, to gather them and forge them into something greater. She gave them Singing. But it wasn't hers to give. All of humanity—the good, the bad, the accepted, the outcast—it is all *mine*."

They aren't looking at me anymore. I follow their gaze down a line of pedestals, each holding a different treasure of Singing. I recognize the first two even before they begin speaking again: a cube of pink halite the size of my head, and a bright white tower of selenite.

"Halosinging. Crystallosinging." They gesture to each pedestal as they list off the magic behind the items. There are so many more than I ever imagined.

A tornado the size of my hand, dancing on its pedestal. "Aerosinging."

A flame born of nothing, something I've seen El do. "Pyrosinging."

A chunk of ice glowing in the dim light, white mist pouring off its supercooled surface. "Cryosinging."

A globe of water, hovering over the crystal pedestal. "Hydrosinging."

Chunks of earth and stone swirling around each other. "Geosinging."

Sparks of yellow light, cracking and dancing in the air. "Electrosinging."

We come to the final pedestal, where a water globe hovers, containing clouds and tiny bolts of lightning. "And of course, Atmosinging."

I feel my heart sinking, seeing evidence of my mediocre magic. There is so much more to the world than even El's Atmosinging, and they all seem much more useful, more powerful, than mine.

I am weak.

Ivlene-Mom is looking at me, and the gleam in their silver eyes is full of greed.

"She gave to all Singers, you see, though differently. Have you not felt the strength as you raised your most beautiful shelter? The power as you reinforced buildings and created tools and weapons? As you fought off every beast and terror this world had to throw at you?"

As Ivlene-Mom lists each accomplishment, I see them in my memory. My ability grew so much, even from when I only had Halosinging.

A cold, wet hand rests on my shoulder, and they look at me with that look again, the one of love, of belonging. One that seems like a mask or a veil. "But no matter Sefella's theatrics, all of this is still mine."

I clear my throat and step back from them. "So you would have us cast out? Reviled?"

Ivlene-Mom sighs, clutching their hand made of water with the one of crystal. "I created greatness. But humanity makes its own choice."

"And then what? What of us?" Tears burn my eyes. How could Ivlene herself—the one who I was always promised would love me—care so little of my fate?

Ivlene-Mom's face turns amused. "Itano and his prophecy. He wasn't wrong, though the ones who interpreted it did not understand the destruction they saw."

"They destroyed the kingdom."

"Yes. And in so doing, they weakened Sefella. Enough that I had a chance to put her back in her proper place."

"But we still exist." Again, it's not a question.

"Yes. For now. Sefella's work cannot be halted. You cannot halt change. You cannot deny a part of life. Whether a person wishes to acknowledge it or not."

There it was again. Sefella is change, not merely Death.

My head is reeling, and a chill fills my blood. None of this fits with what the priestesses teach the people. There is no record, at least not one the priestesses share, about a religion run by Sefella before the Great Culling. Why? Where has it all gone?

And what exactly is Ivlene planning to do to our world?

"Why don't we continue the tour?" Ivlene-Mom says, not unkindly. "There is more to see."

More? What else could possibly be here?

But Ivlene-Mom is already leaving the room with the pedestals. We follow a maze of corridors into the heart of the palace, the dim daylight growing darker and the air growing colder as we go, the light replaced by lavender and cyan light of crystals and plants. I even see the little friends that led us from the caverns, their bright fronds waving against the crystal walls.

The purple glow grows brighter, and then we stand before the gaping arch of a doorway, the edges lined with glowing points of crystal as tall as me. They Sing unfamiliar Songs, deep and dark and mysterious.

They Sing of places I have never been, of hope and life and tragedy.

"What is this place?" I breathe.

"I think you know," Ivlene-Mom says, extending their hand. A black hound with deep amethyst crystals poking out of its coat, similar to Teklari, steps out of the shadow and pushes its head into her palm.

The Hounds of Sefella are beautiful. As is the Underworld.

Ivlene-Mom smiles, confirming that I've guessed correctly. This is, indeed, a gate to the Underworld.

"Don't worry. I will close this gate soon. Humans don't need it. Or they won't, once my work is finished."

I turn back to them, searching the eyes so like mine and Elodie's. "Why can't I speak to her?"

Ivlene-Mom's smile fades, and they turn their face from me, like they are hiding something. They begin to lead me away from the gate, back toward the entrance. "There wasn't much left when Sefella found her. I can't promise how she would react to you."

I feel myself going cold, even as the air grows warmer the farther we walk from the gate. And something about their words feels false. Mom is still there. There is more to her than what Ivlene claims. I know it. I feel it.

But Ivlene doesn't want to let her free, to let her speak for herself.

We step out onto a patio near the entrance, and the Flats open up before us again in all their deadly barrenness. The storm still roils overhead, lightning flashing brightly.

We stop at a crystal banister, gleaming bright in the dim light as if it captured the storm inside it.

Perhaps, with Mom's Atmosinging, it had.

Ivlene-Mom is speaking again. "I will finish my work. Singers are still human, and they are mine. I will squash this rebellion of theirs, one way or another. I will purge Singing from this world, re-create Nasmarya—no, all nations—in my own image." That light of greed glimmers in her eye again. "It will be perfect: no death, no illness, no Sefella…and no Singing."

"Purge…Singing?" My lips feel numb as I speak. The anger, the fear, everything I felt all along—Ivlene hates us.

They don't answer, merely stare at me, unblinking.

"What of my mom?" I say. My heart is pounding in my chest so hard that my head feels light, the blood pumping too fast to be useful.

"You should forget her and go home. When Sefella found her, she'd been beaten down, nearly destroyed by the combination of her magic, the boost of the call from the Burning Rains, and the loss of her home. She was nothing but magic, her mind almost entirely gone. She was nearly dead."

That explained the visions. The rumors from Ryth Hollows. The journal—and death—at Cliffreach. Was she truly lost?

Or…was this just another lie? Was the destruction really caused by Ivlene all along?

"I want to speak with her." Tears burn my eyes, and I blink them back.

Ivlene-Mom hesitates a moment. "You won't like what you find."

The tears spill over. "Please. Let me at least try. Please."

They nod, but there is cruelty, not compassion, behind their eyes. "Very well. If it will convince you."

I can almost see Ivlene's retreat from Mom's body as their shoulders slump, their eyes grow bright with light, unfocused on anything for more than a few moments.

"Mom?" I say.

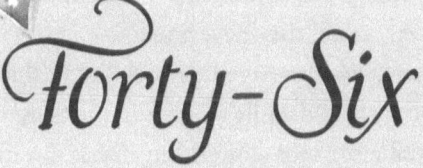

Forty-Six

ELODIE

Remember not how I have wronged you, but rather the things I have done for you.

Excerpt from *Ivlene's Prayer of Redemption*

*H*urry, Sefella says, back in my head again. Her voice is faint, weak.

I rush forward, scrambling down the rocks. Loxy has been inside the crystal palace for at least fifteen minutes by the time I reach the path to the palace. I leave Raiden hidden by the rocks and run between spires of tourmaline as lightning flashes with such intensity, such power, that I feel it in my veins.

Whatever just went inside that building with my sister could not have been our mother.

I reach the steps and take them two at a time, shoving at the door to the palace with all my might and gasping as it slides forward with little resistance. I stumble forward, catching my weight just before I fall to the ground, and pause in the middle of a grand entry. In front of me stand two grand, curving staircases flanking an arched hallway, and above me shines a crystal chandelier sparking with the energy of a lightning storm.

Which way would they have gone?

I desperately wish to have Loxy's ability in this moment, to perform the feat she did while we were in the Glass City and find them by crystal resonance alone…but that is not my power.

I really am jealous of her.

I shake the thought away. There's no time for that, not now, not when some *thing* is with my baby sister.

I duck into the arched hallway, but it quickly becomes maze-like. The light changes with every twist and turn, but otherwise every new corridor looks the same as the last.

I burst into a long room lined with reliefs that seem to be alive on the walls and pedestals holding bits of the world, like salt and crystal. But they must be as magic as the pictures on the walls, as they require nothing to suspend them in the air.

I race through the room to the door at the far side and continue my search of the building. I can't hear any voices, can barely hear the storm outside, but the air turns cold and the light changes color as I walk until I stand before a glowing break in the wall, surrounded by jagged, tooth-like crystals. The cold emanating from within makes me think of the deep rainy season, the cold of death.

I am transfixed and take a step toward the entrance, but a low growl stops me in my tracks. A dog, similar to Teklari but with darker coloring, steps from the shadows, baring bright white teeth in its dark, dark mouth.

I stumble backward, away from the creature. I don't belong here. I turn and run away from the gate, deeper into the hall. The light shifts toward daylight again, and a warm breeze wafts down the corridor. I can smell the ozone of the storm, the damp of rain.

And, most importantly of all, I can hear voices.

Forty-Seven

LOXY

May the rain guard you from the fire.

Excerpt from a Limutrian traveler's prayer

"Mom, it's me," I say again. "Loxy."

Mom—for she truly is my mother now—blinks, her eyes glowing with the same blue light as the building behind me. Why doesn't she understand? Does she not remember her own daughter?

I tamp down the unexpected hurt that blossoms in my chest. Of course she remembers me. She has to. Ivlene can't have been telling the truth—that Mom isn't who she once was.

Maybe if I could just show her.

I hold up the pendant at my neck, the necklace that had been hers. With my other hand, I display her wedding ring. "Remember?" A stray tear slips from my eye, falling onto Teklari's crystal back. Teklari shakes, her crystals tinkling.

Mom's eyes lock onto the jewelry, like I'd hoped. She reaches for it mutely, gingerly touching the alexandrite stone swinging from my hand. I let her take it, let her look at it. After all, it had been hers first.

The clouds shift around her, and the sky boils as her face contorts. Is she remembering? Trying to remember?

I reach into my pack cautiously, extracting the quartz statue that she herself made. Like the necklace, she takes it, studying it with interest but not familiarity.

I swipe at my eyes. How can I bring her back to us? To me?

Sefella speaks in my head. *Your mother is nearly lost. You must help me to return, before we lose what remains of her.*

I catch my breath, afraid at the words. I can't lose her now, not this close to bringing us all back together again, to saving her. I shift on my feet, and my toe scuffs against a crystal pebble on the patio. If I can save her, could we really have a place as we are—truly accepted, truly loved, perhaps for the first time in my life?

I shake away the thought and look back at Mom. Perhaps showing her my magic would help?

I wouldn't, Sefella says, her voice distant with a strong note of warning.

Ignoring her, I bend down, and Mom's head snaps up from the pendant as she watches me retrieve a chunk of quartz. I hold it out in front of me, like an offering, like a sacrifice, and command it, Sing to it, breathe into it. The quartz morphs into a model of Teklari that couldn't be any more perfect had a jeweler carved it by hand.

Her eyes glow brighter, and she drops the pendant and the statue to the ground. Her gaze is fixed solidly on the quartz wolf. She grabs it out of my hand, studies it for a moment, then turns those terrifying, crazed eyes to me. She is hungry, and the way she looks at me tells me it is the magic that awakened this hunger.

The quartz wolf drops to the ground, the delicate pieces shattering on impact, and she lifts a hand toward me, crackling and sparkling with blue arcs of electricity. Her face shifts again, shifts to the face of a person neither man nor woman, yet somehow both. Her face and this foreign face are enmeshed, indistinguishable.

Loxy. Stop this. You must banish Ivlene! Now, while you have the chance, while she has retreated!

There is no recognition in Mom's eyes. No humanity. Only hunger, greed, the need for power.

My heart stutters, and I take a step back. Her hand reaches for me, her fingers barely brushing the skin on my cheek.

Then electricity jumps from her fingertips to my face, and I am filled with fire.

Forty-Eight

ELODIE

And in those days, Sefella will build a new kingdom.

Excerpt from Itano's 300th Prophecy

N o!" I scream, my voice echoing across the crystal walls of the palace. I see it all in slow motion: the statue falling to the ground, the look on the woman's face, her hand stretching toward Loxy.

But I am so far away, too far to stop what is happening. I rush forward at the same time Teklari jumps at the woman. Neither of us is fast enough to stop the electricity from surging into Loxy, and I watch helplessly as she falls to the ground.

My scream of fear turns to one of rage. No one hurts my sister, not even my mother. *Especially* not my mother.

Elodie, wait! Sefella says.

"No!" I scream.

I barrel toward them, still screaming. The electricity of the storm, of the woman, buzzes around me, lending me strength to fuel my sprint. For the first time the buzz and hum of magic is welcome, a relief even, as it is a reminder that I have the power to fight back. I gather it toward me, allowing it to build under my skin.

The woman drops Teklari to the ground with one violent motion, then jerks her head toward me, snarling, her teeth bright against her oilslick skin. The horrifying truth of what magic has done to her, to Mom, sinks in as I draw closer. She's barely even human anymore, half made of elements. I can't see any real human flesh; even her hair seems to be made of something like water and fire.

And her face. There is nothing human in her eyes, no recognition, no trace of my mother. Just a power-hungry beast intent on consuming us.

White paint covers her face, the markings of Ivlene that High Priestess Cydia wears.

And suddenly I know. I know how to banish Ivlene, how to give my mother back to Sefella.

There is another face, fainter, fighting Mom's face for control. It is cool and familiar. A face full of anger, cruelty. A face I always thought would love me.

But I was so wrong.

Ivlene.

"Let her go!" I yell, surprised by my own words. After all this time, after she left us and joined with Sefella, I want her back?

I slide to a stop beyond Mom's reach, and she lunges toward me. I can barely spare a glance for Loxy writhing on the ground, her body shaking with pain or electricity, I can't be sure. Then

Mom is upon me, reaching for me, tearing at me, grasping for my magic.

I jump back and raise my hands, feeling the energy crackle around me. I reach toward her, releasing all the magic, all the years of pent-up frustration, all the fear, the hurt, at her in one beautiful, musical wave.

This is why it's called Singing.

The magic of the storm dances around me, rushes to meet me. It Sings back to me with a voice sweeter than honey.

Mom stumbles back, shock written across her face like text on a page. The storm pummels her with lightning and rain and wind.

And then she disappears in a whirlwind.

Part Six

FOUND

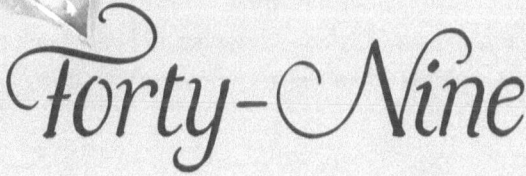

Forty-Nine

LOXY

Alone, you can do much. But together, you can do so much more.

Excerpt from *The Tome of Sefella*

My body is on fire.

Every nerve screams in pain as the electricity from Mom's attack dances through my flesh. It takes time, so much time, for the surge to dissipate, and I am finally left on the ground, panting but alive.

But Mom is gone.

I blink, seeing another form encased in storm. I rub at my eyes, sure that the residual electricity is showing me lies, but the woman remains.

El came back. She came for me. Like Mom didn't. Like she...couldn't.

I brush tears from my eyes and shakily push myself to my feet, grabbing my necklace and the statue and tucking them both safely away. I am about to run to El when lightning crackles overhead, illuminating the form of a woman inside the crystal palace. Glancing at El one more time, I lunge for the doorway.

Inside, the voice of the storm is muffled, but wind dances through the halls, furious like it hadn't been before.

Before I demanded Ivlene release her so I could talk to her. I thought if I could get Mom free, together we could drive Ivlene out.

I was wrong.

Light glimmers in every wall, every shining floor, disorienting me like I am encased in ice or trapped underwater.

And just ahead, in one of the corridors spiking off this one, is Mom's shadow, fleeing into the depths of the palace.

El slides through the door next to me, glances at me and Mom's retreating form, and then we take off after her as one.

"El, I'm sorry!" I yell over the wind rushing through the halls.

She glances at me but doesn't slow her own sprint. "Me, too! I should never have abandoned you!"

"I'm the one who abandoned you!"

"I promise we'll talk about it later!" she shouts as she runs faster. I pick up my pace to match hers, gasping for breath.

We slide around a corner, and a blast of cool, wet air strikes us, slicking the ground with moisture and pushing us back. I slide to my knees, and El grabs my elbow, pulling me back up as we pick our way across the slippery quartz floor.

Then we burst through an arch into a large, open room. Here, the ceiling is open to the roiling clouds and rain is beginning to fall on the already slick crystal floor.

We made it back to the courtyard, table still set for dinner.

"Watch your step," El says softly. "I've got your back."

My heart warms to hear those words, words I've ached to hear for so long.

"I've got yours, too," I say, tears of happiness at her words burning in my eyes, and we trade a smile.

There is no time to say more, not now.

Mom stands in the middle of the room, Ivlene visible whenever lightning flashes. Did Ivlene regain control?

She raises one hand, and a bolt of lightning streaks down and strikes the floor between us and her. I duck, expecting another blast of hot electricity to seep into my bones, but it doesn't come.

El throws up an arm, and the bolt dissipates away from us. "Let her go!"

Mom doesn't answer, but I hear Ivlene's snarl in my head and wonder if El hears her, too. *You belong to me, as she does.*

"No!" El yells. "I won't let you have her!"

I'm not sure if she means me or Mom, but there's little time to wonder. Mom shoots another whirlwind in our direction, and El and I barely manage to step out of the way before it's barreling into the wall behind us.

"We have to disrupt the bond!" El yells over the noise of the storm.

"What?" I yell back.

"The paint on her face. We have to smudge it! It will stop this!"

Stop this? Stop what? Mom's rampage? Is it the markings that are holding her in this state, giving Ivlene the power, sending her after us like a rabid dog?

"I can't do it without you," El says.

You can *do this*, comes Sefella's soothing voice. *Together!*

I'm not sure exactly what will happen, but I listen to the Song of the palace, then call forth crystals from Mom's creation. Spires jump out, trying to trap her limbs, but air pushes up under her and drops her farther across the room. The spires slip out of my control, and I curse under my breath.

No matter what El thinks, I don't have the control. I'm just as new to this as she is. The only control I ever had was over…me.

And I squandered it. I let everything around me sour me to the world instead of finding a way *I* could do something, could help.

And all along, I could have helped. I could have healed, with my Singing or with my kindness.

Yes! Sefella says.

I can't stop Mom. I never could. And as much as I want to, I can't heal her, not the way things are now.

All I want to do is heal the wounds of the world. But I'm not ready.

My heart sinks at the revelation, but I glance at El, fire in her eyes and determination in her stance, and I know that perhaps she can. Perhaps together, we will be enough.

But Mom is showing no sign of stopping, no sign of being brought back under Sefella's control, Sefella's help. With every passing moment, I feel more of her seeping away, leeching out of her like water in a parched desert.

I see Ivlene coming back, bit by bit, desperate to wipe out what is left of Mom and use her for the goddess's own selfish purposes.

"This has to end!" El says, and for once, I'm glad she speaks for me. Because I agree.

El sends a blast of wind at Mom, pushing her back. While she is distracted by my sister's attack, I draw out the crystals again, this time focusing on working with El. She glances at me and nods, and together we drive Mom into a corner with crystals and storms.

Good! Sefella cries in my head. *Good! Together, we can save her!*

This time, the crystals lock into place, restraining her arms and legs. She locks those light-filled eyes on me, and then a blast of wind like no other pummels into me. I slam into the hard, cold wall and crumble to the ground.

Fifty

ELODIE

Come to me, those who are lost, those who are rejected, and I will make you new.

Excerpt from *The Ballads of Sefella*

I vlene-Mom is trapped, but Loxy lies on the ground, motionless. I begin to breathe a prayer to Ivlene, begging for all the help I can get—but then my words shift.

My prayer is to Sefella. Now, and forever more. And it is time to end this.

Casting a worried glance at Loxy, I approach slowly, wind still howling around me. But I subdue it, force the storm to grant me safe passage to the snarling woman-avatar, trapped like an enraged beast. They turn their hate-filled eyes from Loxy to me, but I'm not sure Mom is cognizant enough for true hatred.

As I walk, I dig in my pack for my last gift from Cliffreach, a pot of face paint I had packed from the guest room. I thought I could use it again once I reached a temple of Ivlene.

I will never use it for that now. I do not want to.

I pull the top off the jar and dip my finger in the white paint, eyes locked on my mother's face. As soon as I am close enough, I grab their jaw and force their head to hold still enough to paint new lines, new invocations, across their skin.

With one final swipe, the pattern of Ivlene is broken, and there is a sound like shattering glass. Mom goes limp in the crystal prison, and the form of a person flies out from her skin, out of her body like a spirit.

It hovers over the crystal for several long moments, eyes locked on me, and I shiver. I am looking into the face of Ivlene.

I thought I would cherish a moment like this. To be *seen* by my goddess.

Instead, I shudder, seeing the truth of who this is.

Why would you do this? After everything you've given me, you would take it back now? The form of Ivlene stares into me, her gaze seeing straight into my soul.

I shudder, pain at the reality before me bringing tears to my eyes. For the last twenty years I thought Mom had abandoned us, but the truth is so much worse. "You stole her! You kept her from us all these years! And you want everything you don't deserve now!"

No, Ivlene says. *This was all mine to begin with! You…you and Sefella are the thieves. If you continue on this path, there will be no return. Believe me.*

"Believe you?" Tears slide down my cheeks. "After what you did to my sister? You made the world hate her! Then you broke our family into pieces! How is that worth believing in?"

It is my right!

My mind races. Ivlene is a *goddess*. And I am a mere human, magical though I may now be. I can't possibly hope to save us all.

Eventually, I will prevail.

Sefella appears, more whole, more solid, than she has been in days, and the sight encourages me. *Let me show you the truth, that there is more than what you have been taught. Let me love you.*

Love? Let Sefella…love me. Could it be enough? To stop this? To protect Loxy and Mom?

My mind is racing. I can't think of any other possibilities.

You know what you need to do, Sefella says.

And she's right. I do know. I know how to stop this. And I know now—more than ever before—this is how we save the world.

I was never meant to serve Ivlene. I was always a priestess of Sefella.

My eyes resting on Loxy, I reach for my paint again. My heart swells as tears fill my eyes again.

This could very well backfire. I could be just as lost as Mom, destroyed by the magic. But what choice do I have? How else do I protect my family?

Sefella looks at me, eyes burning with something I can barely understand. Compassion? Understanding?

Love?

"Take me," I say before I can regret it. I dip my fingers in the paint pot. I recall the words from the texts I was forced to read during my training, the words I was always forbidden to offer. "*Sefella, take me as yours. My will is yours. My body is yours.*" I hesitate once more before completing the verse, marking the lines I was forbidden to mark. On Mom's face. Then my own. "*My very life is yours.*"

With those words, those simple swipes of my fingers, Ivlene fades. Her power has no hold here anymore. Not while Sefella is granted a home, is welcomed by any part of humanity.

Sefella does not wait but plunges toward us. I flinch, not sure what to expect, but fearing the pain that may come.

But instead, as Sefella flows through me, back into Mom, filling my veins, my soul, I feel a warmth like the sun on the rocks during the rainy season, like a fire in the hearth after a long day working outside. I feel a comfort I've only felt when Loxy and I were getting along. I feel…acceptance.

You will see how great we can be.

And then the voice, and the warmth, fade away. I am still me. Still whole.

Better than whole.

The wind settles, the clouds dissipating overhead until the sun falls over the landscape, chasing away the shadows. It's over, at least for now.

I turn back to Mom, a cold weight in the pit of my stomach, and begin wiping what is left of Ivlene's paint from her face, cleaning it away to see the extent of the damage the magic wrought on her body.

Her eyes flicker open, wide eyes full of blue light and fear, and then she vanishes in a shower of sparks and dying wind. A ghost-like image of her remains in the crystal cage for another second, but then the crystal cage is empty.

She reappears next to me, free of the cage, then her eyes settle on me, fear dissipating, clarity dissolving. She smiles, reaching a shaking hand toward me. And in her eyes, I see the familiar gaze of Sefella, mingled with a gaze I thought I'd never see again.

"Mom," I say, voice trembling.

Sefella-Mom's eyes fill with tears. "In the flesh. Sort of." Their fingers caress my cheek. "We are both here."

"Sefella?"

They nod and drop their hand, turning to where Loxy had fallen. I follow Sefella-Mom as they lower themself next to my sister, and I drop down next to them as well.

My sister blinks up at me, and now that I'm here, I can't quite keep the panic down anymore. "Where are you hurt?"

She groans and starts to sit up. I support her back, looking into her eyes and trying to gauge her injuries. But she turns to Sefella-Mom, and a smile brighter than the sun overtakes the pain in her eyes.

"Mom?"

Sefella-Mom smiles back, resting a hand on her shoulder. The love rolling off the combined form of our mother and the goddess of the Underworld is so warm I can feel it. "Here, Loxy. Both of us."

There is a tinkling like windchimes, and I turn to see Teklari limping into the room, her sides heaving in pain, every breath a struggle.

We make a sorry lot.

"I'm fine," Loxy breathes, turning back to me. "Just got the wind knocked out of me."

I briefly close my eyes in relief and sit back on my heels.

"Lox, I'm so sorry I never trusted you enough. You had all this power—"

"It was just salt," she cuts in.

"No. It wasn't. It was magic, and you deserved it. You bore our secret well, and when I failed you, you protected us both. I'm…I'm so proud of you, little sis."

I can see the tears in her eyes. "So you don't want to get rid of your magic?"

I shake my head. "How could I? You were right. It can be dangerous, but this is amazing!"

She throws her arms around me, her body shaking. "I'm so glad."

"I should have asked for help," I say.

Loxy shrugs one shoulder, then winces. "Well, I should have been more helpful."

"And the priestesses were wrong. Singing isn't corruption. It's the will of the Bright Ones."

"No," Loxy says. "It's the will of Sefella."

I feel the warmth burgeoning again in my chest and look back at Sefella-Mom. "Yes. It is."

Loxy's body begins shaking with soft sobs. "Thank you," she whispers, but I'm not sure if she's still talking to me or to Sefella.

Because Sefella did exactly what she promised: she brought us to Mom. She brought us back together, as a family.

The three of us hold each other close as Teklari approaches. We break apart only when the wolf sits a few feet away. Loxy scoots across the crystal floor to meet her, digging her fingers into the beast's fur. She holds the animal for a few moments, and I can feel the warmth of their bond.

Loxy really is something special.

"I know what I want," she says. "And I won't let anything stop me anymore."

"What?" I say. My mind is full of Mom, of Singing, and I can't quite follow her.

Her voice is still rough, and I can hear electricity pulsing through her body. She is weak. She needs rest, time to heal.

But I can handle that. We've handled so much together already.

"I want to make a difference. I want to heal people." I remember hearing her Singing the Song of healing to Teklari. "Please, let me do this."

Teklari licks Loxy's face, and she throws her arms around the beast, shoulders shaking. Sefella's presence flutters in my heart with what feels like approval.

I crawl over to her and wrap them both up in my arms, listening to my sister sobbing. I don't speak, don't do anything.

I don't need to.

"I think that's a wonderful wish, Lox," I say into her tangled hair. "I'm sorry it took me so long."

She hesitates before speaking again, sitting up and wiping at her eyes. "Why did you come? How did you know I'd need help, anyway?"

I think of the vision, consider explaining everything to her. Instead, I say, "You're my sister." As if that explains everything.

For us, it does.

She nods, but she looks troubled for a moment. "For what it's worth, I'm sorry. I should have been more understanding. If it wasn't for me, you could be a priestess still."

I shrug, standing and offering her my hand.

But Sefella-Mom stands with us and places a hand on my shoulder. "You are, you know. A priestess. As long as you follow me."

Loxy takes my hand, and I help her to her feet, heart swelling. Tears prick my eyes. I did get what I wanted, just not how I expected, didn't I?

"My plan wasn't the right plan for me. But," I say, a smile twitching the corners of my mouth, "this is better. And now you can get your wish. We can start over somewhere else."

"Where would you like to go?" Sefella-Mom says, voice bright like the tinkling of chimes. There is power there, so much power.

And so much love.

I shrug again, about to ask where we should go next, but there's one more thing keeping our family from being complete. "Can we get Dad?"

"You think we can go back there?" Loxy stares at me, almost open-mouthed.

But Sefella-Mom merely laughs. "You're safe with me, remember? We can find your father. And then we can move on, somewhere new, somewhere just for our people. We can build new temples. Call more Singers. We never need to be alone again."

There's nothing left now but to leave this palace of the Underworld. To head to our new future, with Sefella, all of us together at last. It started with the ending of our time in Limutria, but perhaps that really was for the best.

Every ending is simply a new beginning. Loxy will get her wish after all.

And me? I get to stop trying to make up for old crimes that weren't even mine.

Fifty-One

LOXY

The Age of Sefella will rise from what once was. The world will be at a reckoning, but its ultimate end will be peace.

Excerpt from Itano's final prophecy

Every muscle feels weak, electricity still buzzing beneath my skin, as El helps me to my feet. I still can't believe she's here. After that last fight, I really thought I'd never see her again. But she looks at me with a new warmth, an affection that I don't think I've ever seen, and I can't keep myself from pulling her into a hug.

"So how do we get out of here?" I say, pulling away and wiping at tears in my eyes again.

Gravel crunches behind us, and I turn to see a water horse. But before I have time to wonder how a water horse ended up here, El smiles and says, "Raiden!"

"Raiden?"

El flushes. "Well, Sefella brought him to me. So I could find you."

I can only blink at her. Sefella brought him? And El accepted it? "To find me." I almost choke on the words, more touched than I care to admit.

El presses her lips together, refusing to answer in that El way of hers that says I'm right. Raiden lowers himself, allowing us to climb on, but Sefella-Mom stays on the ground, the earth rising to meet them.

"Which way do we go?" I say, looking out toward the Flats. From here, it all looks the same. I know which way I arrived from, but what if I got turned around somewhere in there?

El's face goes vacant for a moment, then she points. "This way toward Aeglora. We'll head back to the shore, then follow it north."

I nod, and she spurs Raiden onward. He carefully picks his way around the rough ground, and Teklari stays close to his side. I reach my hand down toward the wolf's back, taking comfort in her warmth, in the solid feel of her. Sefella-Mom glides along next to us, content to float on clouds, seemingly happy to be together again.

Oh, to have that much power.

We travel in silence for a long time, mudpots bubbling around us, until the sun is nearing the horizon. Eventually, we talk. Mom is hungry to know everything she'd missed, and El and I eagerly fill her in. A huge mound of hardened mud rises in front of us, extending so far in both directions that we have no option but to climb over it.

I turn my stare to El, to the confident set of her shoulders as she once again takes control of our lives, taking us somewhere safer than the Flats, maybe even safer than Limutria. And for once, I'm okay with that.

"El?"

She glances at me before returning her attention to the uneven ground ahead. "Yeah, Lox?"

I take a deep breath. "I'm glad you came back."

She winces. "I'm sorry I made you think I wouldn't. I'll always come back for you, Lox."

"I…I'll always come back for you, too." I bite my lip. "I know you only ever meant to protect me. To give me what Mom couldn't. And I know at times I resented you for it. But it wasn't all bad."

She almost smiles, but it fades quickly. "I'm glad you think it wasn't. But I never should have kept you from your dreams. I was selfish. Maybe I thought…" She slows to a stop and turns toward me. "I thought if I could learn everything there was to learn from the temple healers, you'd never have to go. To be under their scrutiny. I could take the knowledge to you and spare you the danger. But somewhere along the way, I guess I forgot. I kind of stole your dream, didn't I?"

I blink. I never quite thought of it that way, but I still don't. "No. El, your dream was to help people. It's the same as mine. That doesn't mean you stole it. And you still… Well, you tried."

She laughs, a single bitter guffaw. "I did try."

I take another few steps forward, and she follows. "And whatever else you did, whatever the bad… You brought me Audrey."

My heart lurches at the thought. Audrey. My first love. My best friend. I still don't know if she's all right. But I am going to find out, one way or another. Once we get back to Limutria.

And I'm almost surprised to realize I'm not even mad at El anymore, not one bit. I'm not conflicted, I don't feel guilty.

We were both just doing the best we could.

"I forgive you," I say. "For Audrey. For real this time. You brought her to me, and it wasn't your fault we were banished. It has to be the will of the Bright Ones. Of Sefella. And we still don't really know for sure about her—Audrey. There's still hope."

"There is always hope," Sefella-Mom says next to us. "And as for the will of the Bright Ones?" She shrugs. "It still requires your will to hear the call."

A tear sparkles in El's eye like a diamond, like all the crystals at my beck and call. "I'll never be able to make up for what I did. I've failed you—both of you—in so many ways, hurt so many people."

I stop her, holding up a hand. "And so have I. I've been just as selfish. I've hurt people, too, including you. El, this is our second chance. For real. So let's take it. Together."

She nods, and we crest the mud mountain. The Sea comes into view in the distance, sparkling in that cold, menacing, beautiful way it has. Even from here, I can hear the Singing of its dissolved crystals.

"We'll find everyone," El says, eyes on the glittering waves. Our thoughts are the same. I suppose that's not surprising either, after spending so much time together, truly together. "We'll help Mom and Sefella, and we'll get Dad from Limutria. We'll find out about Audrey, and if we can rescue her, we'll do that, too." She turns back to me. "We're family, you and me, no matter what happens with anyone else."

I nod at her, tears pricking my eyes. She's already crying. I reach a hand for Sefella-Mom, and they take it, squeezing it with a warmth buzzing with magic. "And Mom. And Sefella."

"Yes. Them, too." El clears her throat. "We should stop for the night," she says, ending our display of sentimentality.

We lower ourselves to the ground and set up a camp. Teklari trots off into the Flats, no doubt in search of more rabbits, and Raiden tugs at some scruffy weeds poking out of the cracked earth.

El wanders toward the edge of the rise, her arms wrapped around herself as she stares at the Sea, deep in thought. Maybe even in conversation with Sefella.

I settle down next to Sefella-Mom. All this time, all these miles, it all brought us here. I reach for a strand of watery hair, tucking it behind Sefella-Mom's crystalline ear. Their eyes flick to me, and I see again that fusion of goddess and human. The familiar. The ineffable.

"They're waiting for you, you know," Sefella-Mom says.

I blink. My heart skips a beat. Could they mean what I think they do? "They?"

They smile. "Yes. Your father…and your Audrey." They look out toward the Sea. "And one more thing. I think you know what comes next. What you need to do now. You are one of my chosen, after all."

And I do. I'm not even sure if El would disagree, now that she believes Sefella's words. This was denied me my whole life, far too long. But no longer.

After all, I have permission from a goddess.

A small mudpot splatters white clay on the ground nearby, and I slide over to scoop a handful of the clay up. It is warm with the sun, with the earth's activity, with the life I hope I am about to bestow.

I am not yet a healer. But I have skill. I have potential. I was always meant to be this. To be more. And with Sefella's help, perhaps I will be.

I scoot back to Sefella-Mom's side, dipping my finger in the clay. I close my eyes for a moment, picturing the symbols and designs that had covered Mom's face after Sefella had filled her.

I will guide you, Sefella says.

I open my eyes and drag my finger along my own skin, and, true to her word, Sefella guides my touch until I have replicated the symbols, the marks that allow Sefella to have power.

The marks that make me a priestess-healer of Sefella.

Finally finished, I lean back and drop the rest of the mud on the ground. I look toward the horizon, toward where El still stands staring at the Sea. She looks so strong, so powerful. Another priestess of a new order.

The Sea could not strike us down. Limutria could not destroy us. We are more than they ever imagined now.

We are unstoppable. Sefella declares it so.

Author's Note

This book holds a special place for me. The inspiration came to me with a single photo, and the first draft clocked in as the longest—and fastest—thing I ever wrote—in the quickest time. I think I finished the first draft in about three months. It was something I always wanted but couldn't find: a story about sisters, because I couldn't find enough of them; a fantasy without romance as a central focus—because have you noticed how romance is everywhere, all the time? —and a story about survival, because I always loved the ingenuity and perseverance of the human spirit in every survival story I've ever read. I knew I couldn't be the only one who was looking for these things.

And then I spent five years editing this beast of a book. I shelved it and reopened it countless times. I tried to query it, only to realize I didn't want to give it to anyone else in publishing. It shifted from young adult to adult. It became a queer survival fantasy story, a story just about queer ladies being queer, without any homophobia or aphobia. And by the time I got to the last draft of this story, I realized, with the help of my editor, that there was a strong deconstruction theme throughout Elodie's story. I myself was beginning the process of deconstruction during this time, figuring out why elements of the faith I'd been raised with sat so wrong with me and where I fit now. I'm still in that journey and will almost definitely write more on this topic, and thanks to the internet, I know I am not alone. #purityculturedropout #exvangelical

Another thing I knew I was including even from early drafts was Loxy's relationship with Audrey. It was one of those things that just fit and made sense, and I fell in love with their love story, even though the romance wasn't a focus—the relationship between the sisters took center stage. And as I grew in my own identity, I also realized that both of my main characters were on the asexual spectrum and one is on the aromantic spectrum, as am I. Loxy is somewhere in the demisexual/graysexual area, and Elodie is very firmly aroace, though I would like to point out that their experiences are not the experiences of everyone in the community. Each person experiences their asexuality and/or aromanticism differently.

One reason I wrote this story is because I wish I'd had queer and ace-positive stories when I was Elodie and Loxy's age, or even younger. I wish I'd had the language to understand I wasn't broken when I was a teen, or where to look for answers. I know now, and if any of you relate to this or want to know more about the asexual and aromantic spectrums, I suggest the Asexual and Visibility Education Network (AVEN) at www.asexuality.org. I also highly recommend Angela Chen's book, which includes some intersectionality, titled *Ace: What Asexuality Reveals about Desire, Society, and the Meaning of Sex.*

Thank you for reading, and I hope you enjoyed this book as much as I loved writing it.

Much love,
Jenna

Acknowledgments

It has been a long process preparing this book for publication, and a lot of people helped me along the way.

First and foremost, I want to thank my partner for all his support, brainstorming, musing, and cheerleading over the years. Without his help, all my stories would still be collecting dust on a hard drive somewhere. I also want to thank my sister and my sister-in-law for believing in me and being a couple of the best friends I could ever have, especially in the context of these stories. For my brother, thanks for receiving my coming out to him with genuine happiness for me and acceptance. I also want to thank my friend Steve for reading an early draft and cheering me on, as he has for all my authorly endeavors.

I especially need to thank my author friend, Ann Dayleview, for all her hours of time reading various drafts and giving me feedback. It's been a long process, and she read SO MANY drafts over the years, always giving me valuable ideas and thoughts that helped me fix the gaps and issues I struggled to correct. And I'll always treasure the time we spend together, online or in person, whether it's writing, going to bookshops, or eating dumplings!

Thanks also to the various readers I've had over the years and my other writing buddy, Christine, for all the support and ideas over the years. Your help and support have meant the world to me, and it's so nice to have another friend who understands so much about me and my writing.

Finally, I need to thank my professional team, Savannah at Dragonpen Designs and Arielle, my editor. When I told you both I wanted to publish this not-so-little queer book, when I told you I myself was queer, neither of you batted an eye. Both of you supported me as friends and put as much love and care into the story as I did. Because of you, I had the courage to see this through, fix the problems still plaguing this story, and have one of the most beautiful covers I've ever seen. You will never know how much your support meant to me. Thank you, truly.

And thank you, readers, for taking a chance on me and my writing. I hope you found some hope and solace in the voices of Loxy and Elodie.

About the Author

JENNA PINE is a neuroscientist and writer of atmospheric and sometimes spooky fantasy. She lives in eastern Pennsylvania with her family, and when she's not busy sciencing and dreaming up fictional worlds, she's creating music and art, reading, or gaming. She loves to write about family relationships, gorgeous settings, and magic to make people dream, but most of all, she writes to help people feel less alone.

You can connect with Jenna at www.jennapine.com/links.

Also by
Jenna Pine

Salt in the Wind (A Sea of Broken Glass Prequel)